D1266230

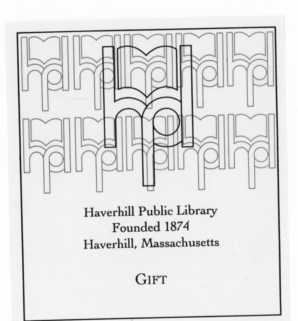

GONE TO EARTH

GONE
TO
EARTH

A DOC ADAMS THRILLER

RICK BOYER

FAWCETT COLUMBINE ▾ NEW YORK

A Fawcett Columbine Book
Published by Ballantine Books

Copyright © 1990 by Richard L. Boyer

All rights reserved under International and Pan-American Copyright
Conventions. Published in the United States by Ballantine Books, a
division of Random House, Inc., New York, and simultaneously
in Canada by Random House of Canada Limited, Toronto.

LIBRARY OF CONGRESS CATALOGING-IN-PUBLICATION DATA
Boyer, Rick.
    Gone to Earth : a Doc Adams mystery / Rick Boyer.—1st ed.
        p. cm.
    ISBN 0-449-90556-X
    I. Title.
PS3552.0895G48   1990   90-34170
813′.54—dc20   CIP

Design by Beth Tondreau Design/Jane Treuhaft
Manufactured in the United States of America
First Edition: September 1990
10 9 8 7 6 5 4 3 2 1

FOR MY FATHER

PAUL FREDERICK BOYER

sine qua non

"There are old soldiers,
and there are brave soldiers.
But there are no *old brave soldiers.*"

—*Special Forces saying*

GONE TO EARTH

GONE TO EARTH

HARLEYS IN THE BARN

We found them in the barn cellar, way back against the far wall, carefully hidden by piles and piles of old junk. Four of them. Mint. Hey, how lucky can you get?

It never occurred to us to think about where their owners were. That is, until we found them still down on the farm. Take it from a physician: they were *never* going to see Paree.

▼ ▼ ▼

S ome people have all the luck," said Jim DeGroot, sweeping his gaze across the far horizon of our new farm in the Berkshires. We were standing on the terrace of the old farmhouse, built before 1800, which Mary and Joe and I had spent the last two months remodeling. We had named the place Pound Foolish Farm. Good name for it; the main house alone had eaten up seventy grand in renovations in the wink of an eye. But the good part was this: the farm was now a knockout. After eight years of abandonment, the place was looking spiffy. Even the grounds had been redone. And there were outbuildings, too. We were looking downhill at the main barn and three smaller buildings. Behind us, adjoining the main house by means of a dogtrot, was the cottage and small plot of land Joe had bought from Mary and me, and was fixing up for his own summer place. The remaining seventy-some acres were in meadowland, pasture, and woods, all of it in the Berkshire range of western Massachusetts, one of the loveliest spots outside Eden.

"You mean the luck of the windfall from Emil's will, or the luck of finding this place so cheap?" I asked.

"Both, for crissakes. First, here's this poor neighbor of yours—who isn't so poor, it turns out—who gets bumped off. And unbeknownst to you, Doc, he's willed his entire estate to you, for trying to help him escape before they closed in on him."

I thought about Emil Haszmanay as the cool evening breeze swept over my face. It was mid-June, but cool at night in the mountains; I loved it. Emil had been my neighbor, and a research scientist at the prestigious Lincoln Laboratory a town away from Concord, where we live. He came to me in desperation, and I had helped him.

But not enough, and he died, murdered by a fearsome Russian revenge weapon known in the spy trade as Moscow Metal. Another person had almost died in that little caper, too. Me: Dr. Charles Adams, oral surgeon. Whenever I recall those events, I still get shaky knees.

"Well, I was glad for the windfall, Jim. But let me tell you, I earned it. You remember what happened?"

"Yeah, I remember. In fact, I'll never forget it. But face it, pal, that's a nice windfall. A pretty hunk of change. You said almost half a million, mostly from the sale of the house and lot?"

"Four hundred twenty-seven thousand."

He gave a low whistle, watching the golden sun drop down behind the far range of hills miles away. "Well, I'll say this, Doc, you and Mary sure invested it wisely."

"You're just saying that because you're in real estate development, Jim."

"Maybe, maybe not. I'll tell you something: the real estate market in Boston is peaking. If you'd made this kind of investment within two hours of Beantown you'd be airtight, but you'd never see the equity appreciation that you're bound to realize here. I mean it."

"So Mary and I were smart to listen to Tom Costello, and not buy stocks?"

He snorted a short, ironic laugh. "*Stocks?* You kidding me? We all know the market's jumpy; it hasn't really recovered from the crash. No, I'd say this is the perfect place to put the money. Perfect. Do you realize we're now standing roughly equidistant from Boston, Hartford, New York, and Albany? Eighty acres of prime, scenic mountain land in the middle of all those population centers? Know what that's gonna mean, Doc?"

"Big bucks, right?"

"You bet. Which is why I'm glad you invited us out here . . ."

"Gee, Jim, we invited you and Janice out lots of times earlier, when the heavy work was being done. How come you never—"

"Just listen, will you? I'm out here to give you some great advice. Now, as you know, my firm specializes in developing rural properties. You take that valley land down there, see that level part? You clear a twenty- or thirty-acre tract, and what you do is—"

"No way, Jim. Not yet, anyway. I know what you're thinking. I know we could make a pile subdividing. But we'll do it later, if we do it at all. We want a few years just to enjoy the peace and quiet out here. And the scenery."

We heard Mary and Janice calling to us as they walked up the hill from the barn. The yellowish light from the big barn's windows was glowing brighter each minute as daylight faded and the air grew bluish and fuzzy around the edges. Crows cawed in the distant woods; swallows twittered above us in circles and dives. A gorgeous dusk. They came up and joined us on the terrace, Mary putting her arm around my waist.

"Charlie, Janice and I went exploring earlier. Did you know there's a camping place down by the river? There's a ring of rocks for campfires, and a lot of beer cans and stuff."

"I know; I saw it earlier, too. Looks like more of a party spot to me. It's on our neighbor's land."

"Doesn't he object?"

"That farm's deserted, Mary, just like this one was until nine weeks ago."

Janice was telling Jim all about the stuff that the hired man, Warren Shaw, was taking out of the barn cellar. We didn't have to be told: the pile of junk had been growing all day outside the big sliding doors that lead to the barn's lower level. Old horse collars, stanchions, pails, harrows and rakes, creaky leather harnesses and belts (stinking of mildew and brittle with age) boards, chains, ancient tools—everything you could imagine at a country flea market. We'd been so busy working on the house and cottage, and getting the lawn and gardens in order, that we'd saved the barn for last. Its upper half had been filled with hay—Lord knows how old—which Warren Shaw and his son had taken outside to the clearing and burned to negate the fire hazard. Now we were attempting to clean out the cellar.

"What smells so good?" I asked.

"Game hens," said Mary. "Game hens with sage dressing and wild rice. The DeGroots brought some Mouton-Cadet to go with them. Let's go inside now, Charlie, and you can start a big fire in the kitchen fireplace, and we can have drinks and pretend we're travelers stopping at an inn. Janice, did you know this place really used to be an inn?"

"I can believe it," she said. "This place is just gorgeous. And the pool . . . was that Joe's idea?"

"Uh-huh," Mary said, looking over at the big excavation taking shape right where Joe's property joined ours. "Can you imagine how much fun it'll be in August when it's finished?"

We went inside, into the thirty-by-fifty-foot kitchen. The fireplace, big enough to hold a yule log, had a twelve-foot oaken mantle above it, as thick as a railway tie. The crane and gigantic ancient andirons were still there. I touched a match to the paper and kindling under the pile of logs, and as the fire crept upward, we poured drinks and drew up chairs. I saw Jim and Janice sweeping their eyes over the huge room, now clean, bright, and cheery. In April, when Mary and I had first trudged up the hill in the chill of the spring thaw to inspect the property, the kitchen was a different story altogether. It was boarded up, for starters; the big swinging leaded windows were covered with plywood. That wasn't cheery. And the fact that perhaps three hundred wee animals of every description had made the place their home, and toilet, during the previous eight years hadn't added to its esthetic charm.

But we'd pulled the plywood down, patched the walls with plaster, tacked sheetrock to the wounded ceiling, filled holes and crevices with joint compound, sanded the wide plank floors, removing centuries of dirt and dents, and done, well, a thousand other major and minor things, and *voilà*! I could tell that Jim and Janice were envious, and I enjoyed it. This was a simpleminded, bourgeois, petty, and materialistic feeling. Nevertheless, I enjoyed it, and felt proud of what Mary and I had accomplished.

"How much for the whole place, initially?" asked Janice. "I know you told me, Mary, but I've got it wrong in my mind. Did you say three seventy?"

"Three sixty-five, five," said Mary, visibly smirking.

"Damn! You're kidding—" whistled Jim softly to himself. "Where the hell am I when these things happen?"

"Yeah, it looks like a steal now," I said, holding up a warning hand, "but if you'd seen it when we did, its charm wouldn't be so obvious. Luckily, we got a sharp architect out here first, to tell us if the foundation, sills, and main beams were sound. It was a real diamond in the rough."

"And even then," added Mary, "we had some scary moments. For a while, we thought the whole left wing was rotten and about to fall down. But it didn't."

"And then we were convinced the well was contaminated. But it wasn't."

"But still, Mary, the *price*," said Janice. "I mean, regular houses in Concord Center are going for that much—"

"Well," she said, watching the blaze before us gather strength, "it had been on the market a long time, and they just kept dropping the price. We came in with a strictly cash offer at twenty less than they were asking, and . . . bingo."

"Of course, Joe's kicking in sixty thousand for his part of the place made the deal even more attractive," I added.

"Yeah," Jim said, leaning over toward the fire and rattling the ice cubes in his glass, "and the fact that your family owns one of Schenectady's largest building supply houses didn't hurt either, right, Mary?"

She admitted that Brindelli's had given us everything we'd needed: lumber, glass, plaster, vinyl flooring, cement, bricks, shingles, copper pipes . . . *everything,* at cost. And since it had come across state lines, we'd even escaped the sales tax.

They were impressed. As well they should be. Yes, I thought, luxuriating in my brilliance, sometimes everything just seems to fall perfectly into place. Before we know it, Pound Foolish Farm will be worth a million bucks. Or more . . . maybe *much* more . . .

As I was sitting before the now roaring fire in the charming inn kitchen of my new country estate, congratulating myself on pulling off the most brilliant real estate deal since the Dutch stole Manhattan Island, Warren Shaw, our hired man, knocked on the door and came inside to tell us all what he'd just discovered in the back of the barn.

He approached us half-apologetically, yanking down the front of his duck hunter's cap with his fingers.

"Sorry to disturb you all . . . Doc, Mary," he said. He said my name like this: *Dawk.* "But you won't believe what I've just uncovered in the barn cellar."

He backed up to the fireplace, his hawklike features, ruddy and thin, easing into a slow grin at our suspense.

"Ooo, hey, don't this fire feel good! Nippy out, eh?"

"Well, don't keep us waiting, Warren," said Mary. "What is it? A big bag of money? A nest of rattlesnakes?"

"Nope. Better'n that, Mary. What I found is motorcycles. Way in the back, behind all the old junk. All stacked up together in the far corner . . ."

"Motorcycles? Real, live motorcycles?"

"Uh-yuh. Harleys. Harley-Davidsons."

"How many?" asked Jim.

Warren, letting his coat flaps out to catch the rising heat under them, held up four fingers at him in reply.

"Four? Holy Christ, Doc, four Harley-Davidsons!"

"Let's go see!" said Mary, jumping up.

We walked fast down the hill toward the barn, now a dark hulk in the night, its small cellar windows glowing amber. From afar they looked like portholes in a giant derelict ocean liner. It was downright cold now; I wished I'd brought my jacket. We walked around the old building to the far side, the downhill side, and went through the barnyard, whose center bore a huge circular blackened scar on the ground where Warren and his son had burned the old hay. Everywhere were stacks and piles of junk. We entered through the big sliding doors and threaded our way past old stalls and manure bins, under low, hewn, whitewashed beams long since turned dusty brown and clogged with cobwebs. The only light in the big cellar came from a bulb in a ceiling fixture at the other end of the building. We groped our way forward in the faint light. I smelled mildew, damp dirt, old straw, and manure.

Then I got a whiff, very faint, of engine oil and gasoline.

"Warren! Where's a light?"

"Wait a sec, Dawk; here I come—"

Warren joined us with his flashlight and swept the beam ahead of us into the far corner of the dank cellar. Brightly painted metal and chrome winked back at us. Beyond that, more paint and chrome, and beyond that, still more.

We followed Warren back there. I was starting to shiver. "Spooky in here!" said Janice with a giggle, trying to make a joke of it.

Warren was standing in the far corner near the machines, shining the flashlight on them. I approached with awe, rather like Howard Carter entering Tutankhamen's burial chamber in the Valley of the Kings. Standing close together were indeed four huge Harley-Davidson bikes. Somebody had hidden them in our barn. A few basic questions immediately sprung to mind: Why? When? *Who?*

"Like I said before," murmured Jim, coming up behind me and looking over my shoulder, "some people have all the luck. What are these worth, Doc? You've got a motorcycle; you should have some idea."

"A couple grand apiece, at least. I wonder whose they are."

"Why they're *yours*, of course. They're in your barn, aren't they?"

I took out my handkerchief and wiped the front fender of the nearest bike. Beneath a light coat of dust, the enamel paint shined like new. Warren squatted down beside the machine, holding the flashlight with one hand and running a blackened thumbnail along his stubbled jaw. His graying hair poked out around the bottom of his duck hunter's cap; his worn overalls were spotted with paint, Rust-oleum, and grease. The quintessential New England handyman. I took the light from him and shined it on the next bike. This one was more customized, or "chopped," as they say in biker parlance. The fenders had been removed, the front fork had been lengthened, extending the front wheel out in a long slant. The rider's seat had a tall chrome back affixed to it. I thought I remembered that bikers called this a "sissy bar," but I wasn't sure. I ride a BMW, and "Beemers," known as gentlemen's machines, are the polar extreme of Harley-Davidsons. Yet Harleys are known for their good construction, power, and comfortable ride. And they're American made—yeah boy! *Milwaukee iron.* They were expensive, sought-after, and cherished by their owners.

But the neatest thing about Harleys is the way they sound. Nothing else on the road goes *Bruummmm! Bruummm! Brrrrrrappp!* Nothing else has that brassy rumble. I wanted one. Now. Surprise, surprise.

I went to the next motorcycle. It, too, was chopped and painted a flashy dark metallic blue. The fourth and final bike appeared older than the others, and was painted metallic green, with lots of sparkle. It looked different in another way, and I soon discovered that this bike was covered with caked mud. Most of it had been wiped away, but it still clung to the engine, caked between the cooling fins on the cylinders. It was all over the spokes and rims of the wheels, too.

Everybody wanted a look; they all came up one at a time and squeezed between the machines, oohing and aahing, leaning over and inspecting each one.

"You're not saying much, Charlie," said Mary. "What's wrong?"

"I don't know . . . These bikes are modified; a lot of time and money's gone into them. I don't know much about bikers, Mare, except that they love their machines. They see their bikes as extensions of themselves. Why did they leave them hidden away in this barn for so long?"

"I'm gettin' cold, you guys," said Janice, jumping up and down. I could see her breath coming out in clouds. We wound our way back out of the depths of the barn and jogged uphill to the house.

We invited Warren in for a drink and all sat around the fireplace.

"Now, Charlie, I know what you're thinking. You want to keep one of those for yourself, don't you? So you can have your Beemer at home and a Harley out here. Well, forget it. One bike's dangerous enough."

"If I were you, I'd advertise them right now," said Jim. "Put an ad in the *Berkshire Eagle* first thing tomorrow. You're looking at ten, maybe twelve grand worth of bikes in there, guy."

"Maybe more than that," I said, sipping my scotch and staring at the logs that popped and spit in front of me. "Warren, did you ever meet the owner of this place?"

He shook his head, reminding me that he was from Otis, a town twenty miles away.

"You might ask around Humphrey Center," he suggested. "But this whole place is new to me."

"Well, didn't you guys meet the owner at the closing?" asked Janice.

"Nope," said Mary. "It was all done through the lawyers.

The previous owner's a widow living in Clearwater. She hasn't been in the state in twenty years."

"How long do you think those bikes have been in there, Warren?" I asked.

"Hard to say," he mused, scratching his head. He said it like this: *bahd ta say*. "Seems ta me, six months anyways. And it sure took a lot of work to hide them there. It took me a whole day just to find 'em."

"So they were hidden, not just stored there?" asked Janice. Warren replied that he thought so. Somebody had apparently removed the junk, wheeled the big machines way into the far corner, and then restacked all the junk back in place.

"But why would they do that?"

"Because they're stolen, that's why," said Jim. I found myself nodding in agreement.

"Well, in that case, maybe you better not advertise them, Charlie."

"Right. And not only that, the first person I'm going to show them to is Joe. I think he and his friends at the state police ought to know."

We sat down to dinner forty minutes later. Warren had already left, lurching down the long gravel drive in his ratty old pickup, headed for his own farm on the outskirts of Otis. After dinner we played bridge for an hour, then went upstairs, showing Jim and Janice to the guest bedroom which Mary had recently furnished with country-style antique furniture from local flea markets. I fell asleep in a happy mood, listening to the racket of the spring peepers outside our window, convinced of the wisdom of our investment, and looking forward to the good times sure to follow.

THREE

Next morning, I woke up thinking I'd dreamed it all. The apparition of four giant "chopped" road hawgs parked in a line, hidden along the far wall of our barn, sealed in there by heaps and heaps of rubble, was a little surrealistic. It was eerie, too.

Again, the question: Where were the owners? Of all the legends, myths, and bold images of the bikers that had come to me in bits and pieces over the years, the one constant that stood out in the hierarchy of priorities was the machine itself: the *bike*. Without it, the biker was nothing.

So who'd put those machines in there that way, and when? Not to mention *why* . . .

"Charlie, Joey's here! He's brought a friend; c'mon down and eat!"

I got up and went downstairs for pancakes and coffee, meeting Joe in the kitchen, who introduced Bryce Stevens, an old crony of his in the Bureau of Investigative Services for the state police. Bryce was about fifty, thickset, and a couple inches shorter than I, with a bit of white around his ears on an otherwise dark head. He shook my hand warmly, and a quick smile passed over his face, being replaced instantly by a serious look. He seemed preoccupied, his expression appearing sad rather than abrupt, and I wondered why.

"Joe says to call you Doc."

"Right," I said, stacking up a pile of Mary's buttermilk pancakes on my plate. She adds a couple teaspoons of dark rum to the batter as well as extra oil; they come out thin, like crepes, and slightly aromatic. Can't stop eating them. Bryce declined food, saying he'd already eaten. I knew Joe had as well, since his first priority in the morning is eating. Now that I think of it, his first priority *anytime* is eating. But that didn't stop him from destroying, in record time, a stack of flapjacks you couldn't pole-vault over.

"Well, here we are, Doc, ready and eager to see those Harleys in your barn; aren't we, Bryce?" said Joe between gulps.

Bryce nodded in agreement, and when we'd finished and helped Mary clear things away, we each took an extra mug of coffee and went down the hill to the barn. Like many barns on hillsides, it had an earth ramp on the high side leading to the main floor. On the low side of the barn, the side farthest from the house, were the big sliding doors that led into the barn cellar.

Bryce stopped at the twenty-foot charred circle on the earth. "What happened here?" he asked, kicking at the burned grass. "Spaceship land, or what?"

We explained that it was where the hay from the barn was burned by our hired man and his son. Then we all walked inside. It was dark without the light on, but pale bluish daylight filtered in now through the small windows. The light came in slanting in soft beams, in which swam hay dust. It resembled a stage set, with the spotlights dimmed very low. We went back to the far wall again, where the bikes sat under one of the small, high windows. They were ghostly in the bluish light.

Stevens went up to the first machine and rapped the fender with his fingernail. *Tink, tink.*

"Have you touched these, Doc?"

"A little. I wiped the front fender there. Maybe some of us touched them here and there, but not much."

Stevens took out his notebook, then worked his way around to the back of the bikes and looked along their rear fenders.

"No plates on any of them. Offhand, I'd say they're stolen, wouldn't you, Joe?"

My brother-in-law nodded, taking out his notebook.

"Just about bet my life on it," continued Stevens. "Motorcycles and motorcycle parts, especially Harley-Davidson, are stolen constantly. These bikes, which are customized, would bring a high price on the black market. Trouble is, being customized, they are instantly recognizable."

"You mean their original owners could identify them on the street?"

"Right. And most bikers aren't the type to simply go tell the police; they're more likely to attack the guy riding the stolen machine and simply bash his head in. Follow?"

"Are you saying that's why they have to be hidden for a while? Until the heat cools off?"

"Yeah. In fact, I'd be willing to bet that these machines came from out of state. Maybe as far away as the West Coast. Probably hauled here in a van, then wheeled in here and covered up. Hell, they could've been sitting here a year or more."

"That reminds me," I said. "Come outside and see what Warren discovered on some old boards."

So we went back outside into the barnyard in time to see Warren himself bouncing down the hill in his old pickup. He got out and showed Bryce and Joe the old planks he'd taken out of the cellar just before he caught the first glimmer of the bikes. The planks were wide, unrotted, and well weathered. Mary and I were saving them for paneling in the remodeled kitchen. Two of these boards I had set aside earlier, and now showed them to

Bryce and Joe. They each had ridges of fungus where it had grown between them.

"Warren noticed this fungus," I said, "and what we figure is this: these planks were moved to get the bikes inside. That's obvious. Then they were restacked back into the cellar to hide them. This fungus has grown in a pattern between the boards since that time; you can see that by the marks it's made. I don't know how fast this type of fungus grows, but you can bet it'd take more than a few weeks."

"Hmmm, not bad. You're right; it'll help give us a time fix," said Bryce. "Not bad at all, Doc. I guess I'm not surprised you're working for us nowadays."

"Part-time only," I said. "As forensic oral pathologist. I do mouths only; no bodies. I was the temporary M.E. down on the Cape until the first body came in."

Stevens looked at me quizzically.

"It was a floater," said Joe. "I saw it, too."

"Oh. Oh yeah, I see why you wouldn't want to stay on," said Stevens, taking out a pocketknife and scraping at the grayish-tan fungus.

"Pretty good powers of observation, though."

"Sure, Bryce. It's the medical training, right, Doc?" said Joe.

"I guess. Anyway, you want to borrow these two planks?"

"If you don't mind, we might take them for a few days. First, though, I'll take down the serial numbers of the bikes and call them in, see if we get a hit on the NLETS line."

"Inlets? What the hell are inlets? The only inlets I know of are small bays," I said, puzzled.

"You remember, Doc. I explained the NLETS network to you once," said Joe. "It's the National Law Enforcement Telecommunications System."

"Oh, that huge computer in Washington that stores data on everything?"

"Right. We punch in information on vehicles, firearms, IDs, bogus bills, whatever, and if we get lucky, the machine spits back a hit."

"You mean a match?"

"Uh-huh, it tells us where such and such happened, or who owns the whatever, or if it was used in a previous crime. Ten to one says that when Bryce sends the serial numbers from those bikes over the wire, it'll come back with a hit, saying they were taken from Newport Beach last year, or something to that effect."

"That's a good guess," said Bryce. "The thieves, and I'm guessing there's more than one, are biding their time until the heat cools down. Then, when they feel the time is right, they plan to scoot back in here and grab the bikes and sell them."

"But aren't they waiting a long time?" I asked. "And isn't that pretty careful concealment for just a theft?"

Bryce shrugged his shoulders and turned toward the house. He looked tired. Tired and a little sad. "Maybe," he said. "But until something else rears its head, we'll assume it's a theft."

"I'm just thinking that it took a hell of a lot of time and work to clear out the barn, roll the machines in there, and then restack all the rubble. Think about that. Think how long it would take. And it couldn't have been much fun, either."

Stevens, a dubious look on his face, began trudging uphill to the house. "Yeah," he said out of the side of his mouth, "it's a little strange."

"Don't you think it's also strange that one of the bikes was buried?" I asked him.

He stopped and turned to face me.

"*Buried?* Where you get that?"

"The one against the far wall; the first one they wheeled in. The green one. I looked at it closely; there's mud packed between the cooling fins on the cylinders. Tailpipe's clogged. There's caked mud and dirt everywhere."

"Maybe it's just real dirty."

"Nope. Buried. Buried and tamped down, then dug up again."

Joe and Bryce shook their heads slowly as we walked up to the house. Just before we reached the terrace in back of the house, Bryce stopped and scratched his head.

"Okay, what I'll do then, I'll call out a lab team to dust the machines for latents as well as take the serial numbers. Just in case."

As soon as we were inside the kitchen, he called Ten Ten Comm Ave in Boston, the state police headquarters building where Joe had his office, and requested a records search for "hot sheets" regarding stolen motorcycles during the previous year. Then he called the Pittsfield office of the state police and requested a lab team ASAP. They said they'd be out just after noon. This out of the way, he accepted a mug of Mary's dark-roast coffee, smoking a small cheroot while he thought things over.

"Are those motorcycles ours?" asked Mary, stirring a big dollop of cream into her mug.

"Probably not," said Joe. "Of course, if we check carefully, and wait long enough, and they don't turn up stolen, and if nobody claims them, then they're yours. But I wouldn't bet on it."

"Well, I hope they aren't," she said, sitting down next to her brother and blowing on the hot brew. "Because if they were, then Charlie would keep them all for himself and start his own motorcycle gang."

"Oh, I don't think he would," said Stevens. "After all, he is a physician. He seems far too mature and responsible a guy to—"

"Ha!" said Mary.

"He's right, Mare," I said. "If you think for a second I'd do a thing like—"

"Ha!" said Joe.

Later that afternoon we walked out to meet the police van grinding up our narrow, rutted road. We followed the lab team down to the barn. The first big surprise they got was trying to move the bikes.

"Sonovabitch! *Wheew!* Are these things heavy, or *what?*" said one of the men, puffing like a steam locomotive as he tried to wheel one of the bikes clear of the others for examination and dusting. They got the machines separated enough to work on them, handling them carefully to save as many prints as possible. They took down two serial numbers for each machine, one on the frame, located up near the machine's "neck," or juncture of the front fork, and one on the engine, on the crankcase at the base of the cylinders. Then they began the slow and careful work of dusting. Bryce took the list of serial numbers to phone them in. He paused and turned back to the men.

"One of these bikes has only one number," he said. "How come?"

"That's all we could find; there was no number on the frame, just the block," said the technician, pointing to the green bike. "I think it's an older model."

The green bike was the one with the caked mud on the engine, the one I was convinced had been buried. Stevens grunted and began his trudge back up the hill to the house. I hunkered down next to the bikes and watched the men work on them. I asked how long they thought the machines had been stacked in the cellar.

"I'd say a year, anyway," said the first man. His colleague agreed. And what were the chances of their finding good prints after all that time? Slim, they said. I pointed at the green bike on the end.

"I say that bike's been buried. What do you guys say?"

"I'd say you're right. Can't figure it, can you?"

"Nope," I said. "I sure can't."

"You the owner of this place?"

"Uh-huh," I answered. "I just bought it."

"Well, who knows? Maybe these will belong to you. What'll you do then? Sell 'em?"

"Hell no. I'll keep 'em and start my own biker gang."

They nodded. They weren't surprised. Not in the least.

"You say you just bought this place?" said a third man in the dark, whose face I couldn't see.

"Yep."

"Bought the farm, eh? Haw! Get it? You just *bought the farm*! Funny, eh? Haw! Haw!"

"Yeah, funny," I said, trying to raise a weak chuckle. It didn't work. Somehow, looking at the mystery motorcycles in the dreary barn cellar, I failed to see the humor in it.

FOUR

The next day I was alone on the farm, sitting with the three dogs in the half-finished kitchen reading the local newspaper, the *Berkshire Eagle,* over coffee. I was waiting for Mary to return from marketing. It was an interesting change, living in the western part of the state. Bay Staters claim there are three states within Massachusetts: the Boston metro area, the Cape, and the West, the West beginning somewhere around Worcester. That might be true, since each has its own distinct flavor and pace. And now, it seemed, Mary and I had a house in each. I liked the mountains. There was a pastoral, unhurried quality here that reminded me of the farms and small towns of Illinois and Iowa, where I spent my youth. Except for the striking difference in terrain, the rhythm, pace, and values were similar.

I found what I was looking for on page two of the local news section:

CYCLE "GRAVEYARD" ON LOCAL FARM?

HUMPHREY—It came as a big surprise to Dr. Charles Adams, a Boston surgeon, when four Harley-Davidson motorcycles were found hidden in the barn of his newly purchased hideaway farm in the Berkshire mountains. Adams, an oral surgeon from historic Concord, purchased the farm for a retirement home with his wife, Mary. Two days ago, while cleaning out the barn, the couple discovered the motorcycles parked together in a far corner of the barn cellar.

"The cycles appear to be in good shape," said state police detective Bryce Stevens, who was called to the scene, "although at this stage it's hard to say exactly how long they've been in there."

He speculates at least several months, possibly a year. Since the bikes appear to have been carefully hidden, the current speculation is that they were stolen elsewhere and hidden on the farm, which had been deserted for eight years prior to the recent sale. The police investigation continues.

Alongside the piece was a photograph of Mary and me standing in the barn looking at the line of choppers. The caption read: "Perplexed couple, Charles and Mary Adams, examine row of customized 'choppers' hidden mysteriously in their barn near Humphrey, Mass."

The reporter who'd visited our place the previous evening had done her job well. For starters, she didn't call me a dentist, as many do, but correctly listed my profession as oral surgeon: a puller of teeth, a straightener of jaws, etcetera. The photo wasn't bad either. The *Eagle*, published in Pittsfield, deserved its reputation as an outstanding small newspaper. I poured a third mug of coffee and lighted a pipe packed with dark Virginia flake tobacco. I strolled outside, the dogs at my heels, and was looking over my estate like an English lord when I heard a car on the gravel. It was an old Toyota wagon, lumpy and dull with age. It skidded to a halt and a young woman got out quickly and ran toward the house. She was thin, and wore her dark hair long and loose over her shoulders. She carried a newspaper under her arm. Oh oh: she'd seen the picture of the bikes and was going to claim one of them for her boyfriend. I made myself a bet on it.

The dogs ran up to her, barking and carrying on, and she flattened herself against the side of the house, a panicky look on her face.

"It's okay," I yelled, walking back up the hill to the drive, "they won't hurt you."

She stood there, frozen, while the barking dogs milled around her. But they give it away every time: their tails were wagging. She reached down and petted Troubles on her head, and then the others lined up for the same. I walked over to her and she looked up at me, trying to smile. But she couldn't; her forced grin had a sour cast to it, and I could tell by her lovely violet eyes that she'd been crying. Still, she managed to shake hands pleasantly enough, and showed a set of teeth that were well cared for, but slightly out of line. She was quite attractive, but not fancy. A real country girl, I thought.

"Hey! Are you the doctor in the—oh . . . yeah, sure you are. I recognize you from the picture in the paper—" She thumped the rolled-up paper nervously against her leg, and shifted her weight from foot to foot.

"I'm Doc Adams," I said, in a voice I hoped was soothing. She could use it.

"Lucy Kirkland, Dr. Adams," she said, holding up the paper and pointing to one of the motorcycles in the picture. "I came here because this bike here looks like . . ." she winced quickly and blinked, "this bike I'm pretty sure is my brother Bill's. I just wanted to take a look at it to make sure."

Well, I'd won the little bet with myself. Except that her manner indicated that something was wrong.

"Where is your brother?" I asked.

She looked up at me, wide-eyed.

"We don't know. We haven't seen him in almost a year."

Oh oh . . .

I led Lucy Kirkland down to the barn. We walked to the back of the cellar to where the bikes were standing, just as the lab team had left them, half-silhouetted by the morning sun that streamed in through the tiny windows. Lucy walked tentatively toward the machines, like a shy girl approaching a boy at a school dance. She held a hand up near her mouth and leaned over the first bike. Then she went on to the next one, running her hand along the seat, then the handlebars.

"This one," she said in a whisper. Her voice was flat, without inflection or emotion. "This is Billy's bike. I can tell by the custom seat and the sissy bar behind it. See? I could tell even from the picture in the—in the paper—"

She did a sharp intake of breath and dropped to her knees, her hands on the seat, her forehead against the big chrome engine as if in prayer at a shrine. The barn cellar, with its ray of sunlight shining in, looked like a rustic chapel. I saw her shoulders shaking and heard her muffled sobs. I knelt beside her.

"Lucy. Can you tell me about this? C'mon; let's go up to the house. We'll have some coffee and you can tell me all about it, okay?"

She stood up, leaning against me. I turned her toward the door, but she stopped and looked back at the bikes. Then I felt her shove me away. She was looking at the far bike, the green one that had the caked mud on the engine.

"Lucy?"

She walked toward the green bike, circled it, like a terrier circling a rat. Looking at it with squinty eyes, predatory.

"Lucy? Lucy, would you like to come up to the—"

"There!" she snapped, shooting out a finger and pointing at the green machine. "That's Franz's bike. I know it!" she said, panting with emotion.

"You know who that bike belongs to?" I asked, still mystified.

"I bet he killed him," she said, crying now.

"Who? Who killed him?"

"Buddy. Buddy Franz. That's who owns that green one.

Franz hated Billy because he took Melissa away from him. And I bet he killed him. I just know it—"

I led her back up the hill toward the house. Mary's Audi came crackling up the driveway and swung to a stop. She got out and met us at the kitchen door. I introduced the two women, and we went inside and sat down at the kitchen table. Mary looked closely at Lucy, giving her an intensive once-over, the way one woman inspects another—especially one twenty years younger. I poured coffee for them and sat down.

"So Billy hasn't been seen in almost a year?" I asked.

"No. We last saw him on Fourth of July weekend last summer," Lucy answered, her head resting in her hands, her elbows on the table. She looked tired now. "He left our house Thursday night on his bike—the very same bike that's out in your barn right now—and we never saw him again. I know he's dead. And I think maybe Franz killed him. Who else could it be? He likes to cut on people. And he sings while he's doing it."

I almost dropped the coffeepot.

"Sings?" said Mary. "Sings while he's cutting people? You mean with a knife?"

Lucy nodded, taking a tentative sip from the steaming mug. Her face was dead serious. I leaned over to her and asked her to give us the background. And as she was warming up for her delivery, I went over to the wall phone and punched in Joe's number in Boston.

"Hey. I don't want any police," she said.

"It's just my brother-in-law," I said.

"**A**nd so this group of bikers called themselves the Aces?" asked Mary.

"Yeah. Like a nickname. It was a bunch of guys from Pittsfield, and some from Worcester and some from up in Vermont. They even had some members from around Albany, even though that's where the Stompers hang out, and they're real bad. But the Aces weren't a bad bunch. They weren't like the Hell's Angels or the Pagans or anything like that. Just a bunch of guys who rode together on the weekends. Their colors are a bunch of cards, like a poker hand, fanned out. All the cards are aces."

"Colors?" said Mary. "What do you mean, colors?"

"You know, their colors. That's the sign on the back of the jacket that tells people what club you're with. The colors are sewn on the back of a Levi's jacket with the sleeves cut off."

"You mean like the winged skull of the Hell's Angels?" I asked.

"Right. The Aces have the four aces fanned out in a hand, with the ace of hearts on top. They didn't want it to be the ace of spades on top. That might make people think it was a black club or something."

"And so what makes you think that this guy killed your brother? This, what's his name?"

"Franz. Werner Franz. Everybody called him Buddy. Great big guy. He must be like almost seven feet tall."

"C'mon, Lucy, that's awfully tall. That's as tall as the Celtics."

"Well, he's real tall, and big, too. And he's mean sometimes. Not all the time; sometimes he could be real nice. But he hated Billy toward the end, and when he got mad, Franz was real crazy, you know?"

"And he cuts people with knives and sings while he's doing it, too," recalled Mary. "Well, Charlie, we've stepped into it again, I see. Buy this place and walk right into a biker gang, including a giant psycho who carves people up for kicks. I *knew* something was wrong with this deal underneath. It felt too good to be true. I had a sneaking feeling in my gut, but I didn't listen to it."

"Come on now, Mare. You were enthusiastic enough when we made the offer. Or are you forgetting?"

She sighed and went to get more coffee.

"Okay," I said, "your brother Bill and this Werner Franz were members of the biker group called the Aces—"

"No. Franz wasn't a member. He was too weird to be in a club. I know because he rode with the Pagans for a while, like for a trial period? Well, they thought he was like too far out so they kicked him out. And that's where the story of the singing came from."

"You mean the singing while he cuts on people?" asked Mary.

"Uh-huh. Mike Church told me about it later. Why I'm so afraid Bill's dead, is that Bill was dating Melissa Hendricks, and Franz wanted her. She kept running away from him because he used to beat on her and everything, but he kept on following her. So finally she wanted to move in with Bill, and that started the whole war."

"And that green Harley, you're sure that's Franz's bike?" I asked.

She nodded, biting her lip.

"And where's Melissa?" asked Mary. "Is she missing, too?"

Lucy nodded. "She's dead. I know. They're both dead. Billy and Melissa. Buddy killed both of them."

"Then where's Franz?" I asked her. "If he's alive, then why is his bike out there, too?"

She thought for a second, and sighed.

"Maybe you're right, Dr. Adams. Maybe Franz is dead, too. He'd never leave his bike behind. Maybe somebody else killed them all. I don't know . . . but I know Billy's dead. We would have heard from him by now if he wasn't."

"What about the other two bikes? Do you know who owns them?" asked Mary.

"The two other guys Billy used to ride with were Mike Church and John Vales. The bikes looked kind of familiar; maybe I can go out there and have another look."

We were just getting up from the table to go back outside when the phone rang. It was Lieutenant Stevens, calling from Pittsfield.

"Well, we ran those serial numbers through the NLETS network, Doc. You're not gonna believe this, but none of those bikes was stolen. Each one was bought and paid for. Each one has an owner. Trouble is, the owners are all missing. They've been missing since last summer—"

"You mean Bill Kirkland and Werner Franz, among others?"

There was a second or two before he could answer.

"Jesus, Doc, how'd you know already?"

"Why don't you come on out here and talk with Bill Kirkland's sister?" I suggested. "She can fill you in on the biker club called the Aces. And she can also tell you about Buddy Franz, I guy I definitely wouldn't want to meet up with. A guy with some kinky habits, like carving people up with knives while he sings to them."

"Holy Christ—"

"Yeah. Interesting country you've got out here, Bryce. Never a dull moment, it seems."

He said he'd be right out, and we walked back down to the barn. We stood there for a few minutes in the bluish light of the barn cellar. I was thinking about what Lucy had said about Werner Franz being tall. I went over to the green Harley and swung my leg over, straddling it. I sat down on the seat, which I realized immediately was very high and set far back. I placed my feet on the pegs, those steel protrusions designed to act as modern versions of stirrups. I could just barely rest my toes on them. But my legs were straight; the normal bent-kneed riding position was impossible. There was a pair of highway pegs mounted on the front of the frame, up ahead of the engine. These extra pegs are placed far forward so that the rider, in the boredom and idleness of highway cruising, can lean back and move his feet way up and rest them on the pegs. Rather like leaning back in an office chair and putting your feet up on the desk. Of course, in this position, your right foot is away from the brake pedal. Dangerous. And you don't get a second chance in a bike wreck.

I tried reaching the highway pegs with my feet. I leaned far back and stretched way out. At six feet tall, I didn't have a prayer of reaching those forward mounted footrests.

Lucy was right; Buddy Franz was big. He was a giant.

FIVE

Test, test, test . . . this is a test," droned Bryce Stevens as he spoke into the tiny cassette recorder. "The following interview, taken this June twelfth, is for investigative purposes only."

He set the machine down on the kitchen table in front of Lucy Kirkland. He asked her to identify herself and she did, speaking into the machine.

Then Stevens read the names spit out by the computer. When Lucy heard them, she jumped up from the table.

"I knew it, Dr. Adams," she said. "The other two bikes are John's and Mike's. I knew they looked familiar. So they're dead. All dead."

"You say you last saw your brother right before July Fourth

weekend?" asked Stevens, leaning over the table. "That's eleven months ago."

"Yeah. See, the biker clubs have two big weekends. July Fourth and Labor Day. On these weekends, they go on runs. They all gather somewhere and just take off for the weekend."

"I know," said Stevens. "Everyone in law enforcement knows about the biker runs. Every cop hopes and prays his town isn't going to be the site of the rendezvous."

"So they came here," said Mary, looking out the window at the valley. "It looks like the Aces chose this valley to gather for their summer run."

"Can you tell us please why they chose to come here? Speak into the microphone please," said Stevens.

Lucy hesitated a second, clearly distrusting the machine and its operator. But the homey surroundings seemed to set her at ease, and she leaned over and talked softly, sadly.

"Well, this place was deserted, you know. We'd known about it for a couple years . . ."

"You knew about it, too?" asked Stevens.

"Well sure. My brother took me out here a few times. It was our party spot. But other people used it, too. It's far away from everywhere. You can, like, raise hell and nobody knows."

"You knew about this spot and came here with your brother, is that right?"

She nodded.

"But last July Fourth, for the run, you weren't with the others? You were somewhere else?"

"Right. I was with my friend Shelly Bancroft over in Springfield. And if you don't believe it, you can ask the police in town about it, mister, because I told them all this last year when we reported Billy missing. We went into town and filled out a bunch of sheets of paper and answered a whole bunch of questions, like I'm doing now."

"Thank you for the clarification, Miss Kirkland," said Stevens politely. "I wasn't in the Pittsfield office then, or we would probably have met. Is this the picture your family brought in?"

He held out a photo, which she took. She nodded and handed it back to Stevens. Looking over his shoulder at the photo, which was in color, I saw a kid with long brown hair and the faint beginnings of a mustache. He bore little enough resemblance to his sister that I would never have guessed they were siblings. And I notice faces, particularly jaws and lower faces. He did have the same haunting violet-blue eyes, though. But instead of being attractive, they were weak and mean and had a sinister glitter to them. The mouth was small and tight, the expression mischievous, taunting. It may have been some prejudice or preconception on my part, but all in all, Billy Kirkland looked like a punk to me. I kept quiet, of course.

"So anyway," continued Lucy, "this place was like a perfect hideout, and big enough to party and raise hell without attracting the law."

We sat and listened to Lucy give her background story on her brother Bill, his girlfriend Melissa Hendricks, the Aces Motorcycle Club, and Werner "Buddy" Franz. Stevens listened patiently until she came to the part about Franz's fondness for cutting people with his big knife and singing to them while he did it.

"Singing to them while he cut them?" he asked, leaning over close to Lucy. "I find that hard to believe, Miss Kirkland."

"It's true. Or, I think maybe it's true; I didn't see it, but I heard about it. Mike Church told me himself."

"What happened?"

"You mean about the singing while he cuts on people?" said Lucy.

"Right. Fill us in on that," said Stevens.

"Does she have to?" said Mary with a shudder. The shudder was real, as was the look of loathing on her face. Mary is a registered nurse and can stand the sight of blood, even lots of it, without flinching. She is unafraid of things that would scare most men half to death. But injustice and cruelty are two things that send her into orbit.

"Okay," said Lucy softly. "Here's what Mike told me. This

was when Buddy was riding with the Pagans for a little while, before they kicked him out. They were on a run, see, and they ran into this guy near Worcester. This black dude, who was walking along a farm road outside town. He wasn't even doing anything, you know, like to piss them off? Well, Buddy gets off his bike and knocks him down and starts kicking him, calling him a nigger and everything. Then he takes out his knife and starts working on him. All the time singing that nursery rhyme."

"A nursery rhyme?" I asked. "A biker singing a nursery rhyme?"

"I think it is, kinda. The one that goes 'black sheep, black sheep, have you any wool?' Remember that?"

"Sure. He sang that to this black guy while he was cutting him?"

"Yeah. Two of the Pagans told Mike about it later. Buddy kept singing black sheep, black sheep, have you any wool? And the guy's on his back, all kicked in and crying and scared to death, but Buddy wouldn't stop. They all thought it was funny at first, but then Buddy was like stripping the guy's skin off his arm with that big knife he carried."

"You mean like shearing a sheep?" said Mary, her eyes wide in horror.

"Uh-huh. And like giving the guy shit for being black? And then the Pagans pulled him off the guy before he like bled to death, you know. The guy got up and ran off, holding his bloody arm with the skin half off. They got back on their bikes and blasted out of there real fast. They didn't stop until they got all the way to Buffalo. They holed up there for a few days, then snuck back and laid low. They never heard any more about it, which was lucky for them. But they kicked Buddy out of the Pagans right then, 'cause he's so weird."

"They kicked him out?" said Stevens, talking softly, as if in awe. "The *Pagans* kicked him out?"

"Yep. That's what happened."

"Lucy, the Pagans are generally thought to be one of the three worst biker gangs in the country; they're right up there with the Hell's Angels and Satan's Slaves. You're saying they kicked Franz out because he was too mean?"

She nodded.

"Did Franz show this behavior all the time?" I asked.

"Well, sometimes, anyway," she said absently. Lucy seemed to add this almost as an afterthought. It surprised me.

"What do you mean, sometimes?" I said. "You said that he killed your brother. You don't think that's bad?"

"I said that, I know. But maybe I was wrong. See, I knew Buddy Franz, and he wasn't always bad. Sometimes he was even nice. He's not—he wasn't—real smart, and sometimes the other guys teased him. But anyway, about my brother, I thought Buddy might have killed him because, like I said, Billy took away his girlfriend, Melissa. But now I'm thinking he didn't kill Billy."

"Because his green bike is in the barn along with the others?"

"Uh-huh. If Buddy did kill Billy, then he would run away on his bike. Far, far away. But he didn't . . ."

"Now wait a second," said Stevens, playing with the knobs on the tape machine. "Why are you so sure he didn't run away without his bike?"

"He would never do that. Even Billy would never do that. I don't know about the others."

We left the house then and went back to the barn. I didn't like the desperate, trapped look on Mary's face. She asked Bryce what would happen to the motorcycles. He replied that they would be returned to the owners.

"And if we can't locate them, they'll be given to the families or heirs. Failing that, they'd be yours, unless you'd want us to sell them at the state auction," he said, going inside the big door. We went into the darkness again. It was cool and musty in there. Troubles, my drahthar bitch, was curled against the wall, her teeth working on what looked like part of an old leather harness.

Lucy walked back to the bikes. After a brief examination of them, she confirmed the identity of the remaining two as belonging to Mike Church and John Vales. Then she explained to us how she used to ride "two up" with her brother Bill around Pittsfield on his bike.

"Charlie," called Mary from the other side of the barn. I told her to wait a minute.

"Charlie, get over here," she said, urgent now.

I asked her if it couldn't wait a second or two, since Lieutenant Stevens was explaining—

"*Charlie!*"

So I went over and saw Mary up against the barn wall, looking down at the dog. I thought I heard her whimper, but maybe it was the dog. Then she was saying oh shit, oh shit, over and over in a little voice.

I leaned over in the dark and looked at the long gray-brown object between the animal's paws. I grabbed it; Troubles gave me a soft warning growl. This is *mine*, she was telling me. I smacked her on the head and she backed off, licking her lips and wagging her tail. I looked down. Even in the dim light of the barn cellar there was no mistaking what it was. There was the chewed crescent of flat bone, joined with another one, bent and curved like a thick twig. Stinky. And then the round joint of the shoulder, called the caracoid process, and the humerus extending from that. The scapula was almost chewed in half. I was looking at a human shoulder, with part of the back as well: shoulder blade, collar bone, upper arm and shoulder joint. All stuck together, still, with ligaments and stinky slime. That just about fit the timetable, I figured: just under a year. A pretty long time, but most of it filled with cold weather. Yes, it seemed reasonable enough.

"Charlie . . . is that . . . what I think it is?" whispered Mary, still flat against the wall, hand to mouth, staring wide-eyed down at the dog and her grisly relic. Lucy and Bryce came up, looking at us.

"Well, one thing," I said, kneeling down and stroking Troubles' head to get a closer look. Too close; I could see with my nose. "I don't think the owners of these bikes are very far off. You ask me, they never left the farm."

was on the phone to Jim DeGroot in Concord, telling him the news.

"A vapor detector?" he said. "What the hell's a vapor detector?"

"Just what it sounds like: an instrument they use to detect gases. In this case, gases from decomposition. It's a box with electronic sensors inside, and a tube snaking out of it. There's a hollow metal probe at the end of the tube. They stick this probe into the ground and see if the needle jumps. And let me tell you, pal, the needle's jumping out here. Jumping like a kitty on coals. Mary's gone bonkers."

"How many have they found?"

"Three for sure. But they've only just started. Isn't this fun? Isn't this just *swell*?"

"But you say it's not on your property, right?"

"Not officially; it's maybe a hundred yards over the line, on the deserted neighboring farm. But so what? It's right down there in that copse of trees by the stream where the campfires were. Remember?"

"Yeah. Well . . . too bad."

"Too bad is right. Jesus, Jim, and after all the work and expense on this place. I just can't believe it. Looks like we might have to sell this place; get out while we still can. And just when we were getting it—"

"Sell it? *No way*, guy. Listen, you put it on the market now, you'll take a terrible beating. Trust me; I know. What you've got to do is wait a year or so until the stigma goes away. No way it'd move now."

"Thanks, Jim. Thanks a lot."

"Hey, don't blame me, for crissakes. I'm just trying to give you good advice—"

We terminated this dreary conversation and I wandered, shell-shocked, back onto the flagstone terrace to try and comfort Mary. It was a labor of Hercules.

"Well, so much for our foolproof investment, Charlie," she said, wiping her eyes and staring out toward the distant grove of trees up the valley around the river's bend. From our meadow, all you could see of the spot was the tops of the tall trees. But she couldn't take her eyes off that haunted place. "I just kept having this feeling from the start that it was too good to be true, Charlie. And now look!"

"C'mon. It's not on our property. It's over on the neighbor's place—"

"So what? It's close enough. Bryce left a few minutes ago; he told me they just found another one. That makes four. Maybe more. Good God. We're gonna have to change the name of the place, *if* we keep it."

"Of course we're going to keep it," I said, trying to sound upbeat. And indeed we were. According to Jim, we hadn't a snowball's chance in hell of unloading it now, even for half what we'd put into it. "And what's wrong with Pound Foolish

Farm?" I continued. "It's a neat name; it's got a ring to it."

"It's got a mass grave on it, is what it's got. I was thinking of some more fitting names. How about Babi Yar? Or maybe Little Big Horn?"

"C'mon, sport. It'll pass. The place is beautiful. And in time people will forget."

"Yeah, in maybe fifty years. Tell me: who the hell would buy this place now? *Who?*"

I shrugged my shoulders and turned to see another police truck coming up the drive. The place was a regular parking lot now. The new vehicle was a black van with a flashing blue light inside the truck, right behind the windshield on the dash. It winked out at us, as bright as Boston Light. Why the hell do they always turn the light on? Why? Do we really need the light, guys? They're all dead, for crissakes—there's no rush. Do we really need to advertise it, as if everybody in the whole damn county isn't going to hear about it anyway?

Mary and I walked back to the house. I had my arm around her. Lot of good it did. I felt sorry as hell for her. We stopped at the side of the house and looked at the lower wall.

"That's where we had to jack the whole frame up and replace the rotted sill, remember, Charlie?" she asked, wiping away a tear.

"Yeah . . . and look at the shrubbery, where Mr. Isimoto pruned and fed it those two months in the spring. Look how lovely it is now—"

We walked on, rounding the corner and looking at the attached cottage, built once upon a time to house the servants. Joe had bought this from us and was almost finished remodeling it. This was to have been his place, his own little country retreat. The farm was going to be the family retreat, the place where the entire clan could gather with plenty of room. It was sad; we both felt terribly cheated.

"But look at it this way, honey," I said, giving her a squeeze around the waist, "we didn't expect this windfall in the first place. It just came to us out of the blue. The Lord giveth, and the Lord taketh away. We must try to be philosophical about this."

"*Bullshit!* The hell we do, Charlie. We worked our asses off on this place, dammit!"

"Maybe I should have bought that fifty-foot steel ketch instead."

She turned to face me, sighing, hand on hip, and regarded me with a look of exasperation.

"Oh, right, Charlie. That was the dumbest idea ever. I think Jim was talking you into it. It was over two hundred grand, and you said yourself it needed another hundred in repairs and options."

"To make her fully seaworthy and safe, yes. It's still for sale, you know. In Bath, Maine. We could go up and look—"

"We'd have to sell this place first, and you know we can't get fifty cents on the dollar for it right now. What we should have done, we should have bought that villa on the Amalfi coast. It was only three hundred and sixty, which is what we paid for this place."

"Oh, great, Mare. Sure, it was huge and beautiful, and we both love Italy, but how often could we enjoy it? Two weeks a year, max? And are you forgetting the fact that the marble was crumbling, and it didn't have a few of the minor necessities, like plumbing, electricity, and heating? You forgetting those little tidbits, Mary?"

She leaned into me, hugging me. I was afraid she was going to cry again, but she didn't.

"You know, the truth is, this was the ideal investment, Charlie. Two hours from home, gorgeous setting . . . the works. Why . . . *why?*"

We sighed, girded our loins, and went inside. There was quite a crowd in the kitchen now, including Joe. I had the bones laid out on a clean sheet of freezer wrap. I know, I know, it was a poor choice. And I got a lot of ghoulish comments, too. But it was clean, white, and the only stuff I could lay my hands on at the time—

"You take it *off* the kitchen table, Charlie. *Off!*" Mary said, starting to cry again and stomping off to the stairway. She needed a break.

There was no arguing with Mary. A few years earlier, when some bad guys killed our little dachshund, Angel, and left her head in our oven as a not-too-subtle warning, Mary insisted we go out and buy a new oven. Didn't matter that it was practically new and cost a mint; she said she simply couldn't bear the thought of cooking anything in there again. Not to mention *eating* it afterward. I saw her point, and went out and bought a new oven. So now I took the bones into the dining room and laid them—still on the white paper—on the window seat, where the light of day could fall fully on them. Some treat. Most of our guests—people with substantial experience in law enforcement—stayed in the kitchen sipping coffee. Joe was one of them. But Bryce stayed at my side, leaning over, hands resting on knees, peering down at the brownish-gray limbs.

"They let you keep these?" he asked me. "The coroner's office doesn't want them?"

"Sure they do, but they're also in my domain, now that I'm working in forensic pathology."

"But they're not teeth or jaws."

"True. They'll take them this afternoon; I'm sure Mary won't miss them."

"Tell me what you see, Doc," said Bryce. "Tell me all you can."

I leaned over close, finding the odor bearable now. However, I did not take this to mean that I was going to rush into my new avocation with the Commonwealth of Massachusetts with renewed enthusiasm. I took a pencil and began to point out significant details.

"These leathery-looking things are ligaments, tissue that joins bone to bone. This big, thick piece is the scapular ligament. It holds the ball-and-socket shoulder joint together. When it's torn you have a separated shoulder. I'm sure you can imagine why it's so painful. The ones up here hold the clavicle, or collarbone, in place."

"I'm surprised the bones are still connected, Doc, after all that time in the ground."

"We're assuming the murders happened in July. There would be a lot of decomposition in the heat of summer, but then the cold weather that comes in September and extends through March kept the remains well preserved. But that's not the interesting thing about this set of bones, Bryce."

"Oh really? What's so interesting about them?"

"Their size. Look here—"

I took the steel tape out of my pocket and gave it to Stevens, asking him to measure my upper arm. It read just over eleven inches, which is about average for a six-footer. I then held the tape along the humerus lying on the window seat. Just under fourteen inches.

"Wow. A big'n," he said.

"Very big. I'd guess his height at over six and a half feet. You know who this is—er, was—don't you?"

"Werner Franz, the singing butcher. Have you read the sheet on this guy?"

"No."

"You don't want to. And just be glad he's dead."

Joe came in blowing on a fresh cup of coffee, lighted cigarette in his left hand.

"Lady Luck smiles on us again," he said, strolling over and peering down at the bones. He shook his head and muttered something I couldn't understand. "I just heard the body count's up to *six*. Who knows? We could be going for a record here. Anybody called the people at Guinness?"

"Not funny, Joe. And please don't tell your sister."

"Hmmmmph! As if she's not gonna find out. The state M.E., Tarkington, just arrived a few minutes ago. Didn't you get to meet him last fall?"

"Uh-huh," I replied. "Nice guy, too. Was that him in the black van with the searchlight?"

"Yeah. He just came back from the dig. Says it looks like a cult murder."

"Cult murder? You mean devil worship? Stuff like that?"

"Could be. The bodies were arranged in a pattern, he says. And one of the skeletons is female. Maybe that's the girlfriend Lucy Kirkland mentioned yesterday. By the way, where's Lucy right now? Some people want to talk to her."

"She decided to go visit her mother. She's a widow who lives in a nursing home in Pittsfield," said Stevens.

"Sweet of her. Can't imagine why, though," mused Joe, shuffling back into the kitchen. Somebody had just brought doughnuts, and he wanted his share, or more. Somehow, the refreshments seemed slightly inappropriate. I could imagine an engraved invitation:

COME JOIN MARY, DOC, AND JOE

FOR OUR ANNUAL SPRING EXHUMATION.

RUSTIC RURAL SETTING.

REAL BONES.

REAL STINK.

MASS MURDER.

COFFEE AND DOUGHNUTS.

RSVP . . .

"*Eewwwwww! Ewwwww!*" people started saying in the kitchen. What was wrong? Stale pastry? Then I caught a faint whiff. *Ewwwww!* I said to myself. The wind had shifted, and the warm spring air brought a little reminder of that wooded hollow a quarter mile away, just over the fence. I went upstairs and found Mary on the bed, lying on her stomach. I sat down on the bed next to her and saw that her eyes were open. She had the Thousand-Yard Stare, aiming it at the wall. It was the look of total devastation, utter defeat. You can see the same expression in the faces of shell-shocked GIs in photos by Robert Capa. In the eyes of the Dust Bowl migrants in pictures taken by Dorothea Lang. I rubbed her back, and her eyelids fell a little. She wanted badly to sleep.

"Our boys are fine," I said softly. "We're in good health. And we still have our dogs and cats, our two other houses, Joe, our friends, and . . . and that's a hell of a lot."

She stirred, and talked slowly and softly, as if to the walls. Her newly papered walls.

"I know, Charlie. And it's not just the money and all the time and effort. I'm thinking of Joey. This seemed to be the first real commitment he's made in a while. I knew he was really excited about this family compound in the country. And his own house and everything. Does that mean anything to you? His own house next to ours? What does that say to you?"

"It says maybe Joe's sick of being a houseguest every weekend, and now he wants his own place to invite us to."

She turned away from me and hid her head under her arm. Wrong answer. I kept rubbing her back. She lifted her weary, worried head and spoke.

"Go over to my dresser and look at the phone bill there. Take a look at the circled number."

I went over and looked at the phone bill, our first in the new residence. A number was circled. There was no three-digit area code prefix, so I assumed it was a local call.

"So?"

"Joey made that call. It was to Pittsfield. He never mentioned it to me, but the number looked vaguely familiar. You know who lives in Pittsfield."

Instantly, I knew what Mary was getting at. There was only one person we knew who lived in this western Massachusetts town. And that person had been, once upon a time, very special in Joe's heart. Martha Higgins had been the only ray of light in Joe's devastated life after losing his wife and son fourteen years previously. Martha Higgins, who was a secretary at the state police headquarters, the Department of Public Safety at Ten Ten Commonwealth Avenue, had been in love with Joe. But when she developed cancer, Joe dumped her. He dumped her not because of her, but because of himself. The loss of his family had been a double curse for him. The loss itself would have been grievous enough; I doubt many people could have ever recovered. But the other fallout was this: Joe was convinced that he somehow caused their deaths; that he was a jinx to other people, particularly those close to him. He became convinced that this curse had somehow caused Martha's malignancy, so he broke off the relationship.

That was a long time ago. Martha moved back to Pittsfield to be with her folks. Although she and Joe still corresponded now and then, on those safe, formal holiday occasions, there had been no resumption of the relationship, even though her cancer had responded to treatment, and even though it was apparent to both Mary and me that Joe still had intense feelings for Martha Higgins.

"Why are you so sure it's her?" I asked. "Maybe he just called Pittsfield to get hold of Bryce Stevens or some—"

"Nope," she said in a monotone. "I looked up her name in the Pittsfield directory when I got the bill. Same number."

"And you haven't talked to him at all about—"

"No. Not a word."

I thought for a second. A second was all it took. I went back over to the bed and stroked her head.

"Okay then, we stay. We don't put it on the market or anything. We don't even talk about it. We stay as upbeat as possible. Remember: the shock is at its worst right now. Right this minute. It'll dim with time. And we'll get right behind Joe and help him with his house. Speed up construction on the in-ground pool. Say we want it ready by August . . . at the latest—"

She reached up and hugged me, crying softly.

"I was hoping you'd say that," she said. "I was afraid you'd think that continuing would just be pouring money down the drain."

"No way. And keep remembering this: the bodies are on the *neighbor's* land. The bikes may be ours, but the skeletons aren't."

Mary put her head back down on the pillow. I rubbed her back again, and she melted into sleep. The sleep of relief after a vigil. I returned downstairs to find everybody gone except Joe and his old buddy, Bryce Stevens. They seemed deep in private conversation, so I went out the front way, working my way around the house. As I passed the kitchen window, though, I overheard poor Joe trying to make light of a grim situation. Thank God for his sense of humor.

"Well shit, I don't know, Bryce. Way my luck's been running, maybe I should call the *National Enquirer*. Think so? I'd say, 'Hey, you guys, this is *the* Joe Brindelli calling. You remember me, right? The guy who brought you the Black Death, the Mongol Hordes, and the Johnstown Flood? Well, you oughta come out here and see my summer place—"

I walked part way down the slope. The nasty aroma was lingering, but diminished. I knew once they carted off all the remains in plastic bags and cleaned up the clearing, it would disappear. But in the meantime, the best thing for us to do was head back to Boston until the thing blew over. Pun intended.

I went back up to the kitchen and announced to Joe that whatever his thoughts at present might be, Mary and I had irrevocably decided to stay at Pound Foolish Farm. We hoped he'd do likewise. And if so, to get off his fat ass and get the damn swimming pool *finished*, for crying out loud, as summer was here already!

He sat stunned for a few seconds. Then a wide grin spread across his stubbled face.

"Hear that, Stevens? My marching orders. Hey, you seen the inside of my place lately?"

Stevens replied that he hadn't ever seen it. Joe stubbed out his cigarette and took him by the arm.

"Well, let's get goin', then. You'll like this place, Bryce. It's gonna be *dy-no-mite!*"

SEVEN

We stayed away from the farm for the next ten days. During that time, Mary recovered her equilibrium and Joe and I buried ourselves in our work. What occupied most of my time at the beginning of the week was fixing a third molar extraction that was terribly botched by a man down in Randolph claiming to be an oral surgeon. He had the title, and the sheepskin, too. He'd even done a residency at a respectable hospital. But I'd heard horror stories about this guy before, and now, when poor Mrs. Morrison came in with a fever from a secondary infection as well as a swollen cheek, I knew they were well founded. He'd left tooth fragments in the socket, for starters. The incisions were all done wrong and had opened. Anyway, it wasn't pleasant, for either doctor or patient. But

unpleasant as it was, I welcomed the diversion that work offered; it took my mind off the farm.

I went back out to Humphrey alone that next weekend to
check up on things. Warren Shaw and a few helpers were putting the finishing touches on the kitchen plumbing and install-
ing the new countertops. They seemed to approach the work
tentatively, uncertain as to the permanency of their employment. I sat them down over beers after work on Saturday and
reassured them that this macabre incident was only a temporary setback, and that we'd be up and going again full tilt the
following weekend. They were mighty relieved.

On another high note, the caravans of the curious, which we
had envisioned clogging the highways for miles around, never
materialized. Warren told me that there had been a few specta-
tors who dribbled by, hoping to see the grisly site. These are the
same high-class rubbernecks who gather like buzzards at fires
and highway wrecks. They're the same ones who gather in
downtown city streets, gawking at the potential suicide cling-
ing to a ledge ten stories up, screaming *jump*, for crissakes, you
chickenshit or *what*? No doubt their own worlds are so dismal
and squalid that they'll go to any lengths to see someone in a
worse situation, and receive some sick sense of comfort or supe-
riority by doing so. The patrolman in attendance had informed
them that the site had been cleared of all remains, that it was
very far from the road, and that it had been sealed off by order
of the police. The gawkers filed away, disappointed and cussing,
most likely en route to their fallback entertainment of professional wrestling.

Bryce Stevens stuck his head in the kitchen when I was sitting at the table with the workmen.

"After the guys leave, can you come down the hill with me
for a minute, Doc? I'll explain what we've found so far."

I was about to ask him if I really had to, but it would have
been poor form, especially for a sometime medical examiner. So
I excused the work crew, then got up and followed him down
the hill, across the pasture, and along the lazy stream to where

it puddled wide in an alder thicket surrounded by tall pines. The clearing was covered with old leaves and pine needles. Devoid of undergrowth, covered by a canopy of trees, and right on the river's edge, it was a perfect camping and party spot. There was no smell left in the place, but I could see big white blotches here and there—caustic lime spread in the shallow graves by the lab people after they had finished. A ribbon of yellow polyethylene four inches wide had been strung around tree trunks in a wide circle surrounding the eerie spot. Printed on the ribbon was the message STATE POLICE SEAL DO NOT CROSS repeated endlessly over and over.

We ducked under it and walked along the mushy earth to the fire-blackened camping area. The ground that was previously littered with old beer cans, aluminum foil, and assorted trash was now mostly picked clean by police looking for evidence. But judging from the kitchen midden of relics that had been there earlier, I assumed the place had been popular for a number of years. Stevens stopped and swept his arm in an arc over the clearing.

"You can see where the graves were. See how they're placed in a semicircle? It seems the bodies were carefully arranged in this pattern. This makes us think it may have been a cult killing."

"You mentioned that earlier. You think it's a satanic cult?"

Stevens nodded. "We also found animal bones. Three sets. One's a dog. That's for sure. The other two are either sheep or goats. We suspect sheep, since they're common around here. But they could be goats; they're associated with witchcraft."

"Good God," I said, sitting down on a fallen tree, "will all this be in the papers?"

"I don't see any way to keep it out."

"That means that we'll have every looney-toon in five counties on our doorstep for the rest of the year."

"No, you won't; the bodies are all gone. It's history now, practically forgotten already. The only people who can't forget are the relatives of the deceased, and us."

Bryce led me up the glade to a cowpath. It had been worn

there by the animals, but it was fairly wide and free of obstructions, and now showed deep tire ruts. The path wound out of the hollow and over a far hill, heading away from our property. Bryce pointed at the hilltop in the distance.

"This is the road the bikers used to get to this place, Doc. They didn't cross your property to get here. The bikes were ridden or pushed up this path to the road on the far side, then to the connecting road that joins Route 8, and over to your place, where they were taken up your gravel drive and down into the barn."

"What about the green bike? The one that was buried? What does all that mean?" I asked him.

"That's a puzzle," he said. "What we're thinking now is that the killers first tried to hide the machines by burying them. But it didn't work; the soil is too rocky, and they couldn't make the hole big enough. A motorcycle obviously requires a much bigger hole than a body. They had a half-buried bike on their hands, and were running out of time. So they abandoned the idea and decided to hide the machines elsewhere, like the nearest abandoned farm building. That turned out to be your barn, Doc."

"Lucky me. But wouldn't this indicate that they hadn't planned the killings very far in advance?"

"Possibly."

"Okay, you found six sets of bones, and there are only four bikes. I take it then that two riders doubled up, carrying passengers?"

"That's the current speculation. It's reinforced by the fact that the lab is now telling us that two of the skeletons are female. So that would seem to fit: two of the bikers had their girlfriends riding on the back."

"And one of them was probably Melissa Hendricks, the girl who Bill Kirkland and Buddy Franz were fighting over."

"I don't think they were fighting over her, Doc; I think Bill Kirkland and Melissa were both on the run from Franz, and he caught up with them."

I thought about this for a second, but something was out of

place. "Well, okay then," I said, "but if that's what happened, then who killed Franz and buried him? And isn't it more than coincidental that his bike was the one that was buried?"

Try as we might, we couldn't make a dent in this riddle, so we made our way slowly back to the house. My spirits had fallen again. Each time I had hopes of putting this grim business behind us, some new gem cropped up. Now it was satanic cult killings, complete with animal sacrifices. Great.

"Joe says you'll be doing the dental forensic work. That true?"

I nodded. "I'll do the follow-up Wednesday morning in Boston, at Ten Ten. Mostly, it's for positive IDs of the victims. They're waiting for dental records now and should have them all by the middle of the week."

We reached the house. I could hear the workmen inside the kitchen. We sat down on the terrace, reclining in two big wooden Adirondack chairs. Bryce seemed very tired and reticent. Perhaps this violence was a shock to him, since western Mass is hardly a hotbed of crime. Dusk was falling. I asked Bryce if he'd like a drink and he said sure. So I came out with a couple of scotches and we sat and sipped.

"Sure is a nice place here, Doc. You made a good buy, and a smart move."

"Thanks. I thought so, too, at first. Now I'm not so sure."

"Don't worry; in the long run you'll be glad you did."

"What about this thing, Bryce? Every time I turn it around in my head, I hit a roadblock. Lucy Kirkland was sure that it was Werner Franz who killed her brother Bill. But we've found Franz's giant skeleton along with all the others. So the question now is: who's the killer?"

"Killers, you mean. One person could never have killed them all alone. And with a guy as big as Franz, it would be doubly hard to pull off. Here's the scenario, as far as we've been able to piece it together from the evidence: The motorcycle club called the Aces came out here last Fourth of July for their annual 'run.' They partied and camped out here. Maybe even cooked a meal over the fire. Then later, probably in the dead of night when they were zonked from drugs and booze, somebody sneaked up on them and killed them outright or else overpowered them, tied them up, and killed them in a sacrificial manner."

I thought about this for a minute. There was a piece, a big piece, out of place.

"I don't think that Lucy Kirkland would agree with that scenario, Bryce. Of course, she wasn't here; she was at her friend's house over in Springfield. But according to her, Franz, the musical butcher, hated Bill Kirkland's guts for stealing his lady friend. And she's in a position to know. Therefore, the idea of Bill Kirkland and Werner Franz sitting around getting drunk together doesn't fit. Have you talked to her recently?"

"I will on Monday, and let you know what she says."

I took a sip of the whiskey and soda and looked out at the valley. The valley of the shadow of death. Sure was pretty, though. The meadows looked very "birdy." Brady Coyne and I could stalk the alder and birch thickets with dogs, gunning for grouse and pheasant. And the stream held trout; I knew it was true because I'd seen them. Maybe it wasn't so bad after all; when the business was forgotten, we could recoup our dream . . .

I turned to look at Bryce and was stunned to see a tear falling down his cheek. His eyes looked terribly sad.

"Bryce?"

He looked at me, wiping his cheek with the back of his hand.

"Sorry," I murmured. "I didn't know it upset you so much."

"It's not that, Doc. Don't worry," he answered in a thick voice. Then he sniffed, cleared his throat, and took a swallow of his drink. He took out a small tin of dry Dutch cigars and lit one.

"Can you keep something to yourself?" he asked me through a cloud of cigar smoke. "I ask because I have to tell someone."

"Sure. In my work, I have to keep a lot of secrets."

"Good. Here it is: my wife—"

Then he caught himself, his throat too trembly and thick to speak. After a few seconds, he continued.

"My wife is having an affair with one of my best friends. She told me last night. She's going to leave me to go with him. I don't want to burden you with it, Doc, but I just had to tell somebody. I couldn't stand to have it all inside anymore. You seem like a nice guy and a . . . a guy I can trust."

He wiped his face a little more. I didn't look at him; I kept looking out at the valley.

"Good Christ. I'm very sorry."

"Yeah, so am I. And my kids will be, too, I think."

"Is there any chance she'll . . . change her mind?"

"I'm not counting on it."

"You want me to tell Joe?"

"No. I'll tell him."

Bryce left then. When he got into his car I reached my hand inside and squeezed his shoulder, then patted him on the back of his neck, telling him to call anytime if he wanted to talk. I liked him a lot—what I'd seen of him—and I felt very sad.

After Warren Shaw and the work crew left, I went upstairs to the master bedroom and began to unpack my overnight bag. But somehow, being there alone didn't feel comfortable. It was awfully quiet, for starters. The spring peepers were gone now, and it was too early for cicadas. Cheeping sparrows and clucking robins were few and far between. And the house was big. Too big to sleep alone in. I considered driving back to Concord. It was a two-and-a-half-hour drive. No, I'd stay the night. I took the submarine sandwich Mary had made for me and popped it in the oven. It was an old favorite: Italian cold cuts and provolone packed into a foot-long sub roll. After I retrieved it from the baking rack, steaming with melted cheese, I opened the plastic sandwich bag and put on the shredded lettuce and sliced tomatoes, then covered it with crushed hot peppers, the wet kind packed in vinegar. I washed it down with two beers and a mug of coffee, and headed upstairs to bed.

I undressed and sat naked on the edge of our bed. I was thinking of Mary and how I would die if she left. I felt very sorry for Bryce. A week ago everything was coming up roses. Now it all seemed a wreck. Kids killed and put in shallow graves in a bog. A family shattered. Hearts broken. And I seemed in the middle of all of it.

How'd you get *here*, Adams? I asked myself. It all started out so nice.

I lay down and closed my eyes. I had been careful to lock all the downstairs doors and windows. And I had bolted the bedroom door as well. But I knew the next time I came out, I'd bring the Browning.

EIGHT

I sat in the cool of the basement of the big police headquarters building at Ten Ten Comm Ave. While it wasn't the location of the main morgue, there was a small one down the corridor, with a bank of twelve refrigerated drawers—three high, four wide—that opened like giant filing cabinets. Then there was the autopsy lab, where the big cutting and weighing was performed (spare me). And finally, the forensic pathology labs, a cluster of smaller rooms, each with its own specialized gear. I sat in one of these windowless cubicles at a marble-topped table with six skulls staring at me. The experience was less unnerving than I'd imagined. But still, some interesting dreams might come of it.

My job was to examine the teeth and jaws of these six heads and confirm, or refute, positive identification of the decedents by comparing the teeth and bones with the data supplied by their relatives and dentists. Mouth casts weren't available for any of them. This was not surprising, since full casts are made in preparation for major mouth work. Usually such work is associated with advancing age and/or substantial means. None of the decedents were middle-aged or rich, so all we had to go on were X-rays and dental charts. Most of these were minimal and of poor quality.

I had tentatively identified four of the skulls as belonging to Melissa Hendricks, William C. Kirkland, John Rooney Vales, and Michael E. Church. But the Hendricks ID was sketchy at best. Bryce had obtained these records from a dentist in Pittsfield who had worked on her mouth when she was a child of ten. She had not been to a dentist since that time, and her parents were nowhere to be found—in Massachusetts, anyway. Lucy had said that she thought they moved to Florida a few years back, but she wasn't sure exactly when, or to what city. When Ten Ten put the name Hendricks on the wire with no results, Lucy then recollected that Melissa's mother had remarried shortly before departing to the Sunshine State.

"And I just never knew their last name. She didn't see her folks at all when I knew her."

So we had a bit of a dead end with Melissa Hendricks, and if it was a pun, it was a sad one; most of the kids seemed to have one thing in common: a disintegrated home with parents who either didn't care, or who had thrown their children out. I know this sounds unbelievable to us upper-middle-class types, but it happens. All the time. I know because my friend Moe Abramson, who has devoted most of his free time to helping runaways and castaways, keeps me up to date on the sad statistics.

There were no dental records at all for Werner Franz, though a missing persons report was on file. And finally, the other female skeleton remained a Jane Doe, with no clues as to who she was. For me, that one was the saddest of all.

My report on Mike Church, handwritten on a legal pad, typified the group:

Here is a male Caucasian aged mid-twenties whose
mouth exhibits nothing remarkable except general
indications of a lower-income status and medically
deficient childhood, as evidenced by the poor condition
of the teeth and a small abscess in the mandible on the
distal root of the left six-year molar. Also in evidence
are eight teeth with caries. Three of these are severe,
and show acute pulpal pathosis. Additionally, the
misalignment of many of the teeth, coupled with poor
occlusion (slight prognathism coupled with a cross bite),
are further indications of a deprived childhood without
dental care. Finally, the ossifying scar tissue on the
mandible, right side, late evidence of a broken jaw left
unset, is probable evidence of a severe blow to the jaw,
incurred perhaps in a fistfight or minor cycle accident.

Positive identification was made by matching the
amalgams in the left premolar in the maxillary arch, the
amalgams on both six-year molars, upper and lower, on
the right side, and a smaller, Class V amalgam at the
root of the upper left bicuspid on the buccal surface.
These amalgams are of generally poor quality, and two
of them are temporary fillings composed of IRM
material. Additionally, matches were made via the
deflection of both lateral incisors and the lower left
cuspid.

Cause of death may not be determined by this
specimen. The generally poor condition of the mouth
and substandard dental work suggest that dental care
was infrequent and marginal, and absent in later teenage
years, coupled with poor oral hygene and diet.

Charles Hatton Adams, M.D., D.D.S.
Forensic Pathologist
Commonwealth of Massachusetts

And so on, for each of the identified skulls. All the jaws and
teeth I examined were remarkably similar in their deplorable
state. It might surprise many people, but twenty percent of
Americans never see a dentist. Never. And less than half see one

regularly. Perhaps it's this statistic that leads to the next one: of Americans over fifty-five, one-fourth have no natural teeth left. None. This in the richest country in the world, with the best trained and equipped dentists in the world. If these aren't figures to be ashamed of, I don't know what are. So it goes. And nothing reveals the vast gulf between the haves and the have-nots as clearly and powerfully as the inside of a mouth.

I can look in a mouth and tell instantly the socioeconomic status of the owner. No matter what he's wearing and driving, or how he talks. Teeth don't lie. You can fool people with words, clothes, cars, and fake pieces of paper, but not with teeth. They tell the truth.

With this in mind, it wasn't long into my examination of Werner Franz's teeth before I knew something wasn't right. I went over to Franz's rap sheet and checked it again. First there were the charges and convictions. Franz was wanted in three states for larceny and extortion, in two states for possession and sale of marijuana and for distributing cocaine. He'd been charged with armed robbery but beat the rap. Then the interesting stuff: two counts of cruelty to animals, two assaults (simple, not aggravated), two instances of illegal cockfighting, and miscellaneous complaints stemming from violent behavior and confrontations with the law.

I wondered idly, as I looked at the big skull, if by chance Werner Franz wasn't an XYY man. A man with an extra male chromosome tacked on. Such specimens are generally very tall, with low body fat, heavy beard, and acne, and possess great strength. Supposedly, a tendency toward violence and crime goes along with these physical attributes.

But now I was less interested in Franz's criminal record than I was in his personal background. This I found on another sheet, a form that was filled in during a deposition connected with one of his many brushes with the law. Franz grew up in a tenement house in the industrial section of Pittsfield. His father, when he wasn't drunk or in jail, worked as a porter and dishwasher. His mother was a spinner in a yarn plant twelve miles out of town. She contracted tuberculosis when the boy—

he had no siblings—was twelve and was sent to a state sanitarium, where she died.

Young Franz was left to fend for himself and got into petty crime in his early teens. After two incidents of severe beatings by his father, he was removed from home—if such it could be called—and sent to live with his maternal grandmother before she died when he was seventeen. In his late teens, he drifted from pillar to post, working when he could at fast food places, junkyards, service stations, and lumberyards. He never finished high school, and his scholastic record was dismal. His IQ on the several standardized grammar school tests he took was below 100, but this was not surprising considering his squalid background. His height, by the way, was six foot six and a half. His weight, 204 pounds. Big boy.

There was no telling what Werner Franz would have developed into if he'd had a decent chance. But he hadn't had that chance, and wound up murdered and buried in a shallow grave with five other dropout misfits in a bog on a deserted farm in the Berkshire hills.

At least, that's what we'd all thought.

But examining the set of teeth in front of me on the marble-topped lab table in the forensic-pathology cubicle at Ten Ten Comm Ave that warm June afternoon, I doubted it. I doubted the hell out of it, for one simple reason: the teeth I was looking at were near perfect. Straight, clean, well shaped, filled, and the entire mouth and bone structure showing good hygiene and expensive care. There was ample evidence of well-applied orthodontia as well. By the degree of attrition on the enamel and the position of the third molars, which were unerupted, I judged the subject's age to be roughly between seventeen and twenty-three.

As far as anyone knew, Werner Franz had never sat in a dentist's chair in his life. There was no way, therefore, that his mouth would be in the kind of shape that this one before me was in.

Ergo: The remains before me now were not those of Werner

Franz, but rather they belonged to an upper-middle-class youth of roughly the same age and size. This conclusion set off other syllogistic progressions in my head, which bounced around in there like billiard balls off green felt cushions . . .

"Well, Doc?" said a voice behind me. Joe came up to the table and peered over my shoulder. A 100-mm cigarette was dangling from his lips, bouncing up and down as he talked, spewing little wavy lines of blue smoke. He checked his watch. "C'mon. Lunchtime. Let's go over to the Greek's and get a sub. Or would you rather I take you someplace real fancy?"

"You know I don't eat lunch."

"Yeah, but I do. And you could use some grub, stuck down here in the chill by yourself all morning. Find anything?"

"Yes, I have. The big boy in the mud isn't Werner Franz. Same dimensions, but not a snowball's chance in hell it's him. So I say this: maybe somebody grabbed a big tall kid and stuck him down in the slime to throw us off the track."

Joe's eyes softened, lost their focus, as he stared at all the bones. The Thousand-Yard Stare again. Joe's job is full of it.

"No shit. How about the others?"

"They check out. I'm not totally sure about the Hendricks girl, and the other female is still Jane Doe. But this skull here belongs to somebody a lot better bred and raised than the likes of Mr. Franz. Which takes us back to Lucy Kirkland's story, doesn't it?"

"How so?"

"Well, she kept insisting that Franz killed her brother because he took the girl. Remember? For a while there we thought Franz was also a victim. But now it seems that's not true, so we come back to what Lucy said, and that makes Franz a very likely suspect."

"You're saying he got some big kid, took him to the farm and killed him, then buried him with the others so that when the graves were discovered, which wouldn't take long, given where they were, we'd think it was him in there . . . and that he was dead."

"Yep. And he even went so far as to give up his most prized worldly possession, his Harley-Davidson, to give credence to the story."

Joe took a big drag and shook his head slowly.

"Uh-uh. I doubt he'd leave his bike there. It was the only thing he had. And from what we've been told, I doubt Franz had the intelligence to mastermind a scheme like that. But, if by chance he did, then it would make sense, because he'd been fingerprinted, but he knew he had no dental records. So the burying of the substitute stiff would work. You sure this isn't Franz?"

"Joe, it'd be a miracle if it were. This is a two-thousand-dollar mouth, minimum. That's what's been put into it over the years. I say you go back to your teletype and punch in a query for a missing white male around six foot six, who disappeared last summer around the Fourth of July. See what you come up with."

Joe picked up the phone and punched an inner-office button on its base, then made the request. We left Ten Ten and went across the street to the Greek's.

Usually, I don't eat lunch except a carton of yogurt and a cup of coffee. But once I smelled the aroma of baking subs, my willpower went all to pieces. Joe ordered first.

"I'll have a small steak and cheese with tomatoes, lettuce, oil, and hot peppers," said Joe.

Small? Did I hear that right? Joe ordered a *small*?

"And what else?" said the kid behind the counter.

"Uh . . . lesseee, a large Italian cold cuts with tomatoes and extra cheese," he said.

Better. That's my brother-in-law.

I ordered a large Italian sausage with the works. When completed, the thing was a foot long and weighed maybe three pounds. The kid wrapped it in white paper and I toted it back to the booth. Damn thing felt like an artillery shell. I keep my weight at 174, a couple of pounds heavier in winter, lighter in summer. But I wouldn't have a prayer of doing that if I worked across the street from the Greek's. The subs were fantastic. We used up six of those little pullout white napkins apiece, and each downed a tall iced tea and a big cup of coffee afterward. I could barely move, and finally managed to waddle across the street and down to my cubicle again, belching all the way. Joe shuffled along in his rolling elephant walk, his eyes glazed over with that contented look that comes upon his face with a full tum.

"Hey, Joe," said a swarthy short man in uniform, "you just got a hit on the NLETS. See Sally in the wire room."

"Thanks, Chris. Well, Doc, let's see how good your instincts are. By God, you're getting to be a better cop than any of us. That Chris Popodopoulos is a great cop. Just lost his brother to Hodgkin's disease. Thirty-two years old, wife and four little ones. Keeee-*riste*, life's a bitch. Makes you stop and drink . . ."

We walked down the long corridor and into a glass-walled room filled with electronic gear. Most of it was connected to the many aerials and antenna dishes on the roof of the building. Sally in the wire room sat amidst a half-dozen clacking, buzzing, and beeping machines, each one spitting out or gulping down data. She looked up at us and quick as a wink tore off a sheet from a printer and handed it to Joe.

"Bingo!" she said, smiling.

Joe scanned the sheet. "Bingo," he said, and handed it to me. The sheet was a description of a missing person, specifically a twenty-three-year-old white male from Lenox, Massachusetts, whose name was William Worthington. His height was listed as six foot six, and he disappeared mysteriously from downtown Lenox the previous July 2. Bingo.

I didn't want to say the word out loud. Bingo was what you said when you won a prize at a church bazaar. Somehow, although it furnished a lead we needed, I didn't think the word was appropriate. And certainly, I wagered to myself, poor Bill Worthington's parents wouldn't jump up and shout "Bingo!" when we called them to say we had their boy's remains here in the pathology lab at Ten Ten Comm Ave.

"When and where can we get this kid's dental records so we can make a positive before we call his folks and get them all bent out of shape?" I asked. Joe replied that since a full missing persons report had been filed by the father last summer, a copy of the dental records was in the missing persons bureau, right down the hall.

"I'll look 'em up and have 'em for you in a few minutes, Doc," he said, heading for the glass doors. I called him back.

"While we're doing all this, I'd like printed copies of everything we've got on Werner Franz. Everything. Depositions, statements, mug shots, prints, accounts from interviews, the works," I said, leaning over Sally's desk. "Can you do it?"

"No problem," she said with a wink. She had bright gold-blond hair in a neat, stiff arrangement that didn't even flap around when she moved her head. She worked her keyboard deftly, and I followed Joe into the corridor again.

"If possible, I'd also like to find out from somebody how tall Franz's parents were," I said.

"How come?"

"Just curious. A question of genetics."

B y the end of the day I knew a lot more. Joe handed me the dental records of William Worthington of Lenox. Even the records themselves showed care, arranged chronologically and placed in an expensive envelope with the Worthingtons' address engraved on the back. In my mind's eye I could see his parents carefully placing the records in there, double-checking to make sure they'd collected everything, hoping against hope that the records wouldn't be needed and that their son would come bouncing through the front door any minute now, saying he was sorry, he'd just gone off on a lark . . . It was a heartbreaker.

I made the ID immediately and confirmed it irrefutably by numerous proofs in ten minutes. So now Joe handed Bryce Stevens the unpleasant task of visiting the senior Worthingtons in Lenox and informing them that their long wait was over, that they could come into Boston now and pick up the remains of young Bill.

What else did I find out? I found out that Werner Franz's parents were of average height: mother was five eight, father, five nine. Now, a boy from this union raised in a fine home with lots of love and a sound diet might shoot up to a height of over six and a half feet. Unlikely, but possible. But one spawned in a slum, missing his sick mother and living in terror of his drunken father, would not, in all probability, ever achieve that kind of growth.

Sometimes medical people use the word *thrive* to describe their young patients. It's a good term because it reflects the patient's vigorous growth, healthy appetite, rapid learning ability, emotional well-being, and so on. Children of poverty don't thrive. Abused and neglected children *can't* thrive. Something else, then, accounted for Franz's freakish growth. Accordingly, I decided to ask Moe Abramson, my psychiatrist friend, about the latest findings on the XYY syndrome.

Richie D'Angelo, from Chief M.E. Tarkington's office, came in around three o'clock and told me they'd finished the workup on the animal bones, so we walked down the hallway to one of the bigger labs and looked at the three skeletons.

"Those turned out to be sheep, not goats," he said. "But John guesses that they used sheep because there are more of them out there and they're easier to catch and steal than goats. But goats are the preferred item for Satan worship. That's what they tell us in research."

"Has a vet looked at the dog yet?"

"Yeah. On the basis of the jaw size and shape, he makes it to be a pit bull. Take a look."

I studied the heavy mandible and the high ridge along the skull where the chewing muscle, the masseter, had been attached.

"A fighting dog, for sure," I said. "Looks as if it could chew through steel."

"The AKC name is the American Staffordshire terrier. The

UKC, which does more to promote the breed, calls it the American pit bull terrier. Either that, or a close relative thereof. Notice the wide placement of the shoulder blades, low angle of the front legs . . . wide stance, extremely heavy skull . . ."

I stood there, looking down and nodding. My imagination clothed the bones in flesh and fur. It would be a low-slung animal with heavy shoulders and neck, tapering to narrow hips with powerful hind legs. Powerful not for running, but for lunging and leaping. But most of the muscle would be concentrated around the forelegs, neck, and jaws, so that the dog could seize its victim in a crushing grip that wouldn't let go, then tear it apart with vigorous shakes of its wide head.

"Franz is a dogfighter. That's what one acquaintance told us. And he's been arrested for cruelty to animals and for cockfighting. Nice hobbies."

"Dogfighting's come up here from the South," said Richie. "I hear there's big money in it. Sometimes ten or twenty grand on a single match."

"From what I've heard, 'match' isn't a very good word for it," I said, "since most of the fights end only when one of the combatants is either dead or mauled so badly they've got to put it down. I'm just wondering why Franz, or whoever the killer was, would kill one of his fighting dogs."

"Maybe it was already dead from a fight, and he just buried the body along with the others to make it seem like a ritual killing," Richie suggested. I liked this idea. The more I considered it, the more sense it made.

Joe and I walked out of Ten Ten together, and I asked him out to the house for dinner. He never turns it down. It was warming up in Concord, and the humidity was high. We sat out on the sunporch with the ceiling fan swooshing down on us, playing an Ellington CD called "Digital Duke." We sipped gin and tonics and dipped corn chips into fresh guacamole that Mary had made.

"I got a call from Lucy Kirkland today," she said, popping a heavily laden chip into her mouth. "She said she's finished wallpapering the end bedroom, and now she's going ahead and sheetrocking the shed where Warren's men framed it in. I tell ya, Charlie, Joe, is that kid a whiz, or what?"

"What do we owe her so far?"

"She said a hundred and eighty bucks."

"That's *all*? That's *it*?"

She nodded. "Plus the room and food."

"That's nothing. You ask me, we're getting a caretaker in the bargain. What gets me, though, is how she can stand the place."

"I wondered about that, too. Working on the farm near where her brother and friends were killed. But the answer's simpler than we think. Basically, she's got nowhere else to go. She was laid off her waitressing job in Pittsfield and she can't find work anywhere. Not even swing shift in the factories. Her father's dead and her mother's in a nursing home run by the county. She broke up with her boyfriend in February; she's all alone."

"Well, before she leaves, let's have her come over and wallpaper my upstairs," said Joe, munching. "I like her rates. And speaking of the farm, what are you going to do with Franz's green Harley? It's yours, you know. The other bikes were claimed by the relatives of the deceased. Billy Kirkland's bike had a huge lien against it, so the bank's got that one. But nobody's made a claim for the Franz motorcycle. Nor are they about to. Both parents are dead. Therefore, since it was left on your property, it belongs to you."

"Well, I know it's a disappointment to both of you," I said, leaning back in my chair, "but I've decided to hand the bike over to the Commonwealth of Massachusetts. Bryce told me there's a state vehicle auction in Pittsfield next month, to be held at the county fairgrounds. I'll have the bike sold off and donate the proceeds, writing off the gift. I just want to be shut of the whole thing. Until then, the green Harley-Davidson stays locked in my barn."

"You've put a lock on the door?" said Mary. "When and why?"

"I told Warren Shaw to put heavy-duty locks on all the barn doors and windows, and to keep all the doors and windows of both houses locked, too. I don't want any more people going in and out of our buildings, *period.* "

"How about Franz himself?" said Mary with a shudder. "The evidence now says he might still be around somewhere, missing his prized bike."

"It's unlikely," I said. "If he is, he's been away from it for a long time. That's why auctioning off the bike is the best idea. That way we wash our hands of the whole thing. I don't want it sitting around as bait."

"You ask me, Doc, Franz is dead. Now, we still don't know if he committed the murders. Frankly, he looks good for it, but . . . BUT, that was a year ago, and the bikes were still in your barn, untouched, until very recently. That makes me think he's dead. A guy with Franz's upbringing would never have the patience to wait this long before retrieving his bike. He's either dead or inside somewhere."

"Inside?" said Mary.

"Yeah. You know: in prison. We've got a call out on him. But so far, no hits. We should have gotten one by now if we were gonna get one. So I say the prison shot is unlikely. Therefore, maybe he's in his own shallow grave somewhere."

"Uh-huh . . . or maybe not," said Mary, getting up to go into the kitchen. I asked her if we could have another guest for dinner, namely Morris Abramson, M.D. She said sure, and since we weren't having red meat, maybe he'd even eat some of it.

"The double Y syndrome . . ." Moe said as he speared the pile of linguine on his plate and twirled it with his fork. "I assume you want me to tell you about the behavioral implications rather than the strictly genetic ones. So I went through my notes and files at the office after you called. Now, what I'm giving you mostly is stuff remembered from journals and from convention papers and t'ings; this isn't a specialty of mine."

"We were required to do some reading on it three years ago," said Joe through a mouthful of pasta, "but I've forgotten most of it. I know that one of the signs is tallness."

"Right," said Moe. "The final proofs must be done in a laboratory, but some outward signs are extreme height, low body fat, active hair follicles . . . sometimes there's an increase in muscle strength, and then there are the behavioral changes that may or may not be present."

"You mean excessive aggression?" I asked.

He nodded and shrugged his shoulders at the same time.

"That may or may not be true," he said. "The thinking now is that maybe they aren't as aggressive as everybody's thought. But XYYs *do* show elevated levels of testosterone. Much higher than average. This is what probably causes the height, the leanness, and the muscle strength. And maybe what leads to the aggression."

We ate for a moment in silence, absorbing this.

"In addition," continued Moe, "they show slightly lower intelligence, while scoring significantly higher on the schizophrenia and prejudice scales on the MMPI test. You heard of that, Joe? The Minnesota Multiphasic Personality Inventory?"

Being in the fields of medicine and law enforcement, we'd all heard of it, the standardized test for measuring personality and tendency toward psychosis. Used worldwide.

"The study found that the XYY men were more toward the edge than the control group."

"So they're more likely to be nuts?" asked Mary.

"Maybe a little."

"You think that this guy Werner Franz is crazy?" asked Joe. "Or just nasty?"

Moe held up his hands in disclaimer.

"Listen—I have no way of knowing for sure. Yeah, based on what you've both told me about his file, I'd say he's unstable at best. But remember: insanity is a legal term, not a medical one. And no subject fits all the criteria of the syndrome, either."

"Maybe not," said Mary. "But Franz seems to fit most of them, including the aggression and the low IQ."

"I'd say that given the boy's size and strength, and his criminal record to date, it's safe to make one inference about him," said Moe.

"Which is?" asked Joe.

"He's dangerous."

We went back to eating in silence. Silence that was oppressive. To boost my spirits, I clung to Joe's theory that Buddy Franz, at last a victim of his own brand of sadism and violence, was rotting in a crude grave somewhere in the Berkshires.

After dinner the phone rang and Mary got up to answer it. I had the cappuccino machine gurgling and blasting away and couldn't hear her end of the conversation. I set the frothy little mugs down on the table in front of the guests.

"Charlie? Warren Shaw's on the phone. It sounds important."

"Hi, Warren," I said, grabbing the receiver. "What's new?"

"Hey, Dawk, I have to tell you. One of my cows is dead. I found her in the pasture this morning, and I was wondering about the insurance, you know . . ."

"Dead? What happened?"

There was a pause.

"Well, it's kinda hahd to say, Dawk. She got tangled in some loose barbed wire and panicked, looks like. Then she kinda wound herself up in it . . . tried to jump the fence and made it worse. That's what I *think* happened, anyways. Like I say, hahd to tell . . ."

Another silence. I grew uncomfortable and wanted him to speak. I heard him working his mouth and making little nervous noises in his throat.

". . . when I found her, best I can say is, she looked hamstrung, then spun around in the wire, cutting herself more so she bled a lot. Then she must have smelled her own blood, I think, and panicked so bad she wound the wire around her neck someways, and strangled herself. Horrible thing. So what I wanta know is, since the wire was left on your farm, could I collect?"

"Well, I suppose so. But there shouldn't be any loose barbed wire around the pasture; I thought we'd picked it all up that weekend before you brought your cows over. Remember?"

"I remember, Dawk. But we must've missed some."

"And this was accidental? Just a quirk?"

"Uh-huh. But so what? A quirk, maybe, but the result was the same: my cow's dead. Listen, I want you to hear somethin'—"

I heard the telephone at his end bumping around, then the unmistakable bleat of a cow. It came hard, over and over and over again.

"Hear that?" he said.

"God, that's awful to hear. But I thought you said she died."

"She did. That's her little calf."

"Listen: I'll get out there tomorrow as soon as I can, okay? Tell me, did you find anything else around there? Any sign or—"

"Nope. A dead cow's enough, though. A dead cow's plenty, you ask me."

"Right. I understand. Well, we'll settle up, and also, I won't charge you anything for the summer pasturing."

"Well, a'course you won't, Dawk. Me and Mary agreed it'd be *free.* She wanted the cows there to keep the grass down, and because they looked nice and peaceful. That's exactly what she said: nice and peaceful. Ask her yourself—"

"Oh, sure. Don't worry. Listen, I'll be out there tomorrow. We'll make it straight; I promise."

"All right, and Dawk?"

"Hmmm?"

"That Lucy girl. Quite a worker."

"Isn't she though? See you tomorrow."

ext day, after my last morning patient, I went out to see the dead cow.

I could see it from forty yards away because it was hung up on the fence in mid-jump, frozen dead in acrobatics, not lying on its side in the tall grass. What happened seemed clear enough: the animal had somehow become entangled in a very long strand of rusty barbed wire. It had turned and circled repeatedly to dislodge the wire from its legs, but only succeeded in further entangling itself. As its fear grew, it no doubt turned and hopped, spun and kicked, panicking with the pain and confinement, and then tried to clear the fence in a futile effort to escape its predicament. But its legs were hobbled, and it could not jump. And now, there it was: stiff and silent, its hind legs planted on the ground, its front legs pointing straight ahead, resting on the top strands, the nearby fence posts bent inward, pulled down by the sagging wire. Its head was on the wire, too, tucked down between the forelegs, as if trying to perform a dive off a springboard.

I crept up to the animal in hushed awe, as if not to disturb it. Why, I didn't know. When I got close enough to see its reddish fur clearly, a siren drone of flies erupted in black specks. I walked around to the side of the animal, leaning over the fence, looking at its face. The cow's eyes stared balefully out, blank, from the frozen head. The whites showed all around the big brown eyes, like a target. Then I thought I had a revelation in word origins: *bull's-eye.* Make that cow's eye. The eyes had lost their spark in death, and now were dry and dull, staring in horror at the birch tree twenty feet away. The pointed pink tongue was sticking out of the mouth, swollen. Flies crawled in and out of the nose and mouth, and flipped and jumped over the eyes. A heavy odor was beginning to come off the stiff body. But there was no bloating, no beach-ball ballooning of the carcass that would set the stiff legs pointing out like pins in a cushion. There was none of this because the animal's belly had been rent asunder by the strands of rusty wire that had sawed cruelly through her in her death struggles.

I heard Warren Shaw coming up behind me. He knelt in the grass, playing with a sprig of straw held in his hands. Then the wind shifted and he jumped to his feet again.

"Whew!" he said, waving his hand in front of his nose and backing off.

"What do you want to do with this, Warren?" I asked. "You want me to get the backhoe man to dig a hole and we can put her in there, or would you rather drag her away, or what?"

"Oh, I called the undertaker already, Dawk. They'll haul her away later on today. You want the police to see this first?"

I shrugged, staring at the animal.

"I don't really see the need, do you?"

"Nope. Just wanted you to see it, so we could figure out a settlement, or whatever."

"I could've sworn we cleared out all the old wire, Warren. I just don't see how we could have overlooked a piece that long."

"Me, too. But remember, that grass is tall. It was even taller when we brought the animals out here."

"You sure this was accidental? You ever see anything like this before?"

"Never seen it before now, but I've heard it happens. If you want to know, it was because of the fence and the loose wire. That's why I asked you about an insurance claim. See where it cut through her down there? She bled to death, finally. If it had happened during the day when we were working out here, I would have heard her bawling and we could have saved her. Tough luck it happened during the night."

"What about the little calf? Will it be okay?"

"I reckon so. I took him back to my place and we've got him on formula. Shame, though."

We'd reached the barn now, and he paused a second, leaning against the big smooth stones of the foundation. He rubbed his fingers over the rough white stubble of his chin.

" 'Course, I sorta can't figure out how the calf escaped that wire, Dawk, bein' so close to his mother all the time."

We walked around the barn, down to the far side where the sliding doors led into the cellar.

"I'm just thinking about that cow," I said. "The more I think about it, the more I'm positive we cleared out all that old wire. But I do remember seeing some lying around on the far side of the fence, outside the pasture, and thinking that would be a chore for the end of summer. Now, if this area is frequented by the biker crowd, I'm thinking maybe somebody could've sneaked up here in the dark and wound some wire around your cow. Done it out of spite or vengeance, since this place was their hangout before we bought it."

I heard a faint rasp as Warren stroked his beard stubble with his thumbnail.

"Well, I must say I thought of that, too. But I don't see how anybody would be strong enough to do that, Dawk. A cow's protective when she's nursing a calf, and weighs, oh . . . nine hundred to eleven hundred pounds. Now, who could be strong enough to grab her, wind her up, and lift her onto the fence? See what I mean?"

I nodded, looking up at the barn. It sure was big.

"Now, if you don't want to talk about that insurance claim, just tell me so."

"What? No way do I want to get out of that, Warren. That's not the issue. I was just wondering . . . forget it."

"Tell you what. If you're worried about kids coming around here and bothering the stock, or the buildings and such, I got a neighbor wants to sell his big dairy bull. That animal's bigger 'n meaner than a rodeo bull. There was a pack of dogs that was killing calves and sheep last summer, and he killed two of them. That stopped the whole thing. You want me to truck him over here?"

I scratched my head and thought.

"Well, I'm not sure; it might multiply the troubles around here. And I wouldn't want my dogs getting gored to death. But that won't be a problem. Mary and I are leaving them in Concord from now on; turns out the constant traveling back and forth is too much for them. Tell you what: if you put the bull and the others in the far pasture and fix the fence so they'll all stay there, that's fine with me."

He agreed, and I kept circling the barn, looking up at the weathered clapboard sides.

"Can we get by for a couple years before we repaint it?" I asked. I hoped so. My wallet really hoped so.

"Oh, sure. See, Dawk, these old barns were built right. Oak beams and sills. No nails or screws to rust out, either. They framed them with oak that was mortised and tenoned. If the roof stays intact, they last forever."

"And you've checked the roof?"

"Uh-yuh. And repaired it with those tin patches you see up there. You're fine for the—"

He stopped, staring at the small window in the stone wall of the barn foundation. He moved closer and reached his hand up, running it along the wooden windowsill.

"Somebody's been at this window," he said softly. "See the marks between the frame and the sill?"

"Uh-huh. Looks like a screwdriver was stuck in there and pried—"

"Not a screwdriver; a knife," he said. "A knife with a thick blade. This has happened since I put the locks on, Dawk. I know because I refastened the window bolts inside, extra tight, and checked the outsides at the same time."

"Well, they didn't get in. Makes me mad, though."

"Know where this window is?" he asked.

"Yes; it's right over where the motorcycles were parked."

There were smudges on the pane, dark streaks and specks where the fine coating of dirt on the glass had been rubbed off. Warren came up behind me.

"Somebody was lookin' inside, Dawk, trying to see if the bikes were still in there."

He grunted and backed off, and I looked closely at the smudges on the windowpane. Thinking they might be fingerprints, I told Warren not to touch anything until Joe came out and had a look.

"So, you think they were trying to get inside?" he asked.

"Yep. But it wouldn't have done them much good. The doors are locked from outside; they couldn't have stolen the bikes if they'd wanted to."

We walked around to the big sliding doors and looked closely at the two massive bronze padlocks he'd put on the doors, one a foot above the ground, one a foot below the top. Each was as big as my fist and as heavy as a box of pistol cartridges. And each showed the rough marks of scraped metal. Someone had tried to pry them loose, in vain.

"Yeah," I mumbled, turning to walk back up to the house, "maybe bringing that dairy bull over here isn't such a bad idea after all."

"Dawk, look!" said Warren, dropping to one knee and pointing at the soft dirt. There, underneath our own footprints, were the marks of enormous boots. They had waffle-type treads, and seemed to be a full fifty percent bigger than my size ten-and-a-halfs. I knelt down and looked at the prints closely. They were recent. Careful now not to disturb any of them further, I went back around to the window with Warren right behind me. There they were again.

The biggest footprints I'd ever seen.

ELEVEN

I t was the second half of June. In the Berkshires, both the days and the nights were warm now. Crickets chirped in the hedgerows and meadows; the cows' coats were slick and shiny; the trees were fully leafed out and green, and bluejays darted around the farmhouse, scolding and fighting. The ugly burned spot near the barn had grown over with fresh green grass. The place looked great. The sun went down beautifully each night. Cool, crisp breezes woke us in the morning.

So much for the good stuff. The bad news was this: within four days of discovering the dead cow and the footprints outside the barn, the state lab made a twelve-point positive make on the fingerprints gathered from the windowpane. Werner Franz, without a doubt.

We took this jolt in silence, for the most part. Mary fidgeted uneasily. Joe grumbled and swore as he thumped on heavy feet around his cottage, directing workmen who were decorating the interior. Lucy Kirkland, whom Mary had hired for a few odd jobs, paced solemnly from room to room, wearing a look of dread, and seemed on the verge of proclaiming dire prophecies for Pound Foolish Farm.

As for me, I've always found that when confronted with something like this, the best thing is to get out and do something. Anything is better than sitting around worrying and moping. So I unlocked the barn and wheeled out the big green motorcycle, which was the only one left. Lucy, who was, with the exception of her invalid mother in a nursing home in Pittsfield, the only relative of the deceased Billy, had his bike on consignment sale at a local dealer. We loaded Franz's bike onto a state truck. We left the bike and the truck in the clearing in front of the barn for a day and a night so it would be seen by any midnight skulker. Then we had the bike taken to the state warehouse to await the auction. The barn stayed unlocked from that day forward. We did all this in the hopes that Franz would observe, directly or indirectly, the exit of his prized machine and leave us alone.

Whether or not this plan worked none of us knew, but each day we stayed at the farm, I would begin the morning by walking around and around the outbuildings, looking for the big footprints. I told Mary I was taking the dogs for a walk. I think she knew better, but she didn't say anything. Joe stayed with us. His place was almost finished, but he stayed upstairs in the room next to ours. With all that had come down recently, we all felt better under the same roof.

We busied ourselves furnishing the house and making the thousand and one minor repairs and improvements that needed doing. Although only three of the upstairs bedrooms were furnished, the downstairs was more than comfortable, with overstuffed chairs and two big couches in the living room, and a kitchen that was both cozy and huge. The major activity centered around the big excavation between Joe's place and ours, where the forms were laid prior to the pouring of the concrete for the pool. Though we never said it, Mary and Joe and I knew that the beehive of activity was vital. The constant motion and effort drowned out the grim business that hovered continually in the back of our minds. To slack off the work would allow those disturbing thoughts to intrude, and eventually sap our enthusiasm.

Sunday morning over after-breakfast coffee, Bryce Stevens stopped by and told us that the state vehicle auction in Pittsfield was scheduled for the next Friday, the last day of June. It would be part of the Berkshire County Fair to assure maximum attendance. He leaned forward and talked to Joe and me in a low voice so only we could hear.

"I've been thinking about this auction," he said. "I'm thinking it might be a good way to lure this Franz into our reach. Follow?"

"You mean he'll show up there and try to buy his bike back?" said Joe, lighting his after-breakfast cigarette. "I doubt it, Bryce. I really doubt it."

"He won't try to buy it, but he might show up to see who does buy it. I think it's perfect bait; it's worth doing a stakeout for, don't you think, Joe?"

"Yeah, you put it that way, I agree. Sure; perfect stakeout."

"I've been talking to the guys in vehicles," continued Stevens, still talking in a low voice. "Something they discovered about that motorcycle, Doc, is that it is old and coveted. It's a configuration of Harley-Davidson known as a 'pan-head.' The term refers to the panlike appearance of the valve covers on the cylinder heads. Anyway, we're confident that there'll be active bidding on the machine next week. I'm thinking that if we got the people from the *Berkshire Eagle* over to the warehouse to do a feature story on this rare bike that's in mint condition, Franz might get wind of it. I assume he's under the assumption that his scheme worked, and that we haven't made the prints he left on the barn window. Therefore, he believes we still think he's dead. Now, I for one think there's a good chance he'll attend the auction. We could have a stakeout team ready to nab him when he shows up."

"Well, I agree that he'll get wind of the sale," I said, "but I don't think he'll be there. He stands out in a crowd too much."

"Maybe. But it's worth a shot. If nothing else, we think there's a good chance he'll be there, lurking in the background, to see who buys his bike."

"We'll be there, Bryce," said Joe, biting a croissant in half and swallowing it. "Won't we, Doc?"

"We sure will," I said.

"Great," said Bryce. "But listen: don't tell anybody, not even people around here."

The Berkshire County Fair was typical to those familiar with them. There was the usual grandstand and track for the bands and awards ceremonies. Off to one side were the horse and cow barns and the smaller buildings housing sheep, fowl, goats, and swine. One section of the fairgrounds gave way to the inevitable carny and amusement rides that had arrived on flatbed trucks. A parade of riders on horseback stamped around the track, flags fluttering. Following them were rows of majorettes, followed by two high school bands playing marches by John Philip Sousa and tunes by George M. Cohan.

Joe, Mary, and I sat on apple crates at the extreme edge of the grounds, watching the men set up the PA system in the midst of an assortment of cars, trucks, vans, trailers, and motorcycles. Lucy Kirkland had come along, too. Bryce thought it would be helpful to have her with us, since she knew Franz by sight. We didn't tell her about Bryce's secret plan until we were inside the gate; then Joe sprang it on her. She recoiled in horror at first, and got scared as hell, saying she wanted to leave because Franz might see her. We all assured her that there was a lot of protection around and she calmed down a bit. But not completely; she was still nervous and kept pacing in front of us, looking this way and that with anxiety on her face. Then we headed to the auction area, leaving Bryce to get into his cruiser, which was parked way back near the main gate, out of sight. He was in touch with Joe via the small two-way radio that Joe wore beneath his sportcoat, fastened on his belt. Finally, the local police overseeing the function had been put on alert for a big tall guy, twenty-three, blond hair, blue eyes. And we'd showed them all the mug shots, too.

When Lucy finally seemed calm enough, Joe and I managed to persuade her to walk around the fairgrounds a bit on her own, not going too far, but keeping her eyes peeled.

"What do I do if he sees me?" she asked, hopping on one foot.

"Come back here and tell us," said Joe.

"What if he grabs me first?"

"He won't; not in a crowd like this."

"What if I'm all alone somewhere?"

"Don't be all alone somewhere, Lucy; stay in the crowd."

"Well, what if—"

"Aw, shit, Lucy, do whatever you want."

"No, I'll go; I'll do whatever you say. I want to help. Really."

"Just keep your eyes open, Lucy, like Doc and I told you. You see him, you run back here and holler. Jeez, Doc, we shoulda gotten her a radio."

"Frankly, I don't think he'll even be here, Joe. He's probably too cagey."

Lucy took off, about as comfortable as a deer in a forest fire, twitching her head this way and that, flipping her long dark hair around.

"Don't go too far," cautioned Mary.

I looked again at the vehicles arranged in a giant semicircle behind the microphone. There were six bikes to be auctioned. I noticed that one of them was an old BMW; I was tempted to bid on it. All morning long sharp-looking men in sunglasses and polyester sportcoats pulled into the area, bouncing out of their late-model cars toting clipboards and notebooks. These were the wholesalers, professional car buyers who traded in used metal. Their ancestral counterparts were, of course, the horse traders. These men swarmed over the vehicles as slick as garden snakes, flicking their eyes and hands over the metal and uphol-stery, making split-second appraisals and rough estimates, which they scribbled on their little pads. Then they stood in small groups talking softly, laughing at private jokes. Obviously, they knew each other well, covering the same beats in their gypsylike profession.

They paid no attention to the bikes.

"Well, Lucy, did you see any good-looking guys?" Mary asked her as she came up and sat down on a crate next to us.

"No, Mary. But I wasn't looking for them. I—" She bit her lip, glancing sideways. "I was looking for . . . you know . . ."

"And I take it you saw nothing interesting?" asked Joe, leaning over her and speaking softly.

"Yeah. Hey, how long will this take, anyway? I'm still a little scared; I can't help it."

"It ain't over till it's over," said Joe softly, trying to soothe her. "Do you want to roam around a bit? Maybe go on one of the rides? If he's here, he won't be anywhere but around here."

"No," she said, sweeping her eyes over the scene. "I want to stay here and see what comes down."

The auctioneer, a fat man with a Stetson and wire glasses, holding a clipboard with a sheaf of fluttering papers fastened to it, grabbed the mike and cleared his throat. Then he began reading from a prepared statement:

"We'd like to welcome you to this summer auction of vehicles from the Commonwealth of Massachusetts," said the booming, echoey voice over the PA system. "The Commonwealth of Massachusetts reminds you that these vehicles have largely come into our possession through seizures in lieu of revenue owed, from the unclaimed recovery of stolen property, from charitable donations, and from other sources and events outside our purview. Therefore, the Commonwealth of Massachusetts, being a transient owner of said vehicles, is in no way liable for their condition. Any defect or malfunction of said vehicles, or injury sustained as a result of such malfunction, shall in no way be held against the Commonwealth of Massachusetts in a civil action . . ."

Joe lighted a Benson & Hedges and blew smoke into the summer breeze. He'd just gulped two sandwiches bought at the main refreshment stand: an Italian sausage with meat sauce and a Polish sausage with green peppers, onion, and half a jar of hot brown mustard. His system was showing no reaction to this bombardment of acid and fat. The folks at NASA should study his stomach lining; it would be great material for covering the reentry surfaces of space vehicles. I listened to the fat man in the Stetson continue his spiel.

"And now we'll proceed with the sale, beginning with this new Ford F-150 truck confiscated in April. As you can see, ladies and gentlemen, it's a half-ton pickup in almost mint condition. Costing over ten thousand dollars new, we'll start the bidding at eight and a half thousand. Do I hear eight thousand five? Eight thousand five, anyone? Look again at the paint job, everybody. Why, you can tell it's hardly been used. The drug dealers who bought this truck won't be able to use it until 1997, so let's see if we can't move it—how about eight even? How about it, folks? Do I hear eight thousand for this prime truck?"

I scanned the bleachers over to my left. Nothing stood out. Nobody caught my eye. Just a few hundred gawkers looking at the majorettes and the high school bands. The crowd at the auction was even more lackluster, composed of the wholesale sharks mentioned previously, and an assortment of farmers and "motor heads" watching for a good deal. The fat man's voice droned on and on in a rolling, singsong cadence.

"Six five. Do I hear six thousand five? C'mon, everybody, if I don't hear a bid soon, I'm gonna set this one aside and come back to it later. Now, who's gonna be first?"

"Lucy, see those men over there in that little group? See that tall one there in the plaid?" asked Mary, trying to point discreetly. "Could that be—"

"No. Much taller. And not fat, either. Besides, that guy there's got black hair," Lucy answered. This brought something to mind, and I leaned over to Joe.

"Think he'd dye his hair? Something like that to change his appearance?"

"Yeah, he might," he said, nodding. "He's apparently clever enough to do a number of things to change his looks. Grow a beard. Shave his head. But he just can't hide that giant frame."

"Okay, this is it. Five even. Who'll start off at five? C'mon now, that's *half price!*"

The bidding started there, went up for a while, leveled off, and finished at sixty-four hundred. Not a bad deal at all, if you could overlook things like warranties. The next item was a late model Chevy Camaro, a "muscle car," as Detroit calls them. The bidding was fierce for this number, with all kinds of young men getting into the action. The bikes still sat there. Joe stood up and dusted off the wide seat of his pants.

"Think I'll go skulk around the edges for a while," he said quietly. I immediately stood up, too, but he waved me back down. "Stay here, sport, and watch the womenfolk. Two of us will cause too much attention anyhow." He ambled off, covering a lot of ground fast with that lazy walk.

Womenfolk? Did I hear that right? Womenfolk? My God, Joe had been out in the country too long. I saw him disappear behind the grandstand, watching the crowd from below and behind. Joe knew his business, all right. He didn't talk much about his expertise, but it was there; you could see the professionalism as he worked.

I saw a big panama-type straw hat at the far end of the grandstand and stared at it. Why was I staring at it? Then I realized, finally, that I had seen it twice before. But the hitch was this: when I'd seen it earlier, it had been in different places. I couldn't remember where.

Four young men ambled into the auction area, wearing worn blue jeans and cutoff T-shirts. Two of them had tattoos, and all had long hair. They went straight to the bikes, then singled out the green Harley, swarming over it. The fat man saw them out of the corner of his eye and made a mental note.

"Forty-three hundred. Do I hear forty-five hundred? Forty-four? Forty-four, sir. Going once then at forty-four hundred . . ."

Joe was trudging back along the front side of the bleachers this time, rolling like an elephant in the Great Rift Valley. I looked for the straw hat again. It was gone. Shaped with a low crown and wide brim, it resembled a Mississippi riverboat gambler's hat. It was now nowhere to be seen.

"Going twice . . ."

The guys in blue jeans were caressing the Harley's fenders, kneeling down to look at the chromed engine, squeezing the clutch lever. They paid little attention to the other bikes, and none to the BMW R100 RS. Oh well, you can lead a horse to water . . .

"*Sold!* Sold for forty-four hundred, even. I remind you, young man, that this is a *cash* transaction. No personal checks are accepted . . . a ten percent deposit holds the vehicle for ten days . . ."

"Well, I can't say I saw anything," said Joe, puffing slightly, as he sat down on the apple crate again. "Nothing that drew my eye, anyway."

"You see a guy in a wide straw hat? Gambler-type straw hat, like a cowboy hat? Know what I mean?"

"Know what you mean, but didn't see it."

"Charlie, look. Those guys want to buy the bike," said Mary, sitting next to me bouncing her legs up and down on her toes. Our oldest son, Jack, does the very same thing when he's nervous. Heredity speaks in strange quirks. Tony, who looks like his mother, doesn't do this. Nor do I.

"I know," I said. "Only they're not tall."

"And now let's move to a two-wheeled vehicle for a change, ladies and gentlemen," said the fat man, pointing to the bikes. "Let's start with this 1962 Harley-Davidson 'pan-head' classic motorcycle. It's old, but in great shape—hey, fellas, please don't touch the bike, okay?"

The young men backed off from the machine, sulking. I saw another man approach them. He was older, perhaps forty or forty-five. He wore denim jeans and a matching jacket. I looked for the "colors" on the back of the denim jacket but saw none. The young men eyed him suspiciously.

"I think," the fat man said, consulting his sheet, "that we can start off the bidding at fifteen hundred dollars. Do I hear fifteen hundred—yes sir. Okay, fifteen hundred it is—do I hear sixteen hundred? Sixteen? Fifteen five? Fifteen five, okay—"

"Where did you see this straw hat?" asked Joe.

"Over in the grandstands. It moved around a few times, then disappeared."

"Was the guy tall?"

"Couldn't tell. I think he was sitting down, anyway. But the hat stood out, you know? And the guy kept facing this way from the grandstands, as if he were watching us from a distance."

"Fifteen five, going once—sixteen hundred. Okay, we're moving now on this classic road machine. Do I hear sixteen five? Sixteen five it is. All right! Do I hear—you sir? Seventeen hundred. Okay . . ."

"Gee, Charlie, they really like that bike, eh?"

"Yeah, well it's a classic and it—"

I sat there, staring out past the auctioneer at the swine sheds and horse barns.

"Charlie?"

"We've got eighteen five on this Harley classic, ladies and gentlemen. Eighteen five going once . . . going twice . . . nineteen! Nineteen even. Do I hear two thousand?"

"Charlie, what is it?"

"See that second barn over there? There's a window in it to the left. See? Now look in the window."

She leaned forward and squinted.

"I see a man wearing a hat. A yellow cowboy hat."

"That's the one." I nudged Joe and pointed. Then I took Lucy by the elbow and pointed. The barn window wasn't high, and the hat was scarcely peeking over the top of the window frame. It couldn't be the same person who had peered into my high barn window in the dead of night.

"Naw, forget it," I said. But I saw Lucy's face, and she was staring at the hat, and the vague, distant features of the face below it. She took a sharp intake of breath, as if in shock. Then she looked at me for an instant, and I saw the hate return to her face. The same hatred that was on her face that first day she came out to the farm and saw the Harleys in the barn.

"Well?" I said, but she said nothing.

Then she jumped up, pointing, and shouted.

"There he is! *There!*"

She hopped and ran sideways, pointing and screaming. The auctioneer stopped and stared. Everybody at the auction stared at her. Mary went over and put her arm around her. Lucy was trying to get free. It looked as if she wanted to run straight for the barn. Did she want to personally attack her brother's murderer? Had her hatred seethed and grown in her enough to turn to rage?

The hat in the window was gone now. I took Lucy by the shoulders and shook her slightly to stop the hysteria.

"Is it him?" I asked.

"I . . . I don't know," she blurted, beginning to cry. "There was something about the face . . . a feeling I had—"

I handed her over to Joe. He put his huge arm around her and looked at me, puzzled.

"Does she think it's him?" he asked.

"I don't see how it could be, considering the height. I think Lucy's a little hysterical. Just keep her company while I look around the barns a little, okay?"

I headed for the barns in the distance. Mary called my name and I turned and waved at her, saying I'd be back in a second. Behind me came the voice of the fat man, on a roll with the green machine:

"Twenty-three five. Do I hear twenty-three five for this one-of-a-kind motorcycle?"

I walked up to the barns. The first one, housing swine, had the rich stink of pigs all around it, and the guttural burping and snorting of hogs rooting in the dirt and straw. I went right up to the building and hesitated, then jumped inside and spun around. Nobody there but a farm girl, moving three sows from one pen to the next, batting them on the rump with a cane.

"Did you see a guy in here with a straw hat on?"

"Nah, sorry," she said, giving the last pig a hard swat.

"Reeeeent!" it said in protest. "REEEEEEENT!"

"Did you see a very tall man around here?"

Again the head shake. I went through this low barn and toward the horse barn. I wished I had my Browning stuck into

my belt. Rather than going in the near door, I went around the
back of the building to its far end and looked in the open rear
door. There were maybe twelve or fifteen horses in there, all in
stalls. They looked like quarter horses, buckskins, and Mor-
gans—your average-type working horse breeds. Nobody else
was in there. At the far end, the one facing the auction, was the
window in which I'd seen the straw hat. Its lower sill couldn't
have been more than five feet from the stable floor. So a guy as
tall as Franz couldn't possibly have been staring out at us from
in here.

Unless . . .

Unless he were sitting on a hay bale. On the hay bale that was
in fact directly under the window, right against the barn wall.
Yeah. For a guy Franz's height, it would be just about perfect.
I went inside, standing near the door. I could hear my own
breathing, and perhaps my heart. A horse snorted. I heard the
muted grinding of molars as the animals fed. I smelled the
ammonia tang of urine, and the heady aroma of droppings. The
smell of stables is a favorite of mine. But not now. Far off on
the wind I heard a marching band playing "Strike Up the
Band."

The horse in the far stall snickered, then whinnied, jerking
back against the halter and its lead rope to get out of the stall.
He stamped his foot, and it made a hollow, echoey sound. It was
a tense silence, and I was nervous. The horse snickered again,
moving his ears back and forth, back and forth, stamping his
feet.

I began to walk down the center of the stalls, looking in each
one as I passed it. Nothing in the first stall on the right. Its
opposite number on the left held a chestnut mare. Two horses
in the next set, a black on the right, a gray dapple on the left.
The dapple was a stallion: the full sac between his flanks pro-
claimed it.

Testosterone, I thought. Bad stuff.

Ffffffft! Plop, plop. Light brown goop was emerging beneath the tail of the horse two ahead of me. Another foot stamp.
I looked up, and froze.

In the far stall, the one near the window and the one with the startled horse in it, I saw the very tip-top of a straw hat peeking above the boards.

At the same time, I heard footsteps swishing in the grass outside.

"Doc?"

"In here, Joe!" I yelled, and watched the straw hat sink down out of sight. Outside the barn, the footsteps swept past me, heading for the rear door. Then I saw the hand come up, holding a very big knife.

"Joe!"

The knife slashed at the lead rope. I saw the horse scamper backwards out of the stall, screaming in a fit of panic. And behind the animal, bent in a crouch, a pair of long legs and big feet. The hidden man was pushing the horse in my direction. Then the face, as I had seen it in the mug shots. Only leaner, harder, meaner. The eyes too close, the pinched look of poverty in the nose and mouth. The glare of hatred from the small bright eyes. The faint acne scars on the cheeks. And, too, the baby-faced look. The look of arrested emotional development in the childish frown of rage.

The horse faced me now, working his front legs. The knife went up, then down fast, sinking deep into the animal's rump in a spurt of bright blood. The horse squealed in pain and fright, and charged.

I turned and ran for the door, hearing the pounding at my back and Joe's voice calling for me beyond the wall. Then the animal's hugeness went into my back and I was down. A monstrous pain on my hip and then my upper back. Oh Lord, I thought, the hoof going right through me.

Then nothing but Joe's voice coming nearer, then beside my ear. Then growing fainter and fainter. Then nothing at all.

TWELVE

There were images after that. Faint sounds and fuzzy shapes. A lot of white. White linen. White uniforms. White walls. White noise.

Then there was Mary, leaning over the bed with all her luscious darkness blocking out that white. Her olive skin and black eyes. Her dark eyebrows knit in a frown over them. Dried tears.

"Charlie?"

"Hiya, babe."

Fresh tears then. Lots and lots. And holding my hand and kissing me.

"Where's Joe?"

"He left as soon as they said you were going to make it."

"Make it? Going to *make* it? Was I that bad?"

"Not really, as it turns out. But for a while we didn't know that. It looked worse than it was. But listen, macho man: you got banged up pretty badly. You've got two splintered ribs on your back, and they're separated, too. Your pelvis is bruised, maybe cracked. And you've got all kinds of bruises and contusions, mostly in the shape of horseshoes, all over you. Lucky as hell he didn't stomp on your head."

"Yeah. Would've busted his foot. *Ohhhhh—*"

A wave of pain hit me, then the giddy, floating feeling of nausea. The room rocked as if we were on an ocean liner. I hated that.

"He stabbed the horse, Mary. Stabbed it right in the ass, deep, to make it run me down."

Her eyes lowered.

"I know," she said. "And to get away, he cut loose four others and stuck them, too, the same exact way. They were running all over the place, screaming and spurting blood. It was awful. Joe called him a maniac."

"Not a maniac, Mare," said a booming voice behind her, "I called him a *fucking* maniac. 'Cause believe me, that's what he is. How you doin', pal?"

"I've been better. Did you get him?"

Joe looked down at the floor and ran his hand through his hair, sighing.

"Naw, we didn't. There just weren't enough of us, Doc. He set that herd of wounded horses loose on the crowd. In the panic that followed, he slipped away, very fast. By that time I was busy looking after you—I thought you were dead, for crissakes—and by the time I got Bryce on the radio Franz was gone, up the hill and into the trees, where we couldn't take a cruiser."

"Do you have a dragnet out?"

"Oh yeah. I'm confident we'll nab him before nightfall. I just don't see how he can slip away."

I thought for a second about this. Thinking wasn't easy; it never is when you're in pain.

"I'm not so confident we'll nail him, Joe. For a big guy, Buddy Franz moves awfully quick. And for a guy who's supposed to be borderline retarded, he seems cagey and sharp. Remember when you went walking over to the grandstand? Well, Franz was sitting up there when you began your walk; I saw him. You walked all around the grandstand. You, a trained professional. And yet you never saw him. Somehow, he knew you were the heat. I—"

I stopped and groaned; a terrible jolt of pain stabbed me along my spine where the ribs had pulled away.

". . . I guess it wasn't that hard to figure out. But the thing is, a big guy like that sneaking from the grandstand to the horse barn under our very noses is impressive. It's also scary."

"Know what you mean. I'm thinking of how he got out of that barn with all of us around. Using those frightened, wounded animals as a shield. Maybe you're right; it might be awhile before we lay our hands on him."

"Swell," said Mary. "But what do we do in the meantime?"

We looked at each other in silence. It was a good question.

Next day, after maybe twenty hours of sleep, I was recovered enough to receive a gaggle of visitors to my hospital room. The room I would be vacating the following morning for the ride back to Concord. Concord never sounded so good. Werner Franz was still on the loose, incidentally. Sitting in a circle around me were Bryce Stevens, Joe, Mary, and our sons, Jack and Tony. These last two were brought from points far afield by news of my mishap. One might suppose that they would be shocked and concerned at seeing their father bedridden and in pain. Concerned, yes; their faces showed that clearly enough. But they weren't surprised; they were growing accustomed to seeing their dad step in over his head.

"Okay, here's the story," said Stevens. "Yesterday, after the fireworks ended, we got in touch with the guy who bought the bike. The man's name is Harry Phelps. Works over at the Sweetheart plastic plant. He's forty-two, retired military, a divorced father living alone in the country right outside Lanes-

boro, just above Pittsfield. We got his address from the auctioneer's slip and met him at home last night. Lives in a cabin up
in the mountains. We told him about Franz, and what he might
be up to. Phelps saw enough of what happened yesterday, and
heard the rest, to know what we meant."

"Did he seem scared?" Joe asked.

"Not really. Phelps is a pretty big guy, I guess he's about six
two or three, a former marine, and looks like he's in good shape.
He's a bike rider from way back, he says, and no stranger to the
biker way of life. We said we'd keep a watch on his place for
a while."

"That's fine," interjected Joe, "and it's S.O.P. But what are
the chances, realistically, that Franz will show up there looking
for the machine? What are the chances he can even find out who
Phelps is, or where he lives?"

"I say there's no telling what a guy like Franz can or will do
next," said Stevens, nervously flipping through the pages of his
little notebook. "A sensible person would have gone to earth.
But from his actions so far, I say we've got to be careful on this
thing."

I picked up the *Berkshire Eagle* lying on my bed. Just underneath it was the *Worcester Telegraph*. Both papers, and the *Globe*
as well, had early mug shots of Franz and a pencil sketch of how
he appeared at the Berkshire County Fair. The Pittsfield paper
carried the headline *Suspected Killer Escapes Manhunt*, and underneath, in smaller type: *Man Eludes Police After Slashing Horses at
County Fair*. It was a grisly piece, sure to attract wide reader-
ship. Now everyone in the state had a good look at Franz's face,
and knew of his giant size as well.

"But at the same time," I added, "I just don't see how he can
remain at large much longer."

"Oh, don't worry," Bryce said. "We'll have him wrapped up
before the week's out. You can bet on it."

His words reassured me, and I was feeling pretty good until
I glanced back at the newspaper and happened to see a smaller
article:

CONCORD PHYSICIAN MASTERMINDS TRAP

PITTSFIELD—It was no accident that police were on the scene in the futile attempt to capture mass murderer Werner Franz. The idea of using the motorcycle as bait to catch the killer was the brainchild of Dr. Charles Adams, an oral surgeon from Concord, on whose Berkshire County farm the motorcycle was first found. Adams donated the vehicle to the Commonwealth to be auctioned at the fair, correctly assuming that Franz would be eager enough to regain his prized classic Harley-Davidson that he would show up at the fair to observe, if not to bid on the machine. Adams was seriously injured by a horse as Franz escaped authorities and is recuperating in good condition at a local hospital.

I put the paper aside, suddenly feeling dizzy. "Great," I sighed. "Just great."

"Uh, I know how you feel, Doc," said Joe. "It was a dumb thing to put into the paper. We're trying to find out which cub reporter did it."

"Yeah, and we're going to get a retraction in the next issue. Just you wait," said Bryce, trying his damnedest to be upbeat. But it was too late now, and we all knew it. If Franz saw the paper, or found out about the tag article indirectly, he'd know exactly who tried to set him up.

"And the worst part is, you guys, it's not even *true!*" sputtered Mary, flinging the paper aside in anger. "Christ almighty, it was *your* idea, Bryce. You cooked it up."

"Uh, like I said, Mary, we're going to get a retraction—"

"A lot of good that'll do; it's already too late. All I have to say is, you guys better give us some surveillance and protection, because as soon as Franz can catch his breath, we know where he'll be heading. Not to mention the fact that he now knows exactly who Charlie is and what he looks like. Sweet Jesus!"

"Lay off Bryce, Mary," I said a trifle harshly, as I could tell by her face. "It was an accident." Then I turned to the men.

"But Mary does have a point; we would like a patrol car hanging around the farm if you can swing it."

"Don't worry," said Joe in a soft voice. "Bryce is right; he can't stay on the loose. We'll have him in custody before the week's out. You can bet on it."

I should have taken that bet—the other side of it—because three weeks later, when we'd all returned to the farm to watch workmen put the finishing touches on the pool, Werner "Buddy" Franz was still on the loose. Not only that, but there weren't even any promising leads on him. Joe thought he was long gone, perhaps to somewhere far away like the West Coast or the deserts of the Southwest.

"He's not around here anymore, that's for sure," he said as he sipped his coffee on the stone terrace and gazed out over our gorgeous mountain valley.

It was late July now, and I was healed enough to return to work on a part-time basis. But since I could not stand for extended periods, serious surgery was out, so I had to stick to my baseline profession of extractions. What fun. It was bad enough that I was thankful for my short hours. I could walk without a limp now, but I couldn't run, so I was grumpy and edgy. Also, I couldn't lift my right arm higher than my shoulder without it killing me. And I tired easily. But I was getting better each day, and we were spending more time at the farm.

The concrete had been poured for the pool, and it was scheduled for filling in early August. The other big development was Lucy Kirkland. In the intervening weeks, she had proven to be such a dependable and tireless worker that Mary had cornered Joe and me privately to ask if we could hire her on as our caretaker.

"We know how good she is," she said, "and I know she's got nowhere else to go."

"Never hire out of sympathy," I said. "I read that in some business magazine."

"Oh, Charlie, you don't know the first thing about business."

"True. That's why I've been reading the magazines. It's sound advice. Just like 'never hire relatives.' But I agree that she's a good worker. I just still find it strange that she can hang around here and not get the creeps, since they dug up her brother's remains less than half a mile from where we're sitting."

"Well, she's almost like one of the family now. I've grown really fond of her. And besides, she's a local; like Warren, she knows the people and the country. I just think it's a great fit all around."

"Okay, Mary," said Joe, "but where does she sleep? Upstairs with you and Doc?"

"Uh-huh, or up in one of your spare bedrooms, Joey, until we have the shed near the barn remodeled. Remember, Charlie, that was going to be the caretaker's cottage?"

The more I thought about hiring Lucy on, the better the idea sounded. The woman could mow, rake, paint, clean, and almost cook. And that skill she was quickly learning from Mary. And what Mary had said about her being homeless was also true. By hiring Lucy on, we were helping her fill several needs at the same time.

"I'll go along with it if you want, Mare," I said. "How much does she want to be paid?"

"She said whatever we decide would be fine with her. I'm thinking about a hundred or a hundred fifty a week."

"Let's try a hundred for starters," I said.

"No, c'mon, you guys, that isn't diddly shit," said Joe. "I've seen her work, and she's helping me out lots. I'll put in fifty a week. That's fifty from each of us."

So we made Lucy the offer after dinner, and she accepted. Accepted is hardly the word; she practically cried with joy, and I got Warren on the phone that very night to discuss the completion of the little shed down by the barn.

Mary confided to me that the phone bills showed that Joe had called Martha Higgins four more times. That in itself was reason to stick by our investment in the country and enjoy the progress we were making. Still, unpleasant reminders crept into our country life. One afternoon a tall, quiet man and his thin wife drove slowly up our driveway, asking if this was the Adams place. It was Lonnie Worthington and his wife, Eileen, the parents of the slain boy, who wanted to see the site. We thought it was a strange, not to say macabre, request. But Joe, no stranger to such things, told us it was not uncommon. A way of putting the past to rest. The couple walked solemnly down the hill and over to the grove of trees with Joe, who brought them up to the house afterwards for coffee.

It was the kind of visit I dread, and the hour spent sitting around the big trestle table in the kitchen seemed like five. But Lonnie, in his slow, soft, deliberate voice, told us how that "great big blond boy" had met their son at the bowling alley and had come over to the house twice just to listen to records and to shoot baskets in the turnaround in back.

"Then he didn't come over for a couple weeks," said Eileen, "and Bill thought he'd lost a friend. Then one night he came over in a pickup truck with a ladder and paint cans in the back. Said he'd found himself a new job and was moving up to Vermont. Said he'd just come by to say good-bye."

"What did the truck look like?" asked Joe.

"Light blue. Old. Maybe fifteen years old, and rusty in places."

"Did it have Massachusetts plates?"

"I don't remember," said Lonnie. "We all thought he was gone for good then. And he was. Then, a week later, Bill was gone."

They sat there, staring blankly into their empty cups. Get me out of here, I thought.

"You told Lieutenant Stevens that your son left the house that Thursday afternoon, saying he was going down to the bowling alley. Right?"

They nodded in silence.

"And that was the last you saw of him. The thinking is then that he ran into Franz in downtown Pittsfield and maybe went for a ride with him in the truck, or maybe on his motorcycle?"

They nodded again.

"Or maybe even that Franz asked Bill to meet him somewhere, and not to tell you."

Another nod. "And he seemed like the nicest boy in the world, Lieutenant," said Eileen, wiping her eyes. "We never thought anything like—"

She couldn't continue, and Lonnie put his arm around her and led her back to the car. After they left, the three of us just sat out on the terrace, not saying much. We offered theories as to what would happen next.

"I think a good thing to do would be to alert the people up in Vermont," I said.

"We've done that, Doc. All the neighboring states, and a national bulletin, too. I think the big question is, does Franz realize how deep he's in this now?"

"He knows," said Mary. "He damn well better know by this time, no matter how dumb he's supposed to be."

"Thing is, we're not dealing with a normal mind here, Mare," said Joe. "The normal criminal would say to himself, hey, I'm in real deep shit here. I better hightail it out to New Mexico or California or someplace and lie low. But a psychopath like Franz, maybe he can't wait to sneak back here some night and burn the barn down. That's if we're lucky. Maybe he'll light the house on fire some night. With us in it."

There was silence before I replied.

"You really think he'd do that?"

"Who knows?"

"I think maybe we better put the place on the market," Mary said. "I know it seems like we're just giving up. And we really like the place and everything. But holy Christ, maybe there's just too much bad stuff that's gone on to . . . to recover, if you get what I mean."

"I hate giving in to this guy, Mary. I say we at least give it another month or so. See if the police can't nail him. Joe, you're a part owner; what do you think?"

He shifted nervously in his chair and drummed his fingers on the wooden arm.

"Well, I, uh, wasn't going to bring this up so soon, but, uh, do you remember Martha Higgins?"

We stared at him, nodding slowly. Mary wore a big smile.

"Well, we've been . . . talking. And a couple of times I went to visit her over in Pittsfield. You remember, Mary, she went back to Pittsfield?"

Mary put her hand to her forehead, as if trying to concentrate.

"Uhhhhh . . . lesssee . . . yeah. Yeah, if I try *real* hard, Joey, I can vaguely remember that—"

"Well, Marty lives in Pittsfield now and—"

"Charlie, do you remember? Is it coming back to you?"

"I think so. Slowly but surely . . ."

"And so, uh, well, I asked her to come out here for a visit next weekend. She said she can't wait to see you again, Mary. Oh, and you, too, Doc. I don't know if you realize it, but it's been over ten years."

Mary jumped over onto Joe's lap, threw her arms around his neck, and hugged him.

"So if it's okay with you guys," he muttered from underneath his sister, "I'd rather we not sell it for a week or so, anyway."

That seemed to settle the question. I eased my tired body back in the Adirondack chair, closed my eyes, and listened to the birdies sing.

THIRTEEN

I was lounging in the sun porch of Chez Adams in Concord. It was late Tuesday afternoon following our most recent sojourn to the country. I was sitting underneath the humming, whirling ceiling fan sipping a cold Hackerbräu and smoking my pipe, trying to relax after work.

It wasn't working; I needed help.

I reached for the phone and punched in Brian Hannon's number at the Concord Police Department. Brian, one of my best and oldest friends in this small town, is Concord's chief of police. He's an irritable, affable, bright, bullheaded, stubborn, kindhearted Irishman, with all the attendant strengths and liabilities of that spirited race from the Emerald Isle. After my injury at the fair, Brian had paid me a bedside visit full of sympathy, and also full of some choice words concerning my lack of common sense. But since then he'd been on vacation and we had not been in touch. He answered on the second ring, which meant, knowing his routine, that he was at his desk doing a crossword puzzle. I greeted him warmly and said we'd been having a pretty good time out at the farm, all things considered.

"Yeah, well, thanks a lot for asking me out there, Doc, now we're on the subject. I been wanting to mention it, but you know me; I'm too polite. You only been out there the whole friggin' summer, for crissakes. Thanks *loads.*"

"You're welcome, Brian. No need to thank me."

"You got no idea how good it makes me feel. What do you want, anyway? You know I'm doing my afternoon crossword. You always call at the most inopportune times."

I told him about Joe's latest thinking regarding Buddy Franz. There was a pause at the other end of the line after I finished. Then I heard a sigh. A worried sigh. Brian said he'd stop over at six.

"Okay, here it is, for what it's worth," he said, lighting a Lucky and staring at me over the coffee table in the sun porch. Brian's face looks like Darren McGavin's. Or maybe Ed Asner's. It's thick, with a putty nose, black-gray eyebrows, grayish blue eyes, and very thin sandy brown hair on top. He looks like an aging Irish boxer. But at least his nose isn't beet red anymore; Brian gave up the booze years ago.

"From what you say, I agree with Joe and this Bryce Stevens. The guy's a psychopath. A maniac, pure and simple. As such, he won't show predictable patterns. That's what makes him dangerous. Also, he's obsessed, which means standard precautions and threats will have little or no effect on him. Joe's all gaga about the NLETS network. Fine. It works. It works like downtown—against your *typical criminals,* which he ain't."

"I guess you're saying that the electronic networks won't be much help with Buddy Franz."

"Well, they can be. But I wouldn't count on it. See, these computer banks go into action whenever and wherever criminals touch base with institutions. Whenever they rub elbows with a local, state, or federal agency, then you get the lead and its verification. But . . . BUT . . . if the felon doesn't come out of his hole—then you've got nothing. All you've got is a blank CRT screen and an empty printout."

"And Franz doesn't interact with these institutions? How so?"

"Look, you got to him through the motorcycle's serial number, right? Okay, that's what I mean; that's how you got onto him at first. But now the bike's gone. The tags are generally made like this: a patrolman stops a guy for drunk driving and calls in the vehicle description. Vehicle's stolen. They haul the guy in and check further, putting his ID out on the national wire. They find out the guy's wanted in four states for armed robbery. That's a real typical case. Or a guy tries to use a stolen credit card at Jordan Marsh. The salesgirl calls in the card to check the credit limit and gets an alert message. She stalls the guy long enough for the cops to get there and collar him. They take him downtown and soon discover through a fingerprint check that the guy's an escapee from Quentin. See what I'm getting at?"

"Yeah, the crook activates the NLETS system by some action which can be verified or refuted, by something that sets off an alarm in all these records, all these data banks—"

"Exactly. Now, what I'm saying is, what if Buddy Franz has got a hidey-hole somewhere out there in the mountains? And maybe the only time he goes out is to buy groceries once a month. And say he buys with cash, or else maybe he's got a girlfriend to go out and buy the food for him. If this is true, then what are the odds that he'll trigger the NLETS, or any other network?"

"Slim."

"Yeah. So nailing him could take a long time. And what worries me is, it appears this guy has you fingered as the man who mucked up his plans. You're the guy who bought the property, discovered the bikes, discovered the graves, and sold his bike out from under him. Then there was the run-in at the fair. He loves you for that, Doc. And that article. The one that said that you were the one that—"

"Yeah, yeah. I don't need to hear it again."

"Maybe he can't forget that, and maybe he'll bide his time and wait until your guard is down—"

"*Stop it!* Cut it out, Brian. Don't you think we haven't thought about that stuff? It's why Mary wants to sell the place now, even if it means taking a loss."

He held up a hand.

"But wait. How do you know that will solve it? See, what I'm thinking, if the guy's really obsessive-compulsive, he'll track you down here, in Concord. What I'm saying is, there may be no way out of this thing until . . ."

"Until what?"

"Until he's behind bars, or dead."

I got up and went to the window overlooking the front lawn. It was a beautiful summer day. The maples were swishing and swooshing their big green boughs in the wind. Across Old Stone Mill Road, the apple trees in Dean McLeod's orchard sat in pretty rows. Farther down the road, horses and cows grazed in the sun. We were within half a mile of the Old North Bridge, that rude bridge that arches the flood, in the heart of historic New England. Birthplace of liberty. The most decent and civilized corner of this decent and civilized land. Living in this little town that was home to Emerson, Thoreau, Louisa May Alcott, Daniel Chester French, and Nat Hawthorne made you feel protected by all that civilization. It made you feel invulnerable. But that was illusory.

"Joe never told me all this. Is it that bad? And if so, why didn't he warn me?"

"Hey, maybe it isn't. On the other hand, maybe it is, and Joe's just trying to protect your feelings. I don't know."

"Okay, say it's bad. What would you do?"

Brian leaned back against the couch cushions and sucked smoke, thinking.

"I'd say there are basically two directions you can head in. One, you and Mary could spend most of the remainder of the summer down at the cottage. This guy has read the Pittsfield papers, which say you live in Concord, so he can easily find you here. On the other hand, he doesn't know about the cottage, so you could be safe down there until the police catch him, which they will eventually."

"I don't like that. For one thing, we both have jobs here. I also don't like some homicidal nut dictating the way I spend my summer. In short, I don't like retreating."

"Figured you'd say that," he said, flicking the ash off his cigarette into the ashtray, "so that leaves action in the opposite direction. Advance instead of retreat."

"I like the sound of that better. Not crazy about it, but it sounds more like me."

"Uh-huh; running into trouble does sound like you, Doc. This scenario calls for you to spend as much time at the farm as you can, maintaining a high profile. At the same time, you take the necessary steps to ensure your family's safety. I'd recommend you hire the best people in the private sector to help you."

"Private sector? You mean hired guards and private detectives?"

He nodded, stubbing out his smoke. The ashtray gave off a wonderful aroma. Just great. I'm really a pain in the ass about cigarette smoking; most reformed smokers are. Of course, I'm positive my pipes don't stink. Not to mention the cigars . . .

"Did you know that the word *trash* in pig latin is *ashtray*?"

Brian looked a little shamefaced, but only a little.

"See, Doc, the police have a limit on what they can do for you. The limits are legal and budgetary. You've got the dough to hire some good help. If you pick the right people, they can stay out of sight, waiting in the wings, so to speak, while you finish the renovations."

"And while the fuzz is out beating the bushes for him, my private palace guards will be on the lookout for Buddy if he tries to sneak up on us in the dead of night."

"In the dead of night or in broad daylight."

"He's tricky, Brian. I'm a personal witness as to just how sneaky he is."

"I never said it was going to be easy. And it will take a

psychological toll on you, and especially Mary. It's gonna be tough. I have some people I could recommend."

"I've got one or two in mind, myself," I said.

"You thinking of that Nazi friend of yours?"

"Goddammit, Brian, Roantis isn't a Nazi. In fact, the first man he killed was a Nazi soldier."

"Whatever. I'm just going by his rap sheet, Doc. You ask me, he does a dynamite imitation of an SS commando. And those guys he hangs around with now and then. You know the ones I'm talking about, Doc. The guys with the dull eyes. The eyes that wouldn't blink a tear if they saw a bunch of tots getting gang banged."

"Yeah, right."

"And those scars on their knuckles."

I paused; this reference puzzled me.

"You mean from fighting?" I asked.

"No. From *walking.*"

I tracked him down in Somerville. He was jogging around the cinder track right near the ball field in the park off Route 2-A. He was carrying a four-foot section of steel pipe on his shoulder. The pipe was maybe four or five inches in diameter. I knew it was heavy. He occasionally shifted the big pipe from one shoulder to the other as he ran. It was pushing ninety degrees, and humid to boot. I turned to my companion, a huge dark man named Mike Summers, formerly of Chicago. Formerly of the 101st Airborne Division. And formerly of the renowned Daisy Ducks recon team.

"What's with the pipe, Mike? Is it for some purpose, or is he just into pain?"

"He into pain, awright," drawled Summers, chewing on a blade of grass, "but not his own."

"How long has he been doing this?"

" 'Bout a hour. That piece of pipe the exact size and weight of a Carl Gustav rocket launcher. Swedish make. Neutral country so it don't leave a track, if you ain't hip. He got that pipe 'cause it wouldn't be cool to practice with the real thing, dig?"

"I take it then, that Roantis has a gig coming up?"

The big man nodded. Mike Summers was six three and extremely solid. Now he was pared down to 220, which made him look almost skinny. Almost.

"Where's he going?"

"Someplace hot, you ain't figured it out, Woodrow."

"My name's not Woodrow," I said. Mike grinned down at me.

"Ever-body name Woodrow," he said. He went back to chewing on blades of grass again for a minute, then turned to me and said: "My woman's coming here in a minute. You ain't met my main squeeze."

I recalled Mike Summers's girlfriend, an "exotic dancer" from a strip club up on Route 1 named the Golden Banana, who billed herself as *Nastie Thang.* She was, too.

But I was in for a surprise. I heard a car door slam behind us and turned to see a magnificent-looking woman walking toward us. She was tall and lithe, dressed in running shorts and a thin cotton jersey. I saw the long, stringy muscles in her thighs flex with each gliding step. Behind her was the powder-blue Jaguar XJ-S convertible she'd been driving. She had her hair done up in cornrows, with long braided strands of it falling down low on each side of her head. The ends of the strands were woven with white beads. Her eyes were greenish-blue, her skin a deep glowing tan.

Move over, Tina Turner. Watch out, Whitney Houston.

She walked up to me and put her hand on the side of my head, giving me a hard stare with eyes that were level with mine. Her gaze went deep into me, like a laser beam from her bright turquoise eyes.

"Are you Doc Adams? The man who took care of Michael when he was all messed up?"

"Well I, yeah. I guess. But it was a while ago, ma'am."

She leaned forward and kissed me on the cheek. Be still my heart.

"I heard about you . . . from him," she said, jerking her thumb over her shoulder to point at Mike, who wasn't even looking at us. He was staring off over the playing field. Then he spoke.

"Doc, meet Rowanda."

"My name's Rowanda Williams," she said, extending her hand. "I'm delighted to meet you, if you can't guess."

"Hi, Rowanda; call me Doc. You know this nut out there?" I asked, pointing toward Roantis, who was finally puffing his way in to us.

"Yes, I've met Laitis several times. But you're the one I was waiting for. What you did for my man was a wonderful thing, Doc."

"That's true, Rowanda. Too bad he wasn't worth it."

"Hey, Doc! What's up?" said Roantis, throwing down the pipe, which clanged against a rock at his feet. "Fuckin' t'ing!" he muttered under his breath.

"Where are you off to?" I asked.

"Someplace hot," he said, taking off his bush hat and wiping his forehead.

"I thought you gave that up."

"Well, this job is special. They really need me on this one, dey say. The cause is good. Also, the pay is too good to pass up."

"When are you leaving? There's something I'd like you to do for me."

"I take off Friday," he said, still panting, "and won't be back for a couple weeks."

This wasn't good news. We all sat on the grass under a shady tree while I told them what had been happening.

"Your friend Hannon is right," Roantis said finally. "He's a guy the cops won't nail for a long, long time. He's what we call a boonie stalker, right, Summers?"

"Uh-huhhh."

"He's got a secret place somewhere, just like Jusuelo and Royce had down in North Carolina. He's made a retreat for himself. It's secret and invisible. From it, he comes and goes, returning by a different route each time to leave no worn trails and to alert nobody. Follow?"

I nodded, looking at Rowanda, who was lying on her back doing slow leg lifts. She was easy to look at. A guy could stare at her forearm for maybe twenty minutes.

"So what I say to do, take Mike with you back to the farm. He can help keep the wolf from the door until I get back. Den I'll go hunt him down and kill him. Mike, he's on vacation this week anyway, and he could use the scratch."

I looked at Summers, who stared ahead at the empty baseball diamond without saying anything.

"How do I know he's eager to go?" I asked.

"Hell, I'd go, Doc. That is, *we'd* love to go. Wouldn't we, Rowanda?"

"Says who?" she said through clenched teeth, holding her legs and body off the ground, balancing on her hips in a V sit. Strong lady.

I stood up and brushed off my pants. "You two want to come join our merry band in the mountains, let me know, okay? I'll give you some time to think it over. I don't want to pressure anybody."

"You serious, Doc?" asked Rowanda, getting up and coming over to me. "You really mean it?"

"Sure, I mean it. I wouldn't say so if I didn't."

"Michael?" she said, turning around and addressing Summers.

"Okay, I'm cool."

"Yeah," she said, "we'll come out and baby-sit for you until Laitis comes back."

"Great. I'll pay you five hundred—"

"No you won't," said Summers.

"Come over to dinner with us tomorrow night and we'll tell you all about the place," I said, starting to walk back to the car. But I turned around and looked at the woman again. She stared back at me with those killer blinkers. She came up and extended her hand. I shook it.

"That's a generous offer, Doc. We're pleased to accept."

I noticed her diction and speech. Flawless, with almost a British ring to it.

"Where did you get your education?"

She giggled. "Skidmore, class of '78. I guess I'm being rather a dropout now, though. I majored in pre-law and went on to law school at Yale. But suddenly, I just got fed up with being so serious. Right now I'm working as an aerobic dance instructor at the Somerville Y. That's where I met Michael."

"He's lucky."

"And you're sweet," she said, winking. Then she went back to her workout.

I got into the car and drove home, a little wobbly in the knees. Ms. Rowanda Williams was quite something. If she worked at it a little, she could give a guy the fantods.

FOURTEEN

"Well, I really appreciate you stopping by here, Lieutenant, uhhh—"

"Brindelli."

"Lieutenant Brindelli. I shore do. But listen, fellas, I ain't seen anybody around here," drawled Harry Phelps. He was a big man and stretched his long legs out as he leaned the chair back. He had black hair, cut short in military fashion, and a very flat stomach. He wore a short-sleeved knit shirt that showed a tattoo on his left forearm, high up, just underneath the elbow. The forearms were large and gnarled, with stringy blood vessels all over them and a lot of muscle under the skin— no fat here—that bunched up and jumped around like snakes when he moved his hands and fingers. Watch out for this guy, I thought. Probably does a hundred push-ups each morning, on his fingertips. I couldn't see what the tattoo was; it was old and blotched. I was tempted to roll up my sleeve and show him mine, the Daisy Ducks tattoo that I got down in Fayetteville, North Carolina, a few years previous. I scarcely remember getting it, since I was full of high-octane jet fuel at the time.

But I've matured since then; now I'm fine.

Joe, Bryce, and I were sitting with Sergeant Phelps on a small covered wooden deck that adjoined his "double-wide" premanufactured home in Lanesboro, the little town just north of Pittsfield. I'd asked to come along with Joe and Bryce on their interview. They hesitated at first, until I reminded them that as an official police investigator, my presence was well within regulations. Joe agreed, adding that, given the circumstances, perhaps it was even my duty.

Phelps's place was located halfway up a wooded slope on a little parcel of steep, rocky land. It was off the beaten track; you had to hunt around to find it. Phelps, obviously a southern boy by his lazy drawl, said he wanted it that way. And it was isolated, too; the nearest neighbor's house was barely visible a hundred yards away on the same slope, with a lot of tall pines in between.

"So nobody's come asking about the bike?" asked Bryce. "I know you'd remember him, Mr. Phelps," he said, leaning forward with a concerned look on his face, "but maybe it was somebody else. We're just checking here—"

Phelps leaned back, then blinked his eyes suddenly as if in recognition. He brought his chair back down on all four legs with a bang.

"Now you mention it, there was a lady come by, looking at the bike. Not bad lookin', either."

"Can you describe her?" asked Joe.

"Describe her? Well, she was pretty tall, with dark hair. Good-lookin' woman, I'd say. Just came up and started asking me about the green bike."

"Was anyone with her?" asked Stevens.

"Nope. She come up alone."

"What was she driving?" asked Joe.

"A truck. Pickup. I think it was blue and white. Old model, maybe eight or ten years old. At least, I'd say."

"Blue and white? Did you get a look at the tag?"

"Naw."

"Make and model?"

"Can't recollect for sure. I know it wasn't a Jap truck. I think maybe a Ford, but I'm not sure."

"Did you see anything in the back? Like maybe paint cans, ladders, tools, or anything—"

"Yeah, there was some old cans of something in there. Paint or something. And no ladder, but there was one of those frames over the bed? You know, metal supports for carrying ladders or boards?"

We nodded. Joe and Bryce wrote furiously.

"And there was one other thing. In the back of that truck, that is . . ."

"Well?"

"It was kinda like a crate? It had a door in the front, with wire mesh on it. I thought it mighta been some kinda cage."

"How big was this crate?" I asked. "As big as, say, a dog-house?"

"Yeah. Maybe. But a little one. Maybe three foot square and maybe two foot high."

We sat out on Harry Phelps's porch awhile longer and then went inside for some iced tea. The little home was sparsely furnished, but cozy. A big wood stove dominated the living-dining area. A low, horizontal model that ate logs lengthwise, it seemed too big for the place. Phelps poured us big tumblers of tea that was too sweet. Even doubling up on the lemon didn't help. I nursed mine very slowly as he lit a cigarette and tried to describe the young woman to Stevens. I looked around the house. It was obviously factory made, but not too bad: nice wood-grain paneling, efficient double-glazed windows that cranked out, thick brown shag carpeting that I was positive hid an exterior-grade plywood floor underneath, and a kitchen and bathroom that were serviceable. It seemed that Harry Phelps had himself a nice little set of digs on the mountainside.

"Well, I hope you'll stay in touch with us, Harry," said Bryce as we left. "We'll keep the stakeout going all the rest of this week. Call us if you see or hear anything strange. Anything."

"Y'all don't worry," he said, waving at us from the deck as we climbed back into the cruiser. "I'll keep a keen eye out, and I can take care of number one, all by my lonesome."

We returned to Stevens's cruiser and wound our way back down the mountainside to the main road, Route 7.

"Okay, Doc, there's a guy I want to see," said Stevens. "I got his name from the police files, a guy named Pete Becker. Lives about an hour and a half from here, up north of Greenfield, right near the state line. It's to hell and gone, so I don't know if you'd want to come along or not. I could take you back to the farm and double back, but I'd rather not."

I told him I didn't mind, and settled into the backseat for the ride.

"You say you've called him?" asked Joe.

"Uh-huh," answered Bryce. "He said he'll see us, talk to us about Buddy."

"He remember him fondly?"

He thought for a second. "You know, it's funny. One of the first things he said when we started talking on the phone was that Franz is crazy. 'Completely nutso,' was the way he put it. But on the other hand, he had sort of a warm regard for Franz and started talking about some of the fun times they'd had together."

"Fun times, eh?" said Joe. "I wonder what that means. Carving people up, or what?"

"They were fighting dogs for money," Bryce answered. "He admitted it over the phone, which is strange. So I checked his rap sheet again; he was busted for dogfighting last year. Paid the fine and is on probation for two more years. I wondered why he was so willing to see us, and that's the reason: it's part of the probation. Which reminds me, you guys; he said not to open the gate until he gets there to let us in. I wonder why he said that?"

We took Highway 7 south to Route 9, east to Interstate 91, then north on the four-lane road all the way up past Greenfield, where we left the interstate and headed toward Turners Falls. Becker lived eight miles beyond that. It took us almost two hours to find Becker's place. During that time, Joe used Stevens's radio to call in the description of the blue-and-white pickup truck so that it could be put on the wire. But the description was feeble, he said, and we shouldn't expect results on what we had so far.

We got to Becker's place at three. The sign on the fence post wasn't exactly subtle:

IS THERE LIFE AFTER DEATH?

TRESPASS HERE AND FIND OUT!

"Oh great," sighed Joe wearily. "We got a hard-on here. Just what I need. This makes my fuckin' day—"

"Should we take the shotgun?" asked Stevens.

"You kiddin'? That's just what a guy like this wants. Just what he dreams about at night, for crissakes. He's probably got a whole roomful of equipment he can't wait to try out. He's probably inside there right now, watching us get out of the car, feeling his whanger get hard. Leave the high-profile stuff here. C'mon, let's follow Doc; he seems to know where he's going."

I was already out of the car and peering over the fence. The place sure wasn't pretty. It didn't seem like New England. Of course, everyone's image of New England countryside is the one passed around at holiday season, showing a white church on a snowy village green with an old-fashioned sleigh going up the main street. Or a cornfield in autumn, with all that gorgeous foliage. Well, the countryside sure was pretty; it was a knockout. But the dwelling place of Pete Becker was not going to be found on any of those postcards and calendars. The old farmhouse was covered and re-covered in tar paper and fake brick shingles. Junk was piled along one entire side, obscuring the windows. Junk in the yard: old appliance parts, tires and wheel rims, stacks of cardboard boxes and rolls of linoleum. Old cans, some rusted, some shiny, most in between. The place stank. It stank primarily of dog shit, that sour, malty smell of droppings that is one of my least favorite, despite my love of the critters in general.

Looking over the fence, I saw the first dog. It was standing maybe forty feet away, back between the two big pines, a heavy chain fastened around its impossibly thick neck. Red, with yellow eyes. The feet placed wide apart and curved, bowlegged. The mouth was open, the dog doing a slow pant, looking dead at me.

What struck me first was the dog's expression. Dog's faces are wonderfully expressive. Comedian George Carlin claims it's because dogs have eyebrows that are mobile, making them frown, weep, or ask silent questions. The dog that stared at me from the trees at the end of its stout tether had no expression. Just those cold, blank eyes. Robot eyes. Killer eyes. I see the same flat eyes on the faces of some of Roantis's friends, and occasionally, on Roantis himself. Not cute.

The animal didn't bark or growl a warning. There was no dark patch of raised fur on its back. There was no wiggle in the tail or twitch in the ears. There was no trace of emotion on that blank, wide face.

Then I saw another dog, farther off in the trees, chained in the same fashion. And another off to the left. Then two more. Most were reddish-brown in color. But one was white, two were brown with white markings, and another was brindle, with a black muzzle. I wanted no part of any of them.

Joe came up and joined me at the gate.

"Son of a bitch, Doc. Look at those, will you?"

"Yeah. Hey, Bryce? Honk the horn, will you?" I said.

A couple of beeps, a wait of ten minutes or so, and Pete Becker appeared on the dilapidated porch, fastening his belt. He was short and dumpy looking, with a paunch and long blond hair over a face that was too full and lined for a man his age, which I guessed to be under thirty. I read a life of dissipation in his body even before he was at the gate. He wore an old tie-dyed T-shirt that was dirty and aromatic. He hadn't shaved in several days, and hadn't washed or combed his hair in maybe a week.

"Hey," he said in a low monotone. "Hey, what's up? You the cop who called me?"

"Yes," said Bryce, watching Becker fumble with an iron bolt on his side of the fence, then swing it open. As he did so, a black-and-tan coon hound rushed down the porch steps, barking and growling. Normal dog behavior. But the pit bulldogs on their chains remained silent and watchful. Their silence unnerved me. Becker and the coon hound led us through the gate and up the rickety stairs to the porch. There were bad smells all around us. Garbage, rotten wood, mold and mildew. Either Becker didn't notice or didn't care. Maybe both.

"So Buddy's in trouble again, eh?" Becker said as he lit a cigarette and grabbed a half-finished Pepsi bottle that had been sitting on the porch railing. He sat down in a dilapidated lawn chair whose plastic webbing was half gone. "Doesn't surprise me. Listen: I don't hang around with Buddy no more. Funny, come to think of it. I ain't heard about Buddy in about a year or so. Figured he went away somewheres, or maybe he's dead. But then I seen his picture in the paper awhile back."

I thought this time frame was interesting, since the murders took place about a year previous. I asked Becker to describe their last meeting.

"Well, like I said, it was like about a year ago. He came over to the lumberyard where I work and asked me could he borrow some money. Said he was going away somewheres, like maybe to Alaska."

"Can you remember exactly when this was?" asked Joe. "Was it before or after Fourth of July weekend?"

"Oh . . . lessee . . . can't be sure. But I guess it was after. Not sure, though. Only thing I remember for sure was that he wasn't riding his bike. He had that old pan-head that he restored. Nice. But he wasn't on it then."

"What did he say about that?" I asked. "Where was the bike?"

"Said it got stolen. Said he was out of luck here and wanted to try someplace else, and could I loan him a couple hundred dollars."

"Did you?" asked Joe.

"No. 'Cause I didn't have it."

"How often did you and Buddy see one another?" asked Stevens.

"Well, when we was fighting the dogs, pretty often. Like, every month or so. Sometimes we'd go out of state to fights. Fights where there was a lot of money changing hands. Sometimes seven or ten thousand dollars on a single fight. Don't do it no more, a' course."

Joe looked over his shoulder at the chained dogs, who had now sunk to their bellies in the rest position. Still, they stared at us. " 'Course not," he said.

"And you haven't seen Franz since?" asked Stevens.

"Nope. Not in a long time. But hey, I guess you guys have, eh? Over at the fair, or whatever? A guy like Buddy, you can never tell where he might be. It's anybody's guess."

"Mr. Becker," said Joe, "we happen to know Buddy Franz is alive and probably within fifty miles of us right this minute. We also have strong reason to believe he's committed mass murder. The odds are he's hiding in these woods and mountains. Now, we've got to find him, and fast. You sure you haven't seen him?"

Bewildered, Becker repeated that he hadn't, and added that he wasn't all that surprised that Buddy had done violence.

"He was strange. I mean, he loved animals, you know? And he's good with them. He can ride a horse really good, and he worked in stables sometimes. But then he'd be mean to them, too, sometimes. It was like he was two people: one nice, one mean. And when he'd get mean, nobody would want to be around him because he's so big and strong, and, like, crazy."

"Exactly how strong is Buddy Franz?" I asked Becker.

"Real strong. Strong enough to pick up a hog that's fallen over. They weigh like a thousand pounds."

"A hog?" asked Bryce.

"Yeah. A Harley bike. We call 'em hogs."

"Is he strong enough to wrap a cow up in wire and put it on

a fence?" I asked. The question came out before I could stop it. I sat there, embarrassed.

"Yeah. Think so. He's strong as all hell, mister."

A chill went through me; I gave a tiny, invisible, involuntary shudder. My gaze fell.

Then Becker leaned back and put his feet up on the porch railing. He was wearing new work boots; they couldn't have been more than two weeks old. I noticed the upper surface of his left boot, just behind the toe. There was a shiny worn grease mark there. Nothing on the right one. I knew what it was.

"Were you ever with him when he cut an animal?" asked Joe.

"No. I never saw him do that. But he told me he cut up a nig-uh, a black guy once near Worcester. He said he did it to show off to his friends."

"His friends being the Pagans?" I asked.

"Hey, yeah. Who told you?"

"A woman named Lucy Kirkland. Ever hear of her?"

"Well, I heard of Billy Kirkland. He used to ride with Buddy, I think. But then I heard they was enemies."

"Ever hear of Melissa Hendricks?" asked Joe.

Becker shook his head. But it seemed to me he had to think a second before doing it. The hesitation made me wonder. I decided to try and catch him in a lie.

"You ever do any riding, Pete?" I asked him.

"Naw, not in a couple of years, anyways."

"What does Buddy Franz do to support himself," asked Stevens, "when he's not running dog- and cockfights?"

"Well, he's a painter and carpenter. Not fancy stuff, just, like, fixing up places. And sometimes he'd work in bowling alleys. He loves candle pins. Shit, I never saw a guy who could roll a ball faster than Buddy."

Joe and Bryce were scribbling away in their notebooks. "Anything else?" Joe asked.

"He can weld a little. A few times he worked in junkyards and steel scrap yards, cutting and welding. He can make stuff, like a shack to live in, out of junk and old boards and stuff. And he's a good hunter, too. Way back when I first met him, he lived alone in an old empty farmhouse, kind of like this one. He lived there alone, way out from nowhere, and hunted and fished."

"By the way, Pete, who owns this place?" asked Stevens.

"Mrs. Moffitt owns it, but she lives in Turners Falls."

"And how much rent do you pay?"

"Hundred a month. But sometimes she lets me slide."

"You have any idea, even a faint one, of where Buddy Franz is staying now?" I asked.

"No. Tell you what, though. Buddy could stay almost anywheres he wanted. He knows about living in the country by himself. He once told me that when he was a kid, he'd run away from home when his father beat him. He'd stay out in barns or shacks, or even hideouts he made himself out of boards and junk, like I just told you. He'd steal clothes and blankets off clotheslines to keep warm. He picked up wood to make fires with. He showed me how to make what he called a hobo stove out of an old oil drum and some gutter pipe for a chimney. He stole food. And he could always hunt. Buddy knows how to stay hidden and live off the land, believe me."

"He had a gun?"

"When I was with him, he always had a .22 rifle and a shotgun. They were cheap guns, and old, but he knew how to use them."

"So what you're saying, you're saying Buddy could be anywhere in the Berkshires right now."

"Yeah. Way up some mountainside near a creek."

"Why near a creek?" asked Joe. "For fish, you mean?"

"Uh-uh; for water. And also, if you wade up a stream, you don't leave any track through brush or grass. And dogs can't follow your smell there. He knew that, too, and told me. He knows all that stuff, Buddy does."

"Why did Franz quit the dogfighting business?" Stevens asked. "If it paid well, why did he abandon it?"

Becker shook his head.

"I don't think he did. But he did disappear for a while. I know

I woulda heard about him, at least, through the grapevine or something. But nobody heard about Buddy for a long time after he left last summer."

"What grapevine?"

"Oh . . . you know," said Becker, twitching his feet on the rail and looking down at the rotten boards, "just . . . people I hang around with. Some of the riders who stop by the lumberyard or who hang around at Shorty's place."

"What's that, a bar?" Joe asked.

"Uh-huh. A bar outside Turners Falls. A lot of bikers hang out there. And there are the people in the dog business. I don't do that anymore, of course," he said, "but I still see those people sometimes."

"And none of them saw Franz last year," Joe said, "and nobody's reported seeing him lately?"

Becker shook his head, then stood up. He wanted us to leave.

"How about showing us your dogs, Pete?"

"Naw. Rather not, I guess."

"If it's all the same to you, Mr. Becker, we think we'll have a little look," said Bryce in his quiet, official tone.

Becker moved to object but knew he had no choice. The three of us started along the side yard, but soon the stench, the tall weeds, the trash and broken glass, not to mention the basso growls and raised lips of the bulldogs, caused us to stop. I couldn't understand why—those, cute, cuddly little bundles of joy.

We called back to the porch and told Becker to get off his ass and give us the grand tour of his menagerie. He shuffled down the steps and joined us. I could tell he was just delighted. We followed him around the side of the old farmhouse to the big fenced yard.

"This here's Grumpy," said Becker, pointing to the brindle-and-white animal that sat silently on top of a doghouse made of an old packing crate. A heavy chain hung from its bull neck. The dog showed no emotion as we approached, something vastly different from the animated show put on by my dogs, who whine, wag, wheel around in circles, and can't wait to jump up and lick you on the face. Grumpy sat as Becker petted his head. I put my hand on the dog's wide head. It had a deep furrow running back between the ears, which were cropped short. The animal thumped its tail weakly against the top of the crate.

"He likes you," said Becker.

"Dogs seem to," I said. "But this sure as hell is no way to keep dogs, Becker. Or any animal, for that matter. Keeping them chained is downright mean. You ever been inside?"

He rattled the chain and stomped his booted feet on the crushed weeds underneath. "Yeah," he admitted softly, "once, for larceny. Thirty days was all."

"Well?"

"Yeah, okay. I see what you mean. But I got to keep them chained apart, or they'll fight. It's in a pit bull's blood to fight, you know."

"Well, you could keep their place cleaner, and at least give them longer chains." I ran my hand along the animal's flank until I felt a bump, a patch of rough scab. The dog turned, its lips raised, showing teeth, and a low growl rising in its wide chest. I removed my hand and petted its head again, talking softly to it. I leaned over and looked down at the wide gash in the flesh that was trying its damnedest to heal. I put my hand softly against it. Warm to the touch. Too warm, and I felt the baggy, soggy paunch underneath. Pus and inflammation in there, and spreading.

"How'd he get this?" I asked.

Becker shrugged. But I knew better.

We walked to the next dog, who strained at his chain to reach us. I started to put my hand down, and jerked it away just in time.

"Watch it, Doc!" Joe yelled.

CLACK! The dog lunged, snapping his wide, steam shovel mouth.

"Forgot to warn you; Dopey's a biter."

"Forgot to warn him, eh?" growled my brother-in-law. "Forgot? Maybe we'll just forget your deal with the probation officers and haul you in, Becker. I'd love to hear what the SPCA would say about this setup."

Every now and then, Joe gets protective of his family. Perhaps its his south-of-Naples ancestry.

A quick inspection revealed massive scars on the animal, two on his chest and a long one on the side of the neck. They weren't infected, though.

Dopey? Grumpy?

"These are named after the seven dwarfs? You've got to be kidding."

"Nope. I had seven, so I thought I'd name them that way."

"Well then, which one's Doc?" I asked, anxious to see my namesake. No doubt he was the handsome, civilized, debonair one. That is, if such could be found in this motley crew.

"Hate to tell you, but Doc died last year," Becker said with a sigh. "Got all ripped up in a fight and bled to death over in Saginaw, Michigan."

I said nothing, taken aback by this description of the violent end of the animal named for me. Was it an omen? I hoped not.

"Mr. Becker," said Bryce, "it's obvious that you're still in the dogfighting business. I—"

"No! No, I ain't!"

"Doc?"

"Recent," I said. "Within the last month or so."

"Don't bullshit us, Becker," said Joe, looking around him in disgust. "It pisses me off. And when I get pissed, I get nasty. Come to think of it, that's probably why you've got that nice new phone I saw through the front door. The phone service on the side of the house looks new as well. All this on a run-down house that hasn't been cleaned up in a year. I'm thinking this is how you set up contacts for the fights. What do you say?"

He didn't say anything, just shook his head slowly back and forth. To me, it was as much as an admission. Joe turned to me.

"Doc?"

"You better take decent care of these dogs, Becker, and quit fighting them," I said. "If you can't do that, I'm coming back here and shooting them. I'm not kidding. You hear me?"

He lowered his head but didn't answer. He reminded me of an adolescent kid, although he was probably thirty. A marvelous example of arrested development was Mr. Becker.

"Yeah, okay," he said weakly.

"The first thing I want you to do is ride with Mr. Stevens to the nearest drugstore and get all the things that I'm going to write on a list. Understand?"

He grunted assent and I wrote out a list that included boric acid crystals, hydrogen peroxide, single-edged razor blades, bandages, and so on.

While we waited for their return, Joe and I went up to the porch to get away from the bad smells, and discussed what to do with trash like Pete Becker. Joe was for turning him in immediately, but I disagreed.

"I'm thinking that if we let Becker off the hook for now, maybe he'll do us a favor later on," I said. "I think he's a guy that Franz is likely to contact if he's on the run and needs help. See what I mean?"

"You mean if we go easy on Becker, he might come our way? Betray his old friend?"

"There's a chance. For one thing, I doubt how far loyalty extends in people like Pete Becker. I say we leave him owing us a favor. Then, if something comes up, he may prove valuable in tracking Franz to earth."

Joe agreed the idea had merit. I ambled around to the back part of the property. Far back from the road, well hidden by a copse of willow trees, was a shack that was once probably a garage. I went inside, looking for a muzzle for the pooches. I found several in that old, vine-grown wooden building that was crawling with bugs and trash. I found a lot of other stuff, too, including a treadmill, several leather harnesses, a cattle prod, and a big stack of folded gunnysacks. All these I knew were used in the training of fighting dogs. The treadmill and cattle prod kept the animals on the run for hours at a time to build up their stamina. That is, if they didn't die first. The gunnysacks were especially repugnant to me. As a lover of both dogs and cats (who, incidentally, can grow to love each other in a normal household), I knew that the practice of placing a pit bull puppy and a cat into the sack, tying the end shut, and whirling the bag around until at least one of the animals inside was torn to pieces, was not my idea of training. And it certainly wasn't even remotely connected with sport.

Poking around in there, I stirred up a nest of white-headed hornets, surely the nastiest of all the winged stingers. I beat a hasty retreat, a leather muzzle dangling from each hand. When Becker returned with the supplies, I put hot water into a washbasin while he muzzled the first dog, Grumpy. I had him carry the animal over to an old picnic table in the sunlight and lay him on it. Then I tied the dog down with rope and sterilized a razor blade with my pipe lighter. I made a fresh incision the length of the wound, and the bad juice shot out under pressure at first with an awful smell, then oozed and oozed. I cleaned the wound with hot water and strong soap, doused it heavily with the peroxide, and showed Becker how to apply dressings soaked in boric acid that would draw out the infection. Then we moved to the next dog, and the next. I treated four the same way and was washing my hands, thinking we were through, when Becker cleared his throat nervously.

"Uh, there's one more, doctor. I think it might be safe to try this one in the far back . . ."

I jerked my head up. "Well, let's go get him, then; I haven't got all day."

"This one's big and kinda hard to handle."

"Well, he can't be much worse than these others, can he?"

"Yeah. He's, uh, my champ. Or was. Now I was keeping him just for breeding."

We walked to the far corner of the yard. There, behind a row of wild raspberry bushes, was a barrel on its side. A big chain snaked into it. But no sound came out.

Becker gave the chain two quick flips. A second later, a paw stuck out of the barrel. A huge, rust-red paw. Much bigger than any of those on the other dogs.

"This here's Bashful," said Becker. "But he ain't, exactly . . . if you get my drift."

FIFTEEN

The dog would not, or could not, get out of the barrel. Becker heaved on the chain, throwing all his weight backwards, and dragged the animal out. As soon as I got a good look, I saw why it couldn't get to its feet. I was amazed it was still alive, and spun around and slugged Becker on the jaw. He backed away fast, holding his hands up in front of his face. I nailed him again right below the center of his chest and he went down on his knees. It was all I could do to keep from kicking him. I ran back to the old wooden shack hidden in the trees and returned with the cattle prod shocker. I tapped it on his upper arm, and he screamed. I tapped it again, and again.

"How do you like it, Becker?"

He tried to answer but he couldn't; his teeth were clenched tight in pain. I tapped a couple more times, calling him a son of a bitch. Joe and Bryce, having heard the screams, came running around the side of the house. By that time, I'd taken the batteries out of the device and bent the hollow metal tube over my knee. I grasped it by the end, a crooked, metal boomerang, and whinged it as far into the woods as I could.

"Get up!" I yelled.

Becker got to his feet, shaking all over. I pointed at the dog.

"You guys see this? You see what he's done to this animal?"

The men stared at the dog, who was stiff with injuries and infection, and whining softly in agony.

"Put the muzzle on him, Becker," I said. "Now."

He did, and I carried the dog over to the old picnic table. Danny, my yellow lab, weighs ninety-two pounds. This dog did not feel any lighter. A ninety-pound pit bull. Sweet Jesus. He was a big bag of muscle. He was also ninety pounds of pain and infection. He probably weighed even more before the infection set in.

I worked on the animal for over an hour, with Joe and Pete Becker holding him down on the table. I wished to hell I'd had some kind of general anesthetic or analgesics, but we didn't. We did the best we could, with the animal crying and yelping even through the muzzle. Yet I was amazed at the pain the animal could stand. Bryce stood off to one side, writing out a lengthy citation. He went to his cruiser and used the radio. Becker looked as if he were about to shit his pants. Serve him right.

Shortly before five, I had wrapped the last of the cloth strips around the dog's wounds. The strips had come from my shirt, the cleanest cloth available in that pigsty Becker called home. We unmuzzled Bashful and gave him a big drink of cold water. Stevens had a bottle of aspirin in his car, and I forced four of them down the animal's mouth with Peter Becker's help. This was dangerous, for here was a beast trained to lock his massive jaws on anything that moved. But poor Bashful, running a high fever, was beyond fighting now. Frankly, I doubted he would make it.

"Mr. Becker, I have written out a report and a citation for this incident," said Joe, waving the papers in front of him. "We've got enough here, with our personal testimony as witnesses, to put you in the hot seat. For starters, it would void your probation, and you know it. Now, what Doc here has talked me into, he says if you'll take better care of these pooches of yours, and not fight them anymore, and maybe sell or destroy those you can't take care of, then we'll let you off the hook, for now."

"Thanks, I appreciate it. And I didn't mean to hurt the dog; I just . . . I just didn't know what to do when they got hurt—"

"Another thing we want you to do . . . *are you listening?*"

"Yeah . . . uh . . . yes sir."

"We want you to cooperate fully with us in tracking down Buddy Franz. He's dangerous. No matter how close you two were at one time, you must realize he's wanted for murder now, and he's unstable and dangerous. Do you realize this?"

Becker nodded.

"So, you see or hear anything about him, you let us know, understand? You don't, and you're up shit creek, pal. For now, you can go with us to Shorty's bar and introduce us to some of the guys who hang out there, okay? Maybe we can shake something loose."

Realizing he had no choice, Becker agreed. After a brief and futile attempt to clean himself up, he emerged from his rickety quarters and announced he was ready to guide us to Shorty's. I asked Joe what the reasoning was for taking Becker along, and he said that people on the fringe of the law were uncooperative at best. Having one of their kind in tow might help in getting them to open up. Frankly, I couldn't see how the likes of Pete Becker could help in any enterprise, but I said nothing. We all climbed into Stevens's cruiser and bounced and swayed down that rutted farm road to the highway that would take us into Turners Falls. I had to ride in the backseat with Becker. Some treat. I kept way over on my side of the car and told him to stay on his. He didn't argue, and from the swelling and discoloration emerging on his jaw, I knew why.

▼ ▼ ▼

Shorty's was a typical roadhouse bar: small place, one story, neon beer signs in the front windows, aluminum roof over the front door, and plenty of parking all around. We noticed three "sleds" parked outside. Sled, Becker informed us, being biker parlance for motorcycle. You hang around the right people, it's amazing what you can learn. All the bikes were Harleys. Becker recognized two of them as belonging to guys named Mac and Dragon. Just couldn't wait to meet them.

"Yeah? Well, maybe we don't feel like talking," said Mac, leaning down low over his bottle of beer, looking as if he were trying to sniff at its contents, or perhaps draw the beverage up through his nostrils, like doing a line of coke. He wore faded Levi's and a black T-shirt with the Harley-Davidson wings on the back. But no colors. He had a big chain on his belt holding a ring of keys and a big biker's wallet fastened to the chain. I thought those big chained wallets were just for effect before I started riding myself. But think about it: your wallet falls out of your blue jeans when you hit a bump and you leave it somewhere on the blacktop behind you. That's all she wrote. Mac had long blond hair which he wore blown back over his head, or perhaps stroked back with his fingers. But it wasn't combed. And light brown muttonchop sideburns. He tipped the bottle back and drank.

His companion, Dragon, was looking at a brochure with brilliantly colored motorcycles in it. It seemed to me that the bikers' minds were filled with three things almost to the exclusion of all others: bikes, beer, and broads. I peered over Dragon's shoulder and looked at the bike in the two-page color photo. I read the model description.

"What's a Softail Custom?" I asked.

"It's a new model bike they come out with," grunted Dragon, trying to appear cool and unemotional. But his eyes told the story; he craved that bike in the brochure. Perhaps he would commit murder and mayhem for it. "See, what they did, they hid the rear suspension undahneath the frame, so the bike looks like the old hahdtail Hahleys. It's the machine everybody wants."

"How much are they?" I asked.

"They staht at around eight . . ."

The bartender asked us if we wanted a drink. Joe and I ordered beers. Bryce, officially on duty, had coffee and took a seat next to Dragon, explaining that he'd appreciate any information either of them could give us on Werner Franz, whether they felt like talking or not. He wasn't playing tough, but there was no mistaking the fact that he was a state policeman and needed some information.

"Look," Mac said finally, "that guy Franz, I met him maybe twice. One time he was, like, okay, you know? Like normal. The other time, either he'd been drinking or doing something like acid, because he was, like, real mental? Then I heard from other guys that he was crazy. Now, that kind of guy, most of us who ride don't want to hang around with. Chances are, they're wanted by the law. And I see by you guys being here, that that's true, right?"

We nodded.

"Well let me tell you something, so you'll know: most riders aren't criminals. Sure, we drink and party. We smoke a little herb . . . sometimes we take some pills. But we don't use no needles. You get caught using the needle in *any* club, even the Hell's Angels, and you're out. Okay?"

We nodded again.

"And most of us got jobs. Some only part-time. And nobody ever accused us of wanting to own the company. Take me, for instance. Know what I used to do? Guess."

"I have no idea," said Bryce.

"Try this one: a college professor."

"Ah, come on."

"No shit. I taught over at Salem State. Composition and literature. Was goin' for my pee aitch dee."

"What happened?" I asked him. "What made you leave academia and take up the life of a biker?"

"What happened? Well, my old lady took off, for one. Took off with a young lawyer out of Harvard Law School. Said she was sicka me not making enough money. So she takes off with this young preppie and they're living over in Back Bay, you know? Raking in the dough, being regular yuppies. I felt like shit. Anyway, I was a stringer for a bunch of papers up there, to get extra money and because I liked it. Thought maybe I was gonna be a novelist someday. Ha! Anyway, one of the stories I get sent on was doing a piece on a biker bar up in Gloucester. Place called McBad's. So I go do the piece, and I liked the guys I met up there."

"I was one of 'em," admitted Dragon. "And for paht of the story, I give 'em a ride on my bike. He loved it . . ."

"Yeah, and they loved the piece when it came out, so they invited me back. First thing I know, I'm selling my Buick Skylark and making a down payment on a hog. Two months later, I quit my job at the college. And . . . here I am!"

With a wide grin, he leaned back, gulping beer, then slammed the bottle back on the bar and burped.

"Nothin' like it, man," he sighed. "Nothin' in the whole world like it."

"And what does your ex think about this transformation?" asked Joe, giving a soft beer belch himself.

"My ex is dead," said Mac softly. "She and her yuppie lawyer husband got to doing coke real heavy. I guess that's the drug of choice for the well-to-do set in Back Bay. Anyway, coming back from one of their high-toned parties one night, going along the Mass Pike at a hundred per in their Mercedes, Mr. Harvard Law, who's OD'd bad on the White Lady, has a heart attack. He passes out at the wheel and the car jumps the rail, flips twice, and burns. They're both gone, in the wink of an eye. I ask you, gentlemen, as a sometime student of literature and philosophy: was it fate, irony, God's Wrath, Universal Justice . . . or *what*?"

We just sat there, not saying anything. Suddenly self-conscious, Mac cleared his throat, chugged at the bottle again, and continued.

"Anyway, as I was saying about us bikers, all we want is our machines, our old ladies, and enough bread for good times. Now, a guy like Buddy Franz nobody needs. The Pagans couldn't use him, and they're badasses. So what I'm saying is, don't think because we ride that we're into all that shit."

This little speech finished, he grabbed a fresh cold one from the bartender and sucked on it.

"I know what you're saying," Joe said. "But this guy Franz does ride, and he is crazy. He's a maniac. And he doesn't do the rest of you guys any good. Follow?"

"Yeah, I know. A guy like him on the loose, the cops are alla time stopping us and searching our bikes and all that shit. We don't need it."

"So, we're asking for your help. If you've got any information on where he might be, we'd like to hear it. Maybe you hear stuff from other clubs, or riders passing through . . . maybe they see something."

"Yeah, yeah," nodded Dragon, fondling the pages of the brochure lovingly, "but what do we get in return, eh? That's what we wanta know. What's it worth to you?"

"What you get is our gratitude, and the thanks of the people from this state," said Stevens. "And fewer hassles from guys like us because of your improved image."

He thought this little spiel might impress Mac and Dragon. It did not, and I wasn't too surprised. I peered down at the picture of the Softail Custom again.

"Hey, Dragon, how much down payment would you need to get one of those?" I asked.

"Well, maybe just like a thousand or so. But then, see, the payments would be high. For me, or a guy like me, between two or three grand would be just right."

"How about the trade on your old bike?"

"Nah. They wouldn't give me what it's worth. I'd have to sell it myself, to another rider, you know. And it might take a long time. You never come out square trading with a dealer. You get fucked every time."

"Okay then, here's the deal. Whoever gives me information that results in our finding Franz, I'll give that person three grand. In cash. No questions asked."

This perked them up. Even Mac, the quiet one, lifted his nose up off the bottle of beer. Pete Becker was alert as well.

"Wait a second, Doc," said Joe, "you don't wanta—"

"That's the deal," I said, waving Joe off. "Three grand. There's your Softail Custom."

"I never heard of a cop offering a reward," said the bartender, a very fat redheaded guy with a bushy beard.

"I'm not a cop."

"Doc, I don't think this is a good—"

"So that's it," I said, leaving the beer money and a tip on the bar. I took cards out of my wallet and gave one each to the bikers, and started for the door. The others followed me, and soon we were on our way back up to the dilapidated farmhouse. We let Becker off and told him to behave himself. I got out of the cruiser and went to check on the pooches. All were improved except the huge rust-red brute named Bashful, who we found lying on his side wheezing and panting, his lips frothed white. I petted him and he licked my hand. When I got up to go, he rolled onto his belly and tried to get to his feet. He couldn't do it; he hadn't the strength. But still he tried to crawl after me.

"He wants to go with you," said Becker.

"Well, tough shit," I said, and walked away. But then the dog started whining, pulling at the leash with all the strength he had left in him. The chain was tight as a banjo string. His tail thumped weakly against the damp grass. I doubted he'd last the night in the condition he was in.

"Oh, what the hell," I said, unsnapping the chain. "I'm getting to be a sap in my old age. It's from hanging around Moe Abramson . . ."

I leaned over and shoved my arms underneath the dog, who cried in pain as I lifted him.

"Oh no you don't," warned Joe.

"Is this okay with you, Becker?" asked Bryce. Becker replied it was, since he was probably going to die anyhow. He didn't seem very concerned.

"Well, goddammit, Doc, don't put him in the backseat," warned Joe, his mouth curling down in a sour look. "Put him in the trunk. It's the least you can do—"

"It's okay, Joe," said Bryce softly. I'll put that old blanket down first. Besides, it's not my car; it's the state's."

So we pulled out of there again, headed for home. I decided to stop at a drugstore and get Bashful a massive dose of penicillin at the earliest opportunity. We discussed Peter Becker at some length. We all agreed he'd lied about the dogfighting. Their recent injuries were evidence enough of that. Also, the brand-new phone seemed a giveaway: the means of setting up fights, both locally and out of state.

"He lied about something else, too," I said. "And I don't know why."

"What's that?" asked Joe.

"He said he hadn't been on a bike in a couple of years. But I know better. He's wearing a pair of new boots. I noticed the top of the left one. It has a shiny, greasy worn spot on it just behind the toe. That's from shifting gears on a motorcycle. It's a foot-operated lever right beneath the engine, and it always leaves a worn mark like that on the biker's boot. A dead giveaway."

"So why would he lie about that? No law against riding motorcycles."

"Who knows?" I said. "But he's a liar. Some people lie compulsively, for no apparent reason. Two of our recent presidents have had this quirk. Anyway, the thing to remember when dealing with a liar like Becker is that we can't really believe anything he tells us, right?"

"Right," concurred Stevens.

"Yeah," said Joe softly, "anything he said. Like even the part about not seeing Franz in the past year . . . right?"

"You got it," said Stevens.

Next to me on the backseat, Bashful breathed in ragged pants and sighs, his nose hot, his welterweight body swollen with heat and hurt. But whenever I put my hand on his head, his tail thumped pathetically against the seat.

"Jeeez, Doc," said Joe, turning around in the front seat to eye the big red dog with the yellow eyes lying next to me, "the last thing you need is another dog. Especially *that*—"

"I'm not going to keep him. I just know he'd die if we left him there. What I'll do is, as soon as he's okay, *if* he makes it, is give him to Roantis."

"Listen, Doc," said Joe, "that was a real mistake you made back there."

"Taking the dog?"

"No. Offering a reward for Franz. That was stupid. Here's why. One: it's probably not going to help get Franz any quicker. In fact, it might tip him off ahead of time, and screw us up. Two: your offer is gonna go out on the biker grapevine with the speed of light. Every one of 'em wants that new Harley Softail. With the word out, it just might leak back to Franz that you've put a price on his head. And when he hears that, even if he wasn't pissed at you already, he's going to come for you. Just you wait."

"Aw, c'mon," I said, trying to sound confident and upbeat. But I felt a cold, heavy feeling in the pit of my stomach. There was truth to what Joe said. I had acted rashly, out of frustration, without considering the consequences. I, and my family, could pay dearly for it. I sighed, and felt the big dog's tongue on my hand.

SIXTEEN

As my injuries healed, and the date for Joe to bring his old flame Marty Higgins out to the farm approached, the population at our rural outpost grew.

"Who's that with him?" asked Mary, looking in awe at the tall, lithe figure of Rowanda Williams as she climbed out of the passenger side of the blue Jag. "And where'd he get that car, Charlie? Is he dealing now, or what?"

"No, hon. That's his girlfriend's car. And that is Ms. Rowanda Williams. Skidmore, class of '78. What do you think?"

"Of her, or the car?" she asked, turning to face me. "I'll admit this in my old age, Charlie; I sometimes get a teeny bit jealous of women who are prettier than me."

She wiped her hands on the dishtowel as she leaned toward the kitchen window. "Fortunately, there aren't too many of 'em," she added, heading for the backdoor. She's right, of course.

I made all the introductions as we caught up with our new houseguests near the driveway. But just then we heard a rattle and clang from the pasture gate. There was Warren Shaw with his biggest truck. He'd just lowered the tailgate and pulled out the steel ramp.

Bam! Bumpty bump bump! *Bam!*

The biggest, leanest, meanest bull I'd seen since Texas thundered down that ramp into the pasture. He kept moving until he came to the watering trough, which he attacked. I couldn't figure out whether he wanted to gore it or mount it. Judging from the horns he carried up front, and the sporting equipment he had in back, I knew that either way, the trough was a goner.

I paused then for reflection. With Mike Summers, Warren's dairy bull, and Bashful (now sunning himself in the yard), it seemed that protection aplenty was arriving at Pound Foolish Farm. I felt heartened by this rallying-'round effect. That is, until I saw a cloud of dust on the driveway, approaching fast. Like a dust devil out of the Old West, or perhaps a pillar of smoke from the Old Testament, Joe's cruiser sped up our drive and spun to a twisty stop on the gravel. Joe, who can move unbelievably fast when he wants, hopped out of the cruiser, grabbed me by the arm, and told me to get in quick.

"We're going to Lanesboro, Doc."

"What happened?"

"Somebody tried to make off with Phelps's motorcycle last night. He woke up in time to get his gun, run outside, and see the guy riding away on it. Says he got off a couple rounds from his .45 and winged the guy."

"Franz?"

Joe shrugged. "We don't know one way or another. But who else would it be?"

We said a quick good-bye to Mary and our new houseguests, leaving them staring after us with blank expressions as we hopped into the cruiser and sped down the drive.

"It was around two in the morning," Joe said as we flew along the rutted road toward the main highway. "Reason I think it was Franz is because Phelps had locked the bike. But he told us he hadn't changed the lock on it, just had a locksmith make another key. Now it could have been hot-wired, but Phelps says he was keeping the bike right outside his bedroom window. To hot-wire the machine would take time, and require a light, too. What I'm thinking is maybe Franz still had his bike key."

I thought for a minute.

"I'm not convinced it was Franz," I said. "He just got out of a close scrape at the fairgrounds; I don't think he'd take another big risk so soon."

"I thought of that, too, but remember, he's a maniac. Who else could it be?"

"Remember those kids hanging around the auction? They couldn't get enough of that old pan-head, and they were bidding on it, too. And what about that woman who came up to his cabin asking about the bike?"

"Maybe. Whoever she was. Sure wasn't Lucy Kirkland; Bryce showed Phelps her picture and he said no way."

"Melissa Hendricks?"

"Dead. At least we all think so, Doc. But Bryce is working on getting a picture of her to show Phelps, just in case. But I think the girl who came by was just someone with a biker boyfriend, and she happened to see the machine from her car."

"Well, one thing's for sure: a woman didn't take it."

"You got that right," Joe muttered, spinning the wheel in his big palms and forcing the cruiser around a tight, hilly curve. "A woman doesn't steal a thousand-pound Harley. But if it was Franz, how did he get Phelps's name and address?"

"The state has records," I said.

"Oh, right, Doc. Riiiight. You think Buddy Franz, fugitive from the law, is going to go ask?"

"No, I guess not. But you just reminded me he's crazy. Apparently the rules don't hold for this guy."

"The noise woke Harry up. That's what he told Bryce. He grabbed his government-model .45 and was outside in two winks. He got off a couple shots and swore he saw the thief flinch and lean over a bit before he blasted off into the darkness."

"So what's Harry's frame of mind now?"

"Pissed off, as you'd expect. He's mad as hell he didn't have the lock changed."

Bryce Stevens was waiting for us when we got to the house on the mountainside in Lanesboro. He met us in the middle of the road, showing us where to park.

"I don't want you to run over the spot, Joe," he said, leaning into Joe's window. "There's some blood on the gravel over there. Take a look; Phelps connected all right."

"Where is he?" Joe asked.

"Talking on the phone again. He'll be here shortly."

We parked and went over to the spot on the road that was dotted with blood, each splash about as big as a quarter. We squatted down and looked carefully. Harry Phelps walked up behind us.

"Doc, how severe would you say the wound is?" asked Stevens.

"Hard to say." I looked back at Phelps's place. It was a good forty yards back up the road. "Nice shooting, Harry."

"Yeah, lucky I guess. What happened, he didn't start the machine up near the house; too smart for that. He unlocked it and turned on the ignition, then wheeled it around, facing downhill, and coasted until he got speed up, and popped the clutch."

"You must've been up and ready pretty fast, to even get a shot off," said Joe. There was uncertainty in his eyes.

"I'd been awake. I thought I heard some noises earlier but wasn't sure. Frankly, I've been a little jumpy ever since we talked last time, you know? Guess I been sleeping with one ear and one eye open. I think what woke me up was him unlocking the bike and wheeling it around. Hell, it was parked underneath the deck, right near my window. So I was up and at the door with the gun as he was coasting down the road. I could just barely see his tall shape in the dark. I'm sure he didn't know I was behind him; he thought he was home free. Well, just before I brought the pistol up he turned on the headlight. The new bikes all have headlights that go on whenever the ignition's on. But this old bike doesn't. So when I saw that beam shining down the road, well, I could see him pretty clear then, by the glare. I used instinct shooting and let a couple rounds fly. I'm sure I saw him tip over a bit in the saddle at the second shot."

We all squatted around the small dark stains on the road.

"I think you hit a blood vessel," I said finally. "I say that because a bullet wound often doesn't bleed immediately."

"I know what you're saying, Doc," said Stevens. "The impact of the slug drives all the blood away from the area. It starts to bleed maybe ten or fifteen seconds later."

"Uh-huh. So these splashes here indicate a severed vessel, but not a major one. If it were, we'd have found a corpse at the foot of the hill, and we didn't."

"I just wonder how far he got," said Stevens. "I've never ridden a bike. Harry, how difficult would it be to keep going on a heavy machine like that?"

"Real hard," Phelps said. "Those bikes weigh half a ton. Plus, I tightened up the clutch cable earlier this week. It takes a strong grip just to move it. If I winged him anywhere in the upper body, he'd have trouble controlling the bike. If I winged him in the leg, he'd still have trouble."

I was walking down the road, eyes glued to the gravel and dirt, looking for tire tracks. Now and then they were visible in the fine dirt and dust. But the gravel didn't take tracks. I asked the men how far down the road they'd looked. They answered not more than a hundred yards or so, given the time constraints. But it would be gone over thoroughly later in the day, they assured me. I went for a walk.

It was over the next rise, down in the low curve of the road, where I found evidence of the bike leaving the road. The dark scar of damp earth in the gravel was the initial clue. The curving line of heaped gravel and dirt told me the direction: the bike had swerved off to the right. In the woods I saw matted brush, and white scrape marks on two large rocks that told me something heavy and hard had brushed against there. Blood, too. Two big splashes on the rocks. The wound was bleeding more freely now. But where was the bike? And where the hell was the thief?

"What did you get on the computer network on the blue-and-white pickup?" I asked Stevens when the trio caught up to me.

"Nothing. We got no hits. No tie-ins with Franz or anybody who knew him. Plenty of blue-and-white trucks, though. But none that old."

"Well, you might try looking for one under Melissa Henricks's name," I said.

"But she's dead," said Joe.

"I'm not so positive anymore. Having any luck tracking down her parents in Florida?"

"We're thinking something will break pretty soon."

"I'm going back to Ten Ten this week and take a closer look at the remains and the scanty dental records. Maybe we should also talk with Lucy Kirkland."

"What about?" asked Joe.

"Transportation. Lucy used to ride with the gang; she'll know answers to questions like: How do bikers without bikes travel? What happens when they're on a run and their bikes break down? Whoever the thief was, he was injured when he veered off the road here. So how did he take the bike with him?"

"He had help," said Stevens.

"Right, but who?" asked Joe. "And is it somebody we've already met, like Becker or Dragon . . . or is it some other weirdo? Some demon we don't even know what he looks like?"

For starters, Joe and Bryce called in to have a team come out and make plaster casts of the tire impressions on the dirt. Joe said maybe they could match them to a vehicle later on. "It's a damn shame we weren't on the scene earlier," Joe said, staring down at the bewildering array of tire tracks on the dirt, "but we'll block the road off and see what we can come up with."

"While we're waiting, why don't you come in for some coffee?" asked Harry. So we did.

The cabin looked a mess, with clothes everywhere. I saw a set of Marine Corps dress blues hanging on a door. Starched and pressed crisp as razor blades, the uniform was impressive, as was the white cap that went with it. I'm sure that Harry Phelps could still wear that uniform with no trouble fitting into it. I also noticed a picture frame on the wall right behind the big wood stove. In it were battle ribbons and medals. Several medals, including the Purple Heart and the Navy Cross. Harry Phelps was a war hero.

"Sorry about the place," he said amiably as he poured coffee from an old-style percolator. "My ex-wife's coming up from Alabama next week and bringing our boy. I'm getting the place cleaned up for them. Hell, seems like I'm on the phone long distance an hour a day, trying to make all the arrangements."

"Were those up on the wall when we were last here?" I asked, pointing to the medals and ribbons.

"No," he said with a chuckle. "I put them up to impress my kid, I guess. He's almost fourteen now, and probably all he's heard about Vietnam is how we lost over there, and so on. I thought I'd . . . try to be a little positive about it. More coffee, Joe?"

"So, Harry, who do you think stole your bike?" asked Bryce.

"Who? Why that big blond fella took it."

"How are you sure?" I asked him, and explained my reasons for doubting it.

"Well, maybe you got something there, Doc. But I'll tell you this: whoever took it is big. I haven't fooled with the seat and pegs yet, and I can barely reach when I sit on it. And also, the guy is strong and tough. He took a .45 slug and kept on goin'."

"We'll get your bike back, one way or another," Joe said.

"Sure hope so," Phelps said, slamming down the phone in its cradle. "Damn! Busy again! Ain't she ever goin' to shut up?"

"Who?"

"My ex. How am I ever goin' to get them two up here if I can't talk to her first?"

"It's called the crash truck," said Lucy Kirkland. "On any run, a club will always have a crash truck following the riders. The truck carries the sleeping bags and beer, some tools, you know.

Spare bike chains, maybe two or three gasoline cans, and stuff. Then if a bike breaks down we can fix it, or else just wheel it onto the crash truck and that rider doubles up with somebody, or else rides in the truck. I drove the crash truck a couple times."

"Was it yours?"

"No, it was Melissa's. I think it was her folks' truck."

"What color was it?"

"Blue. Or blue and white, if I remember . . . but I haven't seen that truck around in a long time."

"You see that truck, you call us right away, okay?" said Bryce. Then he asked her if she had a snapshot of Melissa.

"No, I don't think so. Wait! Maybe. I'll look around and see. Why you need it, anyways? She's dead and gone."

"Is she?" I asked. Lucy shrugged, saying that's what we had thought, and why had we changed our minds?

"You sure Franz hated Melissa enough to kill her?" Joe asked. Lucy looked down, shifting her gaze back and forth. It seemed to me she knew more than she was telling.

"You ever hear of a guy named Peter Becker?" I asked. She said she had a vague recollection. What about the bowling alley in Lenox Franz used to frequent? What about Shorty's roadhouse up in Turners Falls?

"Yeah. I been to both places. But I wasn't with Franz; I was with Billy and Mike Church and the rest of the Aces."

We asked if she'd ever heard of Mac and Dragon, the two riders we'd interviewed at Shorty's.

"Hey, c'mon! What is this?" she wailed. "I been trying to help you, Dr. Adams. And all I get is blame and stuff!"

We were standing near the stable barn, at the shed that was, once upon a time, the blacksmith shop. I watched Mike Summers hauling pieces of sheetrock as if they were cardboard. We were fixing up the old shed for Lucy to stay in, now that she seemed a full-time addition to the farm. But still, I had some questions regarding Lucy Kirkland, and these dealt at least in part with the motivation Franz had for the killings in the hollow.

"Lucy, you told us a few weeks ago that you were sure that Franz killed your brother because he stole Melissa Hendricks away from Franz. Right?"

She nodded, but her eyes did not meet mine.

"And you don't think there was a chance that Melissa never really left Buddy? That maybe she even helped him plan the killings?"

"No! Of course I'm sure!" she said, but her eyes traveled to the ground, confused. "Now please leave me alone, Dr. Adams. Please!"

Mike and I watched her stomp off toward the house.

"Can you put the rest of this up by yourself?" I asked Mike.

"No problem, Doc. Part of my job at the Y is maintenance and repairs. Where you off to?"

"I'm going over to Lenox and hunt up that bowling alley," I said. "I'm curious about who stole that green motorcycle up in Lanesboro. If it turns out it wasn't Franz, then I won't care one way or another. But if it was, and if he'd dare to pull something like that so soon after trying to kill me at the fairgrounds, then . . ."

"Then what?"

"Then there might be repercussions here. But you don't have to tell Mary all this, okay?"

"Gotcha."

I told Mary I'd be back in two hours and headed for Lenox. Red Crown Bowl was easy to find, a low, squat building two blocks off the main street in a part of that nice town that wasn't so. I walked in, past the cigarette machines in the entranceway that smelled of stale smoke, on up to the desk where a teenage boy with a bad case of acne was smoking, chewing gum, and sipping a cola. Now and then one of his dirty hands would snake inside a half-eaten bag of potato chips at his elbow and emerge with a fistful of the fried fat and salt. The source of the skin problem was no mystery to me. I wondered if the kid knew it, or was ignorant of the disastrous long-term effects of a poor diet. I decided to mind my own business.

I approached the counter and placed my shield faceup on the

Formica counter. It was, in all respects save one, exactly like the shield that Joe and all other state police carried. The exception was that underneath the blue-and-gold seal of the Commonwealth were the words *special police* instead of simply *police.* This to designate my standing as a part-time medical examiner for the state. But people who saw the badge didn't know the difference, and never asked. To them I was another plainclothesman. I asked the kid if I could talk with the manager.

"He ain't here right now. You wanna wait?"

"May I have his name?"

"Jerry Rapp. He went out to get—oh, there he is now—"

Jerry Rapp was a solidly built man of about thirty-five with long dark hair and a full, heavy beard of the same color. His skin was red, and he had bright blue eyes that looked tired. He looked at the badge without reaction, perhaps even feigning a bored look. A look that said, okay, cop, I've seen your kind before. I'm *real* impressed.

"Yeah?" he said.

I filled him in on Bill Worthington's disappearance a year previous. He had been managing the place then and remembered the kid, whom he described as a nice guy, a little on the quiet, nerdy side, who liked to hang around the place and listen to the stories and try to make friends.

"You say tried to make friends. You mean he didn't?"

"Not really. He was, like, on the sidelines, you know what I mean?"

"Can you remember anyone who directly made an effort to befriend him? Anybody stick out in your mind?"

"Oh, you mean Franz. Yeah, what a weirdo, man. Like, I'm glad he's gone. I read about him in the *Eagle* a couple weeks back. Bad news. I guess now he's wanted he ain't going to come back here no more. I hope."

I looked down at Jerry Rapp's left boot toe and saw the telltale mark of the shift lever.

"You ride?"

"Uh-huh. And you do, too, right? Not many people know what that spot on a boot means. This place has always been a sort of gathering place for a lot of guys who ride. It's not like a biker bar or anything. Just maybe a hangout."

"What can you tell me about the Aces club, and Melissa Hendricks and Bill Kirkland?"

"Not much."

"Not much? What does that mean, Jerry? They're both dead, and we thought Franz was killed with them until the labs proved otherwise. We're now all but positive he killed them, along with four others, one of whom was Bill Worthington. Have you seen Buddy Franz or Melissa Hendricks within the past, say, ten months?"

He scratched his unkempt head of hair and thought for a minute. "I don't think so, now you ask me. I know I haven't seen Franz for a long time. Maybe a year. And I don't miss him."

"Was he mean and violent?"

"Not so much that. It was like he was weird. Scary. Like, you never knew what he was going to do next. Or when he was going to go off his nut. Mostly, he was quiet. But he's big and strong, and he knows how to use a knife. So I don't—hey, did you ask me about Melissa? I thought you said she was dead."

"We thought so. The evidence is spotty. And now I'm wondering if she's dead or not."

"Well, I sure haven't seen her. Anything else you want?"

"I'd like any information on Melissa and Franz. Their relationship, if any. Were they friends or sworn enemies? Were they lovers? What's the story?"

"Well, if I hadda say one way or another, I'd say they were, like, going together. I saw 'em together pretty often, like a year and a half ago, I think. Around then."

"Do you remember either of them driving an old blue-and-white pickup? American made, probably Ford or Chevy?"

"Yeah. In fact, that was what Franz was driving right when that shy kid disappeared."

"You saw them both here? Together?"

"Uh-huh. But I remember they didn't leave together. I remember because they were talking, and I was surprised Franz was talking to this kid that was kind of out in left field. It was like they were getting to be friends, and it surprised me. Then Franz left, and after about a half hour, the kid took off. And the funny thing was, he left in the middle of a line. I thought that was kind of strange."

"That so? Now, Jerry, was this before or after the Fourth of July last year?"

"Right before. I remember, because last summer the police asked me that same question. I remembered when it was because the summer leagues were having an Independence Day tournament. It was right before the holiday weekend."

"Did the police ask you if the kid left with anybody?"

"Yeah. I said no, he didn't."

"Did you even mention Franz to them?"

"Nope. Because I didn't put the two together until just now, when you asked the questions."

"So Franz and the kid didn't hang out together. They weren't friends."

"Nah. Like I said, the kid was kind of a nerd, you want to know the truth. That's why I was surprised when Franz was talking with him that day."

"But you said they didn't leave together."

"No, they didn't. Franz left first, driving that blue-and-white truck you asked about. But now I think about it, maybe he set the kid up—told him to wait a few minutes and then leave, and they'd meet outside, you know?"

"So they wouldn't be seen leaving together, and nobody could pin it on Franz later, you mean?"

He nodded.

"Was anybody else in the truck when he left?"

"I didn't see anybody. Didn't look real hard, though."

"Did the police ask about Franz?"

"Not last year. There was another state cop in here awhile ago asking about him."

"Lieutenant Stevens?"

He nodded.

"Hey, if there's nothing else, I gotta wax those last four alleys, okay?"

"Sure. By the way, there's a reward of three thousand cash, no questions, for information leading to the arrest of Franz."

He listened, then looked at me closely.

"Hey, wait a sec; I seen you before. I knew you looked kind of familiar, and now I remember. It was in the *Berkshire Eagle,* I think. Right?"

"It's possible. I'm indirectly involved in this case," I said, getting a trifle uneasy at Rapp's question.

"Yeah, now I know. You're the guy who bought that farm. I remember I saved the picture because of the bikes, since they belonged to people I used to hang around with. Aren't you a doctor or something?"

"I'm a physician and a state policeman, too. A medical examiner."

"Yeah, that's it. And I remember something else, too: you're the guy who set the trap for Franz at the fairgrounds, isn't that right?"

"Oh that. That was a misprint. I was there, but I didn't set any trap."

He didn't say anything, just kept looking at me.

But my fears were realized; to anyone who'd seen the papers, I was the brains behind the ill-fated capture attempt. That did not help. Not at all.

"But you're offering the reward? How come?"

"I'm just one person in the party offering the reward," I said. "We're offering it for the obvious reason that Franz is a murderer and a danger to the entire region. Wouldn't you agree with that?"

"Sure. Three grand, eh?"

"That's right."

"Ever hear of Lucy Kirkland?"

The question startled me. I paused for a second.

"Now that you mention it, I know her a little," I said.

"Have you seen her lately?"

"I . . . yes," I answered. Jerry Rapp had been forthright with me; the least I could do was return the frankness. Besides, it was no secret to anyone who wanted to know that Lucy was now staying out at the farm.

"Is she still in deep shit with Franz?"

"What do you mean?"

"Way I heard it, she and her brother fingered Franz for ratting on a coke deal with some bad dudes from New York called the Stompers. Franz got his ass kicked good. That's why he killed Billy Kirkland, and I'm sure he'd kill Lucy, too, if he could find her. But I don't know if it's true or not."

"A coke deal? What were they doing, carrying it, or what?"

"Uh-huh. A lot of bikers are couriers. As a cop you must know that. Hey, are you really a cop, or what?"

I told him of course I was, and headed for the door.

"I'll remember about that three grand," he said, heading for the far side of the building to begin his task of waxing the wood.

"You ever hear of a guy named Pete Becker who fights dogs?" I asked.

"Oh yeah. Friend of Franz's. Not to be trusted."

"How about Mac and Dragon? Ever heard of them?"

"Yeah. They're okay guys, I guess. Why, you meet these dudes, or what?"

"Yes, and I think they're after the three grand, too. And one more question. If you were trying to locate Franz right now, where would you look?"

He thought for a second. "Anywhere. Franz can live anywhere. Town, city, or country. He used to work in stables sometimes, and he's always liked to sleep in stables and barns. He can live without a roof over him. Mostly, if I was looking for Buddy right now, I'd look in old deserted buildings and farmhouses."

I'd look for him in a hospital, I thought to myself.

"Thanks, Jerry. Please call me at those numbers I gave you if anything comes up," I said, heading for the door.

But then he turned around, asking me how well I knew Lucy Kirkland. I decided to level with him, and told him that she was in fact an unofficial housekeeper out at the farm.

"Does she seem happy?" he asked.

"As happy as possible, I think, given all the bad stuff that's happened. Why?"

"Well, I was just thinking back a couple years ago, when she was riding with her brother Bill and Mike Church and those guys."

"You mean the Aces?"

"Yeah. I guess that's what they called themselves. They weren't tough or anything, but Billy Kirkland was always trying to be a badass. A mean little guy. He wasn't very big, and he used to mistreat Lucy sometimes. Seems like she was always waiting on him and the other guys, like some kind of slave. So between him and the Aces on one side, and Franz on the other, seemed like she had a pretty tough time, you know?"

"Yeah. She's been through the wringer, all right. I think that's the main reason she likes being with us, Jerry. It's probably the closest thing to a home she's ever known."

"She seemed like a nice kid to me. Well, good luck with the hunt; I see or hear anything, I'll give you a ring."

"See ya," murmured the kid behind the rental counter, scarcely able to talk with a mouthful of chips. Another bag, just opened, was at his elbow. I got in the car realizing I'd learned a lot from Jerry Rapp, who seemed like a decent guy, and definitely the straightest shooter of any I'd talked with. I also realized he was clever and smart, and had learned as much about me as I had about him.

I drove out of Lenox and decided to make a few wide circles in the countryside, keeping my eyes open. I spent over two hours scanning the hills, fields, and woods, including the towns of Great Barrington and Stockbridge. If there's a prettier town on earth than Stockbridge, Mass., I haven't seen it. I was looking for a likely spot for Buddy Franz to lay up and lick his wounds, and wait for revenge. It was a vain effort; there were hundreds of square miles of rolling hills in every direction, all of it perfect for hiding in. It would take search teams and dogs weeks to comb it. So what chance did I have? Unless I became brilliantly lucky, or found some kind of clue, absolutely none.

SEVENTEEN

That weekend, the first one in August, Joe finally brought Marty Higgins out to the farm for Sunday dinner.

Marty Higgins, just as I remembered her twelve years previous. A little different, of course, but not much. Same light brown hair. Same sensitive blue eyes. A little bit over-weight. You might call her sturdy. Attractive in a quiet way. She had a deep contralto voice that was calm, and calming. She was caring and gentle, but there was quiet strength behind her nurturing. She was a little shy in groups. Marty generally didn't offer her opinion unless asked. And then, it usually turned out to be the soundest offered. Who knows? Maybe her reticence is what attracted Joe to her. After growing up with an older sister like Mary, who is all the things Marty is not, perhaps this low-profile woman who didn't say much was just the ticket.

Mary and I were standing at the edge of the newly completed swimming pool and watching it fill up ever so slowly via the thin green garden hose that snaked into its far corner, when we heard the car door slam behind us. We looked up to see the two of them padding up the grass toward us. Joe came first, leading her by the hand. Marty was behind him, almost trying to hide behind his bulk as they drew closer. He kept turning around to her, murmuring encouragement. "C'mon . . . c'mon—" I heard him say softly to her. She wore a white cotton smock dress. Her light brown hair was cut square on the sides, reaching down just below her ears. She had bangs in front, and a face that was well formed, pleasant, and a little pink. She was blushing and biting her lip.

"Mary? Hey! Mary!" she said in her deep, soft voice, trying to smile. Mary ran up and hugged her to death, then Marty was giggling and crying at the same time. I rather had a case of the damp eyes myself. Meanwhile, Joe was wearing the biggest grin I'd seen in years. *Years.*

"Oh, hi, Doc!" Marty said, disentangling herself from Mary and looking at me. "Boy, you sure look young!"

I told you she was nice.

I hugged her long and hard. It was great to see her again, the one bright ray of hope in Joe's shattered life. "It's been a long time, Marty. Way too long," I whispered to her so nobody else could hear. "I'm so glad you're back. You don't know what it means to all of us."

She began crying in earnest then, sobbing into a little, wadded up hanky, and we all sat down on the terrace while she wiped her eyes. Then she said she wanted to go to the "ladies room" to "freshen up." She trotted toward the backdoor, her white dress billowing in the breeze. "What a lovely, lovely place you have here!" she sang as she opened the door and went inside.

I turned to Joe. "I, uh, take it by that comment that you

haven't filled her in on the recent events around here?"

He shook his head. "Thought it better not to. Not right away."

She came back with a freshly washed face and sat, sipping a tall iced tea. I noticed that Joe was also partaking of the amber fluid, in place of his usual gin and tonic. Heavens to Betsy! What hath Marty wrought?

"Starting a diet, Doc," he explained when he saw me eyeing the drink. "Marty's kind of talked me into it."

"Iced tea, Joe? Say it ain't so."

"Oh, that's great, Joe," cooed Mary. "Marty, you know when Joey's thin, he looks like Marcello Mastroiani?"

"I don't know if I'd go so far as to say—"

"Shut up, Charlie. I think it's great about the diet, Joey. Really."

"Thanks."

"Oh yeah?" I said. "Well, for your information, Marcello, we've got a wee dinner planned in Marty's honor. What does the 'diet' say about charcoal-roasted leg of lamb, white beans in butter and garlic, French bread, Greek salad, Lynch-Bages '77, fresh strawberry shortcake with whipped cream, and cappuccino with cognac? Hmm?"

I saw a thin string of drool depart the corner of Joe's mouth and snake its way down to his shirt collar. He quickly wiped it away with the back of his hand, but another came out the other side, and then a third out of the first side again, and so on. Pavlov would have wet his pants.

"Uh, hate to tell you guys, but Marty doesn't eat meat nowadays."

"Sorry—" she said, hunkering down as if to hide in the Adirondack chair.

"So what?" said Mary. "She'll get plenty to eat, won't you dear?"

"Yeah," said Joe, "and I can eat her share. Just this once."

We all looked at him. Then he looked at his drink, regarding it sadly. He sighed and excused himself, going into the house

at a rather brisk clip, and returned with his usual G&T. It was
big enough to float an aircraft carrier.

You can't rush change.

Mike Summers and Rowanda Williams arrived at six, just in
time to help set the table and put the leg of lamb over the
glowing coals. Mary and I made the introductions. Joe had met
Summers earlier, down in North Carolina during the adven-
tures of the Daisy Ducks. Marty Higgins, looking up at the
giant, bronzed couple, was slightly intimidated. Summers can
do that. With his shaved head, King Kong body, and Sonny
Liston glower, he looks much meaner than he is. "Hi, big guy,"
Marty said, eyeing him evenly. "Hello, Rowanda. I'm Marty
and I've just reappeared in this group after a long time out. Like
one of those seventeen-year locusts, I guess." Lucy appeared
and introduced herself to Marty. Since they'd both lived in
Pittsfield, they had something in common. The three of them
settled in with each other remarkably smoothly, I thought.

The meat sizzled and smoked on the grill. I smelled all that
burning animal fat. I loved it. Too bad Morris Abramson, M.D.,
wasn't around to hold his nose and give us a lecture on choles-
terol and man's inhumanity to animals. A real shame. Moe, my
crazy psychiatrist colleague, with whom I am forced to share
professional quarters, can throw cold water on anything fun.
His idea of a high time would be a stretch in one of those
Tibetan monasteries in the Himalayas. One of those stone dun-
geons where they shave your head, make you sit cross-legged for
hours in a flimsy robe in the snow, feed you boiled rice and
dried figs, and hit you upside your head with a big bamboo stave
every five minutes to get your brain straight. He'd love it; he'd
fit right in.

"Charlie, you're grimacing. You're grimacing while looking
at the lamb. I know what you're thinking. You're thinking
about Moe, and what he'd say right now, aren't you?"

"That sap? Fat chance, Mare."

Does she know me, or *what*? Mary always knows everything, without fail. I've long since given up trying to hide anything from her. Between her and my crazy shrink friend, I have no privacy.

She came over to me and said in a whisper: "And while I'm busy reading your mind, pal, I notice that you've been spending an inordinate amount of time watching Rowanda."

I gave her a shocked look and shook my head. The very idea—

"I'm sure it's just because you want to be polite to her as one of our houseguests. To make her feel welcome. Isn't that so?"

"Uh-huh," I answered dubiously. I didn't like Mary's inquisitory tone. Was she trying to paint me into a corner?

"But I can understand why. She sure is sexy, isn't she?"

I held out my spread palm and rocked it back and forth.

"Mmmmmmmmm . . . so, so, I guess."

"Don't bullshit me, Charlie. Don't you ever bullshit me," she whispered with a smile on her face. The guests were certain she was whispering sweet affections into my ear. "And don't ever fool around behind my back. Not that you ever would, right?"

"Right."

"You do, and I'll rip your balls off, throw them on the ground, and jump on them till they pop."

My jaw fell slack. Sensing my discomfort, she put her arm around me and spoke low.

"I didn't really mean that. I don't think. I just want you to have a very clear picture of the boundaries, Charlie. No bullshitting, and no fooling around. There are two pretty women living here now besides me. I can handle it. But I just want you to know—"

"Okay. I get the point, Mary. Besides, if I even laid a hand on her, Mike would clobber me."

She thought a minute, looking at Rowanda setting the table, watching her move with lithe grace around the flagstones, humming a sweet song to herself. She was wearing very short shorts and a sleeveless jersey.

"Let's hope so. Because I'm not sure Rowanda would stop

you; I've noticed her looking at you. So you've been warned,
pal."

"Hey, Eugene!" said Mike. He said it like this: YOU-gene.

"My name's not Eugene."

"Ha. Ever-body name Eugene. Where you want this coffee
machine, Eugene?"

"Lucy knows. *Lucy!*"

She showed him, and we started working on the salad, throwing lettuce, garbanzos, black olives, herbs, cheese, and cracked
pepper into the huge wooden bowl we'd bought in Vermont.
Mike told me that Rowanda made a terrific salad dressing, so we
called her over.

"Oh, it's my honey, mint, and poppy seed dressing that he's
referring to," she said, expertly tossing the lettuce in a smidgen
of extra-virgin olive oil. "I got the recipe from an inn up in
Dutchess County, New York, where we used to summer. Have
you any cilantro, Doc?"

I said sure, if I could just figure out what the hell it was.

Rowanda drifted off to the kitchen with Mary. Their heads
were leaned together in quiet talk, and they were laughing like
old school chums. Women sure are funny.

"That Rowanda, she just drips soul, don't she?" I said to
Mike. He laughed, saying that if she ever saw his old neighborhood on Chicago's South Side, she'd have a stroke.

The meal was superb. Afterwards, while the women were in
the kitchen and we were sipping coffee on the terrace, Bryce
Stevens pulled up the driveway, and came walking fast up to the
terrace. Without a word, he took something from his pocket and
showed it to Joe.

"Is it who I think it is?"

"Yeah. Melissa Hendricks, taken about three years ago. We
finally connected with her mother down in Florida."

"Lucy!" called Joe, holding the snapshot up, "can you come
here a second and verify something?"

Lucy came out of the kitchen and took the picture in both her hands. She nodded, trying to smile, a sweet-sour look in her eyes.

"Well, that's settled at least," said Bryce, taking back the picture. "Now Harry Phelps can tell us for sure if she's the one who stopped by and asked about the green Harley. I finally found him at home; he's been gone all week playing golf."

"Let's get the answer soon," said Joe. "We've been stalled too long already on this lead."

"I know. That's why I'm going out there now; I thought you might like to come along."

"Can't it wait just till tomorrow, Bryce?"

"Nope. Phelps changed his plans. He's flying down to Alabama to see his boy, rather than have his ex bring him up. He's catching a ten o'clock plane from Logan tomorrow, which means he'll leave the Berkshires at dawn. Follow?"

"Yeah," growled Joe, looking wistfully at the table. "It's do it now, or wait another week. God, I just love my job sometimes. But you're in for a pleasant surprise, Bryce."

"What's that?"

Just then, Marty Higgins came out from the kitchen with more of the shortcake. I saw Bryce's eyes light up.

"Marty!" said Bryce. "Martha Higgins!"

"I was waiting to see if you'd remember me," she said.

"I thought you looked familiar, Marty," he said. "My God, this is just like old home week."

"Good to see you, too, Bryce," she said. "It's kind of like the twelve years never happened, you know?"

"Thought it'd be a nice surprise," said Joe. He looked at Mary and me. "Bryce worked out of the Boston office when I met Marty. We were all fast friends. And for the past several years they've been living within forty minutes of each other without even realizing it!"

After Marty and Bryce hugged and talked briefly, Joe asked Bryce to call Phelps and ask him to drive down to the farm.

"Hell, there's lots of food left; he'd have a great time."

Bryce agreed and went inside to make the call, but returned immediately, saying the line was busy.

"Same old story, you guys. That ex-wife of his must love to talk."

"Wait a few minutes, then try again," I suggested. But it was still busy. Meanwhile, Stevens was enjoying a jumbo-sized plate of the dinner that Marty had brought him.

Then it was time to clean up, so I headed for the kitchen. But Mary told me she wanted to "catch up" with Marty. And she had taken a strong liking to Rowanda as well, so she suggested that all the men drive up to Phelps's place and get the picture identified, one way or another. We thought it was a good idea and told Mary and the others we should be back before dark. As the four of us climbed into Bryce's cruiser, Lucy came over to Joe, leaning in the driver's window.

"Can I see it once more?" she asked, pointing to the manila envelope on the seat.

"Sure," said Joe softly, handing her the envelope. Lucy took out the snapshot and gazed at it, biting her lower lip softly over and over again, not saying anything. She looked very young just then. Young and vulnerable.

"We'll bring it back, you know," said Bryce.

"Yeah," she said, and went to join the other women in the kitchen.

We rolled out of the drive, leaving a brown cloud of dust behind us.

"I bet you and Harry Phelps will have a lot to talk about, Mike," said Joe over his shoulder as we headed northwest toward Route 7. "He's a Vietnam vet, too."

"Ummmm," said Mike, working a toothpick in his mouth. "If he like mosta the vets I know, maybe he don't wanta talk much."

By the time I'd smoked a pipeful, we were winding up the wooded road to the cabin. We got out and stretched, and began the climb up the stairs. Phelps was home; we saw his car parked beside the deck. I was right behind Summers, who stopped on the stairs. I bumped into him.

"Mike?"

The big man said nothing. I heard him sniff quietly twice. He was going to sneeze; sometimes you have to freeze to let it come.

I came up beside him, watching Joe and Bryce, who also stopped and turned around, facing us. I passed Mike and joined the other two, and we climbed to the top of the stairs. Then I looked back down at the big man.

"Mike?"

He shook his head slowly, sadly, back and forth, as if about to pass judgment.

"What is it?"

"Dunno," he murmured. "Somethin' ain't right. I got a feelin' . . ."

I listened, and was suddenly aware of the silence. No birds sang. The squirrels were all hiding in their leafy nests. The crickets were on strike. I turned and looked at the house. It looked fine: all neat and trim, buttoned up, and still.

It looked all wrong.

I heard the faint sniffing again and turned to look at Summers. Mike Summers, the boonie stalker who'd survived two years of cross-border fighting in the jungles of Southeast Asia. His keen senses were telling him something the rest of us weren't picking up.

"Smell it? Smell it, Doc?"

"Smell what?"

"Nevermine. You wadn't there . . . you wouldn't know . . ."

Then he came up to us, solemn as a preacher on Good Friday. When he passed us, going to the house, a breeze came up. A thick syrup of a smell caught in my nose, something ugly and horrid.

And then I knew.

EIGHTEEN

The four of us stood at the top of the steps, looking at each other and wondering who was going to be first inside.

"It's your case, Bryce," mumbled Joe, rattling the coins in the pockets of his ample trousers. "We just kind of came along for the ride. I—*whew!*" He backed off, turning and walking fast to get out of the breeze.

"My case? It's our case. All of ours. Hell, it's more Doc's case than anyone's."

They all looked in my direction; I wished they wouldn't.

"What I'll do first is call for some help—" said Bryce, turning to go back down to the cruiser.

"Hadn't we better take a quick look first?" asked Joe. "See exactly what—"

"Yeah, you're right." Bryce stood there, staring at the front door. I could tell he was just dying to go in. Mike Summers sat down on the top step, looking sadly straight ahead.

"Somebody been burned in there," he said softly. "If he was here, Roantis'd say the same thing."

"Burned? Yeah, come to think of it," said Joe in a whisper, "it does smell burned."

"You spend two years with that napalm stink—it stays in your head," said Mike, leaning over now and rubbing his face. "Here, you guys don't wanta be first—I'll go in—"

Nobody put up a fight. Summers opened the front door—it was not locked—and a cloud of thick, hot stink came out, washing over us. We backed off; I heard the droning of flies from within.

"Oh my God—" said Joe wearily, pacing back and forth with a handkerchief over his nose. "What a pleasant job." He stamped his feet and shook his head, as if trying to shake the smell away from him. "And people ask us why we drink . . ."

Summers went inside. We heard him marching around in there, opening windows. He came out fast, his arm cocked over his face, nose and mouth buried in his shirt sleeve. Then we all walked downhill again and sat for fifteen minutes. Joe lighted a cigarette and I positioned myself in the path of the blowing smoke. The longer I sat, the more I thought. The more I thought, the more I was positive I wasn't going inside with the others.

But Joe had different ideas.

"Wrong, Doc. You seem to be forgetting your position with the state police."

"No, I am not forgetting that. But this isn't part of my job."

"You're a surgeon," said Stevens. "Surgeons aren't supposed to be squeamish."

"I am not squeamish about blood," I told him. "I regularly cut people's entire faces in two for reconstructive surgery. There is lots and lots of blood. But it's good blood; it's blood spilled in the cause of healing and improving. I don't mind the sight of it. But blood in a car wreck affects me much differently, for obvious reasons. And any kind of damage inflicted out of hate does make me squeamish. Squeamish as hell."

"Me too," admitted Stevens. "But I'm going in there, if only briefly."

"C'mon, Doc. Let's take a quick look so we'll know what to say over the radio. We'd really like your opinion, too."

We went in. It was dark in there, and it was a few seconds before I could see what had happened. But once the picture became clear, there was no forgetting it. In the far corner of the room, bound to the wood stove with a heavy chain, was the partially charred corpse of Harry Phelps. I swayed at the sight of it. Mike caught me from behind to steady me, but I waved him off and regained my balance. I went over to the couch and sat down, trying to catch my breath. I watched Summers go over to the body. He examined it clinically, with no sign of emotion. Joe was off to one side, standing against the wall farthest away from the stove.

Suddenly I felt as if I were underwater. Underneath raw sewage, unable to breathe in all that thick stink. I got up, wobbly, and ran outside, falling into some shrubs on my hands and knees, losing all that dinner, and the faintest recollection of that burning meat on the grill sent me retching again. I finally got up, teary-eyed, and staggered back inside, only to meet Joe, himself running out for a breath of fresh air. I girded my loins and staggered back inside for another look.

Phelps had been chained against the wood stove by thick steel links passing around his lower chest and around the stove. The chains were secured not by a lock, but by a small crowbar tool inserted into the links of the chain, then twisted around and around, tightening it like a massive tourniquet. The tension was then locked by hooking the curved end of the crowbar around a leg of the stove. Phelps's arms were not bound, and the chain was passed in such a way that the door of the stove could be opened. It was now shut, and the stove long since cold. The body was straining forward, as if to escape the incredible heat. The front of the body, and the entire lower part of the torso, were untouched. The back was charred black from the heat.

Behind me, Bryce's voice said: "See that bruise on the side of the head, Doc? Right below the ear? I'm guessing he was knocked unconscious, then fastened to the stove, as you see—"

I turned to look at him, then back to the grisly spectacle in front of me.

"Don't tell me," I said, my voice a whisper, "don't tell me he fastened Phelps there, then waited till he came to . . ."

"Maybe. Yeah, he could have done just that. Waited until he was conscious again, and could feel everything."

"And then . . . then he lighted the stove . . . standing back then . . . watching it heat up . . ."

"Can we go now?" said Joe, standing at the door, holding it open. Bryce joined him there, but I stayed, riveted by the horror of it. Phelps's face, unmarked, showed no emotion. The eyes were open, the mouth agape. Dried blood was below his mouth; he'd bitten through his tongue in pain. But there were no twisted features. Despite popular belief, the victims of violent death do not have agony written on their features; the total relaxation of the muscles immediately following death erases them. But Phelps's arms, unencumbered by the chains, were drawn up on each side of the body and extended forward, hands clenched in fists. This strange and haunting postmortem position, found often in burn victims, is called by pathologists the pugilistic attitude, or boxer stance. It's caused by the contraction of burning muscles. The victims resemble prizefighters standing in the ring corner, hands up, arms cocked, waiting for the bell.

I looked closer. A fly was crawling in and out of Phelps's left nostril. There was old, dried mucus from his nose all down his face. He couldn't wipe it off. He couldn't shoo the fly. He could not hide himself . . . hide his ruined body from our horror-struck eyes.

Ultimately, it's not just the pain death brings that is so sad and horrific. It is the ultimate, utter humiliation of it. The skewed glasses. The excremental stink. The flumpy clothes. The stains and deformities. The hiked-up skirt that is never erotic, but always clumsy and embarrassing. The corpse with dull eyes and a mouthful of flies, sitting down all wrong in the high weeds amidst old tin cans, exploded mattresses, and trash.

I looked up at the picture frame on the wall, where Harry Phelps's war medals were displayed. Where were his crisply pressed dress blues, and his Marine Corps saber? Where was his relaxed country drawl, his self-confident laugh?

We stalked silently from the house, leaving the blackened hulk behind, and went down the stairs to the bottom of the hill. Bryce made the radio call and then came back to sit on the bottom step with us.

"How accurately can we piece it together at this point?" asked Joe. He spoke in hushed tones, a soft, weary voice that was cracking around the edges.

"It probably happened right there," explained Stevens, pointing to where Phelps's car was parked. "The killer came in the night and hid near the car. When Harry went out to start it, he got bludgeoned from behind. See those parallel scrape marks in the ground? I say they were made by Phelps's heels being dragged across the ground. Then he was pulled up inside the house."

I looked over my shoulder at the tall flight of stairs. Strength, yes. It would take lots of strength. But then, if he could lift a cow . . .

"And then the killer chained him to the stove unconscious," said Joe, "laid a fire in the grate, waited until Phelps was fully conscious, and began his little game."

"But why?" I asked in a whisper. "Why torture him?"

"You're forgetting that Phelps wounded him with his pistol. Caused him pain. Franz paid him back tenfold."

"You're saying it was Franz," Stevens said to Joe. "But we don't know for sure."

"No, we don't; but we can guess. We know that Franz is around, and this sadistic killing fits with the ones committed on the farm," said Joe. "And it certainly matches the M.O. and the mind-set of all the other stuff we've heard about this psycho so far, including the mutilation of that man near Worcester and the killing of Warren Shaw's cow."

"We don't know about the cow for sure," I said. "We don't

know about any of it for certain, even who took the motorcycle and stopped Harry's bullet."

Joe stroked the purplish stubble on his face, staring into the woods, not saying anything.

"Not only was this killing cruel," said Stevens, "but it raises the possibility of another motive."

"What, besides revenge?" I asked.

"Interrogation. With his victim chained to the stove, the murderer could control the tension on the chain, and the level of pain. The sadistic possibilities are obvious, and the revenge motive you mentioned. But also, he would have an opportunity to ask Phelps any questions he wanted . . ."

"Questions? What kind of questions?" asked Joe. His voice sounded strange, different than I'd ever heard it before. I listened intently, and it was awhile before I knew what it was. It was fear. For the first time in my memory, I heard fear in Joe's voice.

Bryce leaned back on the steps and sighed. "Oh, I don't know. I'm assuming, like you, Joe, that maybe it was Buddy Franz who did this. On that assumption, maybe he'd want answers to questions like how did we find out he was alive? Or maybe how did we set the trap for him at the fairgrounds? How many of us are after him . . . and so on . . ."

I raised my head and saw Stevens, Summers, and Joe all staring straight at me.

NINETEEN

We were at the bottom of the hill when I told Joe to turn around and go back. He asked why.

"Noise. What about the noise? A man of Phelps's size and physical condition would make a lot of noise being tortured to death. So why didn't the neighbors hear anything?"

"Hell, Doc, it's ninety yards from his house to—"

"Naw," said Summers. "Doc's right, Joe. Man woulda been loud. I mean, *loud.*"

"I've been thinking the same thing," said Stevens. "But so far, we haven't found anything that was used as a gag. Maybe the killer took the gag with him when he left."

"How do you suppose he came here?" asked Joe. "He ride the bike?"

"You're assuming it's Franz again," I said. "That's problematical at best, Joe. Even if Franz was the one who took the bike earlier, you're saying that he subdued Harry Phelps, who was no wimp, carrying a .45 slug?"

"Yeah . . . guess there are problems with it—"

"And let me tell you," added Stevens, "a gunshot wound does not improve with age. Left untreated, a bullet wound turns ugly real fast. Whoever stopped that slug Phelps fired week before last is in big trouble if he hasn't been to a clinic. I'd be surprised if he could even walk by now. Hell, it may have killed him."

"So who did this? Where's the motivation?" pursued Joe, jabbing his finger into the air at us. "I say it's a revenge killing because of the sadism. It definitely wasn't a burglary; the house is untouched, for crissakes."

"Well, one thing, you guys," said Summers. He hadn't spoken in a while, being naturally a man of few words. We'd almost forgotten him, and turned to see his massive form sitting on the pine needles of the slope, chewing on a blade of grass. "What I say . . . if this dude Franz *was* the one who took the bike and stopped the slug a week ago . . . and if he did this lil' number here, too, then we know one thing: he a bad motherfucker."

We were forced to agree, and spent the next twenty minutes until the lab truck showed up searching for footprints and tire tracks. We didn't find any that looked interesting, or none that matched the ones found earlier, anyway. Then Stevens suggested we spread out and search the woods and underbrush around the house.

We found the gag within ten minutes.

Mike Summers uncovered the feed bag in the low bushes and crawling vines just behind the house. Of thick canvas with leather trim and bottom, the bag was a foot in diameter. The bag's harness had been removed, and in its place a thin nylon rope had been passed through the grommets at its open end, enabling it to be closed tightly like a GI duffel bag. Joe picked it up carefully by the rope and regarded it with loathing before dropping it into the plastic evidence bag held open by Stevens.

"We'll probably find some fluid traces on the inside," he said, sealing the plastic container. "That was good thinking, Doc. You make a pretty good cop."

"Thanks. But right now, I'd settle for being just a lousy gentleman farmer."

"Yeah, but you can't. Not now."

"That bag would be better than any gag," said Joe as we drove back down the hill. "He slipped it over Phelps's head and then tightened it around his neck. Holy Christ. You believe it?"

"I only believe one thing at this point," I said, looking out the window. "And that's that we've got to find Werner Franz. We've got to find him now, before this bad dream gets any worse."

When we got back to the farm and rolled up the long gravel drive, the first thing I saw was the old battered Dodge Dart, circa 1975, parked next to Mary's Audi, tilting over on its worn shocks. A faded lime green, with its rocker panels rusted out, it sure didn't look like a car belonging to a successful psychiatrist who makes hundreds of thousands of dollars a year. Of course, Moe Abramson really doesn't make that much; he gives most of his money away to charitable causes, and chooses to live in a 1957 Airstream trailer at the edge of Walden Pond, a modern-day Thoreau, with a little Gandhi, Tolstoy, Albert Schweitzer, and Florence Nightingale thrown in.

Why, you might well ask, does he choose to do this, instead of spending his loot for self-gratification, idle pastimes, and ego building, as the rest of us do?

Because Dr. Morris Abramson is crazy. Certifiable. That's why.

Despite these shortcomings, I put up with him. Somebody has to. We had invited him out to the farm for a few days. I was glad to see the battered old car; I wanted some of his expertise right now. But before I went inside the house I searched out Lucy Kirkland.

"C'mon, Dr. Adams, I already told you."

"I know you told me, Lucy, but you must have left something

out. You remember two weeks ago when I came back from
talking with Jerry Rapp at the bowling alley? You told me that
what he said wasn't true, that you never ratted on Buddy
Franz."

"So?"

"So, you didn't tell me enough, Lucy. And from what I've
heard from certain sources, I have a hunch why you're so anxious to stay out here with us. It's because you don't feel safe back
in Pittsfield, do you?"

She looked down quickly, averting her eyes. In my experience, that's a sign of admission.

"With Billy dead, and your mom in the nursing home, you
don't have enough protection from Franz. That right?"

She jerked her head up, looking me straight in the eye, her
chin out in defiance.

"No! I—"

But then she lowered her head and twisted her hands together, as if wringing out an imaginary dishcloth. Riding her
vulnerability, I pushed her hard to find the truth.

"Okay, okay . . ." she said finally, on the verge of tears. "It's
true that Billy told some of the Stompers about how Franz and
Melissa kept part of a shipment and sold it on the side. I knew
it because Melissa told Billy about it one night when she was
drunk."

"And what about your brother and Melissa? Which is it?
Were they lovers or not?"

"Yes. For a little while when Franz was gone on one of his
crazy disappearing acts. It was true enough, so I told you that
when I first came out here, Dr. Adams. And I really did think
Franz killed Melissa, too. I haven't seen her in a long time, and
I know he was mad at her."

"So what happened with the business about the coke? The
Stompers, where are they from?"

"From Albany and around there, mostly. Their president's a
guy named Jimmy DeLisle. He's a big-time coke dealer, and a
real badass. He had Franz running a lot of stuff for him a couple
years ago. I know the money was good; Melissa told me so

herself. She said Franz was making a lot of money, and he was like packing it away in hiding places so he could live for a long time out in the country without having to work."

"Where? Where was he living? Did she tell you?"

Lucy shook her head. "But," she added after a pause, "I think it could be over the line in New York somewhere. But, hey, that was a long time ago."

I thought a minute, then asked her if she ever heard of Franz working in stables.

"I don't think so. I thought he worked mostly in lumberyards and stuff."

"And stuff?"

"Yeah, and junkyards. For a while he worked cutting up metal scrap in a junkyard near Worcester."

"Good Christ, Lucy. From New York to Worcester, Lenox, Pittsfield—he's all over the map. How are we ever going to find him if you can't be more specific than that?"

"How can I know where the hell he is? That's all I can tell you."

"Oh no, it isn't. C'mon. We're going to have a nice long talk with Bryce Stevens, and you're going to tell him everything, including why you decided to hang out here on our farm when you knew Franz was going to come after you."

Well, she wasn't keen on this. I practically dragged Lucy Kirkland up to the main house from her semi-finished abode down near the barn. So there we all sat in the kitchen: Lucy and I and Mary, Stevens, Summers, and Moe Abramson, who'd just arrived in his rust bucket. I was hoping his psychiatric expertise would help fill in the gaps in Franz's behavior. Madman that Buddy Franz was, I thought there might be predictable patterns to his actions. If so, they could help direct us in our search, and perhaps enable us to intercept him before more murder and mayhem were committed. We began by Lucy's detailed account of the coke deal that Franz burned the Stompers in.

"So he was to deliver this shipment to a guy in New Haven?" asked Bryce, writing it down in his pocket notebook.

"I think it was New Haven. Somewhere in Connecticut.

Anyways, Franz only delivered, like, half of it. So afterwards, he tells Jimmy DeLisle that the other half of the stash was stolen. I don't know if Jimmy believed him or not. And, with Franz so big and so crazy and mean, you think awhile before you argue with him, you know?"

"Where was the stash hidden?" asked Joe. "On the bike?"

"Usually, they hide it either in the gas tank or under the air cleaner. Sometimes, if the heat's really on, they hide it in the tire."

"How do they do this?" I asked. "The gas tank? Wouldn't that wreck it?"

"No," Lucy said. "They wrap it around and around in plastic bags so it's totally waterproof. Then they dip the packet in hot wax. Then they stick the stash in there, in those big 'fat Bob' gas tanks Harleys have. It's a lot of work, and you don't do it for grass, just stuff like smack and coke. The quickest and easiest place to hide the stash is under the air cleaner. But the cops always look there first. They never look in the tires, but it's real hard to stash it there. First, you gotta take the wheel off, then the tire and the tube, just like changing a flat. You put in the stash inside the tire, stuck between the tube and the inside wall of the tire, then inflate it up, then put the wheel back on—it's a real pain in the ass and takes a long time. We only used to do it on big hauls, or if the heat was really on."

"We?" said Joe.

She lowered her head. "Well, the guys. You know . . ."

"So Franz told Jimmy DeLisle, the badass leader of the Stompers, that half the haul was stolen, when in fact it wasn't?" asked Moe, leaning forward, his fingertips pressed delicately against his mouth. His lean features were intense in concentration. He was a bearded Sherlock Holmes.

"Uh-huh. He told Jimmy that somebody got into his bike at night and lifted the stash from the gas tank, but the stuff in the front tire was fine. But what really happened was, Franz sold the missing stash for himself."

"Does Franz use drugs?" Moe asked.

"Not really. Makes him too crazy. He likes booze and downers. But the other stuff, like, flips him out?"

"And how did Jimmy Delisle find out Franz cheated him?"
I asked.

"Because when Franz went away for those couple of months,
Melissa was hanging around with my brother Billy and Mike
Church and those guys from the Aces. And Melissa didn't think
she'd ever see Franz again, and he'd beat her up real bad a
couple times, too. Anyway, one night we were out riding over
the line in New York, and Jimmy and the Stompers ran into us.
Well, Jimmy being the badass he is, and having this rep and all,
he starts in on Mike and Billy, shoving them around, you know,
being the tough badass, saying that this is Stompers' turf, and
all that shit, and why were we riding in their turf."

"And to save your brother's skin," I said, "you went up to
Jimmy and told him that if he'd lay off, you'd tell him what
really happened to that other coke stash, the one that Franz
swore was ripped off."

"Yeah. Yeah, I told him. So then he starts in on Melissa,
saying is it true? Is it true? And she goes yeah, it's true, and I
don't give a flying fuck about Buddy anymore, anyhow. Those
were her exact words."

"So then she was on your brother's side," said Moe. Lucy
nodded. "But later, when Franz came back, she went back to
him?"

"I'm not sure about that," said Lucy, a confused look on her
face. "I know she wasn't with Billy as much, but I don't think
she went back to Franz. Like I said, he used to beat her something awful."

"Speaking of ill-treatment, Lucy," I said softly. "I've heard
that on a number of occasions, your brother was pretty nasty
to you. Is this true?"

Her head flipped up, and she squinted at me with hate-filled
eyes.

"Who told you that? Who?"

"Who said it isn't important. I want to know if there's any
truth to it."

She clenched her fists and put them on the sides of her head, as if trying to crush her face from both sides. Her hands were purple, her knuckles white. Tears squeaked out the sides of her closely shut eyes.

"He was my brother," she wailed. "Sure he was mean sometimes. And that John Vales—"

She couldn't go on, and sat there, trying to catch her breath and cry at the same time. I looked at the faces around me. Mary and Joe were impassive. Bryce wore a look of deep sadness and sympathy. Moe's face was interesting: he looked as if he might cry himself, so intense was his empathy. And yet, beneath the emotion, I saw the intense gleam of cool, professional analysis.

"When I first met you, Lucy, and you went to see the bikes in my barn, you said that Franz killed your brother Billy and Melissa because he stole her away from Franz. Remember?"

She lowered her head. Caught in a lie?

"Yeah, that's what I thought then. Honest, Dr. Adams."

"But you thought you'd just keep the coke deal a secret, right?"

"Well, sure. Who wouldn't?"

"Wait a sec," said Joe. "Let's back up a bit here instead of arguing. Doc, is Melissa dead or not?"

"I'm not really sure at this point, Joe," I sighed. "As you remember, I went back to the lab last week and had another look at the x-rays and photos. It never was conclusive that the remains were Melissa's. I assumed they were. But that was based on a few corresponding fillings and X rays that were taken when Melissa was ten. Allowing for an intervening twelve-year period in which a lot can happen to teeth, I assumed the remains were hers. But in light of recent events, and the mysterious blue-and-white truck, I'd say there's a good chance that Melissa Hendricks is alive, and with Werner Franz."

"Shit," murmured Joe under his breath. "We were going to take that picture of Melissa out to Harry Phelps and have him say yes or no. But now it's too late—"

"I don't think that question is paramount right now," said Bryce in his soft, professional voice. "What I want to ask you now, Lucy, is why you chose to come out here and live with Doc and Mary when you knew Franz was after you."

"Well, first off, at the beginning, I thought Franz was dead. We all did. And I kept coming back to this place again and again. Billy and I used to ride out here all the time, and I didn't think of the farm as the place where Billy was killed so much as the place where he was last alive, you know? So anyway, then I started doing little chores and odd jobs for Doc and Mary, and I liked them a lot. They were like family to me. And Joe, too. So then, when Doc discovered Franz was alive, I was scared, sure, but I didn't say anything about why he was after me because I was afraid they'd send me away . . . wouldn't let me stay here anymore."

She drooped her head in sadness. Whether it was genuine or put on, I couldn't tell. Mary was looking at Lucy, too. I tried to read her face, but I couldn't get anything definite.

"And with Franz, the killer, out on the loose and hunting you, you still elected to stay here?" pursued Bryce.

"Yeah. For one thing, I figured this would be the last place Franz would show up, since it's crawling with police and everything, right?"

Bryce nodded in agreement, and I had to admit she had a point, the mutilation of the cow notwithstanding.

"But mainly, I feel safe out here with these people. I like Doc and Mary and Joe. They protect me. I don't have any family left; this is it."

She was crying softly now, rubbing her arms, all bent over the kitchen table. Stevens got up from his chair and went over to pour himself more coffee. Mug in hand, he turned to Lucy.

"It's not officially my business. I can't dictate to the Adamses, or Joe, what to do. But my feeling on this is that it's unwise for you to stay here, Lucy. We can take you elsewhere and give you police protection."

"Please! Please don't!" she wailed, looking at Mary with a desperate, trapped look on her face. I still couldn't get a fix on what Mary was thinking. She looked sympathetic, but there was something else going on behind those obsidian eyes.

"Well?" she asked, looking at me. The decision was up to me, then.

"All right, Lucy. You can stay if you want. But you're at risk here. You know that."

"I know," she said, wiping her eyes and sniffling. "But I feel a lot safer here than back in Pittsfield."

I left the room and walked out onto the terrace. I was getting to be a softy. I knew what it was: it was hanging around Moe too much, and listening to his bleeding-heart drivel all the time.

Mary caught up with me on the terrace and called me a sap.

Then Moe came out and put his arm on my shoulder, saying I'd done the right thing. He would say that; Moe's the biggest sap there ever was. Ever.

"I know. But I just couldn't . . . kick her out, Mare. Look, she's scared out of her mind, she's got no family, and, well, we like her."

"I'm not saying you didn't do the right thing, Charlie. But her being here scares me. She's an attractant for that monster; she's live bait, is what she is."

I sat down and looked out across the pasture up the valley, thinking of what Mary had said. The more I considered it, the more I agreed, and the more it occurred to me we might turn this situation to our advantage. If we had the patience, skill, and courage to do it right, that is. And that was a big if. Shit, I wished Roantis would hurry up and get back.

"Can we come out and join you?" asked Joe from the door. I said by all means. "Where's Lucy, and what's she doing now?" I asked the three of them as they came outside.

"She's cleaning up the dinner dishes, humming to herself," said Joe. "She's on cloud nine."

"I have every confidence that Franz will be apprehended in the near future," Stevens said, lowering himself into the sloping wooden chair. "I just don't see how he can evade us much longer."

Joe snorted, swirling a snifter of amber-colored fluid beneath his nose. I got a good whiff. Not brandy; single malt scotch. Apparently the diet was on hold for the time being. "Well, it's nice to know you've got all this faith, Bryce," he said, taking a tiny sip and smacking his lips, "because I'll level with you: I don't. You know, it's weird, the way I'm beginning to feel about this guy. They say we southern Italians are superstitious. I used to laugh at that. But I'll tell you—I'm beginning to think that this Franz is not of this earth."

"Supernatural? Satanic?" I asked.

"Well, yeah. My mind says no. But my gut, my instincts, tell me different. I remember reading about Rasputin, that crazy monk in Russia. Come to think of it, Doc, the experts now theorize he was one of those XYY guys. Isn't that a strange coincidence? Anyway, not only was the guy huge and strong, but he had psychic powers over people. He could make them do anything he wanted, like instant hypnotism. There was this plot to kill Rasputin. Apparently the entire palace guard was in on it. But in the end, they couldn't even kill the guy. Slipped him poison in his fifth of vodka. Enough to kill a couple horses, not to mention all that booze. Nothing. Shot him several times. No dice; guy could still dance the polka, for crissakes. Tied him up, put him in a bag, tied that up, and threw him in the Volga River in the middle of winter. *Whew!*"

We waited for the end of the story.

"Well?" Bryce finally asked. "Did he die, or what?"

"Oh yeah, eventually. But know what? When they recovered the bag later on, guess what? It was torn open! Rasputin had freed himself, broken the ropes that held him, ripped open the canvas bag with his bare hands under freezing cold water, and gotten out of the—"

"*Shut up, Joey!*"

Stunned, the three of us turned to see Mary jumping up out of her chair and stomping off over the flagstone terrace in the direction of Joe's house.

"What'd I say?"

"You've scared your sister, Joe," I said. "Mary's living proof that fear lies behind anger. Usually, when she's steamed, she's really afraid. I wish her fears were groundless, but they aren't. She's got every right to be afraid."

We watched Mary disappear into Joe's house and reappear shortly with Marty. The two walked arm in arm to poolside, where they sat in director's chairs and stared at the water, talking in anguished whispers in the growing darkness.

Joe watched them for a while, then sighed. "Too bad this has to be going on, eh, Doc? Shit. It'd be just perfect if it weren't—"

"Listen to me a minute, you guys. Let's approach this a little differently," I said. "It seems that, whether we like it or not, things are beginning to revolve around this place. Now, we don't know for certain if Franz is responsible for what happened up in Lanesboro—"

"I'm certain enough to suit me," said Joe. "Bryce?"

"The odds say it's him," he agreed. "What are you getting at, Doc?"

"You all feel that Franz, who's nothing if not vengeful, will focus on me and probably Lucy, too, if he knows she's living here—"

"He knows she's here," said Joe. "He knows, Doc. Count on it."

Bryce nodded in agreement.

"So what's your idea?" asked Joe.

"Well, since we can't seem to find Franz through the usual means, let's see if we can't decoy him here."

"No," said Stevens. "Strategically, the idea makes sense. But we don't work that way; Joe will back me up on this. If anything went wrong—and believe me, it could, very easily—then think what we'd be up against. Think of the public outcry: the Department of Public Safety using a young woman and a physician as bait for a psycho killer. No way would the department go for it."

Joe said nothing. Mary and Marty came up and sat down. They had something on their minds.

"Listen, Charlie, we hate to throw a damper on things, but, well, we just don't feel safe here anymore. Marty is too polite to say this, Joe, but she's scared to death. We've decided to go back to Boston until this thing blows over, before you get killed. So you're coming back, too."

"And so are you, Joe," said Marty.

"You can't tell me to go back," said Joe. "We already talked about this, remember? You worked at headquarters; you know the risks. You can't keep me from doing my job."

"It's not your job, dammit! It's Bryce's job! Your region is Middlesex County!" Marty was standing up now, leaning toward Joe. Her eyes were fierce. So much for the "shy" woman who'd reappeared a month ago.

"Marty!" said Joe.

"You said we'd—" She took a half-step toward him, then began to cry.

"I couldn't stand it if anything happened to you now, Joe. Not after waiting all these years."

"Mary?" I asked. "Just out of curiosity, how much leeway do I have in this thing?"

"None."

"Just checking. So we leave Bryce out here all alone to face this?"

"Franz doesn't have anything against Bryce," she said. "He's just a cop to him. But you, Charlie . . . he sees you as the guy who screwed up all his plans . . . who tried to trap him at the auction. He'll come after you next . . . I know it."

"What about Lucy?"

"We can give her protection for a while," said Bryce. "I can have a patrol car stationed here at night, and a close watch during the day."

"Okay then; we'll leave tomorrow afternoon," I said, getting up and taking Mary's arm, walking her back inside. "Maybe a week at the cottage on the Cape will cheer us up," I added. "After all, I can't start a full schedule at work for another week at least. That's the official word from Jim Bartholomew, orthopedic surgeon. So let's just get away from here and forget it for the time being."

180 ▾ RICK BOYER

"Great," she sighed. "Who's going to watch over the place? Just Lucy?"

"No. Mike and Rowanda will be here, too."

"Will they be safe?"

"Look, the police are going to be watching the place; Bryce has promised us that much. And if anybody can take care of himself, Mike Summers can."

"Isn't that what you all thought about Harry Phelps?"

I ignored this and gave her a big kiss when we got to our room.

"God, I'm so sick of all this," she murmured, collapsing on the bed, "It's just . . . no fun. I feel like I'm in a Thomas Hardy novel."

"Gee, that *is* bad. But it could be worse; you could feel like you're in a Franz Kafka novel."

For some reason, this failed to cheer her up. I tucked her into bed and slipped downstairs again. I'd heard Rowanda's Jaguar pulling up the drive, returning from the drive-in movie she and Mike had gone to. I needed to talk to Mike. Privately.

TWENTY

The next morning in Humphrey, Massachusetts, Moe and I sat on a Main Street bench and watched Rowanda walking Bashful along the sidewalk. The local citizenry was gaping and gawking at them. You'd have thought a shipload of extraterrestrials had just landed. In this part of the Commonwealth, where black people are practically nonexistent, this six-foot bronzed amazon, wearing a denim miniskirt, stretch tube top, and pumps with stiletto heels, was drawing quite a crowd. Maybe six or seven people. And if you know Humphrey, that's a lot; that's standing room only. I liked the miniskirt. I loved the stiletto heels, too. I could write a sonnet about them.

"Boy, Doc, what a quaint town," Moe said. "A lot different from where I grew up in Brooklyn."

"Is that why you still can't talk? Why you put hard g's on the ends of words now and then? Or, as you would say, 'now and den'?"

He said rude things to me, explaining for the five thousandth time that the hard g at the ends of words was something indelible from his childhood in Brooklyn.

" 'Cause I dint grow up in a fancy-schmancy WASPy neighborhood like you, Doc. I grew up wit' real people. Street people."

"Bully for you. What do you think of the dog?"

"Dat's a dog? Hoooo boy."

"Not too loud; you'll hurt his feelings. I was thinking of giving him to you."

"Think no more. No deal."

The muscle-bound, rust-colored brute trotted alongside Rowanda, light on its feet. Its mouth was open, panting in the heat. Bashful had a happy grin. Trouble was, the pedestrians didn't think so. One glance at him and they changed course abruptly, crossing the street, reversing direction, ducking into doorways, and so on. We'd bought a heavy leather harness for him, replete with big, sharp studs all over it. Just for looks, of course.

"So tell me, Moe," I said. "You needed some time to think. Any theories?"

"About Buddy Franz? No. Just general thoughts. One of these involves time horizons."

"Time horizons?"

"Points of reference on which actions are based. They're timetables. Let me give you an example. Ben Franklin's essay "The Way to Wealth" contains very little dat is innovative as far as getting rich is concerned. Likewise, his other sayings, as collected in *Poor Richard's Almanac*, are rather simplistic and trite."

"You mean like 'Waste not, want not,' and other ditties."

"Exactly. But how Benjamin Franklin became rich from penniless beginnings is remarkable. What he exhibited was extraordinary discipline in the accumulation and saving of money. He did this by postponing present gratification for future gain. In short, he could do without passing pleasure, keeping his eye on the future. Thus, we say that old Ben had a wide time horizon; he kept his eyes on the distant future, not the present. This is difficult, and has always been the hallmark of extraordinary men and great societies and cultures."

"What's this got to do with Franz?"

"Not sure, but maybe a lot. As I see it, Franz exhibits the lower-class, present-oriented time horizon most of the time. Which is to say that eighty, maybe ninety percent of the time, he lives in the present, with no regard whatsoever for future consequences of his actions. Of course, the extreme form of present-time orientation is the psychopath, who has no concept of future consequences. If he's angry, he kills. If he's horny, he rapes. Bingo. Just like that."

"No conscience."

"Right. No superego, no controls."

"That's Franz in a nutshell."

"Nope; I don't think so. You're only half right. That's the tricky part."

"What do you mean?"

"Sometimes Franz exhibits a wide time horizon. Sometimes he thinks and plans far into the future. Dat's what makes him so dangerous, and what scares me. Now, the killings near your farm. He planned that. He planned it carefully. How do we know? Because of the boy, Bill Worthington. Worthington was abducted before the July Fourth holiday. You told me so yourself. So, Franz planned to kill him and put his body in the ground with the other victims to fake his own death. He also hid the motorcycles carefully in your barn in a spot he thought wouldn't be touched in years. Finally, he dint go back there to get his prized bike for a year. See what I mean?"

"Yeah. Careful, long-range planning. Strong discipline. Especially staying away from his bike. Too strong for Franz, I'd say. Which makes me think Franz took off for somewhere during that year. Someplace far away, maybe to hide from the Stompers, or the law."

"Could be. In fact, I'd say you're right on the money. But anyway, the planning is evident, no?"

"It certainly is."

"That's why the police can't get him. Joe told me the system is designed to catch the average crook. The guy who thinks a day, maybe a week ahead. At the most."

"But Franz thinks weeks, maybe months ahead."

"Sometimes. But not all the time; sometimes he loses it and acts impulsively. The killing of the cow, for example. He gave himself away by doing that, even though it was cleverly done to look like an accident. I'm sure he regrets it now. But it's too late: by killing the cow he proved he was still alive. Then there was Phelps. Franz was so enraged he had to go back and get revenge. Doing so placed him in danger, but he went anyway, driven by hate. See?"

"And you say he alternates between impulsive, psychopathic behavior and disciplined planning."

"Uh-huh. And between love and hate. I'd say, roughly speaking, putting together a profile based on events only, that, having grown up in a home devoid of love and approval, he wants to love and be loved. But because of the terrible abuse he suffered, he cannot fulfill this need. And so, in rages of frustration, he hurts and kills the objects of his love."

"Phelps was hardly an object of his love."

"No, but perhaps he was a father figure, and his murder could be Franz's indirect revenge for his childhood beatings."

"And you have no trouble believing that these recent deeds are Franz in action?"

"None whatsoever; the profile is too familiar. And I think it's a real good idea that we're getting out of here and back to Concord."

"I agree. At least for the women to go back. But I've been thinking of some strategies."

"Ah! So that's why you and Summers huddled together last night in his room."

"Maybe . . ."

"Speak of the devil; here he comes."

Mike Summers came walking down Main Street carrying a paper sack from the hardware store. He spotted us and walked over to the bench, sitting next to me. He opened the sack and drew out a box of twelve-gauge cartridges, high brass, number two buck.

"A bitch gettin' these, Woodrow. This fuckin' state's got regulations tight as a mosquito's ass. Where Rowanda at?"

"Up the street there. See those people staring?"

Spotting us, Rowanda came walking back toward us, moving those long, sinewy legs smartly, pumping herself along at a good clip. Bashful was ahead of her, straining at the leash.

"You sure you wouldn't like to take Bashful, Moe? I'm serious when I say I'd like to give him to you."

"What? What would I want with a dog like dat? It's a mean and scary animal, and I'm not mean and scary."

"That's just the point. You're Mr. Nice Guy, Moe. You're a bleeding heart and a soft touch, and everyone knows it. They know you won't fight back, and they take advantage, sure that you'll turn the other cheek. You need a dog like Bashful, Moe. So, he's yours."

"Hmmmmph! Well, I refuse. So there."

"Take him; he's yours."

"No way."

"Won't do any good, Doc," said Summers. "Dog wouldn't stay with him. He your dog, period. You brought him through, saved his ass. He got better smellin' your smell, lyin' in your arms, and now he love you. And *only* you."

"Well, I can't take him back to Concord with me; he'll eat my dogs alive. If I'm gonna keep him, it better be out here."

"Why not let him stay with Lucy?" suggested Moe. We thought that was perfect.

"Bashful, sit honey," cooed Rowanda, working the leash. "There. Good boy. My, my, you had those people jumping, didn't you?" Rowanda looked at the dog, who sat at her feet. Then she looked up at me.

"Doc, Mary's depressed. I had a talk with her this morning; I think the quicker she gets back home, the better."

"I agree. But you know I'm coming back here alone in a few days. Can you and Mike manage okay out here until then?"

"I wouldn't worry about us."

"Yeah, usually not. But this guy Franz—"

"After what Mike told me happened up in Lanesboro, I seriously doubt he'll try anything else this soon," she said, sitting down with the rest of us.

"Okay, Moe. Sum it up. Based on your theories of Franz, what would you do? How would you catch or corner a guy like that?"

"Run like hell, and stay away."

"Failing that?"

"Catch him off guard. Interrupt his wide time horizon. Arouse his anger. Cause him to act impulsively. Make him blow his cool."

I looked around at the others to see if they agreed, but they were all looking down at Bashful.

Bashful, in turn, was looking down at an ant, trying to trap it with his paw.

TWENTY-ONE

That afternoon, after we'd packed for the trip home to Concord, Rowanda was showing Mary and Marty a few basic steps out on the terrace. They had a portable radio on the flagstones next to the wall, turned up high. It was blaring a reggae beat. The three of them were standing in a line, side by side, with Rowanda in the middle. They were all wearing leotard dance outfits. Mary and Marty stood on each side of her, watching her every move and trying to copy it.

"Now shake it to the left," she said, clapping her hands and moving her legs and torso to the music. "That's it, Mary. Marty, a little faster, hon . . . there you go . . ."

Bashful sat panting, watching the women, getting up every now and then to go lick their ankles and get shooed away. Pit fighter or not, Bashful was turning out to be the sweetest canine

I'd seen in a long time. Even Moe was acknowledging it.

"Okay, *turn*. There you go. Now reach down and try to pick up a brick—"

The women stooped down, gyrating to the music.

"That Mary a killer broad," said a deep voice behind me. Mike Summers.

"Rowanda's no slouch either."

"Some of us just lucky, eh, Eugene? What's Joe say about the plan?"

"He's not too keen on it, if you must know. Thinks it's too risky. But don't forget: *we* won't be here, *Eu*-gene. You're going to be here, all by yourself."

"Not by myself, Doc. Got my squeeze keep me company."

"Turn and turn and turn and *stop!*" said Rowanda, twirling to a stop and bending her right knee, leaning over and stretching her left leg straight out behind her, like a jogger about to go for a run. She bounced on her flexed legs to the music. "And two, and three and *four* . . ."

"Feels great. Just great," said a voice behind us. We turned and saw that Joe had ambled up, his just-packed overnight grip in his hand. He was looking up at Marty, beaming. "You know, Doc, for all these years I been at gatherings with no woman. I was like the only guy without a wife or girlfriend. And now, look at that! We're all three looking up at our women up there. Feels great."

The song—if such it could be called—ended, and so did the aerobics dance. Joe, still beaming, let the bag fall to the ground and took out his notebook, clearing his throat.

"Item one: the oft-seen blue-and-white truck, purportedly belonging to Melissa Hendricks, or her parents, and driven by Franz. The fucking truck we can't find. Just called over to Ten Ten again and the same old shit: can't find the truck to save their ass. Not registered, period. Not here, not in New York, Vermont, New Hampshire . . . not anywhere. Okay, based on my experience, I suspect the truck's carrying stolen plates. What I like to call 'cold-hot' plates."

"What the hell are cold-hot plates?" I asked.

"Freshly stolen tags are hot. There's a list of stolen plates circulated by headquarters and updated constantly, like the sheet listing stolen vehicles. These are called hot sheets. Anyway, you put stolen tags on the vehicle to avoid a trace, everybody knows that. But the problem is that stolen plates are on the hot sheets, which means the cops find you even quicker. But, what happens, after eight weeks, the plates are dropped off the hot sheets. So what you do is use plates that were stolen eight or ten weeks previous and are therefore cold. I'm guessing the truck is real. I think it belonged to Melissa's parents. Whether or not Melissa is alive or dead, I'm betting Franz took the truck, long unused, fixed it up, and is giving us the skip by regularly lifting license tags out of parking lots and putting 'em on the truck, but only after they're properly aged."

"So what you're saying, you're saying we won't make contact with the truck unless we spot it in the flesh, so to speak."

"Afraid so."

"Well, I've got an idea," I said.

"Please don't; we're in enough shit already."

"I'm thinking of that old Harley. Sooner or later it's going to need parts. Parts that are hard to find. So sometime, Franz or his girlfriend will show up at a dealer and ask about some piece for the machine."

"So we alert all the dealers in the area to be on the lookout for the blue-and-white truck, or even the bike itself," said Joe.

"He wouldn't ride the bike up to the dealers. But he'd take the truck. Or better yet, have Melissa, or whoever she is, drive it there."

"And then we follow the truck? Great idea, Doc. But how the hell will we be there in time to do that?"

I shrugged my shoulders and started for the house. I still had my packing to do, since I had spent the remainder of the morning after returning from town looking over the grounds and checking out Lucy's little cottage, the renovated old blacksmith shop next to the barn. It was a slick little building; it even had a john and shower stall in it. Lucy was delighted with it. The pool was now filled, but murky. We had been told that in a few

190 ▼ RICK BOYER

days the filter would clear it. Bryce Stevens came up the hill to the house. He was wearing civvies: cotton hiking shorts and a knit shirt. He wiped the sweat off his brow and folded his arms over his chest.

"Doc, Joe, the place is all set up. We'll have a cruiser near the foot of the drive after dark, staying till dawn, each day. Also, we've located a spot off a back road across the valley where a cruiser can pull off and stay parked out of sight with a clear view of this place." He turned and pointed to the ridge in the distance. "Right up there. You can't see anything from here, but the man in the car can see us right now. We've got that place as a full-time stakeout."

Stevens went over to Summers and put a hand on his massive shoulder. "Well, Mike, that should make you feel better, huh?"

Summers grinned and chuckled.

"I feel a little better, chief, but not much. See, what I say, this guy Franz, he won't come stompin' in here through the front gate. You dig? He'll come slidin' in through the trees, or craw-lin' up to us through that long pasture grass in the dead of night. Maybe jump down on top of me from the barn roof. You hip?"

Stevens and Joe looked down at their feet, scuffing their shoes nervously over the grass. They knew exactly what Summers was getting at. As if to change the subject, Joe went back to his little pocket notebook.

"Item two," he said, "the feed bag. The lab's had a look at it. Manufactured by the J. T. Rawlins Company, Brattleboro, Vermont. Rawlins distributes them to most local feed stores and tack and saddle shops. Most stables, and the Boston mounted police, have them."

"So he could have taken it from almost anywhere," I said.

"Yep. 'Fraid so."

"Have you had a look around Saratoga?" said Rowanda, who was standing next to Mike now and had overheard our conversation. "You know, Doc, Skidmore College is in Saratoga Springs, and that country's full of racetracks and stables."

"Yeah, right, and I—" I stopped before I finished my sentence. Who was it who'd told me that Franz might be spending time over the line in New York?

"Hey, you guys," I asked, "can we get the FBI in on this thing?"

"We've been thinking of that, too," said Joe. "But so far there's no evidence that state lines have been crossed, even though some of the murder victims were from out of state."

"But you guys can't go over to New York and nose around?"

"You know we can't," said Joe.

"Uh-huh," I said. "But I can."

"Charlie? What's that you're saying?" asked Mary, heading for the pool with Marty. She looked at me over her shoulder. I told her it was nothing.

At three, we got into our cars, leaving Mike, Rowanda, and Lucy there to look after things. I shook hands with Mike through the open window.

"I feel uneasy leaving you here. Remember, Mike, you don't have to do this."

"Yeah, but I kinda like it. Been a long time since I had any rush, you know? And Rowanda likes the place. We'll do what you say. We'll stay inside after dark, all of us in the big house. And we've got the dog with us, inside."

"And we've got him, too," said Rowanda, pointing over the fence at the huge grayish-brown bull that stood in the pasture, chewing his cud. Long, lean, and packed with stringy muscle, the animal was placid most of the time. But now and then it would become enraged, set off by small noises or vague movement. Then the animal would charge around the pasture, goring and trampling the grass and fence posts in its anger. We all knew to stay out. I noticed Mike was wearing his Army-issue .45 on his belt. I knew that whatever the risk, I couldn't be leaving the place in better hands.

"And be sure to keep an eye on Lucy," Mary added, leaning over my lap to talk through the window. "Don't let her roam around far away from the house by herself, okay, Mike?"

"Gotcha. She said she might visit her mother—"

"Well, that's different. I don't think much can happen to her going to the nursing home. Bye-bye."

We all said our good-byes, then rolled out the driveway and onto Route 8, headed for home.

TWENTY-TWO

The first priority upon returning to Concord was getting the rest of the bandages off my rib cage and back. The separated ribs were mostly healed now, but there was still pain when twisting my torso, as in swinging a golf club or trying to rake leaves. Since I don't play golf and leaf season was not yet upon us, I was pain free most of the time. The hoofprint on my upper back had also mostly disappeared. I could practice oral surgery full time now, and I did. As usual, the work was good for me, getting my mind off the farm and events out west. Still, I called Mike each night, having him fill me in on every detail. And I thought about the place, and the lurking threats to it, every minute my mind wasn't occupied by something else.

But nothing happened at the farm. Not the first week, nor the next. All was calm and quiet. Mike said that Rowanda was teaching him and Lucy how to swim in the pool, which was now crystal clear. They were swimming twice a day. And while Mike was never without his .45 and his shotgun, Bashful kept a wary watch, his keen ears and nose ever alert for strangers, visible or not, and barked a warning at the slightest disturbance. Mike also told me that Bryce stopped by on a regular basis, anxious to hear of any strange occurrences. But there was nothing to report.

"So c'mon out and enjoy yourself, Doc. It's a blast out here," he said. "Rowanda sends her best. She say when you come out, she gonna make her chicken Dijon for you."

"I'm coming out alone Friday evening after work."

"What about Mary?"

"She's decided to go down to the cottage for the weekend and visit the boys. Frankly, I wish I were going, too, but I think I should be out there with you. You're still planning on leaving Sunday?"

"Hate to, but yeah. I gotta go back to work, and so does Rowanda."

"You going to marry her, Mike?"

"Think she good enough?"

"You should be so lucky. She's smart, tall, strong, gorgeous . . ."

Laughing, Summers half-covered the receiver and I heard his muffled voice saying something at the other end. Then I heard Rowanda's voice, talking to me.

"Hiiiiii, Doc. I heard what you said about me, you hunk, you. Can't wait to see you out here, babe. I'll fix a special dish, just for you . . ."

Then I heard smooching noises loud in my ear, and Mike came back on the line.

"You see any big footprints around?" I asked.

"Naw. Nothin'. Man's smart, what he is. Knows better than to fuck with me. But mainly, I say he split the scene."

"Listen, Mike. I know you're a big, bad sonovabitch. Just don't forget that this is no ordinary troublemaker we're dealing with. He's a boonie stalker, just like you said earlier."

I heard him sigh softly.

"Yeah . . . I know. Fact is, the four of us stick pretty close."

"Four of you?"

"Yeah. Me, Squeeze, Lucy, and the dog. We go around the place twice ever' day, in the morning before breakfast and in the evening before it gets dark. So far we ain't seen nothin'. You hear from Roantis yet?"

"Got a letter from him. He says he's coming back this weekend and will be coming out to relieve you guys Sunday morning. Then the two of us will stay out there the next week to see if we can't shake Franz out of his hiding place."

"Mary know this?"

"Uh, not really. Not all the details," I said.

The fact was, Mary didn't know diddly beans about our plan; I'd made sure of that. If she did, she'd raise the roof. As it was, she wasn't at all pleased that I was going back out there. Only her faith in Roantis's skill and experience was keeping her calm.

"Where the hell is he, anyway?" asked Summers.

"Who knows? I assume it's 'someplace hot,' like he said."

"He mailed the letter, didn't he? Where's it from?"

"From Virginia, which is obviously a drop. One of his friends put it in a fresh envelope so his area of operations will remain secret. So the pool is really great, huh?"

"Outa sight. Killer."

"Well then, save me a raft. I'll see you around six on Friday, which is day after tomorrow, in case you've lost track of time."

"Why would I do that, Woodrow?"

"If I were out there alone with those two women I might, *Eu*-gene."

At quarter past seven that Friday evening, I was floating on an inflatable raft in the center of the big pool, watching the sun sink slowly in the west. The air was taking on that heavy, bluish tint of evening. Since it was now mid-August, the cicadas were in full swing, filling the leafy boughs with their heavy, plaintive drones. The sound always brings me swift, powerful nostalgia.

I felt a bump, and turned to see Rowanda stretched out on her own raft. Her hair was in cornrows again. She was wearing a one-piece sateen bathing suit in hot pink.

"Gee, you look nice," I said. It was belaboring the obvious, but I had to say something.

She inserted a finger into the top of the suit and yanked it down an inch or so. "Better believe it, Doc. And no tan line."

"Tell me something. You scared?"

"At first I was, but not now. It's been two weeks, and nothing's happened. Mike thinks the whole thing's blown over now. If anybody's an expert on trouble, he is. That makes me feel safe, too; I don't figure there's a whole lot he can't handle."

"I agree. They don't come any tougher. But Mike's accustomed to being the sneaker, not the sneakee. I'm just hoping his experience in Nam will enable him to anticipate what's going to happen."

"What's going to happen is, not much. Relax, Doc; you'll unwind over dinner."

She padded away, closing her eyes and humming to herself. Mike was watching Bashful lean over the edge of the pool and drink. Lucy Kirkland, wearing a canvas beach jacket over her suit, was setting the table in the breezeway. The candles were lighted in there, and the soft yellow light oozed out through the screens and timbers, giving a cozy glow. Maybe I was a little uptight, but I was in a good mood. A little booze, some nice appetizers, a pleasant swim, and then we'd go eat Rowanda's chicken Dijon over rice.

Bashful snapped his thick neck up, a growl rising in his wide throat. After a few seconds I heard the crackling of tires on the driveway and the slamming of a door. The dog charged off around the house. I half held my breath, expecting screams or gunshots. But soon Bryce Stevens came around to the pool, with the pit bull sniffing at his heels. We greeted each other and he stood at the edge of the pool, hands in pockets, jingling coins, and rocking back and forth on his heels.

"What's new?" I asked him.

"Nothing, as Mike probably told you. And I say that's good news."

"How about the, uh, other thing?"

He stood, vacant-eyed, a few seconds before replying that it was still the same. In his spare time, he was looking for an apartment in Pittsfield.

"Sorry to hear about it."

"Yeah, but I'm kind of getting used to the idea now, after the initial shock. And know what? I'm coming to realize that the marriage wasn't so great anyway. It's something we just took for granted for so long . . . you know?"

"Well, I'm glad you're adjusting as well as possible."

"Listen, Doc, Jack Bensen's going to be on watch again to-night. He'll be in his car tonight and tomorrow night, but after that, I'm afraid we'll have to discontinue the surveillance. Hope you don't mind, but the budget just doesn't have room for it."

I told him I understood, and asked him to stay for dinner. He declined, saying he had to go back to town and look at an apartment. After he left I floated alone in the pool. The air was getting chilly; I shivered. I looked around, peering into the blue air of evening. It seemed very quiet now. Very quiet indeed.

I left the pool and toweled off, then went up and changed into jeans and a cotton sweater. I came back down and met Mike, who was opening a couple of German beers for us in the kitchen. Rowanda was pouring white wine in big balloon glasses for herself and Lucy. We all sat down at the table and began to eat. Bashful lay on his belly facing the screened door, head on paws.

I looked across the table at Mike and Rowanda. They glowed back at me in the candlelight. If there were two better speci-mens on the planet, I wanted to see them.

"Are you two going to make babies, or what?" I asked.

Rowanda shrugged. "Hadn't planned on getting married anytime soon, Doc. I just—Bashful! Hush up."

The dog had raised his head and was growling. Then he got up and scratched at the door. We watched him carefully, but then he sank to his belly again and yawned.

I dished myself heaps of Rowanda's salad. It was her honey, poppy seed, and mint dressing again.

"Raspberry vinegar, Rowanda?" I said. "Oh oh, the C.C. Syndrome."

"C.C. Syndrome? What in heaven's name is that?"

"Creeping Cambridge. The ultimate yuppie stuff. It's three steps beyond fern bars and Perrier water. You know: stone-washed full-pleated pants. Old tassel loafers with no socks. The return of granny glasses. Foreign newspapers. Angular chins from anorexic diets. Moon-phase wristwatches. And raspberry vinegar. But it's great; no kidding."

BAM!

The dog crashed through the screen and was gone. We heard him growling and snarling as he scooted across the terrace and out onto the lawn at top speed. He continued snarling all the way down the hill.

"What's that?" I asked my three companions, who were looking downhill with puzzled expressions.

"Dunno," said Mike softly. "He musta heard something down there. Anybody hear anything?"

We all shook our heads. Lucy jumped up and dashed out the door, running downhill after the dog.

"Lucy!" I called. "Lucy! Wait!"

But she was gone, swallowed up in the darkness. Then we heard a tremendous crescendo of enraged dog. Beneath it was another sound. Unmistakable and frightening.

"You hear it?" said Mike.

"Yeah baby," said Rowanda, jumping up from the table and knocking over her balloon glass, which shattered on the floor. "Somebody's screaming down there. Is it a man or woman? Oh God—Lucy!"

We were out the door and running down the hill toward the barn. I noticed Mike had the .45 in his hand. The snarling and growling were loud and ferocious.

Then, just like that, it stopped.

There was dead silence at the bottom of the hill.

"Lucy!" I called. No answer.

"Lucy!"

"I'm down here," she yelled back. "Down toward the barn."

"Goddammit, get back here right now."

"But Dr. Adams, I—"

"Right *now*!"

We met her trudging up the hill.

"What was it?" asked Mike.

"I don't know. And I can't find Bashful."

"Who's down there?" shouted Summers. He raised his arms, holding the pistol in both hands. There were two quick flashes in the dark, and big booms that thumped in my chest and shot pain through my ears. Summers was shooting warning shots over the top of the barn. Speaking of warning—could've told us he was going to shoot, for crissakes. My ears rang.

We followed Summers downhill toward the barn. Having left my Browning pistol up in my bedroom, I was a little bit behind him, rather than beside him. Halfway down the slope we froze, listening. All was silent. We waited there in silence for ten or fifteen seconds.

"Where's Bashful?" whispered Rowanda.

"Dunno," I heard Mike whisper back.

"Call him," I said.

"Bashful!" called Lucy. "Here Bash! C'mon boy!"

No answer. Had Bashful chased the intruder across my property into the next county? I doubted it; the commotion had stopped suddenly rather than faded away into the distance. Mike began to move toward the barn. We followed cautiously. Then we heard a car coming fast up the drive behind us, spitting gravel all the way. A big blue beacon swirled in the darkness. The stakeout cruiser, hearing Mike's shots, had arrived. I breathed easier and tapped Mike's shoulder.

"Stay here," I said. "I'm going back for my gun and a flashlight, and I'm taking the women up with me. I'll send the cop down here, so don't shoot him, okay?"

He nodded, and dropped to the prone position, quick as a wink and quiet as a cat, holding the pistol up in front of his face with both hands. I led Rowanda and Lucy back to the house, on a run in a low crouch. We met Patrolman Jack Bensen coming out of his cruiser, carrying his shotgun. I told him what had happened, and he went down the hill to join Summers. Once inside, I raced upstairs for the automatic. At the bottom of the stairway, Lucy handed me a powerful spot lantern. I told Rowanda to stay near the phone and went back down the slope to the men. The three of us sat there on the grassy slope in the dark for maybe five or ten minutes, waiting for any noise or motion. Bensen, just a kid, seemed scared to death. He reached up and put his hand on Mike's shoulder and whispered.

"Where's the dog? I don't hear him."

"Don't know."

"Is he dead?"

"Naw. Woulda squealed first. It like he just . . . disappeared."

We waited another five or ten minutes, I couldn't tell how long it was. Long enough to build a sweat, that was for sure.

"Let's go," Summers whispered, and got to his feet. For a big man, he was awfully quick and quiet. Bensen said to stay put; his orders were to call in if there was any trouble. But in the continuing silence he seemed to change his mind, perhaps because we weren't sure what was happening. He then got up, too, and we spread out and crept toward the barn that loomed over us. Mike and I went around the far side of the barn, leaving Bensen to watch the front with his shotgun. We slid along the building, backs to the wall, pistols ready. I had the flashlight in my left hand but didn't show it; a flashlight makes a swell target, even when held away from the body. We rounded the near corner and kept going. Nothing. We rounded the next corner, working our way along the barn's back wall, the side facing away from the house. Still nothing. We stood silently in the dark awhile, then I switched on the light. I shined it all over the barn. Nothing anywhere. I called the dog. No response. We kept walking around the barn then, shining the light beam in a wide arc. We worked our way along the other side of the building, then around the near corner back to the front wall, meeting Bensen, who said he'd seen nothing. But where was the dog? The three of us went around to the back side of the barn again and started downhill, sweeping the beams of the lights in front of us.

We found Bashful twenty yards from the barn, stretched out motionless in a pool of his own blood. Instantly, we switched off the flashlights and ducked down in the dark.

"Jesus, Doc. Sorry," whispered Summers.

I reached down and felt for the dog, touching him. No motion. No muscle tone. Then, holding the light close, I shined it directly on the dog, and I saw that his skull was split open, right down the middle. The cut was deep, wide, and very clearly defined in the bone, cleaving all the way through the brain.

"That's why he stopped so suddenly, Mike. One second he was raising hell; the next instant he was dead."

"Know what did that?"

"Yeah. A knife. A big knife," I said, turning around as I squatted, peering cautiously into the darkness.

We waited down there awhile, half expecting all hell to break loose any second. But nothing happened, and soon we heard voices up the hill, and saw the shadowy outlines of Rowanda and Lucy.

"Can we come down?" called Rowanda.

"Yeah," said Summers, "but you ain't gonna like what's down here."

They came down and started crying over the dog. Both of them. Meanwhile, Mike and Jack Bensen kept making wide circles around us, watching our perimeter. I was sweeping the light across the ground, trying to pick up a familiar track in the dirt.

Rowanda finally found the big footprints on the dirt and fine gravel of the old barnyard. I wasn't positive they were the same ones Warren had found near the barn earlier, or the ones we'd seen up at Phelps's place. They looked different, but they sure were big. I showed the tracks to the others. Bensen warned us not to disturb them. We followed the big prints up the hill to the barn. Then lost them in the grass. Found them again in front of the barn, standing around in the loose dirt under the—

202 ▼ RICK BOYER

"Doc!"

I turned and saw Rowanda pointing over my head.

"Up on the wall, see it?" she said.

Bensen shined his flashlight on the weathered wooden planks of the barn wall. There, done in white spray paint, was a word:

WELC

"What the hell's that mean?" I asked, noticing how high up the letters were, and how big, too.

"Welcome," said Rowanda, almost in a whisper. "Holy shit, Doc. He was going to write 'Welcome Home.' " See how far to the left the word starts? Maybe he was even going to write 'Welcome Home Dr. Adams.' Oh my God—"

We returned to the house, leaving the scene undisturbed, waiting for daylight when the evidence could be examined properly. The women didn't want to leave Bashful down there, but Officer Bensen insisted. We made a pathetic attempt to finish the dinner, but it didn't work. The women especially were heartbroken over the dog's death, and I had to admit I missed him, too. Bensen called in and reported the incident, then joined us at the kitchen table, where Mike and I were discussing the strange nighttime visit.

"I think Bashful got a piece of him, Doc," said Summers. "I heard somebody scream down there, like they was in pain, you know?"

"Maybe," I said. "Maybe he got a piece of Franz, but remember, Phelps did, too. I'm beginning to think Joe's right; this guy could be supernatural. And what's pissing me off is this: I know that all the time we were down there sneaking around the barn, Franz was over in the tree line watching us. Watching our every move, getting our reaction. I just know it. I had that feeling."

"Well, you're right, Doc. 'Cause I been in combat enough to have that same feeling. And it don't lie. Another thing: I sure gettin' sick of havin' my meals interrupted by that mother-fucker."

"Michael," said Rowanda, "remember what I said about your language. Just because you're a child of the ghetto doesn't mean you have to be vulgar. It's bad enough we have ghettos; it's worse when we play out the man's stereotype of us. No rule says you have to live out the remainder of your life without improvement."

" 'Scuse me," Summers said sheepishly. "I beg your pardon."

"That's much better, dear."

"How kind of you," said Mike. "Thanks awfully."

"I'm not sure those tracks left there even belong to this Franz guy," said Bensen. "Lieutenant Stevens had me look at the plaster cast of the prints a whole bunch of times. The ones left down there tonight are big, yeah. But the treads don't match. I'm sure of that."

"So? Maybe he changed boots," I said.

"Maybe."

"The only other guy I knew with real big feet is Jimmy DeLisle," offered Lucy, sitting morosely with her head in her hands.

"Jimmy DeLisle? Of the Stompers?"

"Yeah."

"What would he be doing around here?"

"I didn't say he was," she said. "I just said he's the only other really big guy I know of."

"Well, whoever it was out there," said Bensen, "he's been watching this place. He knew exactly when you arrived, Dr. Adams. Nothing's happened here for the past two weeks . . . until tonight."

TWENTY-THREE

As dramatic as the nighttime events were, nothing happened the next day, Saturday. Nor the next. Bryce Stevens and his men came and went, inspecting every square foot of turf around the place. He decided, for obvious reasons, to continue the stakeout car after dark as before. Other than that, things were boringly normal again, and that was the killer. I realized the on-again, off-again nature of this grim business was getting to me. I wanted it over with. I wanted it *settled*, and soon, so we could resume our normal lives.

The more I considered the events of the past two months, the more I was convinced Brian Hannon's initial assessment of the situation was correct. Likewise, his proposed solution, though grim and dangerous, was the only way out. I stuck by my guns. Sunday evening, I was on the phone to Mary, then Joe.

"Well, I think I've got to tell Mary," Joe said over the phone, where I'd reached him at his Beacon Hill apartment. "Bryce told me the footprints weren't identical to the others, but they were probably his. And, considering he killed the dog and all, I just think I've got—"

"No, you don't, Joe. You don't have to tell her. You know what will happen if you do. She sounded plenty pissed when we spoke a few minutes ago."

"You blame her? Look, why don't you just come back here, for crissakes, until it blows over? Why put yourself and all of us through this shit? Huh?"

"You know why; I don't have to spell it out for you. It won't blow over. Not now, not next month. I'm sick and tired of it not being resolved. I want to *end* this, once and forever. We won't corner this guy until we can draw him out of his hole. And the only way he's going to come out is if I stay here and lure him out. Summers has been here two weeks and nothing happened. I return and bingo, we get a nighttime visit."

"Hey, that means he's not after Lucy; she was out there with Mike and Rowanda, right? If Franz was skulking around, spying, he couldn't help but see her."

"Yeah. I've thought of that. Franz hated Billy Kirkland, but he's got no grudge against his sister. That means Jerry Rapp was mistaken about Franz being after Lucy, too."

"Well, how would he know everything, stuck out in that bowling alley in Lenox? What we do know is, Franz is after *you* . . . and we know what he does to people he doesn't like."

"We also know this: I confronted him face to face in that barn. I was unarmed; he had a Bowie knife. He could have killed me, but he ran instead."

"Oh, so now you're Davy Crockett? Jesus, pal, all you need right now is a sense of overconfidence."

"I want you to think about something Summers said. Know what he thinks about this latest thing? He calls it a prank, a feeble and desperate attempt to scare us, done by a chickenshit sneak."

"Yeah? Well, I doubt Harry Phelps would agree."

"I think he would. Remember first that Harry shot him. That would make anybody mad. But he didn't confront Phelps head on, he sneaked up on him and—"

"That's what I'm saying, dammit! Does the fact that he sneaks up on people behind their backs make him any less dangerous?"

"I just don't think he's as dangerous as we've made him out to be. I think, like most nasty people, he's a coward underneath, and with Roantis out here with me, we—"

"Can't Roantis stay there alone? Maybe he can sneak out at night and try to intercept him in the woods or something. You keep telling us how goddamn good he is at this stuff—"

"He's the best; that's why I chose him. But Franz won't show himself unless I'm out here, we've all but proven that. He's got a score to settle, and with both of us here I think there will be a resolution within a week. Just please don't tell Mary about Friday night."

"I won't promise, Doc. If she finds out I held back . . ."

I heard a faint, involuntary shudder on the other end.

"When's Roantis arriving?"

"In about an hour; he called me earlier and said he was on his way."

"When did Summers and his girlfriend leave?"

"They're still here. But Lucy's gone. She went to visit her mother in the nursing home in Pittsfield, and she may even spend the night there."

"I'm glad Summers is still there. Just make sure you have company and keep your eyes open. And remember: Mary's expecting you to call her twice a day."

"I know, morning and evening. I won't forget."

"I won't mention last night's episode to Mary, for now. But the slightest thing gets out of line, we'll be out there."

"Thanks, Joe. Bye."

Mike slammed the door behind him, and I leaned into the driver's window to say good-bye. Rowanda was looking at her watch.

"Hate to split, Doc, but we've really got to get back to Boston. So where's Roantis?"

"I'm sure he'll be here shortly."

"You don't suppose that was him on the phone awhile ago," she said, referring to the ringing we couldn't answer, being down by the creek at the time.

"Who knows? He'll be here; you know that. Drive safely, you two, and thanks. See you in a couple of weeks."

"Yeah," said Summers. "Listen: Roantis don't show by dark, I'd take off, I was you."

"I will. But he'll be here, don't worry."

I watched the blue Jag lurch down the gravel drive toward the highway, then strolled back to the house and made myself a cup of coffee. I missed Bashful. I missed the hell out of him, poor guy. It's amazing how much a dog adds to a household.

Actually, I thought as I walked out onto the terrace with my coffee, I'm lonely already. I finished the mug of coffee and went inside to get the newspaper, the Sunday *Globe*, and returned to my chair on the terrace, sitting the refilled mug on the wide, wooden arm on the right side, and my Browning Hi-Power 9mm automatic on the left arm. I finished the paper and the coffee a little after five, stuck the pistol into my belt, and went for a walk. But I hated the feeling of the gun stuck down in my waistband. What if it went off? So I carried it in my hand, muzzle down, and walked down to the barn and outbuildings again, then over to the pasture, watching Warren Shaw's bull taking in mouthfuls of grass with his long tongue, which he snaked out and around the grass, then pulled into his mouth, gulping the grass down. Farther down the slope, twelve head of cattle, mostly steers, grazed in the afternoon stillness. The bull eyed them now and then. He stamped his feet, shaking off flies. The long, elliptic scrotum between his hind legs shook and swayed. Testosterone again. Bad stuff. And then I thought back to the stallion in the barn and the other horse charging at me, knocking me down.

The stillness, I realized, was growing louder and louder as each minute passed. Where was Roantis? Where was my comrade in arms? Wasn't like him to flake out, especially when the promise of danger was in the wind.

I left the grazing cattle and trudged back up the hill. I sure missed the dog. He had been both companion and guard. And needless to say, the manner of his death was upsetting. Bryce and company had combed the woods and the roads Saturday morning, looking for traces of Werner Franz's path. But his footprints had disappeared up over the ridge on the other side of the valley, lost in the undergrowth and leafy debris of the birch thickets. All the local roads had been watched the past two days in the vain hope of intercepting the killer. Either it was too late, with Franz speeding away before the roadblocks were in place, or else he had chosen another way home, a hidden route through the wilderness where vehicles couldn't go.

But what of his wounds? Surely, they couldn't be that serious, if he was up and about. Either that, or he had the strength and vigor of four men. An oversized, terrifically strong freak, driven by lots of testosterone. And hatred.

I approached the house, which now looked frightening in the lazy light of afternoon. The mood change was subtle, but real. The lights were off. No sound came from it. No friendly laughter, no clatter of dishes in the kitchen, or slamming of doors. No cars in the driveway except mine. It was silent and forbidding. Spooky.

When I was twenty yards away from the house, I stopped. I suddenly realized I was afraid. I was afraid to go into the house. He could be in there right now, I thought, waiting for me. Using the same skill and cunning that he'd showed at the auction, born of a lifetime in the woods and marshes, he could have sneaked back to the farm, watched my friends and protectors depart, then slid onto the property and into the house.

And there he'd be, perhaps close to the wall behind a door. And when I walked through it into the next room, he'd come at me from behind, driving the heavy blade of his big bowie down in a chopping stroke, right through my head. And I wouldn't say, hear, or feel a thing. Just a heavy tap on the top of my head and then nothing. Forever.

I stood there, looking up at the house. The dream house that had become a nightmare. Pete Becker's words echoed in my mind.

Doc? Hate to tell you, but he died last year. Got all ripped up in a fight and bled to death over in Saginaw, Michigan . . .

I kept the gun in my right fist, pointing straight ahead like a cowboy gunfighter. I wanted the piece very visible. I walked to the house. It seemed to loom over me. I circled it first, walking fast and spinning around continually to cover my back. I avoided all bushes, large trees, or anyplace that could hide a man.

A man, yes. But not Franz. I was becoming convinced that Buddy, big as he was, could hide almost anywhere. He sure hid in that horse barn in a way that fooled me. Roantis says he can hide in a room so well that you won't discover him until it's way, way too late. I now knew that Franz had the same skill.

A complete circle of the house revealed nothing. Then I looked over at Joe's place. Hell, he could have opened a ground-level window, crawled in, and be watching me this instant from a second-story window. Right up there, maybe, behind those linen cur—

"Dipshit!" I said to myself. Time to stop this mental hyperventilation, Adams. For crissakes, you're letting your imagination get the best of you. So I walked off a bit from the buildings, up near the head of the drive where I could see for sixty or so yards all around, and tried to relax. Wasn't it unlikely that he'd come back so soon? Wasn't it?

Maybe. But look how soon he came back after Phelps. Phelps! Good Christ. Look what had happened to poor Harry Phelps, the former marine. Chained to a stove that fried him. Charred him like a burned marshmallow. And him crying and screaming into that feedbag—

I walked over to Mary's Audi, which I had borrowed for the weekend. A simple solution presented itself. I would simply drive off and go into town for a while. Maybe call around and find out what was keeping Roantis. And if I couldn't raise Laitis, I'd call the police station and get a patrolman and a cruiser to come out here a couple hours early. That's all. It wasn't chickenshit to do that; it was wise.

It was a great idea. Trouble was, the car was locked, and the keys were in the kitchen. So there I was again: facing the house. What to do? I knew the longer I stayed outside, the darker it was going to get. I knew what I had to do. I summoned my strength and courage, walked straight up to the front door, opened it, and jumped inside.

Surprise! Nobody there.

I went into the kitchen, moving very fast, almost on a run, spinning around as I came into the room, holding the pistol in both hands, stiff armed, like those two guys with the bad sport-coats on "Miami Vice." It seemed to work; it gave me some much-needed confidence. I slid the bolt lock shut on the cellar door as I passed it, and spun the turnbolt as well. Good. That way was blocked, at least. Then I went around the perimeter of the lower floor, pulling in the English-style leaded windows and turning the locking levers on them.

Then the part I really dreaded: upstairs.

I went to the foot of the stairs and looked up. No way, Adams. I kept thinking of Alfred Hitchcock's *Psycho*, with the poor cop going upstairs only to be met by the madman at the top of the stairs, sticking him repeatedly with the knife. Oh God. I thought about Franz, sticking the horse with the upraised knife. I pictured him bringing the huge, heavy blade down on top of Bashful's skull, killing the ninety-pound pit fighter quick as a wink. Killing him in midgrowl.

I went up the first step. All was quiet. The stairway was oak, with no carpeting. It curved up to the right and doubled back on itself as it reached the second floor. Therefore, you couldn't see what was up there. Two steps. Three, four. Pause.

I checked to see that the Browning's safety was off. Round in the chamber or not? I was positive there was a cartridge up the spout, a 124-grain, hollow-point, Hydra-shok round. Lethal medicine. But I had to double-check, so I racked the pistol's slide back and let it snap forward, driven by the recoil spring. Sure enough, a round shot out the ejection port and spun around on the wooden steps with a hollow, beady sound. That would let anyone upstairs know I had a gun. Watch out.

Five steps. Six. Almost halfway up. To hell with it. I sprang up the stairs two at a time, gun up and ready. I arrived at the second-floor landing to see the hallway deserted. I yanked open door after door that opened onto the hall. I think I gave a little yell each time I moved; I wasn't sure. Each time, I turned the knob, then stepped back and kicked the door open, making sure it swung all the way around and hit the wall inside. Finally, I came to the master bedroom and searched it, even looking in the closet and under the bed. Then I locked the door, put a chair up against it so that its top was stuck underneath the doorknob, then lay down on the bed and tried to get my breathing and pulse down to normal.

You wimp, Adams, I thought to myself. He's got you scared to death on your own turf. You, who've been through more than one interesting scrape in the past several years. And look at you now, cowering in your bedroom behind a locked door. Shame, shame . . .

After a few minutes of self-loathing I got up and looked out the window. The one that overlooked the terrace and the valley. All was calm and peaceful. It seemed impossible for Franz to be out there, waiting. But still, the vision of Harry Phelps, chained to the stove, haunted me. And then I remembered I hadn't checked underneath the beds in the other bedrooms. I scanned the hills and woods in the softening light. Where the hell was Roantis?

I paced the room and discovered I had to take a leak. I began to unfasten the door when I had second thoughts. I remembered the unchecked beds, for one. Secondly, how did I know Franz didn't sneak inside the house *after* I went inside? I raised the side window and urinated out of it. Zipping up my fly, I was more filled with shame and self-hate than ever. Jesus Christ, Adams. You going to let this psycho run your entire life, or *what*?

And then it struck me that this is how it happens: this is how a recluse is born. Born of fear. First it's the fear of out-of-town trips. Then fear of the town itself. Still later, the fear-captured person realizes it's much less hassle to have the food and necessities delivered, for he has already begun to fear leaving the property. Then leaving the house itself becomes an unbearable emotional burden. Finally, the fear-wracked prisoner with the self-imposed life sentence finds himself crawling between kitchen and bathroom, the rest of his house a jackdaw's nest of debris and filth. Swell. Just swell.

What I wanted to do was call Roantis, but the upstairs phone wasn't connected yet. I lay down on the bed, putting my pistol on the end table, and closed my eyes. I was tired, but too pumped up for sleep. I thought.

BLAM!

I was sitting up in bed before the sound echoed away. In the next half-second I had jumped off the bed and was holding the pistol in my hands, covering the doorway. I heard no sounds inside. I went to the back window and looked out. A figure stood on the terrace in the falling light, holding a shotgun.

"Doc!" he called, looking everywhere but up at me.

It was Roantis, thin as a rail and brown as a betel nut. I saw him cradling the pump gun across his chest—his beloved Streetcleaner, the ugliest, nastiest firearm in the universe. Replete with shortened barrel, extended magazine, and black friction tape wound around the stock. Though I must say it looked pretty good to me right then. Damned good. He shucked the action.

SCHLICK-SCHLICK!

A red-and-gold shotshell flew out of the ancient Remington and spun across the flagstones of the terrace, a trace of blue smoke curling from its ruptured end.

"Don't shoot again; I'm up here."

He looked up at me.

"Where da hell you been?"

"Up here, resting."

"Why's the door locked? Shit, Doc, you got da whole place sealed up like Fort Knox—"

"Wait there; I'll be right down."

I opened the bedroom door cautiously and slid down the hall, back to the wall and watching all the doors. Then down the stairs and to the kitchen door, which I unlocked, letting the wiry, graying Lithuanian inside. The guy who looked like somebody's gruff immigrant uncle from the old country. The rather short fellow with a whole lot of miles on him. The guy whose odometer had turned over twice. The guy you would never suspect was deadlier than a black mamba.

"You hidin' up dere?"

"Kind of, yeah," I said, looking down at the new tile of the kitchen floor. He regarded me for a few seconds, then put his callused hand on my shoulder.

"Well, I guess I don't blame you. You were here alone, surrounded by the unseen enemy. And the enemy you can't see is always the most scary."

He went over to the window and looked out at the surrounding hills and woods. He was watching the tree line. "This reminds me of the A camps in Vietnam," he said. "We had these special forces camps out in the boonies there. They were isolated, most near the Laotian border. Anyway, we'd sit around in these A camps, in plain sight of Charlie, who was up in the hills, watching us. What was hard, we dint know where he was, see? But Charlie, he always knew where we were. So he would pick the time to hit us. He ran the show. It was hell, Doc, being so far away from help, and not knowing if we could trust our IPs."

"IPs?"

"Indigenous personnel. The locals we hired to help us fight. Anyway, the lesson I learned from that—and maybe the U.S. Army dint learn it yet—was that you cannot leave yourself in a fixed position that's visible. Because then you are a sitting duck."

"Right, that's exactly what it felt like. Like there were eyes watching me and I couldn't tell where they were. So what do we do now?"

"We have a drink," he said flatly, eyeing the cabinets.

"Thought you were laying off."

He didn't reply; he just gave me that pit bulldog stare of his and glided over to the booze cabinet, finding the correct door on the first shot. Telepathy. He poured a gin and tonic into a big tumbler, half and half without ice. He'd never made a G&T that way before.

"So where were you, Laitis? You look tan and fit."

"Near the equator; I'm not supposed to say more."

"Well, by the way you just made your drink, I'd say it was someplace British, or formerly so. Correct?"

He nodded, grinning.

"Yeah, Doc. Can't fool you. Sri Lanka. Used to call it Ceylon. But it's a secret, okay?"

"Right ho, old man. Strictly hosh-hosh. Now, what the hell are we gonna do about this threat?"

"Tomorrow, early, we're going to walk all around and look for sign. No matter how good he is, he will leave some sign. Then we set up a perimeter. When we finish these drinks, you can help me unload."

And so I did. We walked out to his car, a late-model Peugeot. This surprised me; I was expecting the old beat-up Dodge he'd been driving since I met him. But there sat the Peugeot. A diesel sedan. A very classy-looking piece of rolling stock indeed.

"Well, I see the Company's paying you well, Laitis. That's good news, at least."

"I never said it was the Company, Doc. You never heard that from me."

We unloaded a duffel bag of clothes, and a heavier satchel with angular edges poking through the canvas that clanked when I picked it up. Big boy's toys. Then there was a long rifle case, and finally, a laundry sack stuffed with some kind of cloth. Roantis took the personal duffel up to one of the spare bedrooms and threw it on the bed. He returned to the kitchen and emptied the contents of the heavy bag onto the table. It was your typical soldiering hardware: spare magazines for the rifle and pistol, Sykes-Fairbairn S.A.S. commando dagger, some exotic-looking scopes, a couple of smoke bombs, coiled wire and electronic gadgets, and three boxes of double-ought buckshot for the Streetcleaner. I wasn't too impressed, frankly. Maybe a year or so earlier I would have been, but not now.

"We're going to need more than these toys, Laitis. I know you're good, but this guy—"

He nodded, sorting out the stuff. "Yeah, I know."

"Not all of it, you don't."

We sat down at the table and I filled him in on the torture and murder of Harry Phelps, and the recent episode at the barn, including the death of the dog. He listened carefully to all of it and interrupted frequently for clarification of details. Then I told him what had happened just before he arrived. How I'd lost my confidence and finally locked myself in my own bedroom, afraid to go out. How I'd even pissed out my own window. I was expecting a ribbing at the very least, or maybe even a stern lecture on my cowardice. Instead he nodded, leaned forward on the table, and rested his head on his hands.

"Don't beat yourself up over it, Doc. Hell, you were just bein' smart. Here all alone, you realized you couldn't cover all the bases. You were a sitting duck, just like we were in those A camps in Nam. It's true. So I say, you did the right thing. Caution is a blessing. Considering my life, do you think for a second I'd still be around if I dint know when to back off and lie low? Remember: dere are brave soldiers, and dere are old soldiers. Okay?"

I nodded.

"But, t'ing is: *dere are no old brave soldiers.*"

"Right."

"Remember, you must never let your defensive perimeter shrink too far. You do and before you know it, the enemy is right in your face, coming through your wire."

"And he knows where we are, but we don't know where he is."

"We're going to fix that," he said, unzipping the rifle case and extracting the Belgian-made assault weapon, the FN-FAL rifle that is the favorite of professional soldiers worldwide. Roantis explained that with the starscope, a scope developed for use in the dark, he would remain outside the house in hopes of intercepting Franz when and if he came stalking up to our buildings in the dead of night.

"Don't be too sure, Laitis," I cautioned. "You haven't seen this guy's handiwork yet."

While he considered this, I lighted the grill on the terrace, setting my Browning on the redwood table next to the burner.

"You ought to get a holster, Doc," he said, leaning back in his Adirondack chair and lighting a Camel, letting the smoke ooze out through his nose. "You should have it at the ready all the time."

"I know, but I never got around to it. You loaned me yours last time, remember?"

"Well, get one. What's for dinner?"

"Something quick: marinated chicken over rice and a salad. Will you please go open me a beer?"

He went inside and returned with two cold Asahi beers while I placed the whole mushrooms and chunks of chicken on the bamboo skewers and placed them on the grate. The chicken and mushrooms had been marinated in peanut oil, teriyaki marinade, lemon juice, wine, garlic, and a dash of *la ma yo*, or hot sesame oil. Smelled great, and Laitis agreed. The phone rang, and he answered it in the kitchen, coming back with a hint of a grin on his lined face.

"That was Lucy. She sounds kinda nice."

"She is nice, and a great help around here, too. See that smallish building down by the barn? That's her own little house; Summers fixed it up especially for her. So what did she want?"

"She said she wouldn't be back tonight. Said to tell you she was spending the night with some friends in Pittsfield."

"Okay. Did she leave a number?"

"No. Was she supposed to?"

"Nope. You'll meet her tomorrow. Nice girl."

"What's she look like?"

"You'll see."

"I wanta know now."

"You'll see her soon enough. And you're married, remember?"

"I never forget it."

"Uh-huh. And you never act on it, either."

"Look who is talking. What about you and my daughter?"

"You mean Daisy? She's not really your daughter, Laitis."

Roantis adopted her in Vietnam back in the fifties after her dad, René Cournot, was killed at Dien Bien Phu. "So anyway, what about her?"

"What about her? How about in North Carolina?"

"What about it? I never touched her, Laitis. You were there; you saw all there was to see."

"No, Doc. I mean *before* the Daisy Ducks showed up. When it was just you and Daisy down dere in the mountains, in your van."

"Nothing, Laitis."

"Not what she says. She says you were in bed together. And she was naked."

"Your own daughter told you that?"

"Like you said, Doc, she's not really my daughter. She's more like my niece, and she tells me everyt'ing. Well?"

Flashback: I thought of the luscious Danielle Cournot, half Vietnamese, half French, who was called Daisy. The ferocious commando team that Roantis commanded in Southeast Asia was named for her.

"Not true. She had her panties on. I was fully dressed. We kissed briefly. That's all. She had removed her jeans because . . . because . . ."

There was a good, legitimate reason for this. I was just trying to think of it—

"Because we thought she might have a kidney injury."

He leaned back, head to the sky, and laughed. Laughed until I thought he was going to cry.

"And so you played doctor?"

"What's this leading up to, Laitis? Goddammit, tell me!"

"What would Mary think if she found out that—"

"You son-of-a-bitch; You're blackmailing me."

He laughed again, and asked me please to describe Lucy Kirkland. I refused, and we ate in silence.

After dinner we took a quick evening stroll around the buildings but saw nothing. The light was falling fast now, and we made it back to the house just as darkness was setting in. We took the dirty dishes in to be cleaned. I saw Laitis checking out my pistol, releasing the magazine, then touching the hollow-point rounds with his finger. He worked the slide like an expert, checking out the action, then replaced the magazine, snapped it home with the heel of his hand, and carefully lowered the hammer on an empty chamber, leaving the pistol in condition three.

"Those Pachmayr rubber grips are new."

"Yeah," I said, walking into the house. "The wooden grips got busted when our friend from the other side threw the gun off the train and it landed on the track ballast. There are some dings on the slide, too. See them?"

He put the pistol back on the grill shelf with a grunt and went back to his chair. "You ought to quit fucking around with nine-millimeter and get a .45," he said.

"You keep saying that. You and Jeff Cooper. But the Colt holds seven rounds, the Browning thirteen. You want coffee?"

"Naw. Another booze."

"Two coffees, coming up," I said. He gave me a dirty look, but I ignored it.

As I was washing the dishes Laitis came inside and poured his coffee, adding a wee taste o' Scotland to his. He then helped me put away everything and clean up the kitchen.

"Tomorrow, bright and early, we take a tour of the place. Set up some watching posts and perimeters. I'll make a few hidey-holes out there to lie up in. Maybe one for the dark, too. We'll get a line on him."

"And if we don't?"

"Den we go for a series of long drives, Doc. We hit those guys you've met—those bikers. I t'ink maybe we should take Lucy with us."

"If she's willing."

"Yeah . . . we go out after him, not let him come in here after us, eh?"

"Sounds good to me. Anything's better than what's been going on around here."

"Let's lock up and you can draw me some sketches—what's that?"

I heard a car crunching on the gravel outside.

"It's the police cruiser, the nighttime stakeout."

Roantis grunted, saying he didn't like cops to begin with, and that maybe they were screwing things up as much as helping. We went outside and waved at the patrolman—it wasn't Bensen, but another guy—who blinked his vehicle's brights a couple of times in greeting, then switched them off and began his night-long vigil. We went back inside and I locked the doors and windows. Then I remembered something; I went back out to the terrace to retrieve my Browning. It wasn't there.

I called Roantis and asked him what he'd done with it, since he'd had it last. He swore he'd left it on the grill shelf, sure that I'd come back out to get it. We searched everywhere: all through the downstairs, out on the terrace, back into the kitchen for a thorough search. The pistol was gone. Taken.

oantis's manner was changed now. Gone was the cocky
nonchalance, the strained aloofness born of a hundred
deadly missions. Now he helped me secure the house in
earnest. Finally, he exploded, at himself as much as at me.
"*Gott-dammit!* I knew you should have gotten a holster, Doc!"

"What do you think of our friend Franz now?"

"I don't like him; that's for sure."

Two other things were for sure. One: as things now stood,
Franz was winning this war. He was batting a thousand, and
against Laitis Roantis, certainly among the world's best. Sneaking up to our place of refuge in the space of several minutes
when our backs were turned and stealing my firearm. Then
gone again. And two: it didn't help my nerves any. That was
also for sure.

Another item that reared its ugly head was this: it was now time for my nightly phone call to Mary. I was to call her when we were all inside for the night and the place was secured, with the police watchers on duty. Then she could go to sleep knowing I was safe. Trouble was, I knew that sooner or later the news of the chopped-up doggie would trickle back to her through the cops, or Joe. I was hoping she wouldn't find out until later, after we had Franz under lock and key. But that was looking increasingly unlikely.

I dutifully made the call and told her all was well. I left out the little tidbit about the stolen pistol. No need to upset her. Roantis came on the line to give his usual guttural greeting and gruff appraisal of the situation, which was as positive as lies could make it. He got off the line early, though. Something about Mary makes him nervous. I'm not sure what it is. Maybe it's that he's accustomed to third world women, who, at least in my experience, seem more obedient to men. Running up against Mary is something he can't handle. With her, all his machismo and battle scars and Tae Kwon Do sashes are useless. She sees right through that kind of stuff real fast.

"She wants you again," he said wearily as he handed me the receiver.

"Charlie, how is everything out there, really?"

"Swell," I said. "Just swell."

"*Hmmmmph!* You don't sound like it."

"I'm not; I can't wait till we get this guy."

"Well, that's Laitis's job, not yours. Let me speak to Lucy."

"She's not here; she's in Pittsfield visiting her mom and friends."

"Sounds like she's the smart one. Listen, Charlie, I'm coming out there tomorrow or the next day."

"Oh no you're not."

"Oh yes I am."

"Oh no you're not."

"Oh yes I am. You just wait."

Then she hung up. I called Joe's number. Busy. I knew it; she was calling him now. Dammit! She'd wring the rest of the story out of her kid brother in two shakes. That meant Roantis and I had very little time left before she'd storm out here and gum up the works.

Laitis read the situation immediately, because he voiced the same concern as soon as I replaced the phone on its cradle.

"We got to move fast now, Doc. Not only because of Mary, but because Franz now has a gun. That shifts the odds in a way I don't like. C'mon, we got work to do now before turning in."

The first thing he had us do was to take our bedding downstairs to the living room, locking all the upstairs windows after us, and all the bedroom doors, too, leaving the old-fashioned-type keys in the locks on the hallway side. With the upper level sealed off, we then moved all the living room furniture over to the interior wall, close to the fireplace, out of the way.

"Out of the way of *what*?" I asked.

"Sounds. We don't want to block any sounds that come at us. Walls funnel sound waves. A good thing there aren't heavy drapes in here."

"Mary hasn't put them up yet."

"Good. Let's roll this rug up and put it on the chairs."

We did this, leaving a bare and shiny floor. All the while I was thinking Roantis had finally flipped out.

"Now watch how I place my bed in this corner, and you do the same in that far corner."

We placed our bedrolls on the floor in the outside corners in such a way that our heads would be tucked up against the very corner where the walls and floor converged. Laitis had me lie down on my crude bed, then walked all around the room, making a tiny clicking noise with his thumbnail as he went.

"Can you hear it?"

"Can I ever. Sounds like a rifle shot."

"Supposed to. In the corner, on the floor, you are at the juncture of three walls. All sounds in the room come right to your ears. What doesn't reach you will not escape me."

"Where the hell you learn this stuff?"

"Japan. Where else? What you can't learn in Japan isn't worth knowing. A master of ninjitsu taught me that and a lot more."

I knew what he meant. In North Carolina, I watched him scale a sheer rock wall backwards, using only his heels and fingernails. Maybe someday I'd go to Japan and learn all this stuff. On the other hand, maybe I wouldn't.

"Now, let's cut all the lights except that little one in the hall. I'm going to open a window in the kitchen so we can hear him out back."

"But he'll come in, dummy."

"No. I'll rig a wire alarm across it. Stay put. Here."

He removed his holster rig and handed it to me, saying the .45 was in condition one, "cocked and locked," which meant that the hammer was raised over a loaded chamber, with the safety engaged. Since I hate this, I slipped off the safety and carefully thumbed back the hammer while depressing the trigger. With the hammer loose now, I gently lowered it down on the full chamber. Now the pistol wouldn't fire unless I first pulled back the hammer to cock it. This is called condition two. Much better. Roantis came back from the kitchen in the near darkness, took his pump gun and placed it on the floor next to his bedroll. He rechecked the security on the first floor again, crept into the hallway and cut the last light, then came back into the room without a sound. I heard him open the big window between us.

"Want to hear outside, too," he explained in a whisper.

"Aren't you going to string the wire across it?" I whispered back.

"No. I want it clear so I can jump outside and kill him if he walks past."

"Oh, great. Had me worried for a second . . ."

I heard a faint rustle as he crawled into his bed on the floor. We kept on whispering.

"Doc?"

"Yeah?"

"Daisy still asks about you."

I felt an electric shiver through my loins. Couldn't help it. When you're pushing fifty and a beautiful younger woman who's been everywhere, seen it all, and done it all asks about you, it feels kind of good. Hell, it feels like a million bucks.

"That's nice."

"Better not let Mary find out, eh? There'd be fireworks. I'd worry about what might happen to Daisy."

"*Daisy?* She's a world-champion karate fighter; she almost killed me down in Carolina before she recognized me. You forgetting that?"

"I know. But she'd be up against *Mary*. Nighty-night, Doc. Don't let the bedbugs bite."

"Where the hell did you ever hear that, Laitis?"

"In the U.S. Army. At the John F. Kennedy Special Warfare School at Fort Bragg, in Fayetteville, North Carolina. Except all of us in S.F. used to call the town Fatal-ville. Cute, eh?"

"Goodnight, Laitis. You keep a watch for those bedbugs."

I closed my eyes and thought of Bashful with his brain cleaved. Of Phelps split open, his cooked flesh pink-gray against the shiny, carbon black of his skin. Of the giant man-child hovering over the terrified horse in the barn, bloody knife upraised.

Some bedbug.

Some bite.

TWENTY-FIVE

Roantis was up and about before I was, making coffee and going over his military hardware, which was strewn over the kitchen counters. After breakfast we armed ourselves and went for a stroll around the grounds, saying good-bye to the departing stakeout patrolman as he left. It was 6:20, and the birds were still chirping. Roantis looked carefully for sign on the grass leading up to the terrace. There was none, and we then went down past the barn and outbuildings, up the valley to the burial site, looking for fresh tracks or anything of interest. Nothing. Laitis carried a shoulder bag of equipment and a pair of military binoculars. Every now and then he'd sneak down through the trees and brush to the tree line overlooking the pasture and valley and glass the entire area. In a notebook we sketched crude maps of the farm and possible vantage points. One small knoll in particular seemed to suit him. It was located past the barns, about a third of the way to the far woods where the bodies were found. It provided a clear view of the house and grounds and most of the approaches to the property. It also provided an excellent field of fire, Laitis said.

A little after eight, Roantis drove several small metal stakes into the ground near the house and strung thin wire between them, stretching it tight as barbed wire on a ranch fence. At the juncture of the wire and the posts he inserted small electronic triggers. On some of these he fastened smoke bombs. On others, loud noisemakers.

"That might slow him down a lil', Doc. Or at least give us some warning."

"What do you think of the layout?"

"What do I think? I think we're sitting ducks. But starting this evening I'm going to station myself out there in my ghillie suit and take the offensive. I can't tell you how pissed off I am dat he snuck up here last night and took your sidearm."

"What the hell's a ghillie suit?"

"You'll see. Let's go for a drive."

We got into the car and made ever-widening circles in the countryside, trying to catch sight of any possible hiding place or hidden approach to the property. Laitis was certain that Franz was coming and going through the woods, not by the roads. I suggested we follow Rowanda's lead and drive up to the Saratoga Springs region, asking around for stables and horse farms. Lacking other leads, we did it, getting up there just before noon. We stayed until three, visiting four of the largest horse farms and stopping at many smaller ones. At each place we asked about a huge blond man, possibly driving an old blue-and-white pickup. Had they seen him, possibly seeking employment in a stable or asking for a place to stay? No, they hadn't.

But just as we were heading back, we stopped at a smaller spread right on the highway belonging to a horse farmer named Mitchell Sams, who remembered, painfully, a visit by "a bunch of hoodlums on motorcycles" two years previous. We explained our errand, and he listened sympathetically, then led us over to a large blackened stone foundation on the edge of his property.

"Bastards burned this barn down after I ran them off," he said gruffly, his eyes lighting up with hate. "There was a big fella with 'em, too, seemed to be their leader. Wasn't blond, though. Had reddish-brown hair, and a big beard. Fat kinda guy, but tall, too. They were trying to camp out here, and I asked them to leave. They didn't, so I called the law. That was my mistake, because three nights later, she went up."

"Were there animals in the barn?" I asked him.

"No; just hay, fortunately. But still, it cost me a bundle, even after the insurance. And the worst thing was that the police couldn't do a damn thing about it. Couldn't go after those punks because there was no proof."

"You sure they did it?"

He regarded me with wonder, arms across his chest.

"Well now, what do you think?"

"Did you see any colors on the backs of their jackets? Any insignia for a motorcycle club?"

"No. Not that I remember. They just had on old jeans, stuff like that. The women, if they should be called women, had on the same thing, pretty much. Some wore leather jackets, too, even though it was in the summertime."

"Well, it's always cool riding a bike," I said.

"You ride a motorcycle? Thought you were a doctor."

"I am, but I ride a little. Do you remember if the plates on the motorcycles were New York issue?"

"Oh yeah, at least all of 'em I saw."

"Sounds like the Stompers, then. And that big guy with the beard would be Jimmy DeLisle."

Sams nodded fast, saying that I was correct; the police had identified the leader as James DeLisle from his operator's license, but he'd forgotten the name in the interim.

"And how many of the riders had women riding with them?"

"All of 'em. Each one had his own woman. Called them 'mammas,' which I thought was funny, since some of them looked barely sixteen, and pretty beat up, too."

"Nobody rode alone?"

"No; I'm sure of that. There was a girl on the back of each motorcycle. A cop told me there was less trouble that way."

"Really? How so?"

"He said that when they parked for the night and got drunk, there wouldn't be as much fighting over the women if the numbers were even. Guess it makes sense."

We exchanged phone numbers with Mitchell Sams and thanked him for his time, then began the two-hour drive back to the farm. Roantis suggested we pursue Jimmy DeLisle and the Stompers to see if we couldn't shake something loose. I told him that Bryce had already been in contact with the New York State guys, who'd questioned DeLisle and found no connection. Still, ideas about the rival biker club, and possible common meeting places, kept floating around in my head.

When we got back and approached the house, the phone was ringing. I unlocked the door and went inside in time to answer it. It was Pete Becker, saying he knew where Franz was holing up.

"I run into a guy who handles dogs, Dr. Adams. He says he saw Franz at the old Skeggo place. You come up here and give me the money and I'll take you to where he is."

"The old Skeggo place? Where's that?"

"Hey, c'mon; I ain't gonna tell you now. I want the money first, up front. Besides, it's dangerous for me. I'm takin' a risk here—"

"Are you at your place now?"

"Yep. Remember how to get here?"

"Not very well. Why don't you meet us at Shorty's?"

"Us? Who's us? I don't want nobody else in on this."

"He's a man you can trust. Now, no bullshitting, Pete: you're really sure you know where Franz is?"

"Pretty sure, yeah. Only you better come up here quick. Guy like that moves around fast."

"Okay, we're on our way. We'll see you at the bar between five and six."

We got to Shorty's roadhouse a little after six. For a weekday, there were plenty of cars parked out front, and a few "sleds," as well. We entered to find the place half full, with most of the patrons concentrated at the bar. I was pumped up, excited and scared at the chance of closing in on the guy nobody could catch. We ordered beers; Roantis took his with a shot of vodka on the side. We went over to a booth and waited for Becker to appear. The place reminded me somewhat of Concord's Willow Pond Kitchen, a quaint, roadhouse-style place that's packed on weekends and features okay grub—fried clams, french fries, burgers, onion rings, and so on—that are served up in the perpetual blue cloud of tobacco smoke that hangs in the air. Shorty's had illuminated beer signs on the wall, a pool table in the back, and two pinball machines that clacked and pinged. Of the forty or so people in the place, I saw only two women. Some of the guys wore riding clothes, but most wore their working duds, having stopped in after work.

"So where is he? You see him?" asked Roantis, draining the last of his beer. I shook my head, disappointed at Becker's tardiness. I was also uneasy because I knew if we didn't get out of Shorty's soon, Laitis would belly up to the bar and begin putting the drinks away in earnest.

If that happened, it would only be a matter of time.

Sooner or later, some boozed-up biker or other macho type would jostle him, make some rude comment about his thick Lithuanian accent, call him 'short stuff,' or make some equally suicidal crack. And then Laitis would give him that pit bulldog stare and tell him in a guttural voice to fuck off, or he'd get hurt . . . bad.

But of course the guy wouldn't believe him. They never do. He'd throw his head back and laugh, and start in on Laitis again, giving him shit loud and clear so his buddies or girlfriend could hear it all. And before I could take Big Shot aside to warn him that what he was doing was about as prudent as tickling a gaboon viper between the eyes with his tongue, it would be under way. The action taking maybe six or seven seconds at the outside, ending with us having to mop up Mr. Macho with a bar sponge, and Laitis in dutch with the cops again, and so on . . .

Sensing the possibility of these untoward events, I went to the bar and asked for directions to Becker's place. Shorty didn't remember me at first, but when I mentioned Mac and Dragon and the reward money I'd put up, it all came back to him. He drew a crude map on a bar napkin and thus jogged my memory. Then, remembering the new telephone service running into the dilapidated house, I thought of calling Becker. Trouble was, he never gave me his number. Shorty didn't have it either, and inquiries around the bar proved fruitless as well. This seemed to confirm my suspicion that the phone was used primarily to set up dogfights and other bets.

I grabbed Laitis just as he was about to order himself another round, this time with a double vodka bringing up the rear.

"Is there life after death—" said Laitis, reading the sign posted at the gate to Becker's place. "Let's hope not." He unlocked the gate and shoved it back hard, walking into the yard barely breaking stride, unarmed.

Apparently, Laitis Roantis didn't give a flying fuck about life, death, or anything before, after, or in between. Keep it simple.

I waited for the dogs to stand up out of the tall weeds and give us toothy, silent grins, straining their thick harnesses and stout chains. Nothing. Where was Grumpy? Sleepy? Dopey?

We saw the first dead pit bull and smelled the smoke at the same time. At first I thought it was a neighboring farmer burning trash or weeds, but the smoke smelled strong and close. Looking up at the house, we knew it wasn't coming from there. Roantis looked down at the dog again. Split skull, just like Bashful. We walked to the next barrel. Same thing. I kicked at the animal. Not stiff yet. Recent killings. Very recent: no flies, no odor, and the blood was congealed but not yet brown.

"Becker's had company," said Laitis, turning to look at the front porch. "Fifty bucks says we find him inside."

"No bet," I answered, "and you go first."

Roantis grabbed the broken half of a rake handle which he found in the grass and walked up the steps. We opened the

broken screened door and walked inside. The place stank of
stale beer and a filthy toilet. There was litter and junk everywhere. On the kitchen table, underneath a circular fluorescent
bulb still burning, was an old pizza carton. A spotted cat was
squatting in it, gnawing at the two remaining pieces. As we
approached, it scampered off in fright.

"Becker?" I yelled. "Hey, Pete!" No answer.

I followed Roantis up the stairs. The two low-ceilinged bedrooms were vacant. And so, apparently, was the house. Becker
had flown the coop, but it didn't look good.

"Hell, Doc, he wouldn't have run away without the money.
He wouldn't leave the three grand behind."

We walked through the downstairs rooms again. It was when
we went out the backdoor, onto the little porch stoop that led
to the jungle growth of backyard, that we saw where the smoke
was coming from. Forty yards from the house, hidden by two
willow trees, the little shack where I'd found the cattle shocker
on my earlier visit was ablaze. We ran up to it but couldn't get
closer than about twenty feet, so intense was the heat. We
watched the yellow flames lick up to the tar paper roof, sending
great clouds of blue-white smoke pouring from the tiny windows of the little building.

"Becker got scared and took off," I said, talking in a loud voice
to be heard over the roar of the flames. "He killed his dogs and
burned all the evidence up. I think maybe the big boys were
after him. Maybe he was holding out on the—"

"Doc!" Laitis yelled, pointing at the shack.

A section of wall had fallen away, allowing us to see in
through the charred studding, each timber crawling with licking flames, into the glowing interior. I saw a man lying on his
side on the ground in there. His body was completely black. But
the charred features were recognizable. I saw the stern, worried
face of Peter Becker, his long hair burned away, staring intently
in death at the ground inches from his face.

Then, to my utter horror, the charred corpse began to move.

The heat was doing it, making the muscles spasm and con-
tract. The body writhed momentarily, then twisted its trunk

around, the man's face—a grotesque, horrid Al Jolson in black-face—staring right at us. Then the corpse turned again, shriveling before our eyes, and lay on its back. I saw the arms come up, boxer fashion, vainly trying to punch vain holes in the glowing ceiling far above.

It was finally enough to make me turn away and walk and walk until I reached the road, trying to catch my breath, and drive away the stench of burning flesh.

TWENTY·SIX

What do you have for Skeggo?" asked Bryce Stevens, speaking intently into the phone. His face showed a lot of strain. I understood why; his beat was becoming a killing ground.

"No," he sighed. "*Ess, kay, eee . . . gee, gee, oh.* I *think.* We're not sure. We just heard the name spoken over the phone. Can you run through all possibilities, with emphasis on those names in rural locations, please, and those living in the western part of the state? Thanks. If we get nowhere, we'll try names for Vermont and New York, okay? Great. Call me back on my frequency or the number I'm about to give you—"

He was calling from the late Peter Becker's residence, his cruiser pulled up on the filthy, overgrown lawn. Off to one side, five dead pit bulls lay stretched out side by side, their compact, muscular forms strangely languid and small in death. Each had its head chopped down the middle. Each had died fast and painlessly. Obviously, the same couldn't be said for the late Becker, whose body, shriveled and blackened though it was, still showed evidence of 'selective and deliberate trauma to the legs, knees, and genitalia.' These the words of the state lab attendant who had carted off the remains as soon as the site of the fire had cooled down enough to get in there.

It was dark now, and had been for some time. The last remaining vehicle of the fire department had left an hour ago. So there we all were, at the scene of Buddy Franz's latest drill in butchery and combustion. All we had to go on was the name "Skeggo." I wasn't even sure I'd heard it correctly from Becker. Too bad I'd never get another chance to ask him. A swarm of lab men were busy looking for evidence in the ramshackle dwelling; they'd even dusted the phone for prints before Stevens used it. Now they were filing through the tiny, dirty rooms, looking for sign. I wished them luck in that unattractive task.

As we walked back outside into the fresh night air, I thought back over the past few months. Lab team in the barn. Lab team at Ten Ten Comm Ave. Lab team up in Lanesboro. Lab team here. Holy Christ, lab teams were following me like yesterday. Not fun.

Roantis and I were pacing in front of the car, waiting for Stevens to come up with a location.

"You told Joe about this?" I asked him as he went up to the car and leaned against the front fender, arms crossed over his chest in resignation.

"No, but he'll find out before the day is through. It'll be on the daily bulletin. Everybody gets it, statewide. Why? Worried about the reaction from the home front?"

"Absolutely. Mary's patience has been strained beyond the breaking point already. Now, we're not positive it's Franz; it's just a ninety-nine percent probability, right?"

Stevens nodded grimly.

"Well, I hope he doesn't mention it to Mary before I talk to him."

"He and his sister are close, aren't they?"

"You noticed. Did you get any addresses that look promising?"

"I'll know in a few minutes. Hey, can I talk with you a second alone?"

I followed him around to the other side of the car. He leaned over close and spoke in a low voice.

"That guy with you . . . that the Lithuanian killer Joe keeps talking about?"

"He is Lithuanian. And, he is, uh, skilled in the 'dangerous arts,' if that's what you mean. But he's no murderer. What he is, he's a good guy to have on your side when the road gets rocky."

"How do you say his name again?"

"LIGHT-us Row-WANT-us."

"Well, keep a leash on him, okay?"

The three of us paced the grounds until Bryce's radio crackled and buzzed, and he hopped inside his cruiser to talk for a minute or so. Then he called us over.

"Doc, if you heard the name right, we're lucky. There's only one Skeggo listed that's anywhere near here. It's over in Plainfield, twenty miles west. Sounds like a good bet, because it's almost halfway to Pittsfield. Lucky it's a strange name. I called for help; by the time I get there the place should be surrounded. We're going in without sirens or lights." He started the car and put it into reverse, then leaned out the window at me.

"You're not allowed to come on the scene, you know," he said. I could feel the regret in his voice. He was doing his damnedest to keep the official look on his face.

"C'mon, Bryce, we called in the killing and the fire, for crissakes. We're material witnesses. We're—"

"—yeah, and you're a state cop now, kind of. Well goddammit, stay clear, then. It'd be my ass if anything happened to you." He spun his tires on the weeds, then leaned out the window again. "Maybe it'll look better if you ride with me. Get in."

It took us forty minutes to get to the old Skeggo place on the outskirts of Plainfield. Bryce was on his radio, being guided in by the troopers already there, who said the place was dead quiet. It was going on eleven o'clock when Stevens pulled to a stop off the narrow road in high grass, using only his parking lights, pulling in right behind a marked patrol car. We cut all lights and waited inside while he got out and checked in with the uniformed officer. Then he came back and stuck his head inside the window.

"From the descriptions given you by Franz's past acquaintances, would you say this place seems like a good bet for his hideout?"

"Can't see much at night," I said, looking up the slope to the dim outline of a farmhouse and barn against the night sky. Even in the dark, the place looked overgrown and run-down. "But, offhand, I'd say it's perfect. Jerry Rapp said look for old deserted farm buildings. From where we are, I'd say this is the place."

"Nothing's moved here in the past hour, and we came in quiet. That means if Franz is here, he's asleep. Or else he's gone. In any case, I want you two to wait here until we check it out. It's for your safety and our protection. I trust you'll understand."

Laitis replied that he was extremely grateful, and that during the next few minutes he would do his best not to shit in his pants. I turned around, facing the backseat, and informed Laitis that he needn't keep up the feigned cover; Stevens knew who he was.

Somewhat relieved, Stevens went to join his men. We sat in the cruiser and watched the thin beams of flashlights play and flicker about the buildings and the grounds. Roantis laughed, then cursed, at the flashlights, saying that they obviously didn't have much experience sneaking in the dark. After thirty minutes, Bryce and an officer returned and said we could come up and join them.

"We checked the house and barn, Doc. The house is still locked up tight, doors and windows intact. Barn's open, but appears normal. Just hay and old junk in there. I think this is the wrong place. Or else Becker's tip was bogus."

I asked him if he were willing to follow us, instead of the other way around. He said that since it appeared to be a dead end, he didn't mind. I told Laitis to lead on, and he did, telling us not to show any lights. We followed his stooped-over form in the dark. We walked and walked.

We saw Roantis stop, holding his arm up. I stopped, being familiar with all of his silent signals. I noticed that Bryce did likewise. Then Roantis dropped his arm, and I fell to one knee, crouching over. We crept forward, low, and there it was: a little house sixty yards from the main one, hidden between two big trees that were either oaks or maples. We watched it in silence until Roantis came back to us, saying he didn't think anyone was inside. We then withdrew back to the main farmhouse, where we could talk freely. During the trek back, I realized I'd forgotten to make my nightly phone call of reassurance to Mary. Uh-oh. And if she got worried and called Joe, and he happened to mention the murder and fire at Pete Becker's, then she would be really worked up by this time. UH-OH . . .

The upshot was that Bryce, who said he'd feel better if we were out of harm's way, said he'd drive us back to our car, leaving a stakeout team to watch the place until daylight, ready to nab anybody who came or went. That was a good idea, and I realized that Laitis and I should hightail it back to the farm. For one thing, Lucy may have returned, and she'd be there unprotected. I made Bryce promise to let us return the next day, very early, to see what was up. He agreed but told us it would only be under his direct supervision, and that we were to tell no one. We went back to his cruiser and drove to Becker's place.

As we parted, I turned to Bryce. "You seem, uh, pretty good to me, Bryce. How are things?"

"She said she'd talk about it before she left. Who knows? Maybe things'll work out."

"Well, I really hope they do. You sure deserve it."

"Thanks, Doc. Tell you what, if she leaves, I think I'm a goner."

I told him it wasn't so, that he would be amazed at the inner strength he had, and hurried to join Roantis. We got back to the farm at 1:30. Lucy was nowhere around. We went down to her little cottage and looked inside. No evidence that she'd returned. Had she come back from her friend's to find the place deserted, and then left again? That's what I would have done. Laitis and I checked the house thoroughly, unrolled our bedding, and slept in the living room again, heads in the corners and alert to the slightest sound.

Next morning I was awakened by the phone. Guess who? I apologized and admitted she had a right to be steamed. I said Roantis and I were out on a little nighttime recon, which had complications.

"I'm supposed to just sit here and listen to all this bullshit? You serious?"

She announced her imminent departure for the farm. I told her that was unwise. She said she was doing it anyway, and she'd like to see how I could stop her. I told her she would be in deep shit if she did. She said "Ha!" and slammed down the phone.

I went into the kitchen, cussing. Laitis was fixing breakfast. He asked what was wrong and I told him.

"Hell, maybe it was just a bluff. Maybe she won't come out here and gum everything up," I said, accepting a cup of coffee from him. Roantis makes great coffee.

"Oh, she'll come, Doc. You kidding? She'll come out here in a heartbeat."

We downed a quick breakfast and headed for the Skeggo place. As we drove we speculated on Becker's death. Roantis thought it strange that Franz would kill his friend, saying he was either a terminal nut case, or else some rift had come between them. I had a hunch I knew what the rift was.

"I think it was the dog, Laitis. I took Becker's dog, and he attacked Franz. I think Franz recognized Bashful as Becker's dog right after he killed him, and thought that Becker was in league with us. In a sense, he was. So Franz sneaked up on Becker and took his revenge. What scares me, though, is that he probably got Becker to spill all, telling Franz about my earlier visit with Joe and Bryce, and our efforts to trap him."

Roantis sat looking at the scenery of the Berkshires along Route 8. Then he said, "You better go buy another gun, Doc. And this time, get a goddamn holster so you won't leave it behind."

"No time for that now. I'll keep your .45 on my hip for the time being. You can carry the shotgun."

There were only two police vehicles at the Skeggo farm: Bryce's unmarked cruiser and one patrol car. Both vacant. We found Stevens up at the small outbuilding Roantis had located the previous night. He told us we could come on in, but not to touch a thing. It was a low shack, barely twenty feet square, without water or electricity. The floor was rough boards. A bed of straw was in a far corner, a heap of blankets thrown in a pile on top of the straw. There was an old dilapidated suitcase, open and empty, turned on its side against the near wall. Otherwise, except for a few objects placed neatly on a clean paper, the place was empty.

"If Franz was hiding here, he flew the coop," said Bryce.

I looked at the objects on the paper. They were interesting. A battered deck of tarot cards, three curiously shaped stones. Some rope, a woman's barrette, a dog leash, and a bullwhip. I bent over and looked at the barrette. I'd seen one like it before. Recently. Who was wearing it? Lucy? No; Lucy wore her long hair loose, like a flower child of the sixties. It might have been Rowanda. Or maybe even Marty. Mary didn't have any like it, or else didn't wear it often; I would have noticed it, I think. It was plastic—fake tortoiseshell. Had I seen it in Rowanda's hair, which billowed out behind her as she walked Bashful on Humphrey's Main Street? I had spent an undue amount of time looking at Rowanda's hair. And at her everything else. Why?

Why? Because you are afflicted with a terrible condition, Charles Adams. You are a middle-aged male, about to begin that downhill slide that will propel you, at an ever-increasing pace, into old age and decrepitude. And you cannot help yourself. More's the pity, old chap.

No. Even if I'd seen a barrette like this, it wasn't the same one. It was a common type, the kind sold at every five-and-ten. Probably every woman had at least a couple of them.

"Can I pick this up?" I asked. Stevens shook his head. I asked him what his thoughts were.

"Shows he had a girlfriend with him. Melissa Hendricks?"

"Could be," I said.

"I don't think they'll be back, Doc. Do you?"

"Nope. They knew that Becker had tipped me about this hideout. They knew because they worked him over before they killed him. Made him tell everything before he died. And so they were warned we were coming. He stays just a jump ahead of us, doesn't he? It's uncanny."

"Yep," said Roantis, in his clipped, guttural voice. "And maybe that's the way to get him. Think a step or two ahead, and head him off. Ambush him."

"Easier said than done," I said. "How would you ambush him?"

"Way I would do it is to make him t'ink we screwed up. Pretend we're vulnerable, that we got a weak spot," he said, talking low, his face close to mine, his blue eyes shiny and intense. "He'll t'ink he can come in and get his revenge, den get out again. But we'll be waiting. Lucy could be the bait."

"We talked about that before. The police are dead against it, aren't you, Bryce?"

"Of course. For obvious reasons. And let me tell you this: Werner Franz's luck has run out. Nobody that violent can stay lucky, and at large, this long. He'll fall, and soon."

We said good-bye and headed back to the farm, arriving there just after lunchtime. We were heartened to see Lucy's old station wagon in the drive, and found her down in her cottage, locked in.

"Dr. Adams! Wow, am I glad to see you! Where have you been? I'm so scared—"

She hobbled over to us, limping, and hugged me. I could feel her tremble.

"What happened to your leg?" I asked.

"Aw . . . tripped on the stairway in the nursing home. I think it's sprained a little. What do you think? You're the doctor . . ."

I felt her ankle, swollen to twice its normal size. Then Laitis and I took her up to the house, limping in between the two of us. In the kitchen I told her a little background information about my companion, who sat smoking Camels across the table from us, grinning at Lucy in that crinkly-eyed way of his, letting the cigarette smoke steam downward out of his nostrils like a dragon. Lucy seemed fascinated. Uh-oh . . .

I wrapped Lucy's ankle, telling her about the death of Peter Becker. She stared wide-eyed at us as we told her what happened. She was still shaking, and looked tired, too.

"That's why I locked myself in," she said, leaning forward and rubbing the bandaged foot. "You weren't here. You know what it feels like to be here all alone, with him out there, sneaking around?"

"Oh yes. I do indeed."

We had a light lunch, after which I removed some frozen sirloin from the freezer to defrost for shish kebab. I was hoping a good dinner would cheer us all up. While Lucy and I straightened up the house, Roantis disappeared upstairs to his room, reappearing with the laundry bag he'd brought with him. This he opened, and withdrew two strange suits. One was a camouflage stalker suit—the kind worn by turkey hunters and jungle fighters. The other was strange indeed. It was a curious-looking cloth cape that consisted of hundreds of burlap strips of different colors and textures fastened to it. It looked like a seamstress's nightmare.

With a flourish, Roantis threw the cape over his head and became a gumdrop-shaped pile of old rags.

"This is a ghillie suit," he said, his voice emerging muffled from behind the folds and drapes of old burlap. It looked like a pile of leaves. "Three-dimensional camouflage. Invented by the English gamekeepers, who call themselves ghillies. It's the best camo ever."

He explained that the burlap strips were fastened to the inner, polyester shell with Velcro, and were infinitely adjustable. He went outside, and we followed him; I was carrying the loaded Streetcleaner for protection. Roantis walked to a clump of bushes and sat down. Even in broad daylight, I couldn't see him to save my ass. Incredible.

Back inside, he removed his rifle from its case and checked the scope, saying that later on, he planned to station himself outside in the various strategic places we'd scouted earlier.

"Now, while I'm out there, glassing the tree line, Doc, you and Lucy will hang around the house, okay? Lucy? How you feel about this?"

She stared dumbstruck. Not too keen on the idea, obviously. I understood; I wasn't exactly jumping up and down in a frenzy of joy, either.

"Let's get the sketches out, Laitis, and go over this thing in detail. Then Lucy and I will decide if we're really going to go through with it. Right, Lucy?"

She nodded, a faraway look in her eyes.

So Roantis sat us down at the table with the drawings of the property and spent forty minutes going over various plans, each with fairly predictable scenarios. All the while, I fidgeted in my chair, and Lucy was sitting vacant-eyed, wondering what the hell she'd gotten herself into. I sympathized entirely. Finally, Roantis sensed our reluctance and flung down the pencil. He got up and headed for the booze cabinet.

"Gottdammit, Doc! You gonna do this t'ing or *not*?"

"I, uh, don't know for sure, Laitis. Sorry."

Fuming, he poured himself a wee dram—half a glass full—and topped it with warm soda. Then he grabbed my Steiner 7 × 50 binoculars and stomped out to the terrace, where he sat with his drink in the afternoon sun, glassing the valley and the tree line with military precision. He knew what he was doing, all right. But did I?

Question, Dr. Adams: *Are you up to it?*

I looked out the window at Roantis, who was plainly irritated at my hesitation. I looked at Lucy, who was obviously terrified for her life. Then I went rambling through my house, stopping before the dining room mirror to look at myself.

Well, Doc? Can you? You talk a good game. You claim you're going to hunt down Werner Franz until he's dead. It's obvious the cops can't do it. And they want no part of this scheme, anyhow. So if you do it, buddy, you do it without their help.

So can you? All the talking and all the bullshit are gone now. It's do or die, literally. So take a good, long look, Doc.

Are you up to it, or not?

God help me. I didn't know.

TWENTY SEVEN

I spent the better part of an hour up in the bedroom, sitting in a chair looking out through the window. The same window I'd pissed out of, hiding from Buddy Franz, the big guy with the big knife.

When I returned downstairs and told Roantis I was ready to follow his plan, whatever the consequences, it was not to uphold some preconceived, manufactured image of myself. It was because, stuck up there alone in that room, I finally realized I had to face this problem, this powerful manifestation of my fear, whether I wanted to or not. It would be difficult putting up with myself afterwards if I didn't. Also, on the more rational side of the argument, I now had the help and expertise of one of the best men alive to see me through it. So the time was now.

So much for me. Poor Lucy Kirkland was another story altogether. At first she agreed to be a part of the plan, trying on the Kevlar bulletproof vest Roantis had brought, and looking keenly down at the drawings and timetables on the kitchen table. But then the doubts set in, plain for both of us to see. She backed off, made a phone call, then returned to the kitchen at about 2:30, saying she wanted to go visit her mother, who had suddenly taken sick.

Roantis and I both knew it was an excuse; it didn't take a genius to see that. It was her way of trying to back out without directly disappointing or angering us. It was now clear that we had to reshape our schemes around a passive, and protected, Lucy Kirkland. Which, I realized, was exactly how it should be. So the two of us huddled in the kitchen thinking up an alternate plan while she went upstairs to do some cleaning. But then she surprised us by coming back down and volunteering for a plan that was slightly less daring but still used her in the role of the only visible person. Then she took off for Pittsfield, saying she'd be back in time to help me with the shish kebab dinner.

"Just get back here while it's still light," cautioned Roantis. "And beep the horn and wait when you get back. I'll come out to get you."

"Let's go over the basics again," said Roantis, sitting down at the table. "The setup?"

"I'm upstairs with the shotgun, going from room to room up there, always keeping her in sight when she's outside. All windows open wide to give me the field of fire."

He nodded, tapping his fingernails on the crude maps he'd drawn.

"Lucy's downstairs," I continued, "going in and out the back door on fake errands, so that he can see her if he's anywhere around. The front of the house, and all downstairs windows, are locked."

"Good. Where am I?"

"You're out in the pasture where you can see everything going on in back, where any action should take place. You're in your ghillie suit, ready to hit him at long range with the rifle, or rush the house to help me out if he manages to sneak through the perimeter unseen."

"Good. I t'ink that's as sane and safe as we're going to get. Don't you?"

"Uh-huh," I said, rubbing my eyes. "As safe and as sane as we can make it. Trouble is, it's just not . . . very."

He clapped his hand on my shoulder and told me to cheer up. I tried, and felt better. Really and truly I did. Until he cautioned about food.

"Better make a real light breakfast tomorrow, Doc. Maybe nothing but coffee. Okay?"

"What's wrong? The tension got your appetite?"

"Naw. Just t'inking about gunshot wounds. You know, a full stomach makes 'em much worse. Better tell Lucy, too. Don't explain why, just tell her. Okay?"

"Sure," I said. Great, Laitis. Just swell.

Roantis set the table, saying he was hungry. He suggested I stay upstairs in the master bedroom, since Lucy was going to sleep in the next room and wouldn't feel safe up there alone. I considered this proposal. While it made a certain amount of sense, I doubted Mary would be keen on the arrangement, assuming she got wind of it. And the thing is, she always gets wind of it. Banking on her not finding out—about practically everything—is like betting the sun will rise in the west.

But, then again, she may not even have to know . . .

The phone rang; Laitis snagged it on the second ring, grunted a greeting, and held up the receiver.

"For you, Doc. Mary."

See what I mean?

"Charlie, what's going on out there? Fill me in."

"Nothing much. We're just getting ready to fix dinner."

"Nothing much? You've got Laitis out there with you and you say nothing much? Where's Lucy? She staying out there, too?"

"Yes."

"Where's she staying?"

"In Joe's room upstairs."

"You mean the room in the big house?"

"Uh-huh."

"Where's Laitis sleeping?"

"On the living room floor, to keep watch and listen."

"Now for the big money: where are *you* sleeping?"

"On the floor with Roantis, on the other side of the room."

"You're goddamn right you are."

Silence.

"Charlie?"

"Hmm?"

"Is there a lot of danger? Be honest."

I answered her as honestly as I could, which was to tell her that if Franz came onto the property, there would be danger. If he didn't, there wouldn't be.

For some strange reason, this failed to satisfy her. Then I heard sobs on the other end.

"What's the matter?"

"Joey told me about what happened to that guy with the dogs. That man Becker—"

She broke off, sobbing again. As for me, I couldn't wait to get my hands around her brother's neck. *If* my hands could reach around it, which was doubtful.

"Joe wasn't supposed to tell—"

"I know; I forced it out of him. Now listen: you're going to come back here to Concord right now, Charlie. Let Roantis handle it himself; that's what he's trained to do."

I told her that was impossible. Without me at the farm, Franz would have no motivation for showing up. This explanation didn't make things any better. She was screaming now, and shouted that if I wasn't coming home, she was really and truly driving out to get me. She hung up. Just great.

"She's bluffing," said Roantis.

"I don't think so."

"Neither do I, now I t'ink of it."

I called Joe and got a busy signal. Tried two more times with the same result. Mary had called him, throwing her plan into motion. What a time to do it, just as we were beginning to close the ring. I called home again. Busy. Again. Same. Then the line was clear. The phone rang. It rang a thousand times. Good Christ, she'd left!

I tried Joe again and got no answer. Either he'd gone out to a bar, or to eat, or was driving his sister out this very minute. Well, I'd learned one thing at least: never enlist the aid of a southern Italian against a family member, especially a sibling. They'll join forces and turn on you, every time. I called Ten Ten Comm Ave and told them to page Joe. Against regs, but they'd see what they could do.

A horn honked outside, and Roantis retrieved Lucy, who came inside looking a shade more relaxed and confident. It was more than I could say for myself.

Considering the episode of my stolen pistol, we thought it best to cook the shish kebabs inside, in the broiler. The meal would have been tasty under normal circumstances, but my appetite was gone. Lucy and Roantis dug in, and I made myself eat more than I wanted, knowing that I had to skip breakfast because of the possibility of food contamination in bullet wounds to the abdomen.

Gee, everything was just peachy. It's amazing what a relaxing holiday in the country will do for you.

After dinner we went over the plans again, mapping out every move on the diagrams Laitis had drawn. We settled Lucy in the upstairs bedroom at 11:30, then moved the living room furniture and rugs and unrolled our sleeping gear, the same as the previous night. Throughout all this, I had been calling Concord every thirty minutes with no result. But finally, after midnight, Joe called from his apartment on Beacon Hill.

"What the hell's this about a page for me, Doc?"

"Where's your sister?"

"At home, last I heard."

"Well, she doesn't answer, and I'm afraid she's coming out here to—"

"Nah. She's at home, sulking and pouting. She told me she wasn't going to answer the phone."

"It's silly, and unsafe, not to answer the phone, dammit. I'm going to wring her neck."

Joe promised he'd drive out to Concord in the morning and straighten things out. Somewhat relieved, I had a small nightcap with Roantis, then turned in, trying to unwind. But I was in a state; Mary was upset and threatening to come out here momentarily, Lucy was willing to help us, but certainly not dependable, and Werner Franz was . . . out there somewhere.

I couldn't sleep and admitted to myself that part of me hoped Mary would show up, even though the danger level was unacceptable. I missed her terribly. What was worse, I knew I'd feel safer, more complete with her around, but hadn't told her so. Maybe that was part of what had her so upset. Did she think I didn't miss her? Oh, God; I wanted to tell her desperately that I missed her and loved her. And what about tomorrow? What if something happened to me, and I could never tell her? I crept out of bed and dialed home. No answer.

I went back to my bedroll. Roantis was breathing heavily, asleep. He hadn't heard me get up, then. Great; Franz could climb in the big double window between us in the dead of night. Chop, chop, two dead guys. Then go upstairs and do God-knows-what to poor Lucy. I lay there staring at the beamed ceiling that Mary and I had so painstakingly restored in the spring. Staring, staring, staring . . .

But sleep must have come, because sometime in the middle of the night, I was awakened by a faint sound from the front stairway. With my head nestled in the corner of the room, my body projecting at an angle between the two walls, I could hear like Superman. I looked at the hump of bedding across the room that was Roantis. He was apparently asleep. By God, it was a good thing I wasn't. Franz could practically leap through that open window and—

Out of the side of my eyes I saw a dim figure on the stairs. When I stared straight at it, it disappeared. I let my gaze wander in the darkness. Sure enough, somebody was standing on the main stairway. It was on the small side, so it was not Buddy Franz. The figure came down, walking straight upright and in utter silence. A ghost? My heart was going lickety-split. I wanted to jump up and wake Roantis, but instead pretended to remain asleep, keeping my eyes open in the near darkness. As the figure drew near I recognized Lucy by her robe and her gait. She approached Roantis, then knelt down over him. I realized I was halfway out of my bedroll, ready to spring across the room instantly. What was she going to do to him?

Roantis stirred, and there was a murmur of voices. I saw Lucy stand up, and her robe dropped off. I was out of my bedroll in a flash, the flat of my palm held up high.

Whack!

Lucy yelped in pain, grabbing her posterior. I saw Roantis roll to his feet in a blur of motion.

"Lucy, get upstairs where you belong," I said.

"Dr. Adams, I was just—"

"I know what you were doing. *Up! Now!*"

She gathered up her robe and marched upstairs, crestfallen.

"Killjoy," said Roantis, sitting down on the floor and fishing for his Camels.

"That's the last thing we need, Laitis—you two shacking up in here while Franz is on the prowl. And by the way, you were dead asleep a few minutes ago."

"So?"

"So? He could have jumped right in here."

He shook his head, dragging deep on the cigarette that glowed bright as he sucked on it. "Nah. I'll wake fast if he tries that. Trust me."

"Tell me how you can wake up when you just slept through Lucy's coming downstairs. I'd be grateful if you could explain that to me."

He shrugged. I could see his shoulders move in the dark. "It's just a . . . sense I've developed over many years, Doc. A . . . feeling. Don't worry; go to sleep. I'll stay up awhile and have a smoke or two."

"Don't go upstairs. I mean it."

"If I go up there and see her, I won't tell Mary about you and Daisy down in Carolina."

"Won't work, Laitis. You won't tell her, anyway. I know you better."

"You don't t'ink so, eh?"

"Nope. I don't t'ink so. I do not. Now let me sleep."

I rolled into a fetal position, squinting my eyes almost shut, but not quite. I was going to watch him, that ferret in human shape, to see what he'd do. Well, he just sat there and smoked, then lay down and went back to sleep. I didn't for an instant believe his threat to tell Mary about Daisy and me in the trailer down in Robbinsville, North Carolina. Although, as God is my witness, nothing happened that night. Cross my heart and hope to die.

—and hope to die . . .

Considering recent events, and what was perhaps to unfold soon, I didn't like the sound of those words. And I missed Mary. Missed her terribly, in every conceivable way. As I drifted off I couldn't help but wonder what on earth was going through Lucy Kirkland's mind.

TWENTY-EIGHT

Two more calls to Concord, and no answer from Mary. I tried to keep her out of my mind and stick to the business at hand, but it was tough.

After hot coffee and a slice of dry toast, Lucy put on the bulletproof vest and then a sweatshirt to hide it. Having left before daybreak, Roantis was already "gone to earth" in the fields, toting the ghillie suit and assault rifle to his hideout in the back pasture. I kept mentally reviewing our hand and arm signals: yanking a fist down twice meant Franz had been sighted. Pointing indicated the direction he was in, and each wave of the hand stood for ten meters. A "come on" wave meant Franz was heading our way. A tug on the shirt collar meant danger. Finally, the one I hoped never to see: the open hand over the face. This dreaded sign meant that danger was close at hand. It also meant ambush, go to earth . . .

"How come we don't get more to eat?" Lucy said, smoothing the sweater down around her hips. "How do I look, anyway?"

"You look fine, Lucy. The light breakfast is so we'll stay awake."

"Bullshit. The light breakfast is so bullet wounds will treat us better; I saw it in a movie."

The phone rang. It was Bryce Stevens, checking in. I told him we were fine, and that not much was happening.

"Jack Bensen just called me; he says he left your place after his all-night stakeout about an hour ago and everything's fine there. That right? You don't want us back?"

"Not for a while."

"Hey, guess who I saw last evening after you guys left? Roweena what's-her-name."

"Roweena? You mean Rowanda Williams?"

"Yeah. Driving in that fancy blue car of hers."

"Really? Where?"

"Up near where we were yesterday."

"Was Mike with her?"

"No. I thought she'd been out seeing you."

"Well, she wasn't. But she's got family and friends in upstate New York. Maybe that's where—"

"Listen: why I'm calling, is the Kirkland girl there with you?"

"Yes. You want to talk to her?"

He said he did, to see personally if she were staying there of her own accord. I understood the legal reasons for this request, and put her on the line. They chatted for less than a minute, then Lucy got off the line and handed me the phone.

"She says she's sticking it out with you and Roantis."

"Yep. Will you be up in Pittsfield later if I want to reach you?"

He said he would, and furthermore, that a phone call to the police would bring a cruiser screaming into the farm in an instant. I hung up and went over to give Lucy her last-minute instructions.

"When you go out, don't go farther from the house than that tree, remember?"

She nodded her head.

"And stay on this side of the barn. Stay right around in back where I can see you at all—"

"I know, I know." She looked calm to me. I hadn't mentioned last night's incident to her. I grabbed the binoculars and swept the far field until I picked up Roantis, right where he said he'd be: in the shade of a big maple on a gentle rise about a hundred yards from the house. Even through the binoculars he was all but invisible, appearing exactly like a small, gumdrop-shaped patch of brush. I was convinced no casual eye could spot him. From his vantage point, he could see the rear of the barn and the other outbuildings, but still had a clear view of us.

"Are we ready, then?" she asked, and I nodded and went upstairs, taking Roantis's scattergun with me.

As Lucy sallied forth from the back of the house every twenty minutes or so, I kept my eyes on and beyond her, the shotgun held at port arms across my chest. As she went from one end of the property to the other, a pair of grass clippers in her hand, I went from bedroom to bedroom, staying directly above and behind her, watching.

We did this from 8:15 until noon, when she came inside and up the stairs, flopping down on my bed with a weary sigh.

"I'm hungry, Dr. Adams. Can't we eat?"

"Sure. Why not?"

We went down to the kitchen and I made coffee and heated up some soup. Lucy made herself a big PB&J and wolfed it down. Peanut butter and jelly sandwich. Spare me. If there's a nadir in cuisine, an absolute zero in the culinary ledger, the PB&J has to take the prize. She sat there chewing, looking like a fourteen-year-old.

"Is Mr. Roantis married?" she asked, as if simply to pass the time. I replied that he was, in a manner of speaking, and let it go at that. "Is he coming back inside soon?"

"Nope. The plan calls for us to keep doing this until nightfall. Are you up to it?"

She shook her head, and asked to lie down for a few minutes. While she went upstairs to her room, I glassed the far hillside again. Roantis had moved; now he was in his fallback position in a hollow near the tree line. The moving sun had robbed him of his shadow. I dialed Stevens's number up in Pittsfield.

"So far, nothing. We'd planned to keep this up for several days, Bryce, but frankly, I doubt if we're up to it. I really don't like the idea of Lucy out there, even though we've got her covered from front and back."

"Way he's been operating, Doc, I doubt he'll come. You could probably wait till hell freezes over and he won't show. Then when your guard is down—"

"Yeah. Well, just letting you know."

Lucy came back downstairs at 1:30, ready to give it another try.

"But if it doesn't work, can we just forget it?" she asked, going out the kitchen door.

"We can forget it now, if you'd rather. I don't want to put you under any pressure, Lucy."

"I don't mind. Mainly, I don't worry because I don't think Buddy's anywhere near here right now. I bet he's left the state, even."

So I waited up in the bedrooms, scanning the grounds below while Lucy waited in the kitchen and outside near the house. Occasionally she would go over to the pool, the outer limits of her boundary, and run the skimmer over the surface, or check the thermometer. I kept my eyes peeled, with and without the glasses. Nothing. The sun was bright and cheerful; the birdies sang; the squirrels jumped and chatted; big white puffy clouds rolled by overhead; the cows mooed in the pasture. I felt like a jerk holding the twelve gauge and watching this girl trotting around the lawn below me.

Then, right around five o'clock, things got real quiet.

▼ ▼ ▼

I don't know if it's what usually happens in late afternoon or not. I do know that along toward dusk, the birds pick up, with clucking robins that hop on lawns, and jays and crows that call each other. But now, at the first lowering of light, at the lengthening gray shadows that crept, like lazy lizards, from the trees and fence posts and spread themselves over the meadow, it grew silent. The crickets that had made a racket all day were quiet. There wasn't the first breath of a breeze; all the trees were still.

Where was Roantis? I searched and searched the fields for him. Was that him there, beneath the maple again? Or just a bush? How about that hollow by the tree line? No; couldn't see a thing down there in the shadows. Was he in the woods? No, that wasn't part of the plan.

Was he in trouble? Had Franz, boonie stalker that he was, gotten the drop on Laitis and killed him? Oh boy . . .

I suddenly felt very alone. I peered out the bedroom. Lucy wasn't there, so she was inside. I waited twenty minutes for her to appear below me. No Lucy. I walked from room to room, looking over the terrace, the walk to the pool, the side of Joe's cottage, the other side of the back lawn. No Lucy.

I went downstairs, calling her name softly. Went into the kitchen to check for her. Nobody there. I called again, louder now. No answer. Then I went into the living room. I was astonished to see the front door open. Wide open.

I ran up and kicked it shut, then threw the bolt.

"Lucy!" I shouted. "Lucy!"

I went back into the kitchen and looked out the backdoor. I turned and saw her purse sitting on the table, just where she'd left it. Where had she gone? What had happened to her? Had Franz sneaked in and taken her? I looked out at the back field again, but couldn't see much because I was too low. I went up the backstairs two at a time, rushed into the master bedroom, and looked outside. I saw nothing. Roantis was nowhere to be seen. Had Lucy panicked and gone away in her car? I started down the front stairs, and was halfway down them, when I heard shots in the distance. Three shots, coming in rapid succession. That was the danger signal that Roantis and I had agreed upon: the way to warn the other if danger was seen.

I ran back upstairs and grabbed the binoculars, sweeping the big lenses back and forth. There he was, plain as day now. But why had he shown himself? Why was he standing up in the middle of the goddamn field, for crissakes? Then I saw him throw off the ghillie suit, jumping up and down now, waving his arms. Oh Christ—

I leaned out the window and waved back at him. I knew he saw me then. And then I saw what I didn't want to see: Laitis jerking down his raised fist, just like a trainman blowing the whistle. Once, twice. He'd seen Franz. But where? Then he pointed. I couldn't see where he was pointing, dammit. And what about Lucy? Where was Lucy? Was she—

Wait. I raised the binoculars. Saw Roantis pointing again. He was pointing at me. At me? Why at me? Then his hand went up to his face, spread-out fingers covering his face. Ambush. Watch out. Then he was running toward me, carrying his rifle. I heard sounds downstairs now, and knew it wasn't Lucy.

Franz was inside the house.

TWENTY-NINE

t was a second or two before I could move. Then I swung around fast away from the open window and was at the door in two steps. I shut it hard and threw the bolt. Heavy feet were coming up the stairs. Standing next to the door, with my ears cocked toward the hallway outside, I flicked off the shotgun's safety and waited. My pulse was pounding in my head, neck, and chest. I realized I was doing a slow pant, and the tips of my fingers felt as if electric shocks were going through them. I crept closer to the door. No sound came from the hallway. Where was he? I'd heard him coming up the steps. Then silence. I knew where he was; he was waiting just outside the door, waiting for me to open it.

No way was I going to. I couldn't handle the twelve gauge

with one hand, and I needed one to open the door. Franz was right there, waiting with his knife and my pistol . . .

I went back to the window fast and peeked out. No Roantis. He was probably closing in on the house now, coming at Franz from outside. We had him trapped. I went back to the door and listened again. Nothing. I thought of looking out through the keyhole. I lowered my head and squinted.

The second my head went down there was an explosion on the other side of the door. I went down on one knee. Above me, right where my head had been seconds earlier, was a hole in the wooden door. Fresh splinters sticking out. I could smell the old fractured wood, and the cordite, too.

Running feet on the other side of the door now. Feet running away. I looked through the keyhole, but all I could see was part of the vacant hallway. I unbolted the door, flung it open, and jumped back. The hall was empty.

"Doc!"

"Up here, Laitis. Be careful!"

I heard feet on the stairs again. Friendly, I hoped. I went into the hall and edged around the corner of the stairwell. Halfway up the stairs, Roantis made a snapping motion, bringing the rifle up. I ducked back behind the wall, yelling at him to watch what the fuck he was doing, and stared straight ahead at the open bedroom door ahead of me.

Did I hear a noise in there?

I edged along the hall again, watching Laitis motionless on the stairs out of the corner of my eye. I held the Streetcleaner tucked under my arm, about eight inches below my eyes, keeping the muzzle pointing dead ahead, just the way Laitis showed me. I would let it go at the slightest sound. Never mind that Franz now had my pistol. Nothing beats a twelve gauge at close range. Nothing; not even a bazooka. I stood right outside the door to the far bedroom, hearing Roantis coming up behind me. Slowly, slowly, I leaned into the room. Empty. Then I looked at the open window.

I saw a hand there. It extended over the windowsill, gripping

it so the monstrous knuckles—the size of golf balls—were bluish white. Franz had climbed out the window and was now
hanging there.

The gun was on target. I felt the thump of recoil against my
shoulder, and a lot of noise and light, too. Deaf and blind for
a second or two following the shot, I looked up to see the hand
gone. Most of the windowsill was, too. Roantis and I ran to the
window and looked out in time to see a tall figure disappear
around the side of the house. We reached the far window as he
rounded the next corner into the front yard. I followed Laitis
as he rushed downstairs and tried to open the front door. But
I had double-bolted it, and when we finally got outside, it was
too late. Franz was gone. Roantis, a professional at bad language, outdid himself.

We spent the next ten minutes trying to pick up Franz's trail,
all the while calling for Lucy at the top of our lungs. Soon we
both knew that Franz was long gone, wounded or not. We
finally found Lucy tucked up in a fetal position inside the well's
pump house. We heard the whimpering as we walked past. I
opened the little door and there she was, snuggled up, clutching
herself in the tiny shed in the dark, crying.

"Is he gone? Is he . . . g-g-gone?"

I picked her up and carried her inside. Roantis walked beside
us in silence, disgust written all over his craggy features.

We sat Lucy down and gave her a booze, then a cup of coffee.
Between her ragged breathing and hysterical sighs, what we
pried out of her was this: she was doing her part in the decoy
game when she saw Franz sneaking up on the house from the
side of Joe's cottage. And he saw her, or at least she thought so,
which was enough to send her scurrying around the house and
in the backdoor, which she locked behind her. Then, hearing
the shots, which she thought was Franz shooting at her, she
panicked and fled the house in the only possible way: by opening the front door and running out in blind fear to the first
hiding place she could find, which was the well house. There
she'd stayed until we found her.

Looking at her crying at the kitchen table, I suddenly felt

exhausted. Clearly, this plan wasn't going to work. Besides getting me almost wasted, we'd almost gotten Lucy killed as well. No good.

"Well, shit," growled Roantis, pouring himself a generous portion of malt. "Now what?"

"I don't know," I admitted. "But what we *don't* do is, we don't have Lucy running around outside anymore. That's for damn sure. I don't know what plan we'll come up with tomorrow, but it won't be more of the same."

We found no blood in the upstairs bedroom near the window. This was disappointing, because although it was possible that Franz was hit in the hand, possibly severely, it sure didn't look like it.

It was now getting dark. I called home twice more, with no results. Joe wasn't home either. The three of us sat around the kitchen wondering if and when Buddy would come back. We all agreed it wasn't likely that he'd appear anytime soon, so I decided that while it was still light, I'd leave Roantis and Lucy at the farm and go out to buy groceries for dinner. This wasn't the most prudent thing to do, but Laitis and I agreed that a good feed would cheer us up, whatever the possibility of bullet wounds. Besides, going about our business was important for morale; we couldn't let Franz hold us prisoners in our own dwelling.

I thought about calling Bryce Stevens and telling him what had happened. Roantis insisted we keep quiet.

"Hell, Doc, he'll show up with three or four cruisers with their lights and sirens going. Franz will take off for the next county right away, and we'll never get him. We're close now. Real close; let's not blow it."

"What about Lucy?"

"Hell, she can go or stay, whatever she wants. But if she's going, she better go now."

Lucy said she was going to stick it out just as long as she didn't have to go outside again. With that settled, I took the car keys and started for the door. Roantis said he'd see me to the car, and back inside again when I returned.

"Don't let her out of your sight for a second," I told him as I left. While I was at the supermarket on the outskirts of Pittsfield, I took out my little pocket secretary and phoned Jerry Rapp, the manager of the bowling alley in Lenox, and talked to him a few minutes about the various biker clubs in the western part of the state. Some loose piece of the puzzle kept rattling around in my head and I couldn't place it. In fact, I didn't even know what the piece was, just that there was something out of joint. Luckily, I found Rapp at home at the number he'd given me earlier, and we chatted about this and that for maybe ten minutes. It didn't help; the unidentified piece of the puzzle was still missing. I called Concord again. Same thing. Damn! Why now, of all times, was she doing this to me? Why?

I swung into the farm's driveway at 7:30 with two big sacks of groceries on the seat next to me. Then I stopped fast and gave a little gasp. There, parked next to Roantis's Peugeot, was Mary's Audi.

I was elated and relieved. I sighed, and felt it catch in my throat. I was also pissed off and afraid I was going to throttle her at the first opportunity. I was supposed to honk my horn and wait for Laitis to come out with the shotgun. I did not do this. I grabbed the shopping bags, slammed the car door with my foot, and stormed into the house. Mary was in the front hall. She turned to face me, and the color drained from her face.

"Don't say anything, Charlie!" she cried when she saw me coming at her. "Don't say—*Charlie!*"

She ran behind Roantis, hiding, holding him by his arms and peeking out over his shoulder. I had dropped the grocery bags on the floor somewhere behind me.

"Don't you ever, ever not answer the phone again," an ugly voice growled. I suppose it was mine. I wasn't in a good mood.

"No, Charlie! If you come one step closer, Laitis will kill you. Won't you, Laitis?"

"I will?" he said. He appeared confused. It was the first time I ever saw him confused.

"Help me, Laitis. Help me!" she wailed. But he just stood there. Then she called him a wimp. Then Lucy joined in, calling me a bully, even though I hadn't done a thing except stomp around. Next we were all yelling at one another. Soon it degenerated into the usual fray: the men against the women. They called the two of us animals. Bloodthirsty thugs. Violent hoodlums, et cetera. Roantis then announced if they didn't shut up, he would slap the shit out of both of them.

There, now. Wasn't that a reasoned, mature, and chivalrous thing to say? A comment that also forever laid to rest any claims the women made about our animalistic and violent natures.

Somewhere in the middle of this nasty scene I sagged onto the couch and put my head down in my hands. I was going to lose it. Then I felt warm hands on my back, and the murmur of apologies. Mary and I hugged while Lucy picked up the spilled groceries and Laitis secured all the doors and windows. I kissed Mary, and she kissed me back. Felt like a million bucks. I was very glad she was with me. But I was afraid for her, too, and she knew it.

I grilled the ribs on the terrace in the fading daylight. The women were in the kitchen, cooking vegetables and watching out the window. Roantis sat outside with me, sipping a glass of whiskey. His Streetcleaner was within instant reach. He kept his eyes moving, sweeping the tree line constantly. I took the meat inside and we ate heartily, with the talk becoming almost cheerful. But after dinner we filled Mary in on what had happened just before she arrived. Lucy even took her upstairs and showed her where I'd blown away the window frame.

"He was in this house?" exclaimed Mary, swaying on her feet. "In this very *house*?"

We tried to think of new strategies, ones that would be both effective and safe. Trouble was, any plan that was truly safe wasn't effective. We had to face the fact that stopping Buddy Franz would involve serious risk. We all agreed that the women would not share in this risk. Mary also insisted that I shouldn't, either. Roantis, she assured everyone, was certainly capable of assuming the risk since he was a pro. Laitis looked at her, not saying a thing. I doubted if this improved their friendship, which has never been on firm ground to begin with.

After the meal Laitis cleared his throat, lighted a Camel, and said: "What we should do now is put the women in Mary's car, escort them in my car to the main highway, and have them drive back to Concord."

"I agree," I said.

Mary flatly answered that no way was she leaving, and that we were full of shit if we thought we could make her leave her own house.

Then Lucy chimed in, saying she wasn't leaving either. She wanted to see her brother's murderer put away, and that now that we were close, we didn't have the right to kick her out, especially after what we'd put her through.

So there we were again, the men against the women.

We had a little kangaroo court then and hashed out our differences as best we could. It was finally agreed that the women would stay, provided they remained inside at all times. In this role they could keep watch from the house, being extra eyes for Roantis, who would be stalking the fields and woods. And I would accompany Laitis on some of these forays, provided I wore the Kevlar vest that Lucy no longer needed, and the camo stalker suit to keep me hidden. And also provided that we wouldn't be gone long. If we failed to return to the farmhouse within two hours, Mary would call Stevens and request every cop and cruiser in the western part of the state. If Laitis went out solo, he could stay overnight if he wished. But with me in tow, we had a deadline.

The sleeping arrangements were changed. Mary and I were upstairs in the master bedroom. Lucy was next door, and Laitis was alone downstairs. As Mary was heading up to bed, I drew him aside for a second and warned him about any sexual romp with Lucy.

I got into bed just before eleven. Mary and I snuggled and talked for a while, and she explained her reasons for coming out to the farm. She had felt totally left out, and was worried and angry. I told her I understood, and she then managed to extract a promise from me that if nothing constructive happened the next day, the two of us would pack up, head for the Cape, and "veg out" for a week, no matter what happened out here.

Then she fell asleep, and I lay there a long time thinking about Buddy Franz and what made him tick. Crazy as he seemed, there had to be patterns to his behavior. I kept trying to move those walnut shells around in my brain, guessing where that pea was. But I got nowhere. Maybe I'd wake up with the solution in my mind. Just as I was getting those crazy-quilt, disjointed thoughts that precede sleep, I heard Lucy's footsteps in the hall, heading downstairs.

THIRTY

Mary nudged me awake at 6:20.

"Charlie? You had this weird look on your face—"

"I was dreaming," I said. "I had the strangest dream."

"What does it mean, Charlie?"

"It means you've got to be careful today."

I went downstairs to see Roantis already pouring coffee. Lucy was asleep in the corner of the living room. He handed me the Kevlar vest, which I put on over my undershirt, then donned the camo stalker suit he handed me. He was wearing his surrealistic ghillie suit. Mary came down, Lucy woke up, and we had toast and coffee.

"You're not saying much, Charlie."

"No."

The dream kept running through my head, over and over

again. I saw people moving around in it. People on motorcycles. People on blankets near a campfire, drinking and smoking and partying. People sneaking through the woods. People being put into shallow graves, the earth dumped over them and tramped down with big feet. The dream revealed to me exactly how Franz had killed those kids in the hollow. Because the dream, devoid of rational thought and free of constricting logic, had allowed the stray pieces to settle into place. Part of the answer had come during our visit to Mitchell Sams, the farmer across the line in New York who'd had all the trouble with the bikers. Then there was the offhand comment Jerry Rapp made earlier that seemed so insignificant at the time. And now that missing piece, the piece of unknown dimension I'd been searching for, had finally appeared. It was in place now, along with all the others; the puzzle was complete.

According to plan, Lucy would remain downstairs, while Mary would station herself in the bedroom where I had been earlier. Both could keep watch over the windows, ready to call the state police if they saw Franz coming. We'd taken every precaution, but I still felt uneasy with my wife in the house. As an afterthought, I talked Roantis out of his .45 before I walked Mary upstairs. She knows how to use a pistol; I taught her myself. I handed her the piece, telling her how Lucy had panicked the day before, fleeing the house and leaving the front door wide open.

"Nothing like that should happen again," I assured her. "But just in case, lock the door and stay in here. Don't let anyone come in except me. If you hear anything on the stairs, squat down near the far wall, not in front of the doorway. Shoot anything that tries to enter."

She nodded grimly. I kissed her, and said I'd return shortly. On the verge of tears, she made me promise. I did. And I meant it, too. As I went down the steps I heard the click of the lock behind me.

A little before seven Roantis and I left the house, telling Lucy to lock up securely and wait until we returned. I told her Mary was upstairs, armed, in the bedroom, and that from where she was, she had no view of the front side of the house.

"So keep your eyes mostly on the front yard, okay, Lucy?"

She promised she would, and Roantis and I slipped outside, headed for the back pasture. We carried our weapons at the ready, walking together, each man watching his side most carefully. We stuck to the woods, walking near the tree line so we could see the fields. Nothing. I put my hand on Laitis's shoulder, and we both knelt down in the scrub.

"I'm going back to the house for a few minutes."

"Why, Doc? You afraid for Mary?"

"Yes," I lied. "I just want to keep watch there a few minutes. If Franz is watching, he saw us leave. Maybe he'll sneak back there."

"That's not the plan—"

"Just wait here. I'll come back and meet you within the hour. You hear gunshots, come running."

He nodded, sitting down at the edge of the forest. He drew on the hood of the ghillie suit and disappeared, blending with uncanny fashion into the foliage.

"There's something you're not telling me," he grunted. "You and Mary make a deal?"

"Give me an hour; if I'm not back here then, go stay with the women."

I made my way back to the farmhouse through the trees, moving as fast as I could. Finally I reached a spot I had chosen on our way out to the fields: a little copse of spruce trees thirty yards from the house. I settled down in there, invisible, and waited. I looked at my watch: 7:09. At 7:21, I saw Lucy come around the front side of the house, moving quickly and without a sound, glancing nervously behind her as she went. I watched until she was almost out of sight down the driveway before I followed.

She cut into the woods halfway down the long driveway. I was already in the trees far behind her, and kept well out of sight as I followed. She was still limping slightly from her sprained ankle. Only now I knew she didn't sprain it visiting her mother. Keeping sight of her was easy; she had on white tennis shorts and a bright yellow blouse. In my camo stalker suit, I was practically invisible. And I had a hunch that once she was away from the house, she wouldn't watch her back trail. I followed her another half mile through the thick woods.

It was unfolding just the way I thought it would. The dream told me so. In the back of my mind, I saw the dream again. The events of fourteen months ago happening in my mind, right as I woke up that morning, the way I knew it could finally click together, every piece in place:

. . . the three Harleys pulling off the highway and up into the clearing in the woods . . . Billy Kirkland, John Vales, and Mike Church, all out for the Fourth of July run. On the back of Billy's bike sits Melissa Hendricks . . .

Stalking the running girl from tree to tree, I soon realized that there was only one place Lucy Kirkland could be heading for.

. . . on the second bike, ridden by Mike Church, sits another girl, the one whose skeleton we could not identify. The bikes roll and lurch along the soft forest floor toward the river, and the camping place . . .

Lucy slowed her pace now, approaching the clearing carefully. She walked up behind a bush and hid behind it. I saw her begin to turn around, and I dodged behind a tree quick as a wink. I leaned against the trunk and was surprised to find myself panting. Was it the exertion? No; it was the excitement, the adrenaline rush.

. . . Vales brings up the rear on his Harley. There is no girl, no mamma, doubling up on his bike. Or is there? If there are three bikes, why not three girl riders? Could there have been a third mamma on that run, a girl who never became a murder victim in a shallow grave?

As Lucy crept toward the clearing I gained steadily on her, trying to get well within range, the shotgun primed, the safety off . . . remembering finally what it was that Jerry Rapp had told me earlier . . . something rattling around in my brain that wouldn't go away . . . something about Billy Kirkland . . . how he'd bullied his little sister Lucy. How he'd treated her like shit—

. . . later on, drunk on booze and crazed with drugs, does Billy

Kirkland grab that third girl, and force her to have sex with the other men? Perhaps even take her for himself, against her will and to her utter humiliation? Does Billy Kirkland, in his infantile bravado and urgent need to become a biker stud, pass around his little sister Lucy to curry favor with the other bikers? Would he do that? Would the weak-eyed punk I saw in the color snapshot really do that to his own sister?

Lucy was in the clearing now, and she suddenly stopped stock-still, staring at the ground in front of her. I hurried through the brush as silently as I could.

And if he did, what would Lucy think and feel afterwards? Lying sore and bruised in the flickering light of the dying fire . . . tear-blinded, trying to hide her face in her arms? What would she be thinking then?

When I finally got close enough, and parted the leaves in front of my face, I saw Lucy kneeling on the ground over the hunched-up figure of Buddy Franz. She was hugging him, crying. And then I knew it was all true. It had happened, right here, fourteen months ago, just the way it had unfolded in my mind's eye as I woke up.

Afterwards, when the partying and the sex are finished, and the ragtag party has fallen asleep drunk on the ground, another bike comes through the trees, stopping maybe fifty yards short of the clearing, its tall rider dismounting and walking silently to where the crude camp is set . . . sneaking up to the prone figures on the ground. He comes into the clearing in silence, with long, angry strides. Then one of the figures on the ground stirs, gets to her feet, and comes over to him . . .

I studied Franz as well as I could. He looked beat up and tired. His jeans had bloodstains on the left leg, no doubt where Bashful had torn into him. There was more dried blood higher up on the leg, perhaps residue from the bullet wound inflicted by Harry Phelps. His face bore the exhausted, hunted look of the escaped felon. Lucy leaned over, talking intently into his ear. But I felt that Franz already knew the urgent message: that there was a trap waiting for him at the Adams place, a trap which he had barely escaped the previous evening, and they would both have to go away now and get help, and forget revenge. Did my shotgun blast connect? I didn't think so; I could see no more wounds on him. But he was out of steam, that was for sure.

I leveled the shotgun, aiming at the chest of the prone figure. At thirty yards the double-ought buckshot, whose pellets were lead balls the size of garden peas, would rip him apart. But at that range, would some pellets also strike Lucy? Just one or two of them would kill her, too. And could I really kill a person in cold blood who wasn't threatening me? True, he had almost killed me the day before. But the idea of blasting him from an ambush did not appeal. Shoot him in the legs and cripple him? No.

Then I saw the pistol, my Browning, stuck in his belt. If I came at them now brandishing the gun, he could grab Lucy and threaten to kill her, shooting at me while using her for a human shield. No good. I sat and watched. Lucy and Franz embraced. Kissed. Was I really seeing this?

And then, suddenly, they were on their feet and walking into the woods. I brought the gun up again, ready to take Franz at the knees, but Lucy was walking behind him, right in the way. Just before I left my cover to follow them, Lucy reappeared in the clearing, alone. She brushed off her clothes, wiped her eyes, and began to retrace her steps back in my direction. I ducked way down and stayed hidden until she passed me, then followed her again. As soon as she got near the house, I circled around the other way and went back to join Roantis.

THIRTY-ONE

told him everything. At first he didn't believe me. But then, as I explained detail after detail, and how they all fit into place, he knew I was right.

"The *gun*, Doc. I kept wondering how anyone would have the balls to come sneaking up to take your pistol right from under our noses."

"He didn't take it; Lucy did. She never went to visit her mother in the nursing home; she stayed around here, and watched and waited until she could run up and take the pistol back to Franz. If we'd caught her in the act, she could simply tell us she'd come back early."

"So she's the reason Franz has been able to stay a jump ahead of the cops."

"Yeah. Staying with us, she overheard everything Joe and

Bryce were planning. Everything except the trap at the fair-grounds, which Bryce managed to keep secret until we were all at the auction. Lucy couldn't warn Franz then; it was too late. So when I finally pegged him in the horse barn and drew her attention to his hat in the window, she jumped and shouted. I thought then it was hate that made her do it, but she was really trying to warn him of the trap and give him time to get away. And speaking of that auction, I'm sure now it was Lucy who gave Franz Harry Phelps's name and address, so he could go steal his bike back. I bet she told him about Pete Becker, too, and that I had one of his dogs—the dog that bit him. That led to his killing Becker for revenge."

"I wish you'd shot Franz, Doc. Having Lucy as an accomplice explains a lot about the guy, you know? Now we know he's not Superman. But still, he's a tough one. You shoulda nailed him."

"Well, I didn't. So now we'll have to get Lucy to tell us all, including where Franz is right now."

"I know how to do that."

"Wait. Let's go back first and pretend we struck out. See what happens. I don't want you to hurt her, Laitis. You do, and the cops will have our ass."

"I may have to. That's the way it is."

"No."

"I may have to make her think I'm going to hurt her."

We walked back to the house together as if coming in after a fruitless search. We said nothing to Lucy as she let us in the kitchen door. She didn't suspect a thing. And, except for a tense, strained expression which she could not hide, she seemed remarkably calm and together. That figured; a person who has helped commit mass murder would be cool under pressure.

"Have a cup of coffee with me, Lucy," said Laitis.

"No, thanks; I don't want any now."

"Oh, yes you do," he said in a low voice, taking two mugs off the counter, turning and winking in my direction. I went upstairs and rapped on the bedroom door, identifying myself. The door unlocked and Mary let me in. I told her what had happened. She sat on the edge of the bed, openmouthed in disbelief.

"So what happens now?" she asked.

"We get Lucy to tell us where Franz is. Then we go get him."

"No!"

"Shhhhh!"

"No, you don't! We find out where he is and call the police. You are so stupid sometimes, Charlie. I just can't believe it."

"It might be better if you stayed up here while Laitis talks to her."

"Talks to her? What's he going to do, make her talk?"

"Wouldn't surprise me. When the chips are down, he grants no quarter. With Roantis, it's go for the jugular and bite and slice until your opponent is neutralized. Period. No pity, no remorse."

"That's awful!"

"It's awful; it's nasty; it's uncouth. It's also why he's the best there is, and still around."

Mary said she still couldn't believe it. Lucy had been so helpful . . . and grateful. I took her over to the door and showed her the bullet hole Franz had put there trying to kill me. I explained how Lucy had left the house by the front door, leaving it open so Franz could come running upstairs for me with my own gun, the gun she had taken.

"Don't be rough with her, Charlie. Maybe Franz forced her to do it. Maybe he bullied her."

"No. She could have told us and gotten help. The two of them were in on it together. Everything."

Mary said she was going to call Joe and tell him. I saw no harm in that, and took the automatic from the bed table and returned downstairs. Roantis had Lucy in a chair against the wall. As soon as she looked up and saw me she put her mug down quickly and looked at the door; she knew. I guess my face didn't hide it. I nodded at Laitis, who leaned forward over her and said:

"You and Franz planned the whole thing. Doc just saw you together. Where is he now?"

"What? You're crazy!" she said, standing up, crossing her arms over her chest. "He killed my brother. My own brother!

That son of a bitch killed my own brother!"

"Come on, Lucy," I said. "Let's not screw around, okay? I should have been a little suspicious when you were so eager to live out here alone."

"He saw you with him," said Roantis. His voice was flat, low, and full of menace. Lucy's frightened eyes darted over to him quickly. I looked at her hands. She was wringing them, as if making pizza dough.

"Look, Lucy, I can put together almost everything. Want to hear it? You and Franz killed those people down in the hollow. You killed Billy and his friends because of what he did to you. Didn't you?"

"No! I didn't do anything," she said. "I was out of town then; you can ask my friends."

"Franz wanted Billy and Melissa dead because Billy *did* take Melissa away from him, and because Melissa ratted on him to the Stompers, and they beat the shit out of him. You told me that yourself, Lucy. Remember? So you both benefited. I'm thinking that Franz put the Worthington boy in there first, maybe a day or so earlier than the others. Isn't that right?"

She walked toward the wall, snapping around, facing us, breathing hard, her hands balled into little pale fists.

"Your beloved brother Billy and his friends fell asleep drunk on a grave they didn't know was there . . . a grave they were soon to share with Bill Worthington, a tall kid who resembled Werner Franz. Only you overlooked one little detail, didn't you? After it was all over and they were in the ground—complete with some dead animals to throw the police off the track—you had the bikes to deal with. What to do with those bikes, eh, Lucy? You'd never thought of that. You tried to bury one of them, but it was much harder than burying a body, wasn't it? A bike doesn't crumple up and bend the way a body does, and it's very big, right, Lucy?"

She stared at me.

"So you knew burying them all would take way too long. Besides, you wanted to keep the bikes if you could. So you decided to hide them, and maybe come back for them a year or two after the bodies were discovered, when everybody had all but forgotten the murders and wouldn't make the connection. You had to hide those bikes fast, and get away. You scouted around until you came to this place. Nobody home. Deserted for years, and a nice big barn full of junk. I bet even with both of you working together, it took you a long time. Anything you want to say?"

She shook her head, a frown on her face. The frown was real.

"The plan was good. The bikes never would've been found if we hadn't bought this place. You were planning on the bodies being found, weren't you?"

Her eyes widened a little. It all but told me I was dead on.

"That's why you'd planned to bury them in the campground. For the plan to work right, they had to be found and identified. That would leave Franz safe forever. But there was a screwup, wasn't there? What happened? I moved in and found the bikes. Found them *before* the bodies were found. Oh oh. Trouble. So what did you and Franz decide? You decided that you should show up here and make a fuss over your poor dead brother, killed by a madman named Franz. Maybe this was supposed to scare me away and sell the farm. Or at least give the bikes to you, or sell them cheap. Of course later, after we found the bodies, we were supposed to believe that Franz was also a victim. But that story of yours would forever separate you and Buddy in the eyes of the law."

Suddenly Lucy lost it. I think it was my mentioning Buddy's name that did it. Her eyes drew up and squinted, and her mouth turned down sour. She lowered her head and cried into her hands.

"Once the dogs found the bones, the plan was back on track again, even though it meant Buddy wouldn't get his bike back. So things were going okay for you. But then I did a couple things to piss off your boyfriend, didn't I, Lucy?"

No answer. Just a glare through her tears—a look of hate.

"One: I found out he wasn't really dead. I discovered it was another kid, an innocent boy murdered in cold blood. That set the cops out looking for Buddy. Then I locked his bike up so he couldn't steal it in the dead of night. That really pissed him off. Pissed him off so badly he went berserk, and before you could stop him, he killed one of Warren Shaw's cows."

Lucy dropped her right hand into the pocket of her shorts, wiping her eyes with her left.

"That was dumb, because even though he tried to make it look like an accident afterwards, it aroused our suspicions. Once we found the prints he left on the window glass, we knew it was him. So it seems the more pissed off Buddy got, the more he fucked up. The more he fucked up, the hotter we made it for him, and that pissed him off still more, and so on. How am I doing?"

"He!" she shouted. Then she was silent, quivering with rage. That was all she said. One word.

"He what?" said Roantis.

"He, he's not mean," she blurted out, crying again. "I know you don't believe me, but he isn't. All his life he's been used. When he cut on that guy, it was because the others were daring him to do it. Maybe he's not real smart, but to me, he's nice—" She clipped the end of the sentence off with her mouth.

"Not mean, eh?" said Laitis, running his callused hand over his chin stubble philosophically. "Well, I'd say tying that guy to a wood stove, den lighting it up and watching him cook to death is pretty mean. Just a lil' bit mean. Hey?"

"He shot Buddy first. It got all infected and hurt like hell. It still looks terrible, even now, and smells like shit and hurts him all the time!"

"What about the Worthington boy?" I asked. "That big kid who hadn't done a thing to your pal Buddy. What about him?"

"He did that before we . . . we were together the first time. I didn't even know about it until it was done. Then we figured out a way to get back at all of them . . . all at once. The worst was Billy . . . the things he made me do—"

"Lucy, you realize that in not turning Buddy in, in aiding and abetting him, you are partly responsible for two recent murders as well as the original six?"

This was the wrong thing to say, because then Lucy Kirkland

must have realized there was no way out. Since we had discovered her terrible secrets, she had no hope of hiding in lies anymore.

She turned facing the wall for a second, then spun back around, swinging her right arm out in a wide arc. As she moved I heard a soft metallic click, and saw a ray of silver flashing at the end of her hand.

The thin blade of the stiletto raked Roantis's left arm as he jumped back, enabling her to jump aside and spring out the kitchen door before either of us could catch her. Then she was outside, running down the hill, screaming "Buddy! Help! Buddy!" at the top of her lungs. We ran after her, and I didn't catch up to her until we were way past the barn. Then both of us dragged her, kicking, fighting, and screaming at the top of her lungs, back to the terrace. Roantis got her in some exotic body hold that hurt her so much she was mute.

Blood was flowing freely from the slice in his arm now.

"Go inside and bring my bag out here," he said. I did, and he extracted a handful of red nylon strips, each about two feet long and half an inch wide. They had a little thick section on one end, with a slot in it. Roantis took one and inserted the free end into this slot, making a circle, then handed it to me. He grabbed Lucy's wrists together with his good hand, holding them behind her back with an iron grip. He instructed me to pass the loop around her hands and pull it tight on her wrists. I did this, and she was fastened as if with handcuffs.

"These Tytons are a great invention," he said, panting and grimacing. "Better dan handcuffs. Lighter, too. You need a knife to take 'em off."

He shoved Lucy down into one of the big wooden chairs and passed another Tyton strip around the center back plank, then around the first strip. He asked me to pull it tight, which I did. Lucy was now tied firmly in the chair. She was also very visible and very loud, crying and screaming. Anyone within a quarter mile couldn't miss her. I had a hunch Laitis wanted it that way.

I peeled back his sleeve and looked at the wound. Five inches long, curving around the tricep area, and half an inch deep. No blood vessels severed, but a lot of blood, anyway. Roantis was standing there, making his own little red lake on the terrace. I told him to follow me inside, where I called Mary down. We cleaned the wound and closed it as best we could with tape.

Then Roantis said he thought it would be better if Mary went back upstairs. She didn't put up a fuss, and went up. We went back out onto the terrace, where Laitis placed Lucy's feet up on a wooden stool, fastened them together with a another red nylon strip, and used a fourth to secure that strip to the stool. Then he took off her shoes and socks.

And then I got scared.

"Lucy, Doc and I want you to tell us where Franz is. Right now."

"Fuck you. Fuck you both!" she screamed, wriggling around in vain.

"If you don't tell us, you're going to be very, very sorry," he said softly.

"Laitis."

He held his hand up, looking at Lucy now. Looking at her intently, his eyes boring into hers, which were wide with fear again. He asked her again, with all the softness and gentle tones of a father tucking his daughter into bed, where Franz was. She said nothing, and Roantis motioned me to follow him into the house, where he took a roll of metallic gaffer tape from his other duffel bag.

"Go out there and tell her time is running out. Tell her once I start, you can't stop me."

"You said you wouldn't—"

"I won't. Not anyt'ing permanent. You have my word, Doc. But gott-*dammit*, we are going to find out where Franz is. And that is final."

I went out there and tried to be the nice one. The guy who offers the prisoner a cigarette. Asks how his family is. Warns him that his buddy is bad to the bone, so he better speak up. I heard Roantis's feet on the stairs inside the house, going up, then coming back down. Mary was yelling something at him. What? I turned to listen. Something sounded different outside, but I couldn't determine what it was. I looked at the trees, at Joe's house. At the pool. What sounded funny? Something was too quiet. Something over toward the kitchen door . . .

Roantis came back out trailing an extension cord from an outlet inside. Then he went back in and returned carrying Mary's laundry iron. Without a word, he took a long strip of the metal-backed tape and fastened the iron across the soles of Lucy's feet, wrapping the tape around and around and around.

She sat in shock at first, then started crying. Roantis held the iron's plug up in one hand, the outlet for the extension cord in the other, and leaned close, very close, to Lucy's face, looking her directly in the eye. He told her softly, intently, that unless she told us what we wanted, and fast, she was going to feel pain such as she'd never known.

"I don't wanta do it, Lucy. But I will. So help me. You can't help Buddy anymore. If you don't tell us, he'll die. He'll die of that infection if he isn't killed by the police. So where is he?"

"No! You'll kill him!" she screamed. Then she screamed for help again, loud enough to wake the dead. Laitis turned to me and whispered.

"Keep the shotgun ready. Put my pistol on the chair there, so I can get it fast. If this won't bring him to us, I don't know what will."

"Lucy?" he asked. "Lucy, you let Franz into the house yesterday, didn't you?"

I listened again at the outdoor sounds of early fall. Then I knew what it was that sounded different: the crickets in the bushes over near the kitchen door had stopped chirping.

"Where is he?"

"In the woods somewhere. I don't know where."

"Tell me where."

"I don't know! I swear to God I don't—*noooooo!*"

Roantis had plugged in the iron. He withdrew it after a second. I doubted the iron was even warm. But I didn't want to stick around. And if he really hurt her, I was going to lower the butt of the Streetcleaner down on his head and knock him cold. I heard something near the backdoor. A click? A thump? What?

"Did you hear that?" I whispered. Apparently he didn't; he didn't even turn his head. He just repeated his warning to keep the shotgun ready.

"Where is he, Lucy? You've been with him out here a lot when we weren't. You know where he is . . ."

I took the shotgun and walked toward the house.

As I got close to the backdoor, the bushes bordering the terrace grew noisy again, then fell silent as I passed them and went inside. Just inside the kitchen door, I heard Lucy scream. Then a thumping and clumping from above.

"Charlie?"

"Stay there! Don't come down now!"

Mary said no fucking way was she going to stay in her bed-room while Laitis tortured a young girl; she came down the front stairs fast, cussing all the way.

I heard Lucy crying now, sobbing, trying to catch her breath, begging Roantis to stop. It made my blood run cold; it made me hate him. I ran back outside to make him stop. Hell with the plan; I'd had enough.

Less than ten feet from them I felt a blast in my left ear, as if someone had stuck a lighted firecracker right inside it. I dropped to one knee, dizzy. The Streetcleaner clattered on the flagstones. I put my hand up to my ear to take the firecracker out of it; it came away shiny red. I looked up to see Roantis working his mouth at me, yelling something. But I could not hear.

His face was scared, and I got scared. Lucy was screaming and thrashing around in pain. Laitis reached for his pistol on the chair next to him, but he was moving all crooked, like a puppet with a busted string. Then I saw it: fresh blood on his right shoulder, soaking through his shirt. Oh shit, I thought, and began rolling on the terrace stones, grabbing the shotgun and holding it close to my body as if I were climbing it. As I rolled I could see Laitis snapping up his .45, firing from a crouch.

Curled up on my side, I turned all the way around and saw Franz standing in front of the backdoor—right near the bushes he'd leaped from, holding my pistol. Then a blast from Laitis and he flinched, grabbing at himself, jumping up and down, squealing. My gun dropped from his fist. I had the shotgun up and let go with it as he jumped back over the terrace wall. Too late; the glass in the kitchen door blew away in a circle of collapsing sparkles and a whole lot of noise. But Franz was gone.

I got to my feet and went over to pull the plug out before Lucy had a heart attack from the pain. But the plug was already out; it had never been reinserted. She was still screaming, hysterical. Keeping my eyes on the house and the fallen pistol thirty feet away, I batted her on the side of the head and yelled at her to shut up. She did.

Roantis was swaying on his feet, his eyes hazy, distant, confused. He looked way beyond tired. I knew in another few minutes he might pass out. Then it would all be up to me. And Mary upstairs, alone, without a gun now.

"Is he in the house?" he asked.

"No. He went around, I think."

"He was inside, waiting for you, Doc. You hadn't turned around and run back, he'd a killed you. Let's go get him."

We walked to the house, leaving Lucy crying behind us. I was trying to feel sorry for her, but just couldn't. I picked the Browning up off the stones, put the safety on, and jammed it into my belt. Condition one: cocked and locked. I breathed deeply to stay alert and calm myself. Roantis stumbled, mumbling a curse. We walked inside the kitchen and started for the living room. But before we got there Roantis did a drunken waltz step over to the wall and spun around, his back resting against it.

"Mary!"

"Charlie?" came a faint, frightened voice from the top of the stairs. "Charlie! Are you okay?"

She was crying, I could tell. I said I was fine but Roantis was hurt badly. I told her to call the cops. She answered that the phone was dead. Great. Franz had probably cut the lines on his way in. Mary came down the stairs now, shaking. I asked her to help me put a pressure bandage on Roantis.

As I pulled open his shirt for the second time in less than an hour, he tried to look at me. But his eyes went up in his head and went all soft. Oh Christ. I looked at the damage closely. Right through the shoulder, and clipped a blood vessel. His legs began to give, and he slid down the wall slowly until he was sitting on the floor, leaving a wide red trail on the white plaster behind him.

Mary bandaged him with his shirt and dish towel. Hell with sterile dressing; we just wanted to stop the blood before he died. I glanced back at Lucy through the blown-away door. She wasn't going anywhere. When the bandage was in place, I walked into the living room to look out the front windows. Something out of the corner of my eye loomed up.

I spun around.

There, frozen up against the wall, arms and legs splayed out like a monstrous spider crab, was Werner Franz.

THIRTY TWO

For a split second we locked eyes. All fear was gone; now all I felt was hatred. I tugged at the Browning in my belt. Franz saw it and cringed. Patches of dark red on his shirt and jeans told me why.

He came off the wall in a giant spring, growling in rage and hurt. I spun around, trying to draw the gun, but he ran back into the kitchen. I yelled for Mary to run upstairs, but all I could hear was the sound of my own shouting.

And then he was standing over Mary, the knife raised high. She was looking up at him with a dead calm face.

He didn't chop her; he ran out the door instead, limping and leaking as he went. I rushed into the kitchen, grabbed Mary, and flung her against the wall, covering her. Where was the shotgun? Had Franz taken it? I held the Browning ready, recalling the image of what I'd seen: the big man, even taller up close than I'd imagined, pressing himself flat, motionless, silent against the near wall as I came in, holding that big blade up high, ready to bring it down as he leaped. And then standing over my wife. He could have cleaved her skull. But he didn't.

I saw the butt of the Streetcleaner sticking out from under Laitis, who now dozed in shock, sitting on the shotgun. That meant Franz had only the huge knife. I moved to the front hallway, holding Mary close behind me. We both stood quietly, listening, breathing fast and ragged through our mouths. There was only silence. Even Lucy was quiet.

I yanked the Streetcleaner free from under Roantis and handed it to Mary, telling her to stay on the stairs, ready to move up or down if need be. Then I looked outside. On the terrace, Franz was cutting Lucy's bonds with the bowie. He cut through the gaffer tape, grabbed the laundry iron, and flung it away. He helped Lucy up and they ran off, holding each other up, stumbling down the hill.

I let them go; I didn't want anyone hurt anymore, and we had work to do. We returned to Roantis and tightened the dish towel, which was now blood-soaked. He needed a hospital, and fast. He moved and grunted in pain when Mary pulled it tighter, which was a good sign. We laid him down flat on the floor, then got some spare towels and covered his chest with them.

"I got through to Joe earlier," Mary said wearily, putting a folded cloth under Laitis's head. "I got him at the office before the phone lines were cut. Joe said he was going to call Bryce."

I sat down, dazed, and rested my back against the staircase. But there was no relief, because before I could catch my breath I heard Lucy screaming again. Mary tugged at me, but I went outside. The screaming was coming from down the hill. I ran down there, finally seeing Lucy standing in the pasture, backed up to the fence, looking out at me and crying. Franz popped up in the air like an acrobat, doing a back flip in midair, and I knew why Lucy was screaming. A long gray shape came to a stop and wheeled around, throwing clods of dirt as it moved. I ran up in time to see the bull lower its head and charge again, bellowing. The enraged animal hit the figure on the ground before it, working and tearing at the limp form with its horns, raking them sideways back and forth fast, like a welterweight who's trapped his opponent in the ropes.

I shouted to distract the animal. It didn't even notice me, but finally backed off, pawing up dirt and huffing in rage. I aimed and fired. Part of the bull's right horn clipped away, and there was a brief shower of blood on its forehead. But it didn't even turn its head. I fired again, aiming below the ear, and the animal instantly went limp, collapsed in place without a sound.

I vaulted the fence and ran over to the man on the ground. As I leaned over him I smelled the stench of rotting flesh. Gangrene. I knew that Franz had been in agony for days. I turned his head gently, seeing him up close. He was so young. As young as my boys. Lucy came over and knelt next to me, looking down at Franz and crying. His blue eyes stared at us, expressionless. His mouth was open. I saw his teeth. Broken, bent, missing, the way I knew they would be. But now red lines collected in between them, little rivulets of blood from his internal injuries. I laid his head back down on the grass and stood up, holding Lucy. She was crying hard now, as if she'd never stop. I held her to me, trying to comfort her. Mass murderer, accomplice, traitor, whatever the hell she was, whatever the courts and judges would ultimately decide she was, I couldn't help hugging her, speaking softly to her.

I walked her up the hill to the house. A police cruiser's bright blue light was winking in the driveway. Jack Bensen got out of the car with his shotgun, running toward us. I waved him back, telling him to radio for an ambulance. I told him Franz was finally dead, and to take care of Lucy. Take her into custody, and treat her gently.

I stumbled inside and collapsed next to Mary on the floor. Roantis came to, cussing and demanding whiskey. Saints be praised, maybe he was going to make it. I gave him the booze. Not medically sound, but I did it anyway. A double shot and three glasses of water. Anything to make people feel good. Lord knows there had been enough pain. I looked around the kitchen. Looked at the blown-out door, at the bloodstained wall. Thought about the boy lying dead in the pasture outside: broken, trampled, and gored . . . lying alongside the dead bull that had done him in. Thought about the shallow graves, the burned bodies of Phelps and Becker . . . the dead dogs. Death everywhere . . .

I sat there on the kitchen floor next to Laitis while Mary washed and dressed the bullet crease on my ear. She poured tincture of Merthiolate all over it. I knew I was spent because I could just barely feel a wee sting. Another inch and a half to the right and I wouldn't be here. That same slug was the one that went through Roantis's shoulder.

I was sitting in a chair at the table now, in the same exact place I was sitting when Lucy first came out to the farm, nervously carrying a copy of the *Berkshire Eagle,* asking to see the bikes in the barn. I forgot how I got there; I think Mary carried me. I looked around at the beautiful kitchen, at the sunlight now streaming in through the leaded windows. It was a beautiful fall day.

I hated this place now. Hated the hell out of it.

THIRTY·THREE

Almost a month later, in October when the leaves are on fire and the Berkshires are the prettiest spot on earth, Joe and Marty got engaged. He brought her out to the farm from Pittsfield, where they had been visiting her parents, and paraded her around, showing off a hunk of ice so big the *Titanic* better watch out. (I don't want to get into Italians and matrimony here.)

Marty was going on and on about all the plans they'd made, including redoing Joe's Beacon Hill apartment so she could move in next June. But if Joe and Marty were happy, it was nothing compared to Mary's joy. The news had her crying and giggling, crying and giggling all weekend. Naturally, Mary and I decided this called for a bash of some kind. We planned to have it at the farm, since it wasn't going to be ours much longer.

We were going to give away Pound Foolish Farm.

Morris Abramson, that monumental bleeding-heart liberal, do-gooder, and soft touch who masquerades as a head doctor, had persuaded me to donate the farm to the Massachusetts Department of Human Resources. Don't ask me how he did this; Mary and I are still mystified. Perhaps being a soft touch is contagious. But anyway, it was common knowledge that Moe had been seeking a halfway house for runaway kids for a long time, and had been begging and saving money for it. I can't tell you how many bills (I'm talking twenties and fifties here, for crissakes) I've stuffed into the slot of that special oatmeal carton Moe keeps in his trailer for the purpose.

So, sensing our trauma over the events at Pound Foolish Farm, Moe jumped in and suggested we set the farm aside in trust for the state, rather than sell it.

"Hey, Doc, Mary: it came to you free, you should dispose of it for free," he told us. "Easy come, easy go."

"Ashes to ashes, dust to dust," I added, and told him he had finally lost all his marbles, and that I was setting things in motion to have him committed to the state facility at Bridgewater. He responded that we could work out an agreement with the Commonwealth of Massachusetts that would give the state use of the farm and still allow us to maintain a private residence there. Furthermore, he said, the tax write-offs, federal funding benefits, and other governmental largesse would astound us.

He wasn't lying; by placing the property in state trust Mary and Joe and I could continue to enjoy Joe's cottage, while relinquishing the main house for administrative purposes.

In return for this magnanimous gesture, we would receive a tax shelter the likes of which we had never dreamed of. So instead of the original scheme of enjoying the farm and watching the equity build, we would give it away, enjoy it more, and get our wealth in the form of disappearing taxes.

But that was less than half the story, of course. What we would get additionally would be a feeling of having done the right thing. A totally new feeling for me, Mary said. We would turn our windfall—which had become a headache—into something socially beneficial as well as personally enjoyable. Despite some misgivings, I knew in my heart that Moe was right. He always is, you know. Moe always does the right thing, no matter how crazy it sounds.

Jim DeGroot couldn't believe his ears.

"What you need, pal, is a straitjacket," he sputtered. "You're crazy not to reconsider, Doc. Hell, my firm can take the property and guarantee a return after taxes that would blow your mind."

But we told him no dice, and went ahead and signed the papers. Moe was almost in tears afterwards, saying his dream was finally coming true.

"And you're going to be on the staff out here in the summers?" Mary asked him. "What about your practice?"

"Just two days a week. I'll be a counselor for some of the more troubled kids. I can't wait. Doc, dis is the wisest move you've ever made."

"A lot of people think it's dumb. They say we're throwing away a fortune."

"I didn't say it was the smartest move; I said it was the *wisest* move."

He then asked me if I'd ever considered that the terrible events at the farm might never have occurred if there had been a place for abused and neglected kids like Lucy and Buddy, and Pete Becker, and Billy Kirkland, and all the other displaced youngsters who got into trouble. It was food for thought, as they say.

And I'll say this much for Moe: he puts his money where his mouth is. Over the years, that special fund he collected amounted to over a quarter million. Now, some of that was from me and others. But most of it was his. He got matching funds from the state, and more from private donors. With all this loot he's going to build the camp's main buildings: the dormitory and the dining hall. And give it to the Commonwealth of Massachusetts.

Not bad, considering he lives in a 1957 Airstream trailer in Walden Breezes park. And drives a 1975 Dodge Dart. I don't know. He *is* crazy, but I like the guy. So does Mary, and that counts for a lot. Mary says I have a Good Angel and a Bad Angel. The good angel is Moe. The bad one is Laitis. I say yes, but Laitis always comes out on top; Moe would get run over and squashed in a second if we didn't look out for him. So what, she says, Moe stands for all the things mankind could become, Laitis for all that we're trying to escape. I say you may be right, but the fact remains that in a fight, I'll take Laitis and his Streetcleaner over Moe anytime.

Then she gave me a little lecture on maturity, which I'm certain was entirely unwarranted.

So there I was, standing on the terrace of my erstwhile country estate on a Sunday afternoon in late October, smoking my pipe, pretending I was an English lord for the final time. It was a heartbreaker.

But I'd get over it.

Behind me Joe was saying: "She was behind it all. What's come out now is, Franz was her own pit bull. He'd do anything she wanted. It was Lucy who planned the killings, anyway. Hell, she'd hated her brother Billy for years. She even thought of the decoy killing of the Worthington boy, and got Franz to do it. Scary. Actually, it doesn't surprise me. It surprise you, Bryce?"

"Not at all, now that we've interviewed her."

"I mean, Franz wasn't all that bright; I doubt he'd be capable of thinking up a scheme like that. It turns out he was just mean and dumb enough for what she wanted."

I turned and joined the law officers sitting around the low table, sipping drinks. Bryce Stevens had lost weight; it was noticeable now. The result, certainly, of his marriage breakup. But he was coping and improving as time passed. Brian Hannon, draining his iced Tab, remarked that it was swell—just fucking swell—that he'd finally been invited out to see the farm.

"Right before you dump the place," he added, rattling the ice in his tumbler. "So you give me a taste of the country life, then take it away from me. *Hmmmph!* I guess I know where I fit on your list of friends."

"Just so long as you know your place, Brian," I said. He glared at me and I turned to Joe.

"But Buddy didn't kill Mary, Joe. And he had the chance, believe me. For a split second there, he had the chance. My pistol wasn't on him."

"Lucy loves Mary, Doc. Franz would never have hurt Mary. But he wanted to kill you, and she was going to let him. Let him kill you, then the two of them were going to ransack this place for everything they could lay their hands on, steal your car, and head for northern Maine or some other remote place."

"She said that? How'd you get her to tell all?"

"What's she got to lose now? There's no death penalty in this state, so that's out. She's facing life any way you cut it. She figures correctly that cooperating now can only help her."

"They really thought they could kill me and get away?"

"Oh, it's true," said Bryce. "Definitely. That bit about painting the barn was designed to scare your friends away, so they could close in on you alone. Once Roantis came out to help you, they moved with caution. Stealing your gun was Franz's idea, she said. Buddy would have killed Roantis there in the hallway if you hadn't been chasing him."

"Closest shave Laitis has had in some time," I said. "But the irony is, if we'd left them alone, the boy would have died anyway. I smelled his leg; it was only a matter of time before blood poisoning would have done him in. But I guess I still can't understand it."

"Understand what?" asked Joe.

"Why Franz hated me so much. It seemed he was out to get me from the start, back when he killed that cow. What had I done to piss him off so much?"

"Oh, I forgot to tell you," he said. "Lucy revealed their biggest hate motive of all. Know what you did right after you bought the farm . . . even before Warren found the hidden bikes?"

"No. What?"

"You had him and his son take all the old hay bales out of the barn and burn them."

"So what?"

"So what? Turns out Franz used to hang out in that barn. Turns out he hid the lion's share of his bankroll—the money he skimmed off Jimmy DeLisle, and other dough—in one of those old hay bales. Lucy told us there was a good cache of hard drugs hidden in there, too. Lucy and Buddy's nest egg, gone ka-blooey. So what you did, Doc, in complete innocence, was to totally fuck up Franz's life from the word go."

I turned around and gazed out over the valley.

"You going to miss this place?" asked Bryce.

"If I do, I can come visit whenever I want. But, no, I won't miss it much. Part of it is knowing that it's going to be put to good use. It'll have a better future than we could ever give it."

Shouts of laughter came to us from down at poolside, where Mary, Rowanda, and Marty were busy preparing the banquet. There was a big fire going in a cooking grill made from welded halves of an oil drum. Mike Summers was doing the heavy labor. We could have watched him for hours. Until he started cussing and yelling at "James, Eugene, and Woodrow" to come help him. So we got up and went. We got the fire stoked and managed to fasten the spit over it. Impaled on the iron was the carcass of a lamb, coated with olive oil and stuffed with garlic cloves.

"Don't let Moe see that," warned Joe. "He'll have a fit."

"Where is Moe, anyway?" asked Mary.

"He inside with Roantis," said Summers, tightening the spit to the drive mechanism that would set it turning. "They becoming friends. Last I saw, they just about ready to fall in love."

"They are, huh?" I said, marching toward the house. "Well, I wouldn't think they'd have a lot in common. But then again, you never know—"

Moe appeared at the doorway, holding it open for Laitis, who still wore a sling on his right arm. The shoulder wound had required two operations, thanks to that hollow-point round of mine. Roantis cussed me out for it in the hospital, saying he

294 ▼ RICK BOYER

wished I'd stuck to military "hardball" ammo, which doesn't expand and would have gone clean through. Hey, how did I know he'd get shot with my own gun? But I promised him I'd buy a holster.

Laitis lurched past, giving me a crusty nod and a wink, mumbling that it was now past noon and time for a drink.

"What have you two been talking about?" I asked Moe as we watched Roantis head for the bar table on the terrace.

"America's greatest world contributions. I voted for t'ings like public libraries, the Salk vaccine, the Bill of Rights, the social security system—"

"What did he pick?"

Moe threw up his hands.

"The machine gun, the bowie knife, and the pump twelve."

"Figures. He always told me America had the greatest close-range weaponry of any country. Ironic when you think of our frontier past, with all the room we've had. Right?"

He shook his head, gritting his teeth.

"You don't find this interesting?"

"Nope. And I t'ink you need a little lecture on maturity."

"Funny you should mention that; I just had one."

"Didn't work, I see . . ."

"We're cooking lamb down by the pool. Don't look."

"I'll try not to."

"Too bad you're not having any, Moe; it's gonna be good. It's—"

"You know I'm not having lamb; I don't eat meat."

"What are you going to have, pita bread and sprouts?"

"Yep. And fruit and yogurt. And a beer. Maybe two."

"Lush."

Sons Jack and Tony showed up at 1:30. Jack busied himself taking lots and lots of slides, partly for the engagement announcement and partly to preserve the farm on film before the construction began. There was croquet, volleyball, and swim-

ming before dinner, which was accompanied by much toasting
and well-wishing. The lamb was great, but I ate less than usual.
Was Moe getting to me? I noticed his look of horror when he
saw the cooked carcass. I thought he might have a coronary, the
way he was staring at it.

Afterwards, during a lull in the croquet tournament, I found
myself way out at the far stake with a pressing need to release
some of the beer I'd guzzled at the banquet. I decided to duck
into the woods and take a leak. I walked twenty or so yards into
the leafy gloom before I stopped. Something caught my ear. It
was somebody talking in a low voice.

"Oh, God, not again," I whispered to myself.

I crept toward the voice, a man's voice.

Imagine my surprise when I came to a small clearing, no
bigger than a boxing ring, and saw Moe kneeling down in it,
praying. He was praying out loud. He was wearing a navy blue
hooded sweatshirt, with the hood bunched down behind his
neck. It made him look like a monk, and this effect was height-
ened by the bald spot on the back of his head. I couldn't tell if
he was praying in English or Hebrew, but I didn't come closer
and I didn't say anything. I just stood there and watched. Then
I got a real shock: on the other side of the tiny clearing, not more
than twelve or fifteen feet away from him, stood a doe. She was
looking right at him, and he was looking right back at her,
talking to her. Then I saw the birds hopping on the ground in
front of him. I think they were finches. One of them flew up and
landed on Moe's arm and cocked its tiny head back and forth,
trying to understand what he was saying. The scary thing is, I
think the bird *did* understand what he was saying. Then another bird jumped up on his shoulder. Damned if he didn't look
just like Saint Francis.

I haven't mentioned this to anyone, even Moe. Somehow it's
too private. I'm afraid to tell Mary because she might think I'm
losing it. But it happened; honest to God.

Later that night Mary was kissing me in the bedroom, getting
fresh with me. She took off her top, then slid off her jeans and

was standing there in her undies. The panties were new. They were French-cut, of black nylon lace you could see right through. They were dynamite.

"Where'd you get those?" I asked her. She pretended she didn't know what I was talking about.

"Hmm?" she said, flipping her dark brown curls over her shoulders. She was standing near the bed. She put one leg up, rubbing lotion on her thigh. God, she looked great.

"Those panties. Where'd you get them?"

". . . ohhh . . . a friend . . ."

"That's nice."

"Hmm? What did you just say, Charlie? I was thinking of . . . something else—" Her hand was rubbing the thigh more urgently now.

I got off the bed and headed for the door. She asked where I was off to. I said downstairs to get a blunt instrument. Then she hugged and kissed me again, laughing. She has a warped sense of humor. But she let me slide those undies off.

Forty minutes later we were snuggled up together with the covers up, reading and listening to the loud rustle of the leaves outside through the open window. When the leaves are dry they make a wonderful sound. I was very, very happy.

"What's that you're reading, Charlie?"

"Nothing you'd be interested in."

She grabbed the sales brochure from my hand, looked at the color photos inside, and groaned.

"Sweet Jesus, Charlie. Aren't you *ever* going to grow up? First it was the boat . . . now this! And you've already got one. Don't you think one motorcycle's enough?"

"This is no ordinary motorcycle, Mary. What we're talking here, we're talking a Harley-Davidson *Heritage Softail Custom!*"

She sighed and rolled over, saying she was going to have to give me another little lecture on maturity in the morning. I fell asleep, and had a dream about Moe and the birds.

ABOUT THE AUTHOR

RICK BOYER is the author of five other Doc Adams mysteries: *Billingsgate Shoal*, for which he won an Edgar Award for Best Mystery from the Mystery Writers of America, *The Penny Ferry, The Daisy Ducks, Moscow Metal,* and *The Whale's Footprints.*
Rick Boyer currently lives in Asheville, North Carolina.